THE
Body
Heist

THE Body Heist

GREGORY D. LITTLE

Cursed Dragon Ship
PUBLISHING

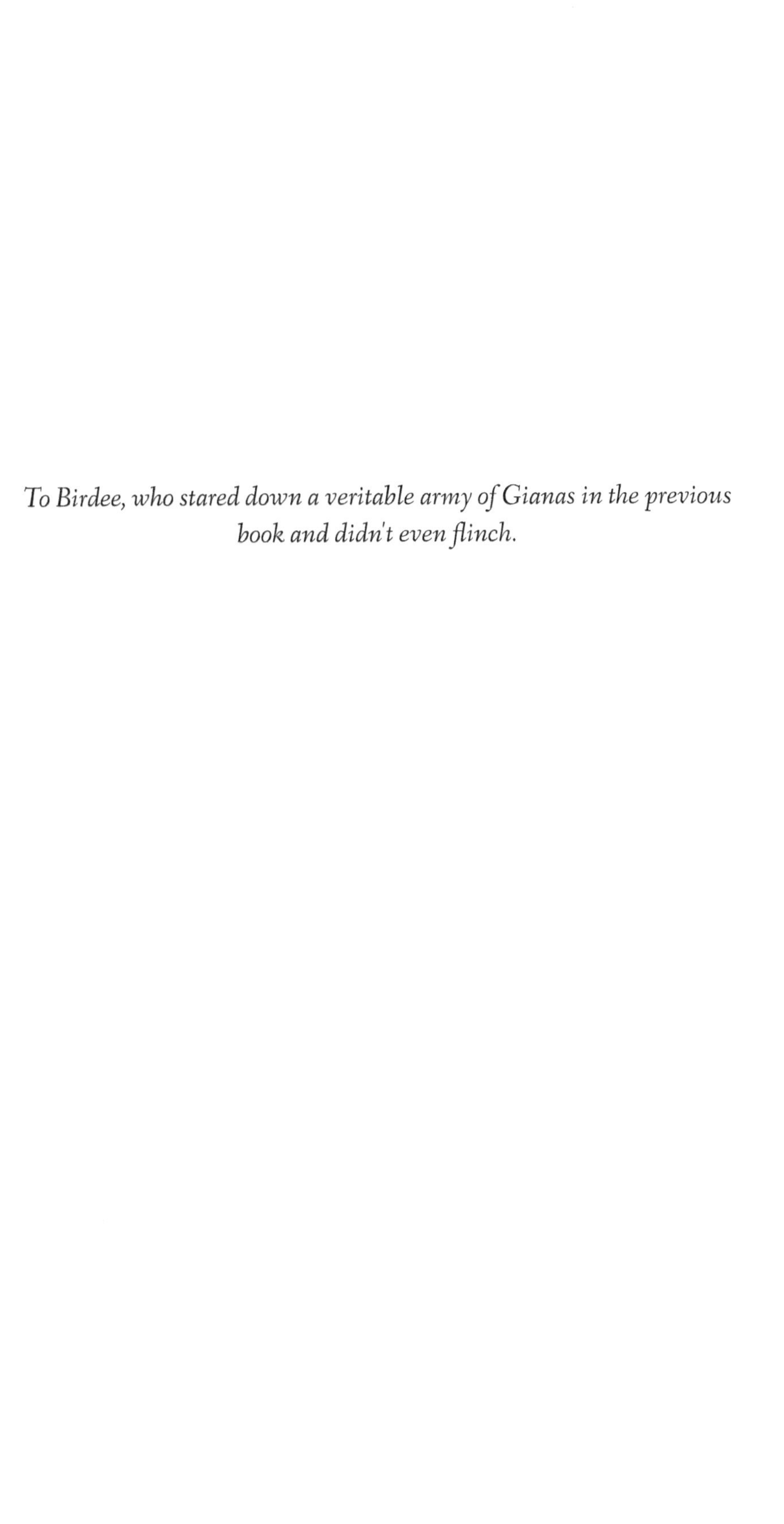

To Birdee, who stared down a veritable army of Gianas in the previous book and didn't even flinch.

PROLOGUE

AAYAN MALOUF WOKE in the permanent twilight of the detention camp, shaking and sweating. He realized by the general stillness of those who slept in the cramped shelter around him that it must still be early, though the light never changed here. He tried not to disturb his immediate neighbors as he forced his racing heart to calm.

The nightmare was the same as ever. Only the intensity varied. This time was one of the better ones, in truth. At least he hadn't woken screaming.

That was good. Perhaps if he could keep this up for a few days running, he could build a habit of it, and his new roommates wouldn't banish him like the last three sets had.

Every night, the dream took him back a year to what he now understood to be Coldgarden's last night. The dreams were full of clarity in the way his memories of that night never were, so much so that he doubted how much of what he recalled in sleep could actually be true. Revenants roaming the streets, but other things, too, things that were in some way worse in how *familiar* they felt, even though he was certain he'd never seen them before that night.

Aayan remembered staring in dumb terror around him as the ground shook and steam-spewing fissures opened, some large enough to split streets in half. But none of that was the worst part. None of that even came close.

No, the worst part had been his desperation to reach his husband and their son, the most profound and urgent desperation Aayan had ever felt. A late night at work had taken him across the city before he'd planned to go home for warmed-over leftovers, hoping only that he wouldn't wake them. He hadn't made it back yet before the rolling disaster began. All he could think about once it had was reaching his family, making sure they were safe and together.

But the night had other plans in store.

As he'd raced home, some external force had seized control of Aayan's body, fogging over his rational mind, leaving only his terror over his family intact. Like a waking nightmare, it frog-marched him to the center of the city and the great, glowing dome of light that had appeared there. The fact he was not the sole victim of this loss of autonomy was the only thing that kept Aayan from going mad that night.

The camp guards told Aayan it had been a year. *A year.* A whole fucking year since he had seen his husband and son. And not for want of trying, of asking, of begging for any information regarding their whereabouts or their welfare on this terrible world.

Aayan did not want to think about what that might mean, did not want to think that every day, there were fewer Coldgardener refugees in the camp. Where the ones that vanished went, no one knew. No one dared ask. Few were willing to even speculate because all of the options were grim.

Sometimes the guards would rush into one of the shelters, all shouts and barked orders and high, tense voices. They would drag out some poor unsuspecting soul, and that would be the last anyone would see of them. Ironically, despite the overall hostility and randomness of the abductions, the thought of simply being disappeared by their captors wasn't the most fearful possibility the refugees faced.

Hypermutation, Coldgarden's most deadly and mysterious affliction, had not seen fit to stay on the world of its origin but had instead followed them to this place. And worse, it had changed since coming to this world, turning people into ravening monsters instead of simply killing them. Monsters that might tear their former loved ones apart before being put down. Monsters that felt familiar in the same way the ones in his dreams did—but no, he tried not to think about that. When he thought about it too much, he felt something he didn't like, a kind of frenzy in his mind, like a building electrical charge. And if he let it build too long, let the potential grow, it might spark.

Aayan didn't know what would happen then, only that it would be bad.

A shadow approached him in the gloaming of the unlit room, a small, dark shape whose silhouette he recognized. He almost spoke before he felt the tug on his blanket intended to wake him, but as ever, the boy was too quick for Aayan's reflexes.

"Time to get up," Bry said.

"Thank you," Aayan breathed. Even a whisper in his deep voice threatened to wake everyone in the room if he wasn't careful.

"It's what you pay me for." Bry was a curiously mercenary child, one who seemed far better acclimated to this form of living than Aayan was or ever would be. Aayan had tried asking him about his past only to discover the boy was slippery as a sewer rat when it came to evading questions.

The truth was, Aayan needed the boy. He had never quite recovered from his brain-fog that night. It still reached out and seized him at the most inopportune moments—such as when it was his turn in the ration line. He'd missed enough meals that way that he'd become malnourished before he'd begun paying people with a portion of his rations to make certain he didn't miss his turn.

Bry had been the only one who had not vanished after only a week or two of the duty.

Aayan rose and the boy followed close behind. Conscientious he might be, but he was not trusting. Outside, the crowds were already moving in the direction of the square. "Square" was a generous term.

Whatever this building had been before—many said it had been a hospital, which was laughable considering the level of medical care the refugees received—this had clearly been a cluster of rooms whose walls and ceilings had been forcibly removed. You could still easily make out the former layout of rooms and hallways, picked out by the uneven places where the last fragments of walls were visible jutting upward.

The lack of roof only drove home that they were not outside. A dark cavern ceiling hung above them, high enough that the only way to gauge its distance at all was the lights embedded up there in regular intervals, like stars placed by an algorithm.

This was the largest space in the entire complex, so deliveries of rations always occurred here. Aayan's heart skipped a beat as he took in the scene. First and most obvious, there were too many ration crates. On normal days there were only ever twenty, max. This time there were easily twice that many—four stacks instead of two.

The second giveaway was those escorting the extra stacks. They wore robes instead of uniforms. These weren't Anaranjadan Colonial Militia. The ACM wore uniforms, not robes. That meant it wasn't a scheduled ration handout. That meant extra food. Just dumb luck that this had happened to be his day.

Some charity group, seemingly religious in nature but certainly separate from the militia, must have taken pity on the refugees of Coldgarden. The lines queued up more eagerly than usual as people realized their good fortune. After so many months, matters were orderly because early on the militia guards had taught the refugees what would happen if disorder occurred.

Aayan found himself staring into the deep cowl of the nearest charity member as he waited. He could make out nothing beyond the occasional gleam of light off some shiny surface. That was not surprising. Everyone on this planet, save the refugees, seemed artificial to some large degree. It made him feel nauseous if he contemplated it for too long, what these people had done to mutilate their own bodies. Still, rumors were rampant that the modifications allowed the natives to actually exist on the surface, actually see the sun.

There were days when Aayan thought it might almost be worth it.

He made it through the line in short order, receiving his double rations and portioning off a double cut for Bry. The boy had more than earned it.

Aayan stored the rations away in the hidden pocket he'd made on his ratty undershirt. Removing two crinkled pieces of paper from the same pocket, Aayan bid Bry farewell and set about the rest of his day.

He unfolded the papers, smoothing them as best he could, trying to draw strength from the images he had scrawled there. In his previous life, art had been his refuge, the one thing—beyond his family—that had replenished his soul.

Now it represented the lone hope he still had for finding them.

He couldn't do this every day. The obsession of it consumed him if he let it. It was how he'd nearly starved himself to death early on. But he also couldn't stop. Couldn't give up. Not now. Not ever.

He walked the ration line as he had many times before, holding up the drawings of his family, asking if any had seen them.

CHAPTER 1

THE MEETING POINT was in the always-strange interstitial spaces between Equatoria and Australis, the central and southern of the Meridian Cities respectively. The place was a restaurant that served as little more than a front itself these days. The restaurant was empty when Stefani Palmieri entered, and despite the sign on the door proclaiming it was closed for a private event this evening, she and the two others with her walked in as if they owned the place.

Iazmaena Delgassi, forming the tip of their little spear, moved as if she intended to do battle. Isamu Hayashi, flanking Iaz on the other side, mirrored Iaz in the tension radiating from him. That was the way of things when preparing to deal with the southern half of the Defective Factions.

The classiness of the sign's proclamation clashed hard with the rattiness of the restaurant's interior, and Stefani couldn't help but wonder what the locals thought. Considering how deep the Defectives had sunk their claws into this area, maybe there were nothing but sympathizers left anyway.

Iaz crossed the empty main room of the restaurant and pushed through the back door, Stefani and Sam on her heels. Inside, Stefani found a wide table partially filled with familiar faces, their expressions ranging from tensely pensive to surly.

"She shows up in person." This from the sourest of the faces. Kestrel was the leader of Freedom's Dawn, just one of the many pompously named groups of Defectives operating at the colony's fringes. "I have to admit I'm surprised." Kestrel swung his head theatrically to either side of Iaz, briefly making sneering eye contact with Stefani. "And you brought your rabid dog." He looked to Sam. "And your boyfriend."

Stefani missed a step at the first comment and hoped it came off as barely constrained rage rather than the gutting, if metaphorical, knife wound it actually was. More troubling, though, was the implication that these people knew more about her role in Iaz's organization than even others in that same organization did. Usually, by the time someone found out about Stefani's role, it was too late.

"I brought people I trust, Kestrel," Iaz said. "Because you and your friends don't leave me much choice. After a year of freedom from that prison, freedom *we* gave you, I'd have thought you'd have managed to dig up a little gratitude from the barren wasteland that is your soul. But I guess not."

It was an accurate expression of her feelings, Stefani knew, if not the most diplomatic start to the meeting.

"Maybe Palmieri's not the only rabid dog after all." Kestrel's face was all smirk. "You were thanked when you freed us. I see no reason to keep having to thank you. It's not as if you faced death-defying odds to do so once our colony's *illustrious* leaders withdrew their forces to the cities to cover their fleeing the planet."

"Another thing that happened because of us," Iaz said. Her tone was calm though. She was keeping herself reined in. It still surprised Stefani. She wasn't certain the woman would have been able to manage it a year ago.

"Lucius, these meetings would take half as long if you could stop throwing out barbs every other sentence." This was Dana Vasquez. If they could be said to have a true ally among this group, she came the closest. "I would think you'd be all in favor of spending less time with these people you claim to hate."

"You'll have to excuse my fellow Defective Anaranjadans, Iaz," Sam said. For all that Iaz had calmed down over the past year, Sam had only grown more protective of her. Maybe that was the answer: she was outsourcing. "We may lack working Harmony parasites, but some of us manage to remember how to be polite regardless."

"You could be rid of us entirely if you'd just help us achieve our goals," Iaz said. "The orbital platforms and then somewhere more hospitable. We'll be out of your hair forever."

Stefani suppressed a grimace. It was lucky Karl wasn't present to hear Iaz talk like that. Stefani knew Iaz was only saying that as a means of convincing the Defective Factions to help—or so Iaz claimed, at least. But of everyone in their little group, it was the mistrust between Iaz and Karl that still festered the most. It was one of the reasons he'd been so eager for his current mission, a chance to get outside Iazmaena Delgassi's orbit for a time.

"Much as it would please me to banish the off-worlders to join their fellows in space, the restrictions on accessing the orbital facilities have not relaxed the way we'd hoped they would over the past year." This was usually the way of things, Stefani had found. Kestrel bitched and moaned to start things off, then they settled into hard-nosed negotiations.

"Which is exactly why we need to move forward with my plan. High probability of success. Zero casualties. And it will force a temporary, but crucial, reallocation of security resources in just the right way to allow us to access the backup shuttle facility."

"Assuming your assumptions—and let's be clear, that's all they are—about redeployments are, in fact, correct," Vasquez said. She and Kestrel did all the talking. The other three, Chao, LaFleur, and Stratton, seemed content to let the pair speak for them as well. Which likely meant it was a tactic: good cop, bad cop. "And of course we can look forward to surge deployment after the initial shock has worn off, at which point everything we do will be harder."

"But that won't be your problem, will it?" Kestrel goaded. "So why should you care?"

Maybe it was bad cop, bad cop today.

"You all claim to want to fight the remnants of the power structure that locked you up," Iaz said. "But I sure don't see much in the way of a rebellious spirit. Maybe those worms in your heads work better than you've been told they do because they sure don't seem Defective." The capital was audible, as was the barb.

The "Defective" prisoners they'd freed from Scenic View Station had gone on to liberate other detention camps, and then had promptly done their best to drop off the radar despite fire and brimstone claims of retribution. Stefani wasn't sure she'd have been brave enough to hurl the accusation at a room full of their leaders, but she'd certainly had the same thought Iaz just voiced.

"We do what we do for our own reasons and in our own time," Vasquez said.

"It's not something your kinds could ever hope to understand." Kestrels use of a plural was intended to be a counterattack to Iaz's salvo, but it felt limp to Stefani, who'd had a year to get used to the notion that theirs was a strange alliance of life forms formerly antagonistic to one another. Maybe that was the problem. Maybe their collective realities—the Coldgardeners and the Anaranjadans—were so different, there could be no common ground between them.

"We're not going to stop you doing what you want to do," Kestrel went on. "But we make no promises of support, either."

"So we take all the risk."

"It's something you want that we don't care about," Kestrel said. "So yes." His shrug was so sarcastic it might as well have been radioactive.

"This is our position," Vasquez said. "Negotiated ahead of time, and one we will not budge on. Make your move, and *if* the planned redeployments happen as you intend, we will hold an emergency meeting and hash out the details of what you want in terms of an escort and aid in taking the shuttle facility."

Stefani could practically hear Iaz's teeth grinding. "That won't give us much time. As you said, any redeployments will likely be reinforced as quickly as they can muster reserves."

"If it's something you care about so much," Kestrel said, determined as ever to get the last word, "I trust you'll make time for it."

After they'd been ushered back out and strode beyond the hearing range of the guards, Iaz fixed them both with a wry smile. "Well, how do we think that went?"

"No worse than when we met with the Borealis factions," Stefani said.

"'No worse than' I can live with for the moment," Iaz said. "Let's show them we mean business. Then they'll have to listen."

CHAPTER 2

THE DOOR to Caroline du Vernay's penthouse suite chimed with gentle insistence. Her lone guest for the evening's festivities was here.

"I'll get it," Caroline called out to her assistant. The words felt odd coming out of her mouth, but the woman had other, more important tasking. Caroline had sent her other staff away for the evening. It would normally have appeared odd for the most powerful Equatorian left on the planet to go without staff for a dinner of peers, but circumstances demanded it.

Besides, she'd decided this last one required the personal touch.

She opened the door to a panicked Barbara Strickland.

"This feels like the last safe place on the planet," the woman said, eyes wide.

"Then come in, dear, come in." Caroline beckoned with urgency, though her liquid French accent did not convey the emotion well. "It's only safe if the doors are closed."

The woman started forward, then paused, looking suddenly guarded. "The others said I shouldn't trust you." But before Caroline could call up one of her practiced responses, Strickland shrugged. "But see where that logic got them. They're all dead."

Caroline smiled as the woman swept inside but only when her

back was turned. That was very nearly the same argument she'd been about to make as a joke.

There was a reason she'd left Barbara Strickland for last.

"I wasn't sure if you'd accept my invitation, but I'd hoped you would come," Caroline said, gesturing her guest to the table. The food was already laid out. "So I've made it up for two. And, just so you don't have to worry I'm trying to poison you or some such nonsense, you get to pick the setting." She smiled to indicate she was joking, hoping Strickland wasn't twitchy enough that Caroline had overstepped.

Strickland went with left. It was just as well Caroline wasn't trying to poison the woman. She'd have guessed right, and then that would have put her poison resistances to the test.

"I swear I was being followed the whole way over." Strickland took a hefty swallow from the glass of wine awaiting her. "I dismissed the last of my staff this morning. I just couldn't trust anyone. Not after what I heard happened to you."

"It was a very near thing," Caroline agreed without going into detail. She couldn't be sure which of the many rumors she'd started the woman had heard.

"I just can't see how they could have infiltrated our ranks this far," Strickland said. "They're alien monsters! How are they this good at pretending to be human?"

"Alien *mimics*," Caroline corrected gently. "And near as we can tell from studying the prisoners, they've been doing it for a long time. So long, in fact, that they managed to convince even themselves they were human."

Strickland almost coughed out her second mouthful of wine. Caroline had to hide her grinding teeth behind her smile. That was a very good bottle she was wasting on this idiot. The least the woman could do was appreciate it.

"So it's true?" Strickland asked. "They really have no idea they aren't human?"

"Hard as it is to believe, that seems to be the case. For most of them, anyway. Safe to say those forming this resistance have a better idea what's going on. And they know their business when it comes to infiltration. Clearly," she added, gesturing as if to encompass the entire world in her statement. "But come, eat your meal. This is real steak, and I don't know how much longer we'll be able to keep the other two cows alive. Now that our dear friends aboard the *Ultima Thule* made off with all our embryos."

Strickland made a *tut* of displeasure at the mention of their peers, the ones who had abandoned them to slowly desiccate on this world.

"Don't worry, dear. They'll get theirs soon enough." It seemed a kindness to give Barbara this much, at least. "Now eat." Caroline suited her own words, digging in with more gusto than decorum called for. She didn't care. The only other person on this rock who had the status to judge Caroline was wolfing her steak down even faster, pausing only to make little sounds of pleasure. The steak knives Caroline had set out scarcely seemed necessary, the printed meat was so tender.

"*How* did you make this without staff?" Strickland sounded half-impressed and half-scandalized.

"I know my way around a kitchen," Caroline said. She allowed a little wistfulness to enter her voice. "My mother, she enjoyed making food. Enjoyed making her family smile. Besides, I wasn't totally without help."

On cue, a noise emerged from the bedroom to her right and Barbara's left. The woman's head snapped in that direction at once, totally focused, her meal forgotten mid-bite.

My, my, but she is twitchy. Caroline tightened her grip around the handle of her knife and rose from her seat, heart pounding.

"I thought you said—oh!" Barbara clutched a hand to her throat, red wetness already sliding between her fingers to cascade down.

Caroline had never slashed someone's throat before, much less from across a table, but from the look of it, she'd gotten the job done. It didn't feel like she'd imagined it would feel. She'd expected a rush of power. Instead she felt jittery, full of jangled nerves firing at random.

She'd wanted to do this last one with her own hands. Maybe that had been a mistake.

"I tr . . . I trus . . ." Barbara could scarcely get the words out around the waterfall of blood flooding her throat.

"I'm sorry, dear," Caroline said, having trouble with her own words as she watched the life drain out of the woman. She kept wanting to laugh uncontrollably. "The others were right when they said not to trust me. It just didn't do them any good in the—"

Barbara Strickland thumped onto the table with a final, gurgling wheeze and lay still.

"End," Caroline finished to no one.

Her aide emerged from the bedroom, garish burgundy scales glinting in the dining room's mood lighting. Her large, dark eyes took in the body dispassionately. "I take it my distraction worked, then, ma'am?"

"Perfect as ever," Caroline said, wiping the steak knife clean on a napkin specifically selected to hide blood. "Now if you could see about cleaning this up, it seems we're finally done with our little side project."

"Certainly."

"And have the rest of her wine," Caroline said. "As a matter of fact, have the rest of the bottle. None of this would have been possible if it wasn't for you."

"You're too kind, ma'am."

Caroline didn't think so. She could still see the moment, all those months ago, in her mind's eye. The line of applicants for the position of aide to the most powerful woman in the newly consolidating colonial government. And hidden amongst them, disguised under false scales and a shaved head, was Bodhi Dwivendi, one of the few remaining Equatorians. He'd smuggled himself into the interview process, intent on killing Caroline and—well, she still wasn't entirely certain. Taking her place? Taking what wealth she had remaining to her? *Taking* of some sort, certainly.

But he'd never gotten the chance. For even as he'd stood up, gun held level at Caroline's heart as she'd emerged to call in the next applicant, another had stood up behind him, a woman with scales in that horrid new style of choosing flamboyant colors over austere black. Caroline had spotted her earlier, resolved to dismiss her outright for her gauche taste, and instead had watched her, face nearly as terrified as Caroline's must have been, hurling herself at Dwivendi and tackling him to the ground.

His shot had gone wide, but in the ensuing scuffle, the next one hadn't. It had blown his head wide open from the underside of his jaw.

Caroline had dismissed every applicant but one. To the woman who had saved her went the job.

"You're too modest, Giana," Caroline said. "But don't change. I like that about you."

CHAPTER 3

STEFANI WASN'T sure what it said about Iaz that most of her own allies among the Anaranjadan locals owned bars. Maybe the less Stefani thought about that, the better.

She ought to be home watching her daughter. In truth, she didn't know which was worse, the guilt she felt at her never-ending neglect of Ella or the certain knowledge that the child didn't really need looking after at this point.

She ought to be home *spending time* with her daughter, at least.

Located amid the fringes of Meridian Australis, a ten-minute walk from where they'd met with the Defective leaders the other day, Stefani had arrived at the bar early and now sat there, totally alone. The owner wasn't even present—plausible deniability—but he trusted them enough to leave them an unlocked back door for them to access.

She looked up as Iaz entered, Sam close at her heels. They had the half-sheepish, half-challenging look of people concluding a walk of shame. Even without Iaz's expression mirroring Sam's, a year on this hellish rock had made reading expressions on the scaled faces most people wore here easier.

No need to ask where Iaz had spent the night last night.

That was happening more and more frequently, for which Stefani was glad. Iaz needed something to ground her in the world, something that went beyond dark emotions. It was just a pity Iaz's blossoming happiness served only to contrast Stefani's growing loneliness.

Karl had been gone a long time now. Even thinking of him somewhere in the bowels of the colony below Meridian Australis forced her to suppress a sigh.

The couple sat without a word.

"As requested," Stefani said casually, holding up a small pack containing the power cell she'd spent most of the night tampering with. Then, because she couldn't resist the temptation, she added, "Not sure why *I* had to be the one to deliver it." She smirked to pull any sting from the words.

"Thanks," he said. "You're sure it will work as desired?"

Stefani could never tell when Sam was voicing his own opinion or when he was simply acting as a mouthpiece for Iaz, but it didn't matter. Stefani's answer would have been the same.

"I make no guarantees. I'm a biological scientist, which is, I shouldn't need to tell you, a long way away from an engineer. If you want a freak polymath, you'll have to hop back across the Bridge and reanimate Kyne Libretta's hopefully frozen corpse."

Iaz's face darkened. "I'll pass, thanks. And I trust you. It's not like you've had much else to do this past year aside from expanding your skill set."

Stefani could have made all kinds of protests to that. *Full-time mother* came to mind. As did certain other, less savory activities. But the former was a pale excuse in Stefani's particular circumstances, and the latter could also count as an expanded skill.

"You're really going through with this today?"

"Not doing anything and expecting to get what we want seems like one of those glib definitions of insanity," Iaz said.

"I just wish we could get more of a commitment from the Defectives for all the risk we're taking." She nodded in preemptive concession. "I mean Sam is taking the risks, but . . . Well, you know what I mean." She could never stop feeling awkward about the man. He reminded her of Damon in important ways, and that just awoke a rash of complex emotions. Both she and Iaz had been literally different people then. She wondered how the other woman could even stand such reminders.

"Sadly, I think if we wait too long, they're likely to back off from even their weak-sauce agreement," Sam said. If he sensed the awkwardness, he never gave any sign of it. In truth, he and Iaz made an effective team, and they always seemed to be on the same page. And on this, he seemed supremely confident. Iaz squeezed his arm affectionately.

"Sam's got this," she said with absolute faith. It was nothing short of a remarkable shift in the woman, even over the course of an entire year.

"Yes," he said. He opened the front of his jumpsuit and inserted the cell into the storage slot in his abdomen with a satisfying click. It had taken Stefani some doing to work up a modification that was compatible with his cybernetics and also the target but wouldn't trip any alarms along the way. "But if I'm not careful I'm going to be late. Got to keep up a normal flow to the day, otherwise it will look suspicious for me after." He exchanged a chaste kiss with Iaz that, even from where Stefani was sitting, promised something far more than chaste later on when the job was done. Stefani felt a stab of pent-up envy.

"I'll see you tonight," Iaz said. "And we can celebrate properly." She let enough heat slip into her tone to make her meaning clear to everyone, not just Sam. Stefani told herself this wasn't the woman rubbing it in. More likely she was trying to bolster her own belief that everything would go off without a hitch.

Iaz watched him leave—practically leered!—and Stefani had just managed to complete the rolling of her eyes when Iaz looked back to her.

"Tell me he'll be all right," she said.

"He'll be fine," Stefani said. "The device will work." She meant it too. For all her false modesty earlier, she was confident she'd rigged it correctly.

"Good. Yes. Thank you." Iaz actually squeezed Stefani's hands in her own.

"I should probably be getting back," Stefani said. "And I'm sure you have a cover job you ought to be maintaining—"

"Not just yet for you, actually," Iaz said, and by her face, Stefani knew what was coming.

"Not again," she said. She tried to pull the weight of dread out of the words, but Iaz's expression told her it wasn't working.

"I'm afraid so. We have another one who needs taking care of."

CHAPTER 4

THE BAR WAS in the part of Shadyside where you were likely to hear the maximum possible amount of gossip. As Karl Yonnel had learned over the many months he'd been embedded—some might say interred—here, that kind of access to information was a double-edged sword. It meant you were almost certain to hear even the most hidden of truths if you listened long enough. But you had to wade through a truly momentous pile of bullshit to find it.

Karl's bodysuit of false scales itched in all the hidden places where it bunched up. That was nothing new, nor was it likely to get better anytime soon. The disguise was far from perfect. Most Anaranjadans possessed synthetic, dehydration-resistant scales in place of skin. Flowmatter body sleeves could recreate the effect so long as no one was looking too closely, but they couldn't replicate the look of having scales covering your entire face. Fortunately, there were enough bare-faced colonials that the look could mostly pass, but it still made him antsy whenever he was out in public spaces.

The sleeve's black scales carried a blurry sheen in the harsh, artificial glare of the bar's unshielded LED illumination. They also never felt like they flexed right when he moved. But it was the only way he was able to blend in enough to look for Marri.

Not that his months of searching had yielded much. But she was down here, somewhere. He knew she was, if only because he kept returning to this bar and, every so often, hearing her name. Even if the visits had become more morale boost than useful intel source.

I'm not going back without her. He'd made that promise to Stefani months ago and reinforced it to himself over and over again in the months since.

Of course, it really wasn't so simple. But much more pleasant to believe than the other reason that skulked in the mire of his unconscious: that he had given up ever finding the girl, and the only reason he hadn't already returned was that he feared what he'd be asked to do when he did. Looking to save Stefani's teenage daughter was an uncomplicated, virtuous task.

Based on some of the rumors he was hearing these days on these very same trips to this very same bar, he could not say the same for what Iazmaena and the others were up to.

"Ruben!" Margie, at least, was always pleased to see him, even if the same couldn't be said about many other places. Karl had long ago learned to hide his distaste for the false name, but his real one was known by too many people he'd rather not raise flags with. She called over to him from the bar. "Your usual?"

"Please," he said. These visits necessitated more drinking than Karl preferred, but it wasn't fair to Margie to squat at one of her tables for hours otherwise. At least he'd gotten used to answering to his alias.

Margie ambled over. Leaving the bar to say hello was not something she did for just anyone, another sign he likely spent too much time here. "And I assume you will once again forgo simply jacking into the feeds like a normal person and would like the goggles?"

"Also, please. And thank you."

"For my most loyal, most old-fashioned customer, anything." She smiled warmly despite the teasing and bustled off to get Karl his drink and his goggles. Every patron but Karl simply plugged in to the newsfeeds and had the information injected directly into their awareness. The sorts of things you could do to your brain—beyond altering it with parasites, of course—were strictly limited on Anaranjado. But plugging directly into data feeds was one area where that clear, bright line blurred a little.

Karl didn't have the implants required for that, and the prospect of getting them was a little too risky. So he used augmented reality goggles to simulate the effect.

The goggles arrived first. He slipped them on with a familiar sense of muscle memory, only inserting one of the earbuds. This left him free to hear conversation going on around him. Dividing his attention in this way was yet another unpleasant thing he'd developed a talent for over the past few months.

Once in place over his eyes, the feeds sprang to life as though screens were constantly hurtling toward his face. That had taken some getting used to. Margie didn't bother tweaking the settings back to default—Karl was her only customer who bothered with the things. He'd have gotten his own set by now, but it would have meant all kinds of registration and account creation using records he didn't have. It would have immediately flagged him as not who he claimed to be. So at least this set was already tailored to his preferences, which meant the first feeds that appeared all had to do with the aftermath of the planet's leadership abruptly departing on a colony ship a year previous, leaving the very hierarchical world adrift and rudderless, at least for a time.

Prior to Karl's departure, Iazmaena had never tired of railing about how they'd wasted those critical weeks of disharmony—pun intended. He doubted that had changed in his absence. But in truth, enough upper-middle bureaucrats had been left behind when the uber-wealthy fled that order had been reestablished relatively quickly. Karl's own brief acquaintance, Dr. Helena Cardiff, the woman who had interrogated him in the hospital and discovered he was not what he claimed, was now one of the most high-ranking people on the planet if the new leadership's frequent public addresses could be believed.

It wasn't the best setup for Karl and those like him, because Cardiff knew entirely too much about what she was up against, and dealing with it was surely high on her priority list. When Karl thought of it that way, it was something of a miracle they weren't already all dead, imprisoned for experimentation purposes, or forcibly transformed into pro-social, parasite-driven drones. He might be slightly biased on that last one, but his own near miss had colored his impressions of Harmony irreparably.

The general murmur of patrons around him stilled, further distracting Karl from the feeds being piped to the goggles. Heavy footsteps marked the only sounds in Margie's bar. Removing the goggles to see who had entered might draw the very attention Karl always hoped to avoid. Still, leaving them on was out of the question. He compromised with a slow removal, trying to make the action look as casual and beneath notice as possible.

The individual who had silenced the bar with his entrance wasn't hard to spot. Even for an Anaranjadan, he stood tall, and even for an Anaranjadan Shadysider, he was far more machine than most. In fact, the only skin Karl could see at all was a few slender swaths across his face, and that seemed red and puffy with irritation or even infection, as though the man's very body rejected the many implants and replaced limbs.

His steps were slow, heavy, and methodical. If they weren't specifically engineered to cause dread in passersby, then they represented an astounding accident in that direction. Karl watched the patrons as much as the man. He saw lots of fear in those with human enough faces to read, but an almost equal amount of recognition as well. This man was scary, yes. But he was also known.

Known by everyone but Karl, seemingly.

His eyes found Margie's. The bartender made a curt gesture directed solely at Karl, one that told him to stay still and stay quiet. It was a kindness on her part, but not a necessary one. Karl was no stranger to combat with creatures bigger and stronger than he, but he certainly didn't go out of his way to seek it out.

The man stumped slowly through the bar, looking more as though he were a robot carrying out a preprogrammed patrol route than a man scouting for an empty seat. His path, Karl bleakly calculated, would take him right by Karl's table. Hopefully, in addition to not looking for a seat, he was also not looking for Karl.

In a desperate attempt to appear uninteresting, Karl did his best impression of the more regular regulars of Margie's, but to no avail. No sooner had the hulking machine-man drawn abreast of Karl when he stopped and turned, staring down into Karl's overly human—for this part of town at least—face.

"I do not know you." No mouth moved. The voice, staccato in accent and heavily distorted as it emerged from a synthesizer. Even aside from that, there was an odd tone. Almost as though he was reading from a script. "Who are you?"

Karl opened his mouth, his prepared lie ready on his tongue. He had no idea if it would hold up to whatever level of scrutiny this man was prepared to bring but answering quickly and easily was always best if you wanted to avoid sounding suspicious.

"That's just Ruben, Mr. Fennec," Margie said, beating Karl to it. "He hasn't been around all that long, but he's a good customer. You don't have to worry about him." There was something in the way she said the words, an implied *I vouch for him* that made Karl profoundly uneasy. No one on this planet should be vouching for him of all people. Certainly no one he'd grown to like.

But he didn't have time to worry after her poor decisions, because the mention of Mr. Fennec put Karl on high alert. *This* was Jürgen Fennec. Of the very short list of people Karl was looking for, Jürgen Fennec stood near the top.

Over the months he'd been searching here, he'd kept his ear to the ground for any unconventional power centers in Shadyside. As a result, he'd kept hearing about some kind of a cult. Only everyone just called it "the Cult," like a title. It took some prodding, but he was able to figure out what exactly their beliefs entailed. And that turned out to be more or less what was actually true.

They'd been the first to know the colony's former leaders, the Equatorians, weren't subject to the Harmony parasite. The Cult reasoned the only way for humans to break free of those chains was to completely replace biology with technology. They had consequently sounded like a great bunch of people to get to know. Karl's faction wasn't out to turn society into machines, but at least a shared grasp of reality might mean their goals didn't run cross purposes.

He'd needed an entry point, though, someone he could approach to get an introduction and meet with an actual member of the Cult. One name kept popping up over and over again: Jürgen Fennec.

Fennec looked between Karl and Margie with almost comically robotic movements. But any sense of hilarity evaporated when Karl saw the man's hands. Mechanical as they were, they were balled into fists, clenched so tightly they shook at his sides. The stories about Fennec were confused. Most agreed he hated the Cult with a burning passion that could only be personal in nature. In fact, most of the stories people had about the Cult's beliefs came from his proselytizing against them to anyone who would listen and a lot of people who wouldn't.

But then there were other rumors, more recent and growing in number. These new rumors said he'd joined with the Cult, that he worked as hired muscle for them now. Mysterious people and organizations often bred contradictory assumptions. That was all Karl had assumed was happening at first. Now, seeing those bunched, shaking fists, Karl wondered if the man himself was confused or under some kind of duress.

"If I'm causing trouble," Karl said to everyone and no one, "I'm happy to leave." He did not want to be on the receiving end of that fury when it crested, and he didn't want Margie to be either.

The entire room was silent for a very, very long time.

"If Ms. Mandalay vouches for you, that is sufficient. For now." Without another word, he turned on his heel and stomped back toward the entrance, as though Karl was the sole reason he'd stepped in out of the tunnel in the first place.

Fennec's fists never stopped their shaking.

There was no time to think, not if Karl didn't want to miss his chance. He stood and followed, grasping Fennec by the shoulder, pulling him around firmly. One of those bunch fists glanced off Karl's as Fennec spun, and even by accident, the blow hurt.

"Sorry," Karl said, practicing a deference he'd had to deploy frequently over the past year. It wasn't hard, given Fennec's sheer size.

He expected the hulking machine-man to bluster, boast, threaten. What he didn't expect was calm, icy regard. It turned out to be far more chilling that way.

"I'd just like to buy you a drink," Karl said. He wondered how much the man could *feel*, whether all that metal could conduct sensation the way skin would have. It seemed hard to believe.

But regardless of whether Fennec could feel or not, he didn't notice when Karl slipped the small device into the pocket of his coat.

"Do I look like someone who partakes of alcohol?" Fennec jerked himself free, turned back to the door, and exited.

Margie made her way to Karl's table the moment he collapsed back into his seat. She blew out a shaky breath Karl was pretty sure was just for show. The breathing, that was. The fear seemed quite genuine. Karl could relate. His sigh of relief had been entirely genuine.

"Why would you do that?"

"I had this crazy idea that I could smooth things over with him," Karl ad-libbed. Margie looked at him as though he were insane. Which was fair. It had been far from his best lie.

"Just please tell me you aren't one of those shape-changers," Margie said with a laugh that said it was almost entirely a joke. Almost. "Or I might be in a lot of trouble."

"Believe me," Karl said smoothly, "I'm the last person you'd want to use as any kind of infiltrator." He made his own laugh sound much more genuine. It was a skill he'd gotten good at, if not especially proud of. Plus, the statement wasn't precisely a lie. "Though it sure would be useful, now that I think about it. Why, the next time I ran into that big fellow, I could just make sure I looked like someone else."

Over the last year, Karl had found that one of the best ways to come across as innocent was to deliberately misunderstand how Coldgardener "shape-changing" worked, especially in very trivial ways even most locals understood better.

"So, uh, who was that, anyway?" It seemed the thing to ask. Karl already knew quite a bit, but there was always a chance he could learn more. Plus, it would be odd if he wasn't curious. His cover was that of a Shadyside newcomer, and so choosing ignorance was always best. Besides, it would be nice to confirm he hadn't risked his life for nothing.

"Jürgen Fennec," Margie said, dropping her voice to a whisper. "He used to be a kind of folk hero around here. Someone went missing, someone didn't pay what they owed, he'd sort it out. Like a private eye, sort of. I think that's the term. Can't think why he'd come in here now. He didn't seem to want anything, unless he was just looking for an unfamiliar face." She stared at Karl then, as though trying to see through his flimsy story.

That wouldn't do.

"So if he's not a private eye anymore, what does he do?" It was the sort of thing Ruben would ask casually, and Karl hoped it might dredge up something he didn't already know. He'd been careful not to over-question Margie—someone he saw often and who might notice such patterns—and now he wondered if that been a mistake.

"Don't really know. Around a year ago, he kind of vanished for a time. When he resurfaced, he was working for this other group. He still sorts stuff out, but it's for them now, not Shadysiders, and now when he sorts you, you don't get back up again, the way I hear it."

"So what's this other group?" Karl used every rhetorical trick he'd learned in the past year to sound only mildly interested in the answer to this question.

"Don't really know," Margie said again. "Don't really want to know. I've heard tell they're that kooky Cult that used to live deeper down, believed all kinds of strange things about Harmony. Hated it, some said. Imagine that! Who could hate peace? But even if they did, they weren't violent themselves, so it's hard to think they could be the same group. How do you take a peaceful group and a peaceful detective, put them together, and get something new everyone is afraid of? Got themselves some young new leader, a young woman I heard, but that doesn't explain anything." She let out a sigh. "Even if you could square the math, that kind of thing's not supposed to happen down here."

Karl had no response beyond shock, so he gave none beyond a remorseful shake of his head. But his mind was working overtime. In the many months he'd been down here, he'd heard Marri's name only a handful of times, always in a hush. And he'd heard about the Cult's new leader. But he'd never heard that leader described as a young woman.

It couldn't be. Surely it couldn't.

He could ask Margie the obvious question. He could ask if she knew the name of that leader, ask if it might be "Marri." The temptation to do so was almost unbearable. But showing such sudden and particular interest after he'd just strained his cover in order to plant his bug on Fennec would potentially burn his most valuable relationship on this side of the planet. Better to wait.

If Fennec really was working for the Cult, then one way or another, that bug would answer his question for him.

CHAPTER 5

THE TWISTING urban canyons of Coldgarden reared up around Marri, as menacing in the darkness as they were brimming with the whispered promise of freedom in the light of morning. Even after so many days of the same sight, Marri felt a peace and well-being she had not fully appreciated until the world of her birth had briefly been ripped from her.

It was not real, of course. Knowing that now—and knowing how long it had taken her to recognize this simple fact about her current existence—always filled her with irritation. Unlike when she'd first worked it out, she was careful to keep that irritation under control. Negative emotions which crossed some silent threshold of intensity she couldn't always predict often resulted in a response from the world.

Or, more precisely, from the entity which controlled this world's every aspect. And, upon thinking of the Professor, she was naturally drawn toward seeking out the day's lesson.

In the early days, drifting into the realization that this was an artificial place, like a computer with the way vistas sometimes lost resolution out of the corner of her eye, had always sent Marri on a downward spiral of resentment, feeling like a caged animal, and finally despair. It had taken quite a lot of the world adjusting to her emotional state before Marri had learned how to predict which emotions would lead to which adjustments.

Stefani would have been proud of the kinds of experimentation Marri had engaged in to learn these limits, and this pleased her. But her science teacher, Ms. Kimball, would have been equally proud, and this did not please Marri.

There was still much about her condition that was mysterious to her, but she was reasonably certain of three things: that this was some kind of computer simulation, that the one controlling it wanted her to know that fact, and that it also didn't want her to experience too much emotional distress over that knowledge.

Her last memory of the world before this one was of the terrible moment when Giana had revealed the truth of her machinations and taken over Marri's body. She had tried to flee into a great, sucking darkness inside her mind, and then there had been nothing. Even these memories she had to be careful recounting, lest they upset her so much they cause her awareness to fuzz for a time.

Based on this sequence of events, Marri had wondered several times if she might be dead. She'd learned very quickly not to dwell too long on those notions if she wanted to keep unbroken clarity of thought though. The Professor was nothing if not overprotective of her mental health.

She had settled on *Professor* as the name for her current god because it seemed so intent on teaching her. Maybe literally thinking of it as a god would be the most appropriate thing. It communicated without words, after all, altering the entire world in response to her thoughts instead. But a stubborn whisper of who she'd been before she came to this place didn't want to give it the satisfaction, as childish as that seemed.

She felt the lesson before she saw it. Beginning one always involved sliding into a dreamlike state where obviously nonsensical things made sense for exactly as long as the dream lasted. Marri allowed herself a moment of self-congratulation at having worked this out before her altered state of mind could take over, but she never let herself feel too pleased.

It had taken her a very long time to learn all of this. She just wished she knew how long.

She scanned the surrounding buildings as the feeling crept over her, looking in vain for some change to the sterility of the place which would indicate where she was supposed to go. The nearest building was glass-fronted, but it stubbornly refused to show Marri her own reflection. The glass always seemed to be angled just so or warped in such a way to distort the image, even if it looked fine out of the corner of her eye.

Another hard-learned lesson: she couldn't recall her reflection, not clearly. But she could recall a memory of how much it had upset her. It hadn't always been that way in this place. Just more recently. And, as expected, even thinking back on the memory of her upset caused the memories to blur at the edges, becoming more dreamlike the more she thought about them.

Or maybe that was just the day's lesson circling her, drawing her in.

"Marri!" Bry shouted, appearing as if from nowhere in the alley just ahead. "You won't believe the haul we found. We'll eat three squares a day for a year, but we need your help to get it."

"Hold on," Marri said, stifling a smile at the boy's enthusiasm. "I've heard this before."

"Yeah, but this time I mean it," he said. Now she was laughing, and she ran on too-long legs—a newfound height she was aware of only in her deepest sub-conscious—to join him.

The truth of this place was already vanishing from her awareness now that this new task had been set before her. It was always this way, but she retained only a dim awareness of this fact, coupled with the knowledge that she would remember it again once the task was done, before even that disappeared completely.

CHAPTER 6

THE ONLY THING worse than Caroline's daily address to the people of Anaranjado was her regular morning meeting with the few people she was still forced to share power with on this rock. It was an even bet Major Helena Cardiff would be in a temper today because she was in a temper at least half the time. Caroline had stopped worrying about playing the odds and simply had Giana order her the largest coffee on offer—the off-menu size—every day from her preferred shop as she, Giana, and her small entourage of personal bodyguards made their way to the meeting rooms.

Once upon a time, this had been an indulgence, one she only allowed herself on days when she had reason to believe every moment would be a battle. The only problem was this started happening frequently enough it had stopped feeling like an indulgence and started becoming a necessity.

Still, at least the shop was still open. They catered to a different clientele now that the Equatorians were gone, but they still remembered their most loyal customer, the one whom it would be wise to stay in the good graces of.

At least some things hadn't vanished in a flare of drive cone along with the *Ultima Thule*. And Caroline remembered loyalty. Remembered it and rewarded it. And, come to think of it, she was still feeling magnanimous toward Giana for that very reason, so she had her aide put her own order on Caroline's tab as well.

Caroline opened the door, pausing for the requisite brain scan from Phelps, Helena's aide. The scan was checking to make sure she had a Harmony parasite. She didn't, of course. No Equatorian did. But she did have an implant specifically inserted to mimic the parasite's biological signature for the purpose of tricking just this sort of scan.

The irony was not lost on her, but Caroline was not about to be mistaken for one of the aliens just because her social class lacked Harmony. And, as she had developed the scan-tricking implant in secret and installed it herself, she was confident no one else had access to a similar trick.

The two most powerful women on the colony waited while Giana performed her own scan of Phelps, and then Phelps of her. Lastly, Giana scanned Helena. Satisfied everyone was who they claimed to be, the meeting could formally begin. Before Caroline could say anything, Helena was already speaking.

"You'll be pleased to know the Bridge team has reported steady progress for the last week. That's three weeks in a row."

All this without preamble. The major wasn't much for pleasantries. Her "news" also wasn't any different from a week ago. So far, nothing about this meeting was more surprising or interesting than its absent party.

Of course your team reported this. We've biologically programmed them to be people-pleasers. They'd believe it, too, whether or not it was true. Their self-conception would allow nothing less. It was different for Helena and her ilk, of course. A functioning society needed tiers of leadership. Pure followers should do just that: follow. People of Helena's formerly middling rank had parasites precisely calibrated to allow them to show some initiative and exercise limited authority while still deferring to their betters.

"And you've seen the data backing this progress up?" Caroline asked. The scientists studying the Bridge were of the follower tier, and people-pleasers erred always on the side of telling people what they wanted to hear, after all. Caroline's own independent agents seeded amongst the teams reported something very different, of course: struggles bordering on stalemate. Not that she would say so aloud and risk compromising them.

"I'm not some amateur at this, du Vernay," Helena said. "Your outsized accent doesn't make you more sophisticated than me."

You're not a scientist, either, and making fun of someone's accent just shows me how childish you are. The trouble was, Caroline was also not a scientist, at least not in this field. Show her the Harmony parasite's genetic structure and she'd talk someone's ear off for hours. But physics of the complexity that Bridge technology relied on? Both she and Helena were hopeless, utterly reliant on a bunch of scientifically inclined lemmings without any Equatorian expert to oversee their efforts. It was a real problem.

"Well, then, that's good news," Caroline said, since she had no evidence to the contrary. No point pushing the matter. Talking too much of Harmony as if she were outside it—which she was—would not go anyplace good. "If this pace continues, in a few more weeks, or months, we can open the Bridge. And once we do that, we can get to the colony site decades ahead of Heller and his ilk, set our trap at our leisure."

"And with enough armament to blow those traitorous rat bastards out of the sky when they finally arrive." Despite her words, Helena displayed no obvious pleasure at their plan apparently going well. Nothing made the woman happy. Nothing satisfied her grudge that they were left here to rot. Nothing short of total revenge ever would. That, at least, Caroline understood. It made Helena's company more tolerable. Marginally more tolerable.

Still, the game must be played.

After all, she won't be making the trip. Caroline was careful not to let this thought show on her face. If Major Helena Cardiff thought she was going to be allowed to run yet *another* colony into the ground, she was delusional. But for now, she was useful enough, if only barely. Her conspicuous and growing rebelliousness further strengthened a disturbing hypothesis stewing in Caroline's mind.

Harmony worked to bind societies together. In theory, it made for a more harmonious human race, hence the name. In practice, however, the Good Doctor's grand project made for more unified and agreeable, pro-social behavior, so long as everyone concerned was in possession of a Harmony parasite.

And, as they had discovered here on Anaranjado, and who knew how many other colonies, you could get more granular than that. Different subtypes of the parasite, something Ana León had never dreamed possible, could recognize one another, forming subgroups of tighter bonds within the broader group.

Helena Cardiff had a Harmony parasite. Caroline had gone to some pains to confirm that to her absolute satisfaction. Even given her higher-tiered status, that should have made Helena deferential to the colony's Equatorian leadership—Caroline, in other words. Always in the past, Anaranjadans had deferred unquestioningly to their Equatorian betters, the acknowledged leaders of their Utopian hellscape. But always before those with any middling level of power in the stratified society had also been carefully insulated from an Equatorian leadership who, after all, did not possess Harmony themselves.

Equatorians had traditionally issued orders through powerless subordinates pulled from the general populace, who possessed Harmony parasites geared toward absolute deference to recognized authority. Those orders then reached subordinates who possessed power—and a different strain of parasite which optimized them to wield said power to the extent permitted and no more. The Equatorians had been careful never to mingle too much with this middle-management layer, lest familiarity breed contempt and their secret slip out.

Caroline had always wondered if that caution was really warranted. Now, with such mingling forced upon her, she was close to concluding that it absolutely had been.

Cardiff might have to be eliminated sooner than would be convenient.

"The only sad thing about our friends in cryosleep transit is we won't be able to see the looks on their faces before we turn them into a minor ring system in orbit," Caroline said, playing her role to the hilt and letting none of what she was thinking show up on her face.

"No, the sad part is we can't just head over there now and leave this dust-ball behind us. But we are needed here."

Caroline nodded agreement. Without them, the colony would collapse before they could abandon it. They only had to keep the place running for a little bit longer. Then they could make their own escape. If the Bridge progress really *was* progress, they would need to start stockpiling resources soon.

Which meant they would need to purge the camps, as they were quickly becoming little more than useless drains of resources. Caroline was a little more convinced each day she'd learned all she could —or at least all she should bother to learn—from their population of refugees.

By contrast, Caroline had not yet decided what she would do about her Helena problem when the time came. Killing Cardiff would be the safest way of course—long term, at least. Far less safe in the short run. But there would be a certain poetic satisfaction to knowing the woman would be left behind again, doomed to mummify on this blighted rock.

But unlike Heller and his overwhelming arrogance, Caroline had no intention of simply assuming the Bridge would never function again. She intended to be the last one through before destroying it utterly.

Thoughts of Halford Heller stoked her rage. "Don't follow," he'd warned in his parting message to her. Well, she wasn't following. By getting the Bridge working again, they would have gotten their first. By the time Heller and his toadies arrived in just about two decades, they'd have quite the surprise waiting for them. Waiting for them, in fact, at the exact site they'd already planned as the start of their own colony.

A colony rendered obsolete before it had even begun. But that was for later. Now, they had more immediate problems to contain.

"You saw this report from intelligence about increased chatter?"

Helena assumed her trademark look of barely concealed disdain which she reserved for when Caroline attempted to talk about anything she deemed under her purview. Which meant she sported it all the time.

"My dear, chatter is always increasing. The day it decreases is the day I'll worry over it."

A bald-faced lie, but coupled with the pet name "my dear," it was another sign of how dangerously free the woman was becoming with her thinking. If Caroline hadn't known any better, she'd think Helena saw her as a proverbial signer of checks and nothing more.

"I find that highly unlikely, since matters have been so quiet on that front recently. But if you see no need to keep me in the loop on the details, Helena, why don't you give me the bullet point summary. What are the Defectives up to?"

"All indications are that they are cleaning house," Helena said. She made it sound like a good thing, as though the fact that their spies had been going dark one by one was a worthwhile price to pay for distracting the Defectives with internal matters for a few months. Never mind that it had taken twice as long to cultivate those spies.

"Our supplies of people willing to betray them are not limitless," Caroline said. This was a painful admission, but a necessary one.

"That needn't be the case if *someone* hadn't lost the Harmony Template to a bunch of Cult freaks a year ago."

And that was why it was painful, but also why it was necessary.

"Cultist freaks who have gone even quieter than the Defectives, need I remind you? Who ever heard of a quiet Cultist? Preaching their delusions is all that gets them up in the morning, surely."

"Yes," Helena said. "And that's the reason they worry me a great deal more than a bunch of malcontents."

"What worries me is the thought of both groups teaming up."

CHAPTER 7

THERE WERE NO TRULY rough parts of town in Meridian Equatoria, but the bar Stefani found herself in might be the closest thing to one. It wasn't her decision though. She was just following the target. Though they didn't know it, this was where the target had decided to die.

The thought brought her no pleasure. But few things did these days. She ought to be out looking for Marri, for all that such thoughts prompted growing doubts that there was any Marri to be found. Besides, that was Karl's job. That had been part of her deal with Iazmaena, that she, Stefani, would stay provided Karl could go searching. Stefani had Ella to think of.

But that only called forth the old, intrusive thought that this was no way to raise any child, even a child as . . . unusual as Ella, in anything approximating a normal life. *Normal life.* The thought prompted an almost frantic hilarity. There was no normal place to be. There was no safety to be found except that which they carved out themselves.

This was why Stefani wasn't looking for Marri, wasn't trying to find more stability for Ella. Instead, she was headed toward a run-down diner, cleaning up another of the resistance's messes.

She didn't like it. Hated it, in fact. But Iaz's logic was as pragmatic as it was ruthless. With so few of them trustworthy, every person had to perform the role most closely aligned with their skill set.

And, as nonsensical as the explanation would sound to almost anyone else, only Stefani had experience as a hitman.

Julian Mikkelsen headed straight for an empty table upon arriving. Still just mid-afternoon, he had his pick of nearly all of them. Stefani slipped through the closing door just in time to see him take his seat.

Bad. Trevor spoke the word in her mind, a different kind of intrusive thought, one that originated from an entirely separate personality from her own. *Difficult to get him alone. We should have taken him in the alley.*

The diner is one of ours, at least, Stefani retorted. *And it's not as if it's packed. Besides, this seems like more of a* you *problem.*

She hated how much it felt like she was bantering with the serial murderer living in her head, but of all the terrible realizations the last year had foisted upon her, the worst of all was the understanding that the harder she tried to suppress Trevor Volkes, the more he tended to come out when she least expected it and in ways she couldn't predict. That hadn't resulted in any disasters yet, but it was maybe the only reason to be grateful Marri was missing.

That isn't how this works, Palmieri. I'm very good at what I do, but my skill set is also very narrow. This guy needs killing. Our boss made that call, and you came here, so you agree. But I just do the killing. Getting him in the position to be killed—that's all you.

You're such a bullshitter. Trevor had killed plenty of people in his day, and Stefani *knew* that had involved its fair share of luring because she had access to his memories. He just enjoyed making her as complicit as possible when he was the goddamned murderer.

Stefani knew she was compartmentalizing—luring a man into danger under false pretenses was not as bad as killing him, but the latter couldn't happen without the former. Ultimately, the only way she could do this and not go insane was to convince herself that the person driving the body doing the killing was more important than the body itself. *And even if you weren't bullshitting, you've watched me do this enough times by now. You could fake it just as well as I could.*

Look, if you really want me driving longer than I already will be, say the word.

No. She did not want that. She also didn't want to admit that, however. So instead, she just set about her task. There were a couple of ways she tended to approach this, but this time, the beginnings of a false seduction were blessedly out. Julian knew enough about Stefani and Karl that he would never believe it of her.

Of course, that just made it harder in other ways.

She caught the establishment owner's eye soon after she entered, gave him a look that he knew all too well, and watched his gaze go flat in response. This was Alex's least favorite part of the job too. But, credit to his professionalism, he didn't give any other indication that anything was about to go down. Stefani hoped he at least appreciated the professional courtesy.

"Hey," Stefani said to Julian, approaching him quickly, avoiding his name because they were in public and that was the standard operating procedure, even in a bar that was part of the resistance. "I was hoping I'd find you here. We need to talk." She let the urgency through only in her tone and the tightness of her face. Urgency was key because she needed him not to think. Her showing up right after him was already abnormal.

She gestured slightly toward the back of the bar with her head.

"Hold my order, Alex," Julian said to the owner. "I'll be right back." He didn't sound so sure about that, but that could either mean Stefani's ruse was working perfectly or not at all. She waited for Trevor to speak up—despite claiming this was her part of the operation, the man had the survival instincts of a junkyard dog and just loved to weigh in on everything she was doing wrong—but he said nothing, which she judged to mean things were working. So far.

With luck, Julian thought he was about to get a juicy tidbit he could report back to his real masters.

They threaded their way through half-full tables and patrons wandering to and from the restrooms. When they reached the supply room Stefani knew would be in the back, she gestured at the lock, then at Julian.

"This is that important?" Julian's voice was a whisper. "It's not exactly a busy time, but enough saw us go back here together that Alex will need an explanation at the very least."

No, dear, he won't. "This is catastrophe level," Stefani said. That was her own terminology. She hoped it would keep him guessing and be the perfect bait, something to keep him cooperative and not let him think too much.

Trevor disagreed. *Too much. It's got to be tempting-big, not suspicious-big.*

I exaggerate when I talk. Julian knows me enough to know that.

"Well, are you going to tell me?"

"As soon as you get us somewhere where we can talk," Stefani said. She had a key to this particular storeroom, but she would never admit to it. That, too, was part of her cover.

Julian frowned but did as he was bidden. Still, Stefani recognized that frown. She was made. It was just that Julian thought he still had the upper hand. As the door shut behind them, she ducked the swing she knew was coming and lashed out with her right hand, slapping her palm and the concealed shock pad it held against Julian's cybernetic arm.

It still could have gone down badly. He might have been hardened against such an attack. But in the end, it didn't. His arms and legs failed him, and if his core and most of his head remained meat, they didn't do much good sprawled on the floor.

He opened his mouth to call for help, but Stefani—Trevor now, in truth—was faster. He drew from their sleeve his custom-made weapon. It was a double-edged knife, long and recurved and stiletto thin. It was technically designed to kill Coldgarden natives which had resumed their true form, but it worked fine on humans too.

Stefani watched as dawning realization stilled Julian's tongue.

"Oh fuck," he said. "It's you?"

"No one ever suspects nice, mild-mannered Stefani," Trevor said in her voice.

"Please, Stefani, please. I didn't—"

"Now, now," Trevor said, slowly lowering down to crouch beside the stricken Julian, whose cybernetic limbs were still twitching. The disabling shock wouldn't last forever, but Trevor was a pro at this. "I already know what you did. What I don't know is to whom. Do you think I would be here, doing this, if we weren't sure? Do you really want to step over into the great beyond as a big, fat liar? So why don't you just tell me, and you can get that off your conscience at least."

"I didn't have a choice, okay?" Julian had tears in his eyes, now. Stefani hated this part worst of all: the begging. Of course, lying there, helpless, there was little else he could do. "We've taken it too far. I couldn't live with the guilt. I don't know what I thought we were doing. Maybe that was stupid of me, but I didn't think we'd actually be attack—"

"Last chance," Trevor cut in. "You sacrificed everything to assuage your guilt. But now you're guilty of selling us out too. So why not go all the way?"

"I'm sorry," Julian said, weeping real tears. "I'm sorry. I can't. I have to look my family in the eye. I—" He cut off with an *urk* sound as Trevor slid the blade home between his ribs. By the staggered sense of various types of resistance, the precisely angled strike had punctured both lungs as well as at least two chambers of his heart. His tremors, far from calming, spread now to the rest of his body, causing his feet to start drumming.

Trevor twisted the knife, and Julian shuddered with newly ruined innards. It was tricky to manage while simultaneously making sure none of the blood got on her clothing, but Trevor was a pro and had long prized the clothes he wore.

"Please," Julian said, his mouth frothing blood. As though he were not already dead. "Please." Then he gave one last, violent shudder, nearly throwing her clear, and lay still.

Stefani tried not to feel the shudder of pleasure that rippled through her. It was Trevor's pleasure, not hers, of course. But he still felt it with her body.

Our body, he corrected primly.

Not last time I checked in the mirror, she said, giving vent to her disgust in what had just taken place.

Recency bias doesn't become you, Trevor said. *Or I suppose, it doesn't become me.* Stefani had to stifle a chuckle and hated herself for it. Trevor did love his wordplay, and he could be funny when he wasn't being awful. *Doesn't become me unless you need someone killed, that is.* It was its own kind of knife-twist.

"Back into the dark recesses you go," she said aloud, just to prove that *she* was the one who could talk.

Yes, ma'am. He deferred to her more frequently now. Earlier on, he'd fought her for control a lot more. But taking on this role for Iaz, they had reached a sort of accommodation. Now he knew that if he behaved himself, he would get his chance to come out and play in the way he preferred.

Stefani had never imagined a mutually beneficial agreement could feel so filthy.

She banished the thought. She had to get home. Ella would have dinner ready by now. At least, she would if she hadn't gotten distracted again disassembling some mechanical device or other to understand how it worked.

It was difficult to say what sped Stefani's feet more, her need to get away from the gruesome scene or her fear that if she dawdled, she'd arrive home to find her oven in pieces on the kitchen floor.

CHAPTER 8

STILL TRYING to shake off the film of murder that clung to her like rancid oil, Stefani walked through the front door of their apartment to the sounds of a conversation happening in the direction of the kitchen.

"I didn't expect you until later," Stefani said to Iaz as she entered. Ella was putting the finishing touches on some kind of stew. It had been a pleasant surprise, and not just because the stew smelled wonderful—potatoes and garlic and onion with a variety of spices swirling between. Ella was a smart girl, and she did well with all her home lessons, but she took her enthusiasm over technology to absurd extremes sometimes.

"Auntie Iaz didn't want to be alone," Ella said. Stefani had read that teenagers were perceptive, but, judging by the gob-smacked look that crossed Iaz's face at the comment, Ella was on a whole different level.

Of course, Stefani's youngest daughter wasn't *really* the thirteen years she appeared to be. She was, in fact, not quite two. But Giana's lifesaving treatment—or whatever one could call it—a year ago had not been without side effects.

Stefani's daughter was not a Coldgarden native, not a revenant.

She was of the same strange disease race as Giana. They were the source of Mutagen Prime. Ella had coined her own term for what she was based on this, and mutaprime seemed as good a name as any. Giana's treatment had "saved" Ella only in the sense that it had completed a transformation that hadn't quite taken and had been killing the girl as a result.

Every parent lamented how fast their children grew up. Stefani just wished it was not quite so literal in her family's case. If this kept up, Ella would soon be subjectively older than her adopted sister, Marri.

That is, if Karl ever managed to find her.

"Auntie Iaz," Stefani said, trying not to sound passive-aggressive. Judging by the look she got in return from Iaz, seated at their kitchen table, watching her "niece" finalize dinner, Stefani's attempt at concealing her emotions wasn't really working. "I didn't really want the apartment to be an operations center tonight."

"I figured we'd do a little viewing party for, you know," Iaz said.

She clearly didn't want to say more in front of Ella, which was good, or might have been for a normal child. But Ella was far from normal. Stefani was about to lay into Iaz and never mind that she could sense how closely Ella was listening. But then she looked more carefully at her old friend, saw the thread of manic energy coursing through the woman. Ella was right. Sam was running the op, after all. Iaz was clearly not okay.

"Well," Stefani said, working from memory. "Nothing's supposed to happen for a couple of hours yet, so let's all sit down to dinner. It smells delicious."

Ella served, refusing all help. Iaz couldn't stop exclaiming how much the girl looked like Stefani had at that age. Stefani suspected this was mostly because the other woman knew it produced such a complex and uncomfortable stew of emotions in her. She had never quite shaken that mean streak that was her revenant-self peeking through.

Not like Stefani was one to hurl criticisms of that sort though.

"And how was your day, Steffi?" Iaz asked. "Get all your tasks done?"

"I'd have said already if not," Stefani said. "It was another day. Nothing of note happened." She tried to make it true by sheer force of will because it was the bitter truth. It was difficult to keep trustworthy allies in this world. But she also hated herself because she couldn't tell if this thought was Stefani trying to deny the magnitude of what she'd done or Trevor encroaching ever further, rotting her morals.

It's a true statement. Stefani was sure it was *her* thought. She was. That damned Harmony parasite made the Anaranjadans so loyal to their own and so unwilling to expand that circle to include Coldgardeners. That was the major reason Iaz's resistance mostly worked with Defectives, but even they were so soaked in the culture that half the time they acted as if they *had* working parasites.

But if Stefani didn't believe her own lie, how could she expect anyone else to? Worse, she didn't miss the knowing glance Ella flicked toward her. Trevor's sense of smugness spiked with Stefani's discomfort.

Best of all would be to recruit more Coldgardeners, but most of those had been rounded up and put into camps months ago. Very few Coldgarden survivors had arrived on Anaranjado with even the slightest inkling of what was going on. It had made them easy pickings, unfortunately.

And Iaz, Stefani, and the rest had faced near total failure getting any insight into what went on in those camps, much less how to get anyone out of them. They were the most well-guarded sites in the entire colony.

They ate in a silence Stefani told herself was companionable but likely qualified more as strained. The weight of worry hunched Iaz's shoulders. Stefani recognized it because she felt a similar weight of guilt and denial upon her own. And between them was the girl who wasn't a girl, whose big eyes missed nothing and revealed nothing.

Stefani couldn't help but imagine her daughter looking into her eyes and seeing not Stefani but Trevor.

At last, the plates were emptied and cleared, the not-teenager was bundled off to bed after logging vociferous protests, and the pleasant but fragile haze of simple domesticity began to erode as the appointed hour approached.

There was no live feed of the structure they'd targeted. That would have made it a pretty lousy target, in fact. So there was nothing for the pair of them to do but sit and wait for news of the incident to show up on the feeds. That was part of the reason Stefani was annoyed Iaz had showed up in the first place. Without Iaz's presence, Stefani could have had an evening pretending at normalcy with her daughter. With Iaz disrupting everything as a walking bundle of nerves, that became impossible.

Stefani chided herself over such callous thinking. *She's worried over Sam.* Two years ago, Stefani wouldn't have had any trouble reaching that thought. But of course, two years ago, "she" was another entity entirely. And she hadn't killed anyone yet.

Was it possible to feel nostalgia over a time you arguably had never lived?

After Iaz surfed the various feeds with a franticness that drove Stefani to exasperatedly turn off the screen, rightly informing Iaz it was still too early. They played cards for a time, stopping only when the lights flickered. Iaz frowned at Stefani and checked the time. It was odd. No power surge taking place in Borealis should have affected them here. Anaranjado had as robust a power grid as she'd ever seen, on top of limitless supply from their looming parent star.

Probably just a coincidence, the timing.

An hour later, an urgent alert at last popped up. These were automatically installed on every newsfeed device in the colony, and any sufficiently urgent news would switch them on automatically, with no override available. It ensured every colonial citizen would be up to date on urgent events as soon as possible.

In other words, the vast majority of the citizenry were all about to see the results of Iazmaena's opening statement in her argument with Anaranjado.

"There are reports of an unusual incident in Meridian Equatoria, where an entire subsector is without power after a freak surge." The voice was a pleasantly neutral copy of the feed's main personality. Likely that person was off this evening. "Cutting now to live footage of the incident."

The image was that of a bustling series of boutique shops which catered to the colony's wealthiest residents. It swarmed now with ACM officials and dazed-looking bystanders. The source of the distress was obvious as black smoke poured from the power relay the camera view was centered on. Stefani recognized the area as not being far from the shuttle complex.

Which struck her as very odd.

"Iaz . . ."

"What the hell?" Iaz glared at the screen as though demanding it answer her question. "That wasn't the target!" Under her breath, she muttered, "Sam, what the hell?"

"We are receiving reports from the scene which indicate multiple casualties in the surge itself. Officials are concerned about air exchange for those people still trapped inside, so it is possible the casualty count could climb higher still. Authorities have offered little comment at this point, but they have not ruled out an act of terrorism."

"That seems like the exact opposite of what we wanted," Stefani said.

Sabotage, not terrorism, Iaz had pushed when arguing in favor of the action to the other Defective factions they were trying to work with. *No casualties. Just a way to manipulate their security arrangements in our favor.*

As peacefully as possible had been their defining stipulation. Hard-edged as some of them were, the Defective's primary grievances lay with the wealthy elite, most of whom had already fled the planet.

And now, every word of Iaz's assurances had been proved a lie with how matters had actually gone down.

Iaz looked as though she was wadding up her rage and fear with her tongue so she could swallow them back down. At last, having apparently done so, she threw Stefani a bleak look.

"You're absolutely right," she said. "In fact, it's so far from what we wanted, the only reasonable conclusion is that we've been betrayed."

Then a new feed broke in, completely cutting off the one covering the attack, and all other thoughts fled Stefani's mind.

CHAPTER 9

MEETING WITH HELENA once a day was more than enough for Caroline du Vernay. So receiving a second meeting request in the same day crossed the outer bounds of what she was prepared to tolerate.

Or it would have if not for the tone. Caroline wouldn't have believed Helena capable of even that minor level of deference. Nevertheless, terse as it was, the message was the message.

Your expertise is needed. Bridge.

Caroline couldn't imagine how much it had cost the woman to say those words. She could only assume she really was needed. Or that this was some sort of elaborate trap. But she didn't believe Helena would dare. Besides, Caroline had brought guards of her own, ones she trusted far more than anyone in the ACM.

The Bridge site was an unpleasant distance from Meridian Equatoria. Even given the shortcut tunnels Caroline had privileged access to, it still took her the better part of an hour before the private tram deposited her at the nearest junction to the site.

When the Bridge site had been an interesting if ultimately

useless historical artifact dating back to—and responsible for—the colony's founding, it had been enclosed in a transparent dome. Broiling hot inside to keep anyone from tampering with it but sealed off from the worst of the planet's weather.

The site had changed a great deal over the past year.

Caroline rounded the final bend in the tunnel and saw Helena. The major narrowed her eyes at Caroline as she approached. Caroline had not told the horrible woman about the private tram network accessible only to Equatorians and had no intention of beginning now. Let the woman think she had simply been elsewhere when she'd received the summons. That she was answering a summons at all ought to be more than enough.

"What's all this about, Helena?"

"Thank you for your *prompt* visit." The woman was obviously trying to figure out just where Caroline had been coming from. She suppressed a smirk at keeping the major off balance. "As to your question, I'm afraid it's beyond any description I could attempt. Follow me."

Helena's guards, a pair of them flanking her, looked twitchier than usual, so Caroline decided to forgo any kind of biting reply about the woman's reading level. Together, they passed through the door separating the junction from the Bridge site.

Darkness greeted them. What had once been a desert hothouse was now an artificial cave encased by a Stone Dome. The enclosing rock was thick enough to blunt Naranja's wrath entirely and even leave a faint chill in the air. No small feat that had been. The colony did not possess a great deal of printers capable of working at that scale and in that medium, and it had needed them all to sculpt stone at this magnitude so quickly. The darkness that greeted them was, Caroline always forced herself to remember, stratospherically expensive.

They could have left their fortunes, but no. Her former peers had drained their liquid assets down to the last cent, transferred them to chits, then carried those chits aboard a colony ship which they had absolute control of. Money was useless to them and might have made all the difference to her now that she was self-financing this venture.

She supposed that had been the point.

"Where is everyone?" The only other time Caroline had been here since dome construction had been completed, it had been abuzz with activity, a kicked anthill of starkly lit gleaming metal concentric rings, a bastion of technology juxtaposed against the primitivism of being buried in a sunless cave. The harsh work lights were still in place, and the control-tower-to-be stood out like a blazing beacon in particular, emerging from the dome's rising side as it did. But she saw not a soul and heard not a sound.

"Evacuated," Helena said simply. Caroline threw her a sharp look. "I thought it prudent until we understand what's happening."

"And what *is* happening, Helena?" Caroline had read more about the history of this device than she'd ever imagined or, more to the point, desired. The Bridge network humans had begun on Earth and spread out among the colony worlds was nothing if not counterintuitive in its complexity. Caroline's most basic tenets of how it had worked had turned out wildly off-base. And she was not alone. This meant that problems were frequent. "We've had nothing but complications since we started this effort. What new thing could possibly have happened to prompt a full evacuation?"

"You'll see. This way." Helena gestured into a dark space between the work lights, a swathe lit only by stray light reflecting off Bridge metal, then set off.

Caroline hesitated.

Helena made it twelve steps before realizing her guest was not with her. She turned back with a sardonic smile Caroline could just make out in the reflected light.

"My, my, so nervous?"

"I'm not the last of my kind on this rock for no reason," Caroline said warningly. Suddenly, she was less certain about what Helena Cardiff would dare. Surely not.

"Caroline, if I wanted you dead, I can assure you I wouldn't be present for it. I'm not that kind of killer." With that, she turned back and continued on her way.

That the woman would even say those words chilled Caroline to the core. Still, there seemed little to do but go on. Reluctantly, Caroline followed. Her mind, shorn of any responsibility save worry, began cataloging what it was seeing. The rings, which had been in their hovering, deployed configuration for as long as she'd been alive, had settled back into their ground receptacles. That alone had been a month of effort. They looked utterly dormant but were paradoxically more awake than the Bridge had been almost since the colony's founding.

You didn't need a site on either end of a Bridge span to build one—using them to colonize worlds would have made little sense otherwise—but each colony had been equipped with the parts necessary to build their own site once they were established. Caroline had always assumed this meant Earth's colony worlds were to be free to trade with one another, but that had not been the case at all.

It turned out the colony Bridge sites only existed because it made both the math and energy requirements less onerous to have each site build half a span and let them meet in the middle. It had not taken long for Anaranjado—and presumably every other colony—to learn the truth. While Earth's Bridge could go anywhere, each of the colony Bridges were slaved to that master site. In other words, they could go to Earth, but nowhere else.

But that was no longer the case.

"Get that light," Helena said a few moments later, and it took Caroline a moment to realize Helena was talking to one of her guards while simultaneously pointing up at the ceiling at one fixture in particular. The man darted off toward a console bathed in gloom.

Once she'd uncovered that particular detail about Bridge limitations, Caroline had assumed the Coldgarden refugees must have been lying. They must have come from Earth. But the Anaranjado Bridge's own logs had confirmed they'd been telling the truth. Somehow, they'd found a way to break free of the Earth site's hold over their Bridge. Using that information, Anaranjado's scientists had worked out a way to reawaken their own bridge from its dormant state.

It was amazing what a bunch of determined experts could accomplish simply by knowing a thing was possible.

A humming sound announced power was flowing again. The major turned from where she'd been staring at her guard with impatience back to address Caroline directly. "The entire staff was off last shift to allow for synching of new upgrades, but the first shift back found it. I thought it best, even with the evacuation order, that we not have the space so visible. Because, well, because of *that*."

The light turned on with a loud *clack*, instantly bathing a large wedge of the darkness in blinding light, and Caroline gasped at what it illuminated.

Two bodies lay sprawled, both mutilated almost beyond recognition. Except that wasn't quite right. Caroline found it very difficult to process precisely what she was seeing and so began with the easiest first.

The form on the right was clearly an ACM member, or had been. They were missing their head, but chunks of it still lay strewn about in bloody gobs. Caroline could make out bits of skull and brain both.

The body on the right was split open and splayed wide from groin to crown. Shorter and stockier than an average Anaranjadan, and utterly bereft of scales that Caroline could see, it wore flow-matter which tried, unsuccessfully, to knit itself back across the wounds. The twitching black cables of the matter flailed as they stretched across glistening, mulched internal organs, desperate to bridge the gap.

The gruesome tableau left Caroline's own guts roiling.

From the height and lack of scales, she almost would have wondered if some Equatorian had stayed behind unbeknownst to her. But it was the third form which most drew her eye. It dug massive, barbed pincers, caked with blood and gore, into the meat of the right body. Its fat, bulbous, segmented form trailed out behind its head, pointing languidly back toward the ACM soldier with the missing head. Like it had burst forth from it, exploding it outward as it went. Only the fact that it was clearly dead kept her from scrambling away as quickly as she could.

It was unquestionably the reason Helena had summoned Caroline here.

"By the Good Doctor," Caroline said, her throat dry.

"My sentiments exactly," Helena said. "Now, will you kindly tell me what the hell kind of Harmony variant I'm looking at?"

Caroline's first reaction, deeply ingrained, was to snap her head around and find the guards, who shouldn't be privy to that kind of talk. But she saw, with a laughably shaky kind of relief, that Helena had ordered them away, presumably while Caroline stood there in rapt horror, taking it all in.

Her second response was to think the woman insane. This was no kind of Harmony, not at all. Only then did she start looking closer. The creature was too large, yes, multiple orders of magnitude too large. And no Harmony parasite possessed such formidable mandibles—the damage they would do to surrounding brain tissue would be catastrophic.

But the segment number and layout, though grossly out of proportion in every dimension, was correct. And the tendrils were there, except instead of terminating in bits of brain analog where the creature made its linkages, these ended in spindly, five-fingered *hands* that looked both disturbingly human and repulsively not.

"At a guess," Caroline said because Helena was still staring at her expectantly, "that thing emerged from your man's head and . . . attacked this other man." She was shaking her head while she spoke, as though already negating the statement, refusing to believe what was right in front of her. "No one else was here?"

"No one else was here," Helena confirmed.

"Security footage?"

"Security systems were temporarily down as part of the upgrade. That's why I had a guard posted." The patience in Helena's voice was as strained as the flowmatter trying to jump across the wound in the second figure.

"Almost makes one wonder if the victim knew that fact and decided to show up. But who is this second person?"

"My people are looking into that. But I didn't bring you here for your forensic expertise. What I was hoping for was an explanation for *how* such a thing could have happened. My God, Caroline, I know I'm not privy to everything you were doing, but *what have you been doing?*"

"Nothing like this," Caroline said, sounding more defensive than she would have liked. "Nothing *remotely* like this. I mean, look at the size of the thing. I wouldn't even know where to begin!" Something in her tone must have been convincing because, after holding her gaze for a long moment, Helena nodded.

"That leaves two possibilities, then," she said. "You know what they are?"

"Yes," Caroline rasped. "Either it's something the Cultists have ginned up thanks to Subject Rho, or it's somehow courtesy of the invaders still at large."

"Or perhaps both," Helena said darkly.

"You assured me you had the latter situation under control, Major," Caroline said.

"There are very few unaccounted for," Helena said, somehow managing not to sound defensive. "And I have difficulty imagining they could be doing *this* without help." And so, she threw the blame right back. Because Subject Rho and the Cult who had taken him were very much Caroline's problem.

A problem she was no closer to solving than she had been a year ago, ever since she'd been abandoned here and Jürgen Fennec had stopped taking her calls.

As if to punctuate the moment, one of Helena's ACM guards jogged over, a phone in his hand. "Beg pardon, ma'am. Urgent call for you."

Helena snatched it from him with bad grace then pressed the

phone to her ear. "Yes? What is it?" She listened for a moment. Then her face went slack before pinching in sudden fury. She turned to Caroline.

"There's been an incident," she said. "Some kind of massive power surge." Her face paled as she listened further. "It looks to be some kind of attack."

"I need to get back there," Caroline said, already turning away. "Now."

CHAPTER 10

SOMEHOW, Karl retained enough discipline to resist checking his newly planted bug until he got back to his hidey hole in this frozen hell. Little more than a small hollow of stone with a bed nook, a space heater, and a charging port that currently provided power for said space heater, it was enough to live in, if only just. Even the lancer barracks back in Coldgarden had felt more spacious. And at least there someone had been preparing his meals.

The stone part was important. Had Karl been forced to rent one of the ice cubbies, he wouldn't have been able to use the space heater without his shelter slowly melting around him. And without the space heater, he would have long ago frozen in his bed, like an odd piece of performance art.

Pausing only long enough to peel off his itchy sleeve of scales and put on every single piece of clothing he owned, Karl unplugged the space heater from the charging port and plugged in his receiver device. He had to hope Jürgen Fennec never wandered out of range of this level's network nodes. Signals did weird things in these twisting warrens of ice and rock, so networks were partitioned by district and level. With limited bandwidth available to transit between networks, only the very highest priority traffic could travel between districts. Illicit listening devices, sadly, wouldn't make that cut.

At least, that was how the shady back-alley Defective who had sold him the device had caveated the situation.

For the first few minutes, all he got was ever-shifting bands of static. Sometimes the soft hiss of white noise, the kind you might go to sleep to, other times piercing squeals of feedback which left him frantically dialing down the volume. Karl began to fear Jürgen had indeed left the district.

At last, though, he heard a word. Then another.

"No. Not my concern." It was Fennec's voice. Had Karl never heard him speak in person, he'd have assumed the sound quality was compromised. But that electronic harshness belonged entirely to the man himself. "If you wish to rethink the arrangement, you can take it up with her in person. Her door is always open, but by the same token, it is unwise to arrive unannounced."

Fennec hadn't stated his purpose for coming into the bar, but if Karl had to guess, based on what he was hearing, he was doing the rounds of local establishments on behalf of the Cult's mysterious new leader.

Half-choked responses seemed to follow Fennec wherever he went. He asked a few perfunctory-sounding questions, but it was strange. It felt to Karl almost as though the man was going through the motions of something with no real purpose behind it. Karl never heard the man sound as unnervingly focused as he had those few seconds where Karl had held his full attention.

At last, after another hour or so, there came a stretch where the only sound was the rhythmic plodding of the man's steps. He had certainly left the main drag of establishments in this area of the tunnels. The next new sound Karl heard was the squeal of hinges on some kind of door, followed by a much louder and more mechanistic sound of what must be a more substantial door opening.

The quality of Fennec's steps changed after this. He was no longer walking on the mishmash of ice, rock, and assorted corrugated metals or synthetic gripping surfaces which made up the tunnels and their establishments. Instead, he trod evenly on something that sounded smooth and hard. There were murmurs of other voices, most sounding as electronically garbled as Fennec's. Then, finally, a new voice, different from all the rest.

Different, and strangely familiar.

"Jürgen. You're almost late for our big moment."

"My apologies." If Jürgen had any excuse to offer, he kept it to himself. Still, Karl pricked up his ears. Even with those two words, this was certainly a more deferential Fennec than he had experienced. Yet there was something underneath that deference. It reminded him of his time in the lancers for some reason.

The other voice, the woman's voice, offered an even deeper mystery. She sounded young, but it was not the voice of a child. And yet it almost sounded like . . .

"I know you become easily confused these days," the woman said, not without sympathy. "But I still require thought from you. I can't be policing your every action anymore. That took too much out of me."

"I will endeavor to do better in the future."

"Regardless, you'll be happy to know the plan went off without a hitch. Our plan, not theirs. It's appeared on the newsfeeds and has started taking up more bandwidth. The erstwhile Magistrate Delgassi will be scrambling, wondering what happened with their attack. The rest of the colony will be reeling shortly, just as soon as the fact it *was* an attack becomes known."

Karl's breath caught. He was not up on precise timelines, but the last time he'd spoken with Stefani, she'd indicated Iazmaena had something big in the works. He would have to check the feeds after this. "We'll give them a few moments more to panic and then make our statement colonywide."

Statement? Karl frowned in confusion at that. That he could pick this up here meant they were in the district. But something going out to the whole colony always came from either Equatoria or Borealis, not down in the depths beneath Australis. It made no sense.

"And then what?"

"For you, Jürgen, I will shortly have another task. A very important one. But that's for after."

"Yes. Of course."

Karl heard it again, then. That thread of some other emotion underneath the deference. It struck him suddenly what it was. He'd heard it before from lancers who were toeing the line of civility and required obedience but deep down hated their commanding officer's guts.

Talk ceased then for several minutes, but there was a general sense of bustle, the sound of some kind of equipment being set up. It was the kind of sound which normally would have been accompanied by someone issuing instructions, likely with some follow-up questions, but Karl heard nothing at all.

"Live in three seconds," Fennec said suddenly, out of the blue. "Now."

"Good people of Anaranjado," the woman intoned, sounding exactly as if she were a news anchor speaking on camera. "My name is Marrietta Palmieri."

Karl fell off his bed.

CHAPTER 11

"Good people of Anaranjado, my name is Marrietta Palmieri, and I wish to speak to you about the future of this planet and everyone on it."

A year of fruitless searching, hope fading to despair, and there she was. Anyone but her mother might not have recognized her, so different had she become. But she was right there on the screen. It was the first time Stefani had laid eyes on her daughter since they'd left the world of their births, and she was looking at, not a child, not even a teenager, but a young woman, one wearing the scales of a local.

Inside her head, Trevor bestirred himself, mentally nudging her to start breathing again. The tunnel of her vision expanded back outward with her shuddering inhalation.

Marri. Marri, what's happened to you?

But of course, what had happened to her was obvious. Stefani had only to think back to her other daughter to see. Marri continued speaking, her face gravely serious in a way that plucked at Stefani's memories, minus the scales.

"For a year now, this colony has suffered. Invaded and then abandoned. Your leaders proved themselves false in your greatest hour of need, leaving you flailing, attempting to rediscover your purpose, your place in the universe. I am here today to return that to you. All I ask is for you to hear me out.

"By now you no doubt know about the terrible attack which took place just a short while ago, cutting short who knows how many lives."

Stefani's ears perked up. Marri referred to the early explosion, the wrong target. *Marri knows somehow.* Then the terrible weight of that realization settled upon her. *Marri is . . . responsible?* With each passing second, what Stefani witnessed became more and more impossible to even accept, much less understand.

"I had not planned on speaking to you today, on revealing my existence, but this terrible tragedy demanded it." Anger crept into Marri's voice and expression. "Because I know exactly how the colony's leadership are already planning to spin matters. They will blame the New Calgarian refugees. They will do so before a proper investigation can be conducted, and they will continue to do so whatever that investigation finds. Because ultimately, what they want is to leverage this attack into exerting greater control over the people of Anaranjado. It is possible that, even now, lockdowns and security cordons are being established. By the time this message goes out, it may already be blocked, and you may never see it.

"But change cannot come without hope. And regardless of what comes after today's tragedy and the response to it, I beg that you not lose hope. Not even after what I'm about to tell you. Because the truth is it was our own people, our Defective brothers and sisters, that coordinated and executed this attack."

"*Shit.*" The word left Iaz's mouth like the hiss of a teakettle on the boil. "She's just scuttled our whole alliance with the factions." Stefani didn't care, *couldn't* care about anything but seeing Marri on the screen. "But what happened to—"

"I know this because my order has the perpetrator of that attack with us, in our custody."

"Sam," Iaz finished, despairing.

"My order offers sanctuary to all who would seek escape from stifling control," Marri went on. "So we will not be turning him over to the authorities at this time. But we have been questioning him extensively, and he has revealed a great deal of information to us about this group of escaped Defectives and their plans. Including their desire to gain access to—and ultimately, control of—this world's orbital platforms."

Iaz moaned, sinking to her knees. Stefani moved by rote over to offer some form of comfort, but she couldn't tell which of them needed it more.

"It is clear this group has dark designs on our world, my fellow Anaranjadans," Marri said, and her face, so full of an adult's grim lines in the way her child's face never had been, broke Stefani's heart. "But this conflict did not start today. Let's wind the clock back one year, to when your leaders, the Equatorians, betrayed their covenant with this world, showed their true colors as traitors. But their abrogation of their duty runs deeper than you know. They abandoned us because they *are not us*, and the truth is they never were. It is a dark truth, one they kept from you. They are not truly human, because they lack Harmony. Our leaders were no more human than the Defectives who just attacked and killed so many of our dear citizens. Today, we see the cost of that abandonment laid bare. Today, we realize that they left us here to die at the hands of their very agents."

The impossibility of the words finally broke through Stefani's stupor. The statement made no sense to anyone who would think carefully about it. The Defectives had been locked up—many for decades—prior to Iaz and her refugees working to free them. It had been the Equatorians who had insisted they be locked up. To hear Marri tell it, they had been in cahoots the whole time, the longest of long cons.

But in the wake of an attack with upwards of a hundred casualties, and after a year of rising societal tensions, how many people would latch on to an explanation that so neatly conformed to their prejudices?

Marri, what are you doing?

"The Equatorians decided long ago that the rules which bind humanity together should not apply to them. They believed themselves greater than humanity, but we know the truth. They are lesser. Their abandonment of this world proves that. And for now, they are beyond our reach. But their sleeper agents are not. We need to find them, Anaranjado. Find them and root them out before they poison our world any further."

Somehow, Giana is involved. It's the only thing that makes sense. Giana had healed Ella, but in the process, somehow accelerated her growth. Seeing Marri this way, Stefani could only conclude that Giana had encountered Marri, either before they had met up or after the other woman had gone undercover among the colony's remaining leadership.

Either way, Giana had been keeping something from her.

"In the meantime, members of my order will be arriving in every settlement. Seek us out if you need aid or supplies. Seek us out if—" The feed cut off abruptly then, vanishing in a flashing blitz of strangely patterned static which lasted several seconds before going dark. Someone had apparently figured out how to jam it.

Stefani turned to Iaz to find her friend already waiting to meet her eye. Cold rage crawled all over her features, papering over the fear which looked ready to burst forth from beneath.

"Don't worry," Iaz said. Stefani wondered which of them the words were meant for. "We'll have a talk with our mutual friend just as soon as I can arrange it." So Iaz had drawn the same conclusions about Giana that Stefani had. It made her feel a little better, like she was not alone in this. "Marri's alive. That's the important thing. We'll figure out the rest as we go." Stefani's gratitude toward Iaz—not a common feeling as of late—surged even as she took in her friend's worry lines.

"I'm sure Sam's okay too," Stefani said.

"That's the hell of it," Iaz said. "I'm worried that he's not, but I'm even more worried by what it means if he is."

Which pretty neatly summed up Stefani's feelings over Marri as well.

CHAPTER 12

CAROLINE RACED back to her offices through all her secret tunnels. No matter how this went, it was already a disaster. Though at least she'd brought her own handpicked guards, so she didn't have to reveal the existence of said tunnels to Helena.

Just prior to leaving the Bridge site, she'd tried to fire off a message to Giana to meet her along the way, but having not thought to bring a unit capable of relaying communication with her, there was no way to know if that message had gotten through. A mistake she would never make again. The only positive was Helena herself had proceeded in a different direction. The latest regional ACM command post was far closer than headquarters back in Equatoria.

Caroline tried to shed her escort as she arrived home, but they were having none of it. She was not in the mood to be charmed by overprotectiveness. On the other hand, Helena's words, sounding more like a warning, echoed in Caroline's ears. She wouldn't be present if she tried to kill Caroline.

Could this all be a ruse? Was this attack just a pretext? Had there even been an attack?

The newsfeed triggered as she entered, which already told her it was urgent enough to override any kind of filters she'd placed on it for the sake of her peace and quiet. She fixed her eyes on the screen as she attempted to raise her own people to get a more detailed take on what had happened and how.

She caught only a few seconds of coverage of the incident itself before the young woman—impossibly—cut into the feed which should have had absolute priority over every other source of information.

Then she began talking, and Caroline forgot to be astounded in favor of being horrified. "No," she said as she watched this Marrietta Palmieri on the pirate signal broadcast all her deepest secrets, plus totally making some up just for fun apparently. "No, no, *no*."

The feed abruptly cut off in a strange burst of static, so it seemed *someone* had taken the necessary initiative to block it. Much too late though.

"Don't . . . move." The voice belonged to Olowe, one of her personal guards. A trap after all, or simply a man reacting on instinct to what he'd just heard? No, the timing was too perfect for it to be anything other than a spur of the moment decision. Caroline was, as of very recently, the last Equatorian. Something in this Marrietta Palmieri's words had triggered the man—her own guard!—to turn on her. She turned slowly, unable to obey even this simplest of commands.

What she saw was exactly what she'd feared.

Olowe and his fellow guard, Vega, formed a phalanx behind Caroline, their weapons level with Caroline's head. These were the new all-purpose weapons, capable of dropping both organic and cybernetic targets with ease, so she had no doubt what would happen if either pulled their trigger.

"Is it true?" Vega sounded shaken. Caroline supposed he had a right to be.

"We heard everything she said," Olowe said. He, for one, didn't sound at all unsure. "She's talking about you. About your *kind*." There it was, the hallmark of Harmony. It bound those who possessed it tightly together but separated them from those who didn't all the more strongly as a result. It was the parasite's double-edged sword.

"I'll give you one chance to come with us peacefully. Otherwise . . ."

Otherwise.

Caroline stood there, trying to process. All these months scheming, worrying over Helena growing too bold, too independent, and now this. A totally random occurrence had undone her in a single instant. It was hard to credit. Maybe even *impossible* to credit. *So fast. This Marrietta Palmieri turned them so fast after just a few words.* Caroline's schemer's brain was reawakening from its shock. This couldn't just be persuasion. Something else was going on.

One thing was instantly clear, though. There was no way she was going with them. She knew better than most what Harmony-infected people were capable of when faced with an outsider they considered a threat.

Hell, she was partially responsible for it, at least on this colony.

Vega's hands still trembled on his gun, but Olowe's were absolutely steady. "Last chance."

He was more right than he knew, if not for the reasons he thought.

Caroline turned and bolted for the door, reaching into her pocket and toggling the little remote she kept there at all times. Her true last chance was in getting away before they got over the shock they were about to receive.

A vase shattered and sparks glanced off the doorframe where their first shots missed and she had been too slow. They were trained professionals. Right about now they would get over their surprise and draw a controlled bead on her. But the door hissed open at her approach, and she was into the corridor and running. They were quick, though, ducking through before the door could cycle closed again.

"Stop her!"

Even over the growing distance, Caroline could hear the clicks as they pulled the triggers and the guns refused to fire. Curses chased her down the hall, and Caroline could have kissed her own paranoia. She had never told her guards she had a device that could disable the weapons she provided and insisted they use. This secrecy had just saved her life.

But they were big, powerful men. They didn't need guns to kill her if they could put hands on her. And she heard their heavy footfalls already in hot pursuit. Caroline had always been thin but never fit. Though she called all the speed she could muster, she knew in that moment it wouldn't be enough.

If she could just break their line of sight, maybe she could duck into one of the vacant suites or even behind some architectural feature. Small hope they would miss her, but small hope was all she had.

She rounded a corner heading toward Heller's old home and found Giana holding up her own gun.

Caroline pulled up short in shock, nose level with the barrel, only to have her aide shove her roughly to one side as two pairs of heavy footfalls rounded the corner.

Two quick shots, two thuds of bodies falling like stones, and it was all over.

Giana turned to Caroline. "Glad I got your call." Her smile was crooked and a little wild at the edges. Caroline, by contrast was glad that her little weapon-disabling device hadn't been powerful enough to cripple Giana's as well. "Why didn't they shoot you?"

"I was either just a touch too fast or they intended to take me alive," Caroline said, thinking fast. "Regardless, thank you for saving my life. Again."

"Don't jump the gun," Giana said. Both women abruptly laughed a matched set of frenzied barks at the inadvertent joke. "We've got to get you to a safer place than this. Small odds they will be the only ones looking for you based on that broadcast."

"I know a place," Caroline said.

All the way to her place of safety, Caroline kept envisioning the worst-case scenario—her lab overrun by traitorous Anaranjadans, invading insect monsters, or Harmony parasites swollen to absurd size. In part, this was an exercise in mental preparation, working through what she would do in any number of permutations of the concept of "worst case."

In part, she did this because catastrophizing was something of an obsession of hers, both an outlet for and a cause of her anxiety.

Giana clung to her like a fly on spoiled meat, head ever-swiveling, gun in both hands pointing downward but ready to swing up at a moment's notice. It was the very picture of expertise, and Caroline wasn't sure she'd ever felt more protected in her life. Thank god for the woman.

At last they arrived. It was not a place Caroline had ever taken Giana. It was not a place Caroline had ever taken *anyone*. Not since her parents died and she had subsequently scrubbed all record or knowledge of this place from every database on the planet. The door opened at her approach, but she was the only one it would do so for. Being the last of her family line, only her biometrics were sufficient to satisfy its sensors.

There was no Helena to look up in murderous triumph as Caroline entered. No revenants or blind Harmony monstrosities. Her secret lab was empty, as she'd known it would be. She stepped right through the door and under the makeshift archway she'd recently built up from scrap parts. It felt like stepping over the threshold of a fortress, and aside from that little frisson of safety, Caroline didn't give it a second thought—she'd never even tested the thing—until the moment Giana followed her through.

The alarm was instant and earsplitting.

Caroline, blood running cold, whirled to see a startled, wide-eyed Giana staring at her in sudden alarm.

"Nothing to worry about," Caroline lied, marveling at how calm she was able to keep her voice. "I forgot it's keyed to do that for anyone but me who tries to enter." She had to shout to make herself heard. "If you'll bear with me a moment, I'll shut it off." She made her way toward a drawer, not as if she was in no hurry—that alarm was awful—but as if she was in no *worry*. Every second, her heart struggled to pump ice.

It can't be. It can't. But Caroline had always trusted anything she'd engineered herself, tested or not. Still, it was hard. The woman had saved her life multiple times.

The drawer opened. In it lay a gun. Caroline picked it up and turned around, one hand in her pocket.

She found Giana's gun leveled at her head. Aha. Apparently she hadn't been as subtle as she'd thought.

"It doesn't have to be like this," Giana said. She looked almost as scared as Caroline felt. Giana's eyes were wide. Her nostrils flared around deep, sucking breaths.

"I'm afraid it does," Caroline said, slowly raising her own gun. Hand still in her pocket, the motion so small as to escape notice, Caroline disabled Giana's gun. She supposed, when it came down to it, she hadn't really trusted the woman after all. "I designed that archway myself, you see. Built the prototype right here. We haven't had time to roll it out many other places, mind, but I know what it means when someone walks through it and it goes off." She almost called Giana a traitor, but that would be the opposite of the truth. "*Something,* rather. Abomination."

Giana pulled the trigger or at least attempted to. It clicked impotently, the same way her guards' had.

"Don't move," Caroline said. "Or I'll get to see which of the creatures you are by the color of the goo that comes out of you."

CHAPTER 13

AFTER THE BROADCAST, Karl had eventually succumbed to a few hours' tortured sleep. He woke no less confused. The broadcast by Marrietta had shaken him deeply, coming as it did over both his listening device and every networked screen in the colony at the same time.

It's her. Somehow, it's her. The answer to that seemed to somehow relate to Giana, or at least one of her kind. But Karl worried what following that speculation to its conclusion would do to his morale, so he tabled it. He likewise dismissed what she'd said. It wasn't that it wasn't important, it was just that he had no explanation for it, and that didn't matter now. What did matter was she was *here*, in the same district as him. Or she had been, at least. The signal on the listening device had gotten pretty garbled by the end, possibly overwhelmed by whatever pirate broadcast technology Marri had made use of to somehow override every comms device on Anaranjado.

But the gist he'd been able to get was that her presence in his district had been a temporary thing. Jürgen was remaining a bit longer, but Karl gathered Marri had already departed.

He woke with at least a partial answer to one of his questions. It was so blindingly obvious he could scarcely forgive himself for not seeing it right away when he might have made it there in time. The question of how she'd performed the broadcast was, in truth, no question at all.

The local comms hub. Every district had one. It was the only way the different Shadyside districts could communicate with one another at all. Each hub provided a direct hardline link between neighboring areas, bypassing the ice and rock that would make normal transmissions all but impossible.

Karl had never been a comms expert during his time with the lancers. He had no idea if a communications hub could be hijacked via direct physical access in order to send a live stream to the whole colony at once. But he certainly couldn't imagine any plan more likely to succeed if that was the end goal and one lacked access to the true heart of the colony.

This being the deepest district with such comms access, Karl was fortunate that he only had one hub to check, that linking up to Middledeep. He saw no reason to waste time and allow the trail to go any colder. If they'd left any clues behind, he would find them. And if Jürgen was waiting there, if it was some kind of trap? That seemed improbable, but if Karl was wrong there, he would just deal with that situation when it arose. He couldn't hold back out of some speculative fear.

This was Marri. He had to find her.

As he prepared to dart out the door, he stuffed his fully charged tracking unit into his outermost coat pocket where he could easily get to it. Then he paused in sudden confusion. There was something already in his pocket, something he couldn't recall putting there. Karl didn't own enough possessions down here to find random things he'd just left stuffed into random pockets.

He pulled the object out, and it was exactly what it had felt like— a cash chit, an utterly anonymous little wedge of metal and plastic that could be loaded up with any amount of liquid asset and spent just about anywhere in the colony.

And despite the fact that they all looked the same, Karl was suddenly sure he'd never laid eyes on this one before. Frowning, he pulled out his handheld. It was always dicey to stick a data device of unknown provenance into something you owned, but he had a simple but crudely effective lockdown protocol installed which would read the results of the chit to the screen and allow nothing else access. Nothing was foolproof but, coupled with the fact that his personal comm unit for reaching back to Iazmaena and Stefani was another device entirely, he felt safe enough to risk it.

He keyed in the lockdown protocol, slotted the chit into the handheld's reader and waited. It took longer than he would have expected, as though his device was confused. It was almost enough to make him pull the chit out of an abundance of caution.

When the number finally came up, he was even more confused than before.

01010011 01101000 01100101 00100000 01101001 01110011

00100000 01100001 01101100 01101001 01111011 01100101

That was no kind of monetary value he'd ever seen. Karl was not now, nor had he ever been, an egghead, but even he recognized binary when he saw it. Binary could translate into text, and chits like this would ignore any letters someone tried to copy over to them, reading only the numerics to reduce any chance of a funds transit being lost in translation between systems.

This wasn't some random amount of cash. This was a message of some kind.

Hoping against hope that the message wasn't some command to wreak havoc on the few files he kept linked to this unit, he disabled the lock down protocol and queried the district network for the translation of the binary. He did it one string of numbers at a time, just in case the full search tripped some kind of watching algorithm. He sighed at how easily that precaution had leaped to the front of his mind.

He hadn't always had to be this paranoid.

At last, letter by letter and in two cases, spaces between words, he had it. It didn't seem to be a code so much as a vague statement.

She is alive.

CHAPTER 14

STEFANI OFTEN DREAMED OF COLDGARDEN. Despite the constant stress she labored under, these were generally quite pleasant dreams of a Coldgarden that never was, one in which she and Ella and Marri and Karl found a kind of happiness, spending their free time roaming and hiking far beyond the city. It was always a wall-less city in her dreams. There were no such things as revenants, no such things as hypermutation, or mutaprime, or even Coldgarden natives.

No cosmic monster in the belly of the planet.

It was just the human Stefani Palmieri, her human children, her human husband, exploring a world that wasn't bent on their destruction, and growing ever closer as they did so. An utterly preposterous dream, but no matter what else was going on in her waking life, she always woke with a smile on her face after having it.

On the night after Marri's broadcast, the dream was a demented, twisted version of itself. The city burned. The land heaved and broke, and terrible things came scuttling and oozing out of the rents in the earth, scalded by the gouts of steam geysering forth.

In this version of the dream, they'd missed the Bridge to Anaranjado. This version of Stefani had no concept of the world to which they'd be escaping. It was merely sanctuary, a place of safety as the world of their birth died around them. But their opportunity was gone, and now darkness, fire, and all-consuming hunger would battle for the right to claim their lives.

Stefani's first thought upon waking was to wonder if this small pleasure had been robbed from her forever and replaced by a small torment instead.

Her second thought was of Marri. *How? How can this have happened?*

Then she was up, full of nervous energy and the desperate need to *do.*

She found Ella standing at the foot of her bed and nearly shrieked.

"Ella! You startled me."

"What's wrong?" The girl's preternatural stare always penetrated deeper than any adult's Stefani had ever seen.

"Nothing!" Stefani said sharply. Then, deciding that was both foolish and unfair, she shook her head and began again. "That's not true, I'm sorry."

The girl's raised eyebrow was an elegant way of saying *obviously.*

"We saw your sister last night, after you went to bed."

Ella blinked but gave no other sign of surprise. There were times Stefani envied the girl her equanimity, but now came the hard part, trying to explain without *really* explaining. Stefani was determined to protect Ella from as much of this world as she could. Sometimes it seemed the only gift she was really capable of giving as a mother beyond the genetic code which seemed irrelevant now anyway.

"There was a broadcast," she said. "We were watching the news for something important Auntie Iaz was waiting for—"

"I know what Auntie Iaz does. What you all do." Ella's nod was meant to be encouraging, Stefani was sure. These little reminders of how un-childlike she really was never sat well with Stefani, but Ella tended to restrict them to times when Stefani was being needlessly circumspect.

"Fine," Stefani said. "We were waiting for some news on something Auntie Iaz had worked on, and it went all wrong, and afterward, when we were still trying to figure out what happened, a rogue broadcast started, and your sister was giving it. Only she looked too old. Much too old for only a year to have gone by."

"Like me, then."

"Yes," Stefani said, and she found saying the word was both harder than she'd imagined yet also left her feeling lighter. "Like you."

"So you suspect Giana."

"We'd like to talk to her, yes." Stefani felt an odd need to soften her suspicions, at least in front of Ella. The girl did owe her life to Giana, after all. That knowledge made any thinking about the woman fraught, as though Giana were Ella's second mother.

In truth, while she'd gone to sleep thinking dark thoughts about the woman, as she examined her feelings now, she realized they'd slipped into something closer to despair than righteous anger. Giana had done what she'd done to Ella before the strange episode that had seemed to temporarily kill her, rocking her with seizures and leaving her bleeding from nose and eyes. Stefani had caught enough of that collapse to believe it hadn't been faked, and she also believed Giana's subsequent amnesia.

So, while she certainly believed it was possible Giana Novak the mutaprime mastermind had done something similar to Marri prior to meeting up with Karl a year ago, she also believed *this* version of Giana would have no memory of doing so.

She was on the verge of calling Iaz, telling her to dismiss any plans of reaching out and risking Giana's cover just to confirm what Stefani already knew to be true when the woman called her first.

"I'm coming over," Iaz said without preamble. "It's not good news."

Iaz arrived with all the subtlety of a profanity-laced thunderstorm. Sam hadn't come home—that much Stefani was able to glean. But then, she'd have been stunned if he did, and she knew Iaz was smart enough to know that, too, however much she might have hoped for it. The newsfeeds reported that cleanup crews were still resolving the issue at the site of the attack. But the most obvious outcome was just that. Even with the little bit she'd revealed, Marri had proven that she had Sam in her custody. Enough to convince Stefani, at least. The way Iaz talked, she felt this was a message directed at her.

But the attack aftermath, which would take time for everyone, Iaz's cell included, to fully unpack, wasn't why she'd come. After making sure Ella was out of the room, she passed a handheld across the table to Stefani.

"From my source," she said simply. No more than that. She was careful to reveal nothing about her source to anyone, not even their code name. Stefani tried not to take that personally. She took the handheld and saw an exchange of text. "The first message is from them," Iaz said by way of orienting Stefani.

You didn't tell me you had an asset in Belt Buckle's orbit.

It's safer if you don't know everything.

Safer for you, maybe. Every morsel of information you withhold makes me that much more likely to get caught. Speaking of caught, your little secret asset has been caught.

WHAT? Is this because of the incident?

That amateur hour? Hardly. Though next time, I hope you actually USE the information I give you instead of ignoring it. Then maybe you can get the results you want.

I just got confirmation. Your asset's codename is Valence, isn't it?

Yes, it is.

Give me what information you feel COMFORTABLE sharing, and I will do what I can to let you know where they are.

Stefani finished with a chill. She didn't need to ask. The information Iaz provided made the answer plain. But she asked anyway. "Is this—"

"They are talking about Giana, yes," Iaz said, face a grim mask. "If this is accurate, she's been captured by Equatoria."

"Shit, Iaz."

"I know."

"Do you know how bad this—"

"*I know.*"

Stefani reined herself in. It was difficult. Totally aside from how badly Giana could compromise them, there was the additional fact of what they'd seen in the broadcast. Come to think of it, that made for mighty suspicious timing. She grasped for something that would deflect the deadly trajectory of her thoughts.

"Your source certainly is brusque."

That earned a snort of laughter. "They are that, yes. But too useful to stay annoyed at. And as many risks as we take, they are taking far more judging by the value of the intel they provide."

"It has to be asked," Stefani said. "Do we think she's really captured? Is it possible she turned?" *Or was never on our side to begin with.*

"I know you think she had something to do with Marri," Iaz said, "but I don't see how that makes sense unless yesterday was a giant false flag operation. Giana was captured by Caroline du Vernay's people. Marri seemed like she was out to tear the whole leadership structure down by inciting the populace to do it for her. How do those square?"

Admittedly, Stefani couldn't see how. She fell back on her own intuition. "The timing is just so convenient."

"At this point, I'm not sure her motivations matter all that much. Giana and Marri. Marri and Giana. Something tells me if we find one, it will be easy enough to find the other."

On that much, at least, they could agree.

CHAPTER 15

GIANA AWOKE STARING outward at strangely distorted light coming from above her. Twice during her march down to these depths, Caroline with a gun to her back, Giana had almost dared try and run. Almost dared Caroline to shoot and kill her. But she had seen the twist of hurt on the woman's face, the rage as she'd understood Giana's betrayal.

In the end, Giana hadn't really believed Caroline would hesitate to kill her if Giana gave her the slightest excuse.

Her scales itched the whole way down. It had been that way all the months since she'd had them grafted on—no simple disguise for her, not with her tasking—but it only seemed to command her attention when she was under pressure.

Maybe she had been under more pressure during her days of lost time, but if so, she couldn't remember feeling it.

Her last memory prior to a year ago had been back on Coldgarden on an ill-conceived dinner date with Arjun Khatri, her former classmate and longtime admirer. That evening had ended in a haze and then a void of awareness, but she still remembered the backdrop of fear of discovery. She had been a former Gene Sequencing employee working for the right-hand scientist of Iazmaena Delgassi, the architect of Gene Sequencing's both figurative and literal demise.

Then, she'd woken up on a slab in a morgue on another world, with Karl and Stefani and Iazmaena all swearing up and down they'd watched her have a brain hemorrhage and die. Coldgarden was gone. In truth, she'd lost only a few days of time, but they felt like another life entirely. Her former boss—the *revenant* Stefani Palmieri, she'd been shocked to learn—had done her best to explain as Giana had done her best not to succumb to a panic attack. Coldgarden had possessed no true humans. Not even Giana herself, though she'd become something even further from human there at the end.

She'd been the assistant to one powerful woman, trying desperately not to let her secret slip then. Now . . . So much had changed, and yet, nothing had.

But if her other self, that person she'd been during those missing days of her life, had managed to keep her secret long enough, *this* Giana had failed miserably. Never more than now did she wish she had the power to "turn" people she'd apparently possessed for a short while. Maybe it could have saved her life.

Once she and Caroline had reached some dungeon-like cavern Giana had never been granted access to before, she'd been pushed roughly through another arch—similar to the first, but far less prototype-looking—and the results had been the same. Giana wasn't sure if Caroline had been disappointed or gratified at the repeat result. Before Giana had time to really process what she was seeing on the other woman's face, she'd felt a jab in her neck, punching past the scales, and all had gone dark.

As awareness returned fully, she had a moment of naïve, dizzying hope that she'd simply fainted, that all the worse possibilities had been the result of fevered brain activity in the last moments before she'd lost consciousness.

Then she saw the way the ceiling lights glared off, not empty air, but some kind of curved glass extending outward and down from both sides of the arch. Everywhere she looked, her eyes took in more of the glass. She was enclosed in a bubble of it.

A cage.

Abruptly, with a lurch, the cage around her began to move, and her with it.

"I suppose I could dock your wages for the cost of the cage." It was Caroline's voice, devoid of any warmth now. "We'll have to destroy it after you're dead. But I'm not planning on employing you anymore, after all."

"Why are you doing this?" Still addled by her forced bout of unconsciousness, Giana was nevertheless aware enough to deny everything, even if it was already too late.

"You needn't waste the energy protesting," Caroline said, sounding bored of this turn of events already. "Even if the new sensors malfunctioned—which they haven't, not twice—the cocktail of drugs we injected you with wouldn't work on a human. On a New Calgarian, though . . ." At Giana's vacant stare, Caroline gave a mirthless laugh. "My dear, we've had a year to study your kind and no shortage of test subjects to work through. Though I will admit I'm surprised you woke so quickly. And I'm especially cranky that those are real scales you are sporting. That negates a lot of our assumptions in a way that makes my life harder."

Well, I'm a bit less mutagenic than your usual test subjects, I'm sure. That could suffice as explanation for both Caroline's questions. Giana would not say as much aloud though. Now was not the time to hand Caroline du Vernay any additional information, especially since Giana seemed to be unique, even among her own "kind."

"No apologies?" The brightness in Caroline's voice was back, but now Giana recognized it for what it was: rage with a veneer of strained civility. "Are your kind even capable of feeling remorse? You certainly had me fooled. Two times you saved my life. Were those even real?"

"They were real," Giana said. *Real enough, anyway. They'd had* intel that the first was imminent, which was how they'd managed to time it so well. The one just a few hours before—or was it yesterday? —had just been dumb-luck timing. Regardless, there seemed no point in playing the part of the aggrieved victim.

Caroline's smile could have meant anything, and Giana was abruptly very tired of it all.

Perhaps she should have been afraid. She was the one stuck in a cage after having betrayed—and, maybe worse, humiliated—the most powerful person on the colony. And perhaps the woman she still thought of herself as would have been. But however much she'd lost her memory of those few, crucial days in her life, she knew she was no longer the physical being she had been. She had not wakened with exactly the same personality as she'd had when her memories of Coldgarden ended. Plus, neat as the solution to imprisoning her was, it revealed an underlying truth which heartened her further.

"You seem awfully afraid of me," Giana said, giving voice to that truth once she'd arrived at her new presumed home, a bare-walled, bare-floored stone cubical of a space. Only a portion of one wall had been covered over, and that with a pre-fab style panel complete with lighting fixtures and several recessed slots in the wall. The entire room had a very unfinished feel to it.

"We've learned the hard way to be wary of your kind," Caroline said in answer. Giana had figured out early on that any kindness the woman showed was an act. Or perhaps it was better described as kindness one might show for a pet they didn't like but which belonged to someone they did. Performative only. If Caroline had ever genuinely cared for anyone other than herself, those people were long gone.

The new, harsh tone, stripped of its veneer, sounded strange in that mellifluous accent, but Giana supposed this was the real Caroline.

"We're going to ask you some questions now," Caroline said. "You have information which we need, and you're going to give it to us."

Giana gestured expansively around her. "Or you'll kill me?"

Caroline barked a laugh. "Eventually, certainly. For now, you will only be killed if you attempt to escape, and lest you think that's an easy way out, I'm talking about a *credible* attempt at escape, which, well, good luck with that."

"Good luck to you too. I mean about getting me to talk without the threat of death." Giana flexed the part of herself that enabled change, and pale, white light shone out from between the scales of her forearms as the part of herself beneath those scales flexed, stretching them ever so slightly apart. It was close to the limit of what she could actually do, but there was no way Caroline could know that.

"I'm going to make this easy for you, creature. The easiest choice you will ever make. And, I might add, a better choice than you deserve. You can answer all my questions, fully and completely, without any resistance. Provided what you tell me proves true, you might even find your way back into my service advising me on your former friends. From inside that cell, of course. This is the smart choice. When I say *former* friends, I mean it because I am the only friend you need concern yourself with now. For your own sake.

"Alternatively," Caroline said when Giana didn't answer, "we can go a different direction." Here she paused, and just before it grew awkward, Giana heard a rhythmic sound approaching the holding area. She might almost have called it the sound of footsteps, but the quality of the sound, not to mention the sheer volume, meant she had to be wrong.

She wasn't wrong.

The thing which stepped through the door filled the space so thoroughly it had to stoop to pass through. This was despite the fact that the door was large enough to have allowed them to wheel in Giana, holding chamber and all.

What entered was a vast machine, some kind of matte black robotic construct, three meters tall and just as wide. It stumped in on two chunky, angular legs, but each leg bifurcated at the knee, providing four contact points total to its plodding steps.

"This is Martin," Caroline said, gesturing vaguely at the thing. "Martin is something of a special case here at the colony. He is very good at what he does, and what he does is very valuable, but also fairly distasteful."

Giana struggled to reorient herself to the concept of this thing as being some kind of *person*, but Caroline went right on talking. "Martin was one of our earliest Defectives, a rather extreme example. He was caught engaged in his . . . predilections. As he was working his way through our system of justice, his case was flagged for further review.

"As a result, we reached an accommodation with him some time ago. We would allow him to be the very best at what he enjoys, even waiving certain of our stricter rules to facilitate his transformation into the most perfect form of that instrument. In return, he would perform that role only when we asked it of him and be put on ice in the meantime. He didn't mind. His calling is truly all he lives for, especially after our experts were done working on his brain."

Her smile was acidic, which matched perfectly the roiling feeling in Giana's gut.

"What Martin does is extract information via the application of pain. And his reward for this is a truly absurd amount of pleasure on his part. So great a pleasure, in fact, that it meets the clinical definition of addictive."

As if on cue, the thing called Martin unfolded its torso into a number of smaller manipulators. Some of these multi-jointed arms ended in gleaming, brutal edges, spines, and probes. The gleaming silver stood out against the matte black of his body, or chassis, or whatever it ought to be called. Others terminated in instruments so delicate, Giana couldn't make them out in the low light.

"You needn't think that your appearing to be a young, pretty woman will earn you any mercy from him," Caroline said. "But you also needn't think it will . . . inflame him further than a different sort of subject would. Truly, we are all just meat to Martin. Meat with the potential to scream."

Giana found she could not tear her gaze away from the thing, much less respond.

"Now," Caroline said. "Which path will it be?"

CHAPTER 16

CAROLINE DESPERATELY WANTED A DRINK, and it was doing nothing to improve her mood when dealing with the traitorous Giana Novak.

But, no. Her relentless pursuit of the proper labels to apply to things, be they matters or people, would not allow that term to stand. Giana wasn't human, so she couldn't be a traitor to humanity. On the contrary, her position as the trusted aide to the most powerful person on Anaranjado suggested she was uncommonly brave in her commitment to her kind. If such terms as bravery could even apply.

But as she watched Giana stare up at the hulking mass of Martin, a relic of an earlier, more openly barbarous period in Anaranjadan history that even Halford Heller and his ilk had apparently not wanted to lug along with them aboard the *Ultima Thule*, she had to admit that if she wasn't watching real fear play out across the woman's entire body, it was the best impression of the emotion she'd ever seen. Award-winning actors going back centuries would have nothing on this performance.

Watching that fear was like a balm to Caroline's jangled nerves. The creature had fooled her good.

"Well, now," she said. Giana jumped at the sound of her voice, like it had been a gunshot in a confined space, like she'd already forgotten Caroline was there. "Last chance before the choice is taken from you. Which will it be? Will you cooperate, or does Martin get to play?"

Giana opened her mouth, her chin trembling, and Caroline's smile grew triumphant. She had the thing. If it was faking fear, it was so committed to the charade it might as well be real. At last, she was going to get her answers.

"I—" But whatever Giana meant to say next was cut off as the door behind Caroline burst open. A figure pushed back the metal plating as though it was the flap of a stiff cardboard box to make room.

And even greater than the shock of the event itself was the fact that she recognized this figure. He was tall, even for an Anaranjadan.

Jürgen Fennec, looking far more robotic even than when she'd last seen him a year ago. Looking barely human at all. Still, it was Jürgen. Far more than an acquaintance, how could she not recognize him, even changed as he was?

"Guards!" Caroline barked before she remembered that she had deliberately avoided guards since two of them had tried to murder her the previous day. It might not even have mattered. Looking at Jürgen now, she was uncertain any of her former retinue could have taken him down.

However insane that still seemed, she sidestepped to put Martin in between Jürgen and herself. Martin was a torturer, not a fighter, and his form was not designed for anything approximating the latter, but he was at least massive. She had to fight down shakes, whether from lack of alcohol or just primal terror, she didn't know. Depending on the answer, she'd resolve never to drink to excess again or, alternatively, to drink herself to death if she could only survive the next few minutes.

"Giana Novak," Jürgen said, his words more electronic squealing than human voice. "I am here for her." No acknowledgement of Caroline at all. Absurd as it was, given the circumstances, the omission stung her.

They'd been lovers, once, after all.

"Stop this, Jürgen." Her voice was at least half disbelief. "Stop this at once!"

But if Jürgen Fennec recognized her, he gave no sign. Aside from the brief demand, spoken as much to the room at large as her specifically, he paid her no attention at all. Then, as if to make specific mockery of Caroline's faith in Martin's bulk, Jürgen struck with the speed of electricity, palm-slapping each of Martin's four leg analogs as he moved in a blur, alternating hands with each hit.

Each time his palm made contact, the affected leg popped and smoked, spraying sparks in two cases. In short order, Martin's suddenly unbalanced weight on legs that would not support him sent him careening over onto what could generously be called his back. His upper manipulators twitched feebly, but they were instruments of precision and delicacy in their extraction of agony. They were never meant to be load-bearing.

Caroline supposed it was fortunate he'd fallen away from her rather than on her.

With her one roadblock down, Caroline twisted to get out of the approaching assailant's path. He batted her aside anyway, paying her no more mind than he would an irritating insect. Her pride burned hotter than her arm where he'd struck her.

"Stop right there, Jürgen!" she shouted, but instead of wounded pride, this time she felt a stab of fear at the words. Then fear at the fear. She had never before been afraid of Jürgen, not even when she had broken up with him.

She needn't have worried. Her former boyfriend had eyes only for the wide-eyed woman in the glass cage. Caroline suppressed a ridiculous spike of jealousy over this single-minded focus and braced for him to smash through that glass with all the difficulty of pushing through wet paper, but instead, he grabbed the entire apparatus and, after making sure its grav-sled features were active, hauled the entire thing, occupant included, around Martin's fallen form and out the door.

The entire encounter had lasted less than thirty seconds.

CHAPTER 17

GIANA HAD CERTAINLY HOPED for some kind of rescue, but this had not been what she'd expected. The entire extraction of her had been so fast, she'd scarcely had time to react before she was being hauled out into the tunnels and floated along, her rescuer moving briskly but not with any particular urgency.

"Caroline du Vernay is having a crisis of trust," he said, as though anticipating Giana's question. "She made sure the complex was empty."

"Who are you?"

"I work for you."

"I'm sorry, what?" Giana was sure she hadn't heard that right.

"Forgive me," the man said in his electronic squawk of a voice. "I get confused in my speech sometimes. I work for someone you know."

"Iazmaena?" She blurted the name without thinking, then bit back naming anyone else.

"No. You will see soon enough." Then, as if deciding he wasn't in the mood to play question and answer games, he pulled a small canister from somewhere in his coat, checked the interface against one on her chamber. It was an air-handler interface, Giana realized with some alarm. But she couldn't do more than open her mouth before the man jammed the canister against the intake, mated the connections, and triggered the release of some kind of gas into the chamber with her.

She swam downward into sleep.

"All will be clear soon" was the last thing she heard him say.

Giana woke inside the same glass-walled cell. Admittedly, she was in a different building this time, and there was no hulking torture machine-man, so it seemed like an upgrade from that perspective. Still, the fact was she couldn't leave. The *other* machine-man was nowhere in sight either. No one was. So Giana attempted to find a comfortable sitting position and waited, arms crossed.

When the door finally opened and admitted a young woman, it took a few beats for the person's appearance to register. Then Giana's basic sense of reality lurched around her, a feeling she was becoming all too familiar with. Even having seen the broadcast which had turned some of the guards against Caroline, it was difficult to credit the woman standing before Giana.

She was looking at Marri Palmieri, but an *adult* Marri.

"This shouldn't be possible," Giana said, stupidly.

"I might say the same," Marri said. "Giana Novak." She shook her head in something approaching wonder. The voice, though a shade deeper, and the familiar cadence of her manner of speech confirmed what Giana's eyes were telling her. This was Marri, somehow. "You're fortunate I determined Lukas was more trouble than he was worth, even loyal to me. If he were still alive and saw you here, you'd certainly be dead. But more to the point, you *should* be dead."

"And you should be a kid," Giana said, breathless. But the renewed sense of shock was wearing off, and her ability to think rationally reasserted itself. This wasn't, in truth, the first time she'd seen someone who'd aged too quickly, even if she discounted the broadcast.

Ella.

"You're like me," Giana said. That didn't make sense. Stefani, Iazmaena, and Karl had all been quite clear that Marri was a Coldgarden native. But she couldn't deny the truth standing right in front of her.

"You have no idea how right you are," Marri said, and there was wry amusement in her words. Despite her appearance and the similarity of her voice, the more she talked, the more subtle differences from Marri Giana noted. And there was something else. Giana and Marri had never gotten along back on Coldgarden: far from it. Yet Giana felt a strange affinity for Marri the woman that she'd never felt for Marri the child, like she was family and not her former boss's daughter.

A realization struck.

"You know something about what happened to me," Giana said. It wasn't a question. "About why I can't remember."

"I think it would be safe to say that I am what happened to you," Marri said. "Or near enough as makes no difference." That was when Giana finally understood what she was hearing. Not Marri's vocal cadence, but her own.

"You're me."

"No. I'm Marrietta Palmieri. But I'm *a little* you too. More specifically, I'm all that's left of the *original* you."

"You took her over. You took over Marri."

"You really are ignorant of your own people's ways," Marrietta said. "I'm Marrietta Palmieri. I've always been Marrietta Palmieri. It's just that *she* hasn't always been *me*. But in this case, there's more of the 'donor' left over than there usually is. Had to be that way. She was special in a way that couldn't be lost. Just like in you, there's quite a bit less of the donor."

"I want to talk to the real Marri."

"That's what you're doing. She's standing in front of you."

The implication was as clear as it was dreadful. *No!* Giana forced thoughts of how Stefani would react away.

"I'm going to need you to walk me through everything."

"And I'm going to be honest with you when I say you aren't here to bear witness to what I'm doing. She—I—tried to kill you a year ago, but it didn't take for some reason. That's all right, though. You can still be useful to me. I might need a backup."

"A backup?"

"Bodies are fragile things. Even ours," she said with a very Marri shrug. "Never know when I'll need to take over a new one. Much easier when there's already an affinity between the two."

"And what will happen to me in that eventuality?"

The look she got was pitying, but it was not the kind of pity anyone would appreciate.

"If it makes you feel better, afterward, you will still be Giana Novak, the person you think you are now."

It was an effort to keep the tears from her voice. "If I'm not Giana Novak now, who am I?"

"Who are any of us, at this point?" Marrietta asked. "You. Me. Stefani. Iazmaena. Karl. Even Ella. None of us are who we thought we were. Do the specifics really matter?"

"Then at least tell me why you are doing whatever you're doing."

"You really don't remember any of it? Nothing about our purpose?" An expression flashed across Marrietta's face, but it was an expression Giana recognized was one of her own. Irritation.

Keep her talking. If nothing else, every word the woman lets slip was information useful to Giana's side. Though the fact "Marrietta" was willing to talk at all didn't bode well for Giana's chances of escape.

"The last thing I remember was meeting Arjun Khatri for dinner. I was looking into the police conspiracy in Renewal Ward back on Coldgarden. But I felt strange that whole day, like I was coming down with something. And that entire evening is fuzzy, like I drank too much and blacked out." She hesitated, but it seemed like a good time for radical honesty. "Then I woke up on a slab in a morgue on a different planet."

Marrietta shook her head in some mixture of disbelief and sympathy. "Well, I'm sorry for the hand I had in that. But rest assured it was all for a greater purpose."

"What?" Giana pressed. "What possible purpose could justify everything they told me about you? What could justify murdering a child and stealing her body?"

"We were created to destroy the creature that formed the heart of the world Coldgarden," Marrietta said simply. "That you don't instinctively know that makes you all the more interesting."

Taken aback by the directness of this answer, Giana nonetheless recovered quickly. "And from what I was told, you succeeded. So, even aside from why you had to do that, what are you doing here? Don't tell me this world has one of those creatures, too?"

"The death of the Host was our specific mandate, but I don't need to be constrained by those kinds of limits. I can help with the broader purpose."

"Which is?"

"Disruption," Marietta said. "The death of rigidity. The resistance to stultifying order. This universe is filled with life desperately seeking to cage chaos, to smooth change out of their existence and enter an eternity of predictable stability. But the only systems that do not change are dead ones. We exist to prevent that from happening."

"You prevent death by killing?"

"We kill some to induce the change needed for others to thrive."

"You say you have a mandate. Who gave you this mandate?"

A rapturous look appeared on Marrietta's face, then, one Giana was quite certain had never appeared on the girl's face before. Or hers, for that matter.

"A god doesn't speak to you in words, doesn't identify itself by a name. A god is simply your everything, or it is not a god."

"You talk to a god."

"I *exist* because of a god. And so do you."

"I'm fairly certain I was born to Herbert and Julia Novak." Both years dead to a hypermutation outbreak while Giana had been in college. Maybe that was for the best, now, as grim a thought as that was.

Marrietta scoffed. "You have my apologies. My attempt to remove you clearly only removed the part of you that was the most me. It would have been kinder if you'd just died, but it seems the rest of you was just human enough to survive and, apparently, to forget."

"If what I forgot was your *holy mission*, I think I'm just as happy not remembering."

"Perhaps soon I can make you remember," the other woman said as though not hearing. "Then you'll understand why we're more now. So much more than we ever thought we could be."

The smile she directed at Giana was both beatific and, Giana thought, a little insane.

"But we have a lot of work to do first."

CHAPTER 18

MARRI AWOKE to the usual disappointment she felt when she was aware enough understand this was a simulated world. On such days, her main goal was to try and get some sense of her true surroundings. Outside the simulation, where was she? She had to *be* somewhere. Computers produced simulations, and computers were physical objects that existed in the real world. So, somewhere, she must be hooked up to a computer, despite not recalling anything like that ever taking place.

On her most lucid days, she suspected the Professor had a hand in that. The last memories she had were pretty traumatic. Whatever had come after to lead her to this place must be even more so for its creator to feel the need to protect her from the memories so completely.

She had to be careful not to drift too far into speculation, lest the hammer of unawareness dumb her down for a time. Marri's pet theory was that her body was in some kind of coma while someone—maybe the Cult, maybe someone else—worked to purge Giana's influence from her. The first time that thought had occurred to her, it had been pretty bad. She had become very upset at pretty much every aspect of that concept, so much so that she'd been temporarily lobotomized for quite a while, as near as she could reckon the passage of time.

Regardless, whatever they were doing to fix her, it sure seemed like it was taking a long time.

But today, for once, something was noticeably different. The city no longer looked like she remembered home looking. It still stood tall and walled, but against an orange sky with a huge, angry sun hovering forever on the horizon, the top sliver of it peeking just above the wall. It was obscured enough to avoid searing her to ash but never enough for her to forget it was there.

It almost felt like she could feel its heat even through the city wall.

"Marri!"

She felt herself tense at hearing her name. Bry's arrival always signaled the portion of her day when she was about to go into her dreamlike trance and forget a lot of what was really going on in her life. Already she felt the haze descending. Despite its ephemeral nature, it wrapped itself around select portions of her mind like a smothering blanket. Bit by bit, her awareness shrank until the orange sky was just another normal part of another normal day.

"Hurry!" Bry said, dragging her along a street full of people, none of whom paid either of them any mind. "We have to hurry."

"What's the rush?" Marri demanded.

"We're running out of time."

"Time for what?" She wasn't hungry, and if she wasn't hungry, no one was, as she was the last one to get fed. She thought hard about the Mice. None of them were sick. They were literally hurrying for no reason. Wasting energy.

"We have to sort through the files before they're gone."

"Files?" She scoffed. Marri's Mice didn't *sort files*. They scrounged tech from Underguts and sold it to stay fed and warm and healthy. "What are you talking about?"

Frustration showed in every line on Bry's face in such a way that he didn't look like himself for a moment. Then he was back to painful urgency. "These files are *important*. They're a part of history."

Marri snorted. "What do we care about history?" Almost as soon as the words left her mouth, she felt a wave of dizzy disorientation and a sense of déjà vu.

"These files are *important*," Bry said. "They're a map of Underguts."

"We already know Underguts by heart," Marri said. "I'm not risking—" But she couldn't even finish the thought she had the briefest sense of recollection, of a portion of her mind being stolen from her in a moment like this, as though she had been smart and was instantly rendered dumb.

"These files are *important*," Bry said. "They show how the new magistrate plans to block off Underguts and how we can get around the blocks."

Marri nodded slowly. So, the rumor was true. This new magistrate, the one who took over for Undel, this Delgassi woman, was going to close off the tunnels. Bry was right. If they couldn't find a way around the blocks, all her Mice would starve.

But wait. No, that wasn't right. Marri shook her head stubbornly. She remembered the tunnels being blocked, but that had been a long time ago, surely? She lived with Stefani now, she—

"My cognitive matrix was not designed to house a second consciousness," Bry said suddenly. His voice had changed, lost all emotion, becoming clipped and robotic. "You are diffusing throughout my substructures and are in danger of losing cohesion and being subsumed into my greater whole. I have to collate and sort individual engram analogs before our selves become too intertwined to separate. I require your assistance in this matter."

A sensation of the entire world lurching rocked Marri. "What? What did you say?"

"That these files are important," Bry said. His normal voice had returned. Marri frowned, not sure what she even meant by that. Bry was Bry. He continued talking. "They're the only way we can figure out who adopted all the other Mice so we can get them back together."

Yes. Yes, that sounded like something Marri had wanted terribly once, even if she'd never admitted it, even to herself. Bry knew her so well.

"Take me to where they are then."

The building with the files was close. Marri could have sworn the low, worn structure had been some kind of a store selling refurbished antiques just yesterday, but she didn't quibble with the urgency bordering on desperation Bry exhibited.

Inside were row upon row of tables, each with arrays of softly glowing monitors atop computer terminals. Each monitor showed a different video file, and the videos were all short enough Marri quickly surmised they were playing on a loop.

"Pick the ones you recognize," Bry said. "The ones you remember experiencing. Touch the screen on those. Leave the others alone."

How was this supposed to—why were they doing this again? Marri suddenly couldn't remember. Oh, well. It was important. She remembered that much. So she set to her task.

Some of them were obvious. She remembered spraining her ankle and worrying for a week while it healed that she was going to starve to death. That had been before the Mice, and indeed, it had helped her see the value of working together for mutual benefit.

She remembered being cornered by two older boys, both of whom wanted the working handheld she'd found partway down a storm sewer that would cover a month's food costs. She remembered tricking them into attacking each other over who would end up with it while she slipped away.

She remembered nearly being caught by revs in Underguts with Bry. She remembered confronting Magistrate Delgassi about her decision to close the tunnels. She remembered meeting Stefani. She remembered getting that boy in her school in trouble, all so she could sneak her school handheld out, hack it, then sneak it back in again. That had been a good one.

She even remembered her mother dying, though the video of that was as fragmentary and incomplete as her memory, for which she was very thankful.

Then some were obviously *not* things Marri had experienced. A few of these depicted human adults doing things, but all the adults looked like she remembered most of the people of Anaranjado looking. None of them were people she'd met.

Many of the others, though, depicted strange things unlike anything she'd ever seen. Bizarre plants that looked a strange sort of glowing purple at the edge of sight. Similar to lights she'd seen before peeking out of nightclubs back in Coldgarden. Even stranger were the creatures. They were not humans, not Coldgarden natives, not revenants, not disease-people. They were bizarre things, with many spindly, splaying appendages, in ways that reminded Marri a little of the strange feather monster she'd encountered in Anaranjado's depths. That had been right before the Cultists got hold of her.

At first, she recoiled from footage of these creatures, but the more she watched, the more they seemed to move and act like they were intelligent. They stalked a strange, wet world, massive trees emerging from a surface of shallow water. She watched the creatures stretch out their mismatched limbs, loping about, moving in and out of obvious buildings, communicating with one another, all beneath a cloud-shrouded sky. Occasionally an orange sun peaked through those clouds, a sun that wasn't nearly as close as the one looming outside now.

But fascinating as these were, they were not what she was here for. And the last few videos proved tricky as well as unpleasant. There was Magistrate Delgassi again, but this time she was not on Coldgarden but the icy tunnels of Anaranjado. Then again, but higher up, in the habitat levels just above the tunnels. Then Giana, her innards still drying on Marri's claws as they shifted back to human hands, except now the woman was whole again, gripping Marri's wrist in a grasp of iron, preventing her from killing the man the Cultists had kidnapped.

These memories were undoubtedly Marri's, but though they were painful to recall, there was also something else about them. Something wrong in a way she didn't fully understand. So she did not tap on these monitor screens either.

At last, she reached the end. It felt like hours had passed, but surely that was all in her mind. The room wasn't that big.

"Thank you," Bry said. And abruptly he didn't sound like Bry anymore. Something was returning to Marri, some awareness she'd forgotten she'd lost. "That was very helpful." He smiled stiffly, and then, just as Marri *remembered*, before she could ask any questions, darkness rolled over her.

CHAPTER 19

"HOW DID THIS HAPPEN?" Stefani paced the room. She knew she looked like a caged animal, but she couldn't help it. "How can things be falling apart this fast?"

It applied to more than just their circumstances. Stefani felt that she herself was unraveling with equal speed. Before Iaz had arrived, she'd actually felt somewhat calmer. Worried, of course. But as focused and determined to find her daughter as she'd been any time in the past year. It was as though just seeing her alive, in whatever state she was in, had been enough to bolster her.

Then Iaz had broken the news about Giana, who was not responding to emergency comms requests. Going by the warning Iaz had gotten from her source, the safe assumption was she'd indeed been picked up and was now in custody.

Stefani had felt herself fall apart like a landslide and had been able to do absolutely nothing about it. At least she'd sent Ella out with an errand to run. The girl wore the scale-sleeve-and-stilts disguise more convincingly than any of the adults in her life.

Stefani's mind raced. "Who did I miss? Who did I need to kill to prevent this?" The answer was obvious. Marri could only have aged one way. "I should have killed her. I should have killed Giana the second we found her and Karl."

Stefani was talking more to herself than Iaz. Iaz answered anyway.

"You're not thinking straight," she said. "If Giana did this, she did it before we found her and Karl. Maybe we were wrong to trust her, but there was no way we were stopping her before we even found her. And even if we somehow could have, where would that have left Ella?"

Yes, of course. It was bad when Iazmaena Delgassi had to point out that you were being irrational. When Stefani forced herself to take a breath, she understood that it was not that she had a sudden new fear of what Giana was capable of or what she had done, it was the knowledge that the woman might have passed beyond their reach.

"Right," Stefani said. "Sorry." *Deep breaths.* "If Giana did this to Marri, she won't remember having done so. Now, whatever she was before she 'died' may have done something and not told us. That I'd certainly believe. But our version wouldn't know anything about that." Unless we think she's a good enough liar to play both of us."

"I sincerely hope not," Iaz said wryly. "Though I suppose that could be my ego talking. But let's not get tunnel-vision here. It's not as if Giana is the only one of her kind on the planet, after all."

"Somehow, she ran afoul of one of the mutaprimes," Stefani said. "If not Giana, then one of the others. I think we can say that much with certainty." She forced herself to stop pacing, took another fortifying breath.

"And just so I'm clear," Iaz said, eyeing her warily, "who am I talking to right now?"

"Stefani, Iaz. You're talking to Stefani." Irritation flared, brushed against murderous rage, and for a second, Stefani doubted her own statement. This prompted another flash of anger, this time around a kernel of resentment directed at Iaz.

They'd known each other for many years, long enough for Stefani to read Iaz like a book. She saw the regret in her friend's face. She knew Iaz had acted with maximum expediency when she had decided to make use of Stefani's unfortunate circumstance. Now, Stefani saw concern in the other woman's eyes. Concern that she'd made a mistake. But Stefani didn't need to worry about that right now. Not on top of everything else.

"Hey, don't worry," Iaz said with empathy and concern. She could read Stefani every bit as well as Stefani could read her. "Whatever is going on, finding Marri has just moved to the very top of my priority list. So that's where I'm sending you. You're going to help Karl locate her. And before you say anything, I will stay here and make sure Ella is safe. I'll guard her with my life, Steffi."

Gratitude flooded Stefani. "I will. *We* will. I swear." She was going to get to see Karl again as well. "We are going to get her back, Iaz. We are getting. Her. Back."

Iaz only looked somewhat pleased by this response. *She thinks I'm too volatile, too moody.* Ironically, this realization made Stefani's mood turn yet again, and she fought down snapping at the woman.

"I'll look into things from this side," Iaz said, seemingly determined to power past the moment. "Whoever is responsible for putting Marri in this position is also responsible for the failure of our op. I'm going to see what I can get from the official investigation, pump any sources I can for access. In the meantime, I've got to try to patch things up with the Defective factions. Taking the heat for this clusterfuck is not what they signed up for. Just promise me you won't do anything exceedingly dangerous before giving me a heads up. I'm not going to try and stop you," she said, holding up placating hands at Stefani's involuntary glare, "but it would be nice to know where the next thing to blow up in my face is about to get going."

Stefani couldn't help but chuckle at this.

"I need to run out and see to a few things, but I'll be back in a couple of hours, so why don't you get set to go in the meantime?"

CHAPTER 20

CAROLINE FRETTED the whole way back to her quarters. She took only the least traveled, most access-privileged routes, expecting a hostile gaze or an outright attack around every turn regardless. Threats would be less likely to penetrate these disused byways, long traveled by Equatorians to move about in secret when necessary. Of course, given the cramped, linear nature of most of the passages, any threats that *could* make it this far would find her easy pickings.

It couldn't be helped. Whatever else was going on, there was still the matter of the extremely mutated Harmony parasite Helena's people had discovered. Caroline had no idea if the thing related in any way to whatever game this Marrietta Palmieri was playing, not to mention Giana's unmasking and Jürgen's attack, but the sheer coincidence of timing meant it couldn't be ignored.

It had taken quite a bit of browbeating—by remote comms, of course—to convince Helena to have her people leave the specimen, rigged for travel, by the entrance to Caroline's apartments. But that was exactly what Caroline found, a miniature cryopod aboard a hoversled sitting outside her front door like some package the deliverer had been too lazy to ring the bell and hand over.

After several concurrent scans confirmed the cryo unit and sled were neither booby-trapped nor equipped with some kind of tracking or listening device, Caroline felt her mood shifting.

Her world had turned upside down more times in the past day than she had fingers on a hand. She had no idea what was happening or who was responsible, beyond a Jürgen Fennec so transformed he didn't even seem to recognize his onetime lover. In obsessing over said Harmony specimen, Caroline's mind clearly craved something that, however strange, at least existed within her sphere of expertise. It was a scientific puzzle. Impossible on its face, but precisely the kind of puzzle she was best equipped to solve.

Something over which she could feel some sense of control, in other words.

Going back to her lab space felt like a risk. The only person who knew about it was Giana, but Giana had now left Caroline's control.

But there was nowhere else she felt even half as safe. Maybe the fact that it was the last place she'd taken Giana would work in her favor. Surely it would be so obvious a refuge that no one would believe she'd return there.

She backtracked her own path, pulling the sled behind, detouring when she reached the junction that would lead her to her own secret lab, the one that had uncovered Giana Novak's deception. Once the door was sealed behind her and she'd hooked up the Harmony specimen to hardwired power, Caroline spent a considerable amount of time sweeping the entire space for cameras and listening devices, and then running as many deep-level scans of the interior of the specimen case as she possibly could without actually opening it.

The events of the past day had convinced her it was impossible to take too many precautions.

The specimen definitely came up as Harmony-related, and it definitely came up as dead. Those were the two most important benchmarks, and they would have to be good enough. Caroline finally began to relax. This made her think of wine, and to her delight, her lab's wine fridge still held a few bottles from her last surge in completing the arch. She unscrewed the cap off a chardonnay while she waited for the wall-mounted specimen test chamber to run through its preconditioning temperature drop. She would be transitioning the specimen from the pod Helena had provided to its new home as soon as the latter was cold enough.

The first three swallows of golden liquid eased the edge considerably, likely only because of how hungry she was. On that score, she was less fortunate. The food fridge was quite empty, and she had a dim recollection of eating through the few emergency nutrient bricks she'd kept on-hand in some all-nighters working on the arch, so absorbed in the problem at hand, she hadn't even cared that she was eating poverty food.

Well, she would have to deal with that later. She had the wine at least. And, sealed up in here, that feeling of safety started to grow. It was reckless to think so, but it recalled the special kind of imperviousness she'd felt when her parents had still lived, when even other Equatorians wouldn't have been able to touch her. The sudden, forceful memory of the feeling drove home just how much harm its lack had caused her through all the intervening years.

She made the calls she needed to make, careful to mask precisely where she was making them from. And, at least on the surface, no one balked or called her out for what Marrietta Palmieri had revealed, though Caroline caught at least a few hooded glances. Regardless, the new status quo was quickly established. In light of the current security situation, her people would henceforth conduct their duties from home until she worked out a better solution. She was not going to cede control of this colony to anyone, but neither was she going to gather herself and all her people together where they could conveniently be killed or rounded up in one fell swoop.

Or where some fraction of them might turn on her without warning.

She left instructions to each of her top subordinates with what they needed to be prioritizing and how often they were to check in with her regarding progress or its lack. An expedited analysis of the attack, independent from anything the ACM was conducting. An urgent alert on the whereabouts of Jürgen Fennec, as well as any Coldgardeners that might have slipped the net a year ago. Any and all information on this Marrietta Palmieri, and any known associates of that name, if it even existed in their records. And, in the process, Caroline subtly tweaked certain tasking in a way that would quickly expose Helena as a traitor on the off chance she grew overconfident and careless.

Unlikely, that, but it would give Caroline time to formulate something better, and the woman had to be dealt with sooner or later regardless of the strength of her transactional loyalty. Caroline was starting to feel invigorated instead of frightened. The wine had something to do with it, but simply taking action to counter hostility rather than merely reacting to it was its own kind of drug. She had to be careful not to allow it to lull her too far. Feeling powerful was not the same as being powerful, and she had lost far too many steps on her mysterious enemy without gaining anything for it.

Her initial countermoves done, she turned her attention to the Harmony abomination. By now the wine was fully at work in her and the test chamber was fully prepped. It was not exactly best practice to hand-transfer and then perform science on a one-of-a-kind lab specimen while under the influence, but the fact of the latter made the former seem acceptable. Besides, she'd made transfers like this hundreds of times, many while drunker than this, if she was being honest.

A few minutes later, it stood suspended vertically in a chilled preservation solution, a gelatinous fluid that would, coupled with the cold, alter its chemical composition as little as possible. The specimen container had also contained blood and tissue samples from both of the bodies found in proximity to the worm, as per her instructions. Her first plan would be to compare samples from the worm to samples from the man it had emerged from to see what could be learned.

She could wish she had samples from the two guards Giana had killed to "save" Caroline, but that might be too risky to procure depending on what had been done with the bodies. And Caroline realized, with a sense of slipping gears, that she had no idea what had been done with the bodies. It was not the sort of thing she would normally have let get by her, but matters had been fast-moving and complicated.

She shook herself. It didn't matter. For all she knew, both bodies might lack heads and therefore their Harmony worms—and considering who had killed them, maybe that was no coincidence—but there were always hormonal calling cards that acted as identifiers to various strains of the symbiont. If there was any recent relation between the two, Caroline was confident she'd be able to identify it.

Let it go. She could dig into that if she had time.

She keyed her automated systems to begin a sampling regime, relishing the muscle memory which she was able to call on for the long-disused devices. She couldn't hold back a giggle. It was only partly the wine. Being here, doing frantic, desperate science, made her feel young in a way she seldom achieved these days. Designing the arch to detect New Calgarians had been the closest she'd come in years. The stakes were so much higher now, but they'd seemed high then too. She couldn't feel any difference in the intensity of the emotion now compared with her memory of it.

Crazy, maybe, but that didn't make it false.

While the sampler worked, Caroline lost herself to the memory, the nostalgia, of those years. Her father's gruff pride, even if he never really gave her the sense she was his equal. He hadn't lived long enough for her to reach the heights of his genius. Everything they'd achieved on this world with Harmony was because of him. The Good Doctor might have created Harmony as a means to advance humanity, but with the benefit of historical hindsight, her flawed ideology had always stood in the way of her scientific genius.

Caroline's father, on the other hand, had abandoned doomed idealism and showed the true path forward: not humanity united, but humanity *tailored.* Each microcommunity on Anaranjado sported its own, separate variant. The entire colony was a giant experiment, and it had been Jules du Vernay's dream to push that experiment as far as it would go.

It was the project of more than one lifetime. But her father had held an answer to that as well, one he'd told Caroline only once she'd come of age. He had never intended to die like anyone else. It was why he'd created a special faction of the parasite, one that would drive those who possessed it to wish nothing more than to free themselves of Harmony. In attempting to escape it, they would pursue radical body alteration up to and including the brain if it meant being rid of their shackles, as they saw them. That sort of tampering with the brain was totally forbidden on this world and likely any other where Harmony held sway over the populace. The body alteration techniques they would develop with such experimentation was what her father had planned to take advantage of once it was perfected to his standards.

Both her parents had died before those standards had been reached, of course. Caroline had no idea what might have happened on other worlds where such ideas were pursued. But on this world, the Cult had been the end result.

CHAPTER 21

GIANA AWOKE with the certainty she was being stared at. That instinct was, unfortunately, correct. At first, she thought it was the man who had not so much rescued her as moved her cell from one set of walls to another.

But after she blinked the sleep from her eyes fully, she realized she was mistaken. She had caught glimpses of the other Cultists since being brought here. They were so completely mechanized they could be difficult to tell apart.

"Can I help you?" She tried to make the question sound confident, even defiant, but all she wanted to do was hunch in on herself. *I shouldn't be here. How is this happening? How can any of this be real?* That sense of unreality that had assaulted her ever since waking on this terrible world threatened to devour her anew.

Considering her overall situation and the very real physical threat any of these Cultists posed should they decide to harm her, perhaps she should listen to her instincts more frequently.

The figure put a metal finger to nonexistent lips, a universal—and surprisingly gentle—gesture for her to keep silent. Giana frowned. The figure produced a tray with food and water. This had happened before, of course, but never with admonitions to silence accompanying it. Giana had a sudden fear she was being prepared for some kind of strange ritual, and her initial instinct, which she'd just sworn to obey, was to reject the offer.

Hunger and thirst, however, were stronger than fear.

She was apparently taking too long to look eager for this offering. The cultist took the finger they had placed to their lips and poked at something else on the tray. Something Giana didn't recognize.

The device was flat and roughly circular, some little piece of unfamiliar technology. The finger went back to the lips. Giana's frown deepened. She hesitantly approached to take the tray. She expected the Cultist's body language to relax as she played along, but they retained their unnatural stiffness as they leaned forward to press the tray through the slot.

At the moment their heads were as close as they were going to get, albeit separated by the glass of the cell wall, the Cultist finally spoke. It was a simulacrum of a woman's voice, staccato and hesitant. However they controlled their electronic voices, it sounded as though the volume had been turned all the way down.

"Look at it with care. Hide it otherwise. You are not as watched as you ought to be, but act on it only during sleep cycles. Most of all, hide it from me as soon as you take the tray."

Giana almost fell backward in shock. As it was, she barely kept from upending the tray's contents. She did manage to palm the device, though, and slipped it under her thigh as she sat to regard the food and water.

A profound change came over the robotic woman as soon as the exchange was completed. She straightened, suddenly radiating the body language of extreme confusion. Her head swiveled left and right, as though trying to figure out how she'd gotten here.

"I . . . Enjoy your meal and let us know if there is anything we can do to increase your relative comfort. If you'll please excuse me, I believe some of my implants must be malfunctioning."

She strode away quickly.

Despite all the fear, confusion, and a newfound curiosity, Giana went straight for the food. It was not difficult tearing into the soft, dense nutrient brick she'd gotten begrudgingly used to eating over the past year. At least the water was just water, about as stale as water could taste, but Giana was thirsty enough that she didn't care.

Once she had wolfed down everything on the tray, she judged she'd been left alone long enough that the mysterious Cultist would not suddenly be coming back to catch her, however little sense that worry made. Giana pulled out the device. In the center of the rough circle was a flat pane of glass or plastic that made her think of a screen. The entire thing reminded her of a flat, mechanical eye.

No sooner had the thought occurred to her than she felt watched in an entirely new way.

There was no trigger or control she could see to activate whatever it was, and despite the screen, or lens, or whatever it was, she couldn't see how to make it *do* anything. She was about to put it away, the fear of discovery overtopping the curiosity, when words appeared on the panel. A screen then.

It was a bulleted list of items. Most sounded technological, and she didn't understand any of them beyond *bio microprinter,* a device more commonly called a nutriprinter, which she'd heard of in great detail over the last year, ubiquitous as they'd become in the colony. Even then, it came appended with specifications she didn't follow at all. She frowned in confusion at what she'd been handed. How could this possibly be meant for her when she didn't have the slightest idea what it was talking about?

The list vanished.

"No," she whispered. "No, no." She was excellent at memorization, even of unfamiliar terms, but she hadn't had time to go through her routine on doing that. "Bring it back," she told the thing lamely. "I just didn't have time to memorize it." As if it could understand her.

Then a new list appeared, totally different from the first one. It was far more understandable, a step-by-step series of instructions broken down into simple terminology, albeit still talking about modifying some piece of technology she didn't recognize from the context.

With a little huff of frustration, she tapped the screen with her thumb, and this list, too, vanished. She almost screamed, but then the first step of the second list appeared alongside a miniature diagram of something. Giana stared.

It was a diagram of the chamber she was being kept in.

The bulleted item pulsed in time with a glow that highlighted a portion of the chamber. She gasped in realization.

It was instructions on how to tamper with her chamber. At first, she felt a thrill of hope that these steps would allow her to escape. But as she worked through the steps, looping them over and over again, watching them refer to corresponding parts of the diagram, she realized with a sinking feeling that she was wrong.

She wasn't being instructed on how to unlock her cage from within. She was being instructed on how to transform pieces of it into something else.

CHAPTER 22

STEFANI STEELED herself as she entered the underground medical practice, unsure whether it deserved such a lofty title even in her head. If Dr. Anastasia León, the ancient creator of Harmony back on Earth, was colloquially known as *the Good Doctor* here, then the back-alley sawbones Iaz had dug up from under some rock would probably be her opposite.

Self-interested and crabby, as scaly and as tall as any of his kind, Doc Cuddles—Iaz's name for him—somehow maintained a clinic of sorts in Meridian Equatoria. The longer Stefani stayed in the ostensibly rich part of town, the larger the seedy underbelly seemed to grow. Perhaps it was simply a function of having so much of its spaces vacated a year ago, but Stefani suspected it had always been present to some degree.

Everyone had their dark little secrets, and the wealthy's tended to be darker and more secret than most.

"Palmieri," he grunted as he admitted her. He didn't bother looking up from whatever specimen he was working on. If he was surprised to see her, he didn't show it, though she'd only met him once before.

"Doc." Only Iaz had the guts to call him *Cuddles* to his face.

Stefani wasn't sure what his name was. He didn't seem keen on sharing it.

"Don't see you around much."

"I mostly try to stay indoors."

He grunted. "That's wise."

"But that's about to change."

"Less wise."

"I need a sleeve and stilts, ASAP." Even from her brief experience, she'd heard enough stories from Iaz to know there was never any point dithering with Cuddles. He didn't appreciate anything less than directness. So at least he practiced what he preached.

"Flimsy disguise. It's worked so far because there are few enough of you that they haven't really been looking. You think that's going to remain the case after that cock-up your people pulled yesterday?" He finally turned to look at her. "I assume that was you?"

Stefani wasn't naive enough to answer that question. Cuddles was a reliable source of many things but not a man to trust with your secrets. That was particularly true when Stefani wondered what Cuddles did to earn a living before the Equatorians fled the planet.

"Can you do it?"

"You'd be better off not needing a disguise. Between Novak's scaling and the tissue samples Delgassi provided me with, I've been practicing. You let me graft a pair of new legs on you, put scales on the rest, and a month from now no one will ever know you weren't born here."

"I don't have time for that kind of work." Stefani hoped she wasn't visibly paling. "I need something today."

Cuddles looked annoyed, gestured testily for Stefani to step into the chamber in the back of the room with a large red kill switch beside it. Hopefully not a literal term in this case. "Suit yourself. But you know the drill."

"If I'm caught, I've never met you," Stefani said.

"Like that will save me." His laugh was rueful. "You're lucky

Delgassi's line of credit is still good and that I'm a greedy, Defective old bastard."

Stefani had been here when Karl got his sleeve-of-scales disguise, so she knew how it worked. She stepped into the cylindrical cavity in the corner, then waited for Cuddles to trigger the privacy screen to circle around out of the wall and block her from view.

"Clothes off," he said. Stefani obediently disrobed, and Cuddles stepped over to pull her jumpsuit from her hand. Her shoes followed suit. "These shoes fit well?" he asked absently.

"Yes."

"I'll use them to size your stilts, then, while the scale sleeve is fabricating. Activating the scanner. Arms out at 90 degrees to the rest of your body. Feet shoulder-width apart."

A pulsing spiral of lights coruscated around her as her body was measured for the sleeve fitting. Stefani did her best to stand very still.

Cuddles liked to talk while he worked, mostly to himself. "You people want to make me into a tailor, a cobbler, a spy. I'm a *doctor*. I could help you better by doctoring you."

"Maybe if you offered some sort of bulk discount," Stefani said.

"No talking while you're being scanned," Cuddles said. "But funny. You need any guide documents for wherever it is you're going?" he asked, for all that he just told her not to talk.

"Who says I'm going anywhere?"

Cuddles was clearly unimpressed by her dissembling. "It's been a year. Your friends all have their disguises. Even your daughter. Not you, though. Easy enough to blend in around here if you're careful. Enough hangers-on and imitators of the Equatorians got left behind, after all. So for you to come here now tells me you're going on a trip. And no talking unless you are actually answering my question."

"I know where I'm going and to whom." That was all he needed to know. More, even. The reasons she'd been the most sequestered of Iaz's people were complicated. Iaz had been a magistrate, and then archon, of course. But the former only for a few weeks, the latter mere days. And by that point, she'd retreated into paranoia, not making public appearances. Stefani, by contrast, had been a magistrate for eight months during a period of heightened outreach to rebuild trust in city leadership. There was no telling what kind of information on her, including pictures or video, might have made the Bridge crossing.

Plus, she was Iaz's fixer. Her exposure to arrest was greatest based simply on what she got up to when she did venture out.

"One year on-planet and you aliens think you know it all," he groused. "Scan's done." He tossed her jumpsuit over the top of the privacy shroud, minus her shoes, and Stefani got dressed.

Once she was back out in the office, he walked the shoes back over to her.

"Put these on and come back in an hour," he said. "They'll be ready."

"Can't I wait here?" Stefani didn't relish spending any extra time with the man, but the idea of walking back home and out here again was even less appealing.

"No," he said. "You aren't buying enough for me to put up with your—"

He cut off at a pounding at his door. His head snapped up in alarm then whipped around to Stefani in mute accusation.

Stefani shook her head. She had no idea who this was.

"Sherman Donnelly! This is the Anaranjadan Colonial Militia. Open your door immediately and submit your place of business for inspection."

"Does this happen often?" Stefani kept her voice to a whisper, trying to control her fear.

"This happens never," Cuddles hissed. "Back in the scanning chamber. And keep quiet."

Stefani did as he bade. She had serious doubts over how effectively she could hide when you could see her feet at the bottom and, for anyone tall enough to have been born on Anaranjado, they could look down from above through the open space and see her frightened face looking back.

But as soon as she was fully within its confines, it shut in a different way, fully enclosing her and drowning her in absolute darkness.

She couldn't see, but she could still hear everything. So she worked to keep her breathing under control, fearing she'd be equally easy to detect.

The door opened. When Cuddles spoke, he sounded so kind and obsequious Stefani almost didn't recognize his crusty voice.

"Good afternoon, sir and ma'am. How can I help you this fine day?"

"You are Dr. Sherman Donnelly?"

"Indeed I am."

"I am Squad-Lieutenant Juan Lewis, and this is Private Luna Jimenez. We are investigating the attack which took place on a power substation less than a kilometer from this location, looking for any witnesses who might have seen anything or anyone out of place immediately prior or afterward. We are also searching all nearby residences and businesses in case anyone is hiding out. I'm afraid I must insist you submit to a search of your premises now."

"Of course, of course. Anything to help the ACM. Please come in."

Stefani heard booted feet enter and begin prowling around.

"Our records indicate you provide low-cost prostheses and cybernetic augmentations, correct?"

Stefani had to resist a snort at "low cost."

"Yes, that's correct."

"I see several machines in operation," Lewis said. "What are you currently working on?"

"Synthesizing scales for a young patient ready for their adult set, primarily."

Someone tromped over to his voice.

"Size checks out," Jimenez said.

"And what are these?" Lewis asked. Metal on metal *tink* sounds told the story of one of the soldiers lifting up Stefani's in-progress stilts.

"The beginnings of some leg prostheses I've just started on." Cuddles was an expert at affecting an air of pro-social obedience to authority. Stefani began to understand how he'd managed to keep under the radar for so long.

"I've never seen frames like these in leg prosthetics."

"Ah, well, yes," Cuddles sounded suddenly embarrassed for the soldier. "As you said, low cost is my aim. Few of my patients are financially fortunate enough to afford ACM-caliber hardware. But I do what I can for them, and by the grace of the common well-being, I'm able to provide them something functional if not especially stylish."

"I—of course. My apologies. It was not my wish to be insensitive."

Private Jimenez chose this moment to speak up. "And what is that cylindrical device in the corner?"

"Body scanner," Cuddles said as Stefani's heart rate spiked.

"Open it, please."

"Oh, I'm sorry, Squad-Lieutenant, Private. It's in the middle of self-cleaning and diagnostic cycle. It's an old, finicky machine. If I stop it mid-cycle, it will force a hard shutdown and all my custom settings will be deleted—"

"I apologize for any resulting inconvenience on your part, doctor. But that was not a request. Our instructions are to search any space large enough to conceal a person."

Stefani heard Jimenez's approach. She prepared herself to transform and strike as fast and hard as possible. She felt Trevor tensing within her his eagerness a counterpoint to her fear. She drew her execution knife just to give herself options.

There was a click from outside the chamber as Jimenez pressed the kill switch.

Stefani almost slammed into the wall in a springing attack before she realized that nothing had happened. The switch hadn't worked.

"I'm so sorry, Private. I didn't get a chance to finish. I was going to say that because of those risks, I disable the kill switch during these cycles to prevent such an incident from occurring. It can't be opened short of tearing it apart, but I would please ask you not to do that. If you return in an hour, the cycle will be complete, and I'll happily show you the inside."

"If an hour is required, then we shall wait an hour."

"That's certainly your prerogative, Squad-Lieutenant, but I will point out that anyone hiding in that chamber would be dead by the time an hour is up. It's airtight when it's sealed up like this.

As if his words had purged the chamber of air, Stefani's breathing grew ragged, and she forced it back under control. Cuddles had to be lying, didn't he? This was just a tactic to convince them to leave.

All the same, she began to breathe as shallowly as possible.

"In that event, I will be happy to log their corpse into our registry and—depending on its nature—bring it back for study. Now, then, we have plenty of discussion points, more than enough to take up an hour of your time, as regrettable as that is."

"Of course. Of course. Though I hope you don't mind if I work while I talk."

"Go right ahead, so long as we can keep an eye on you."

Lewis began asking Cuddles questions about people he knew. The vast majority of these were names Stefani had never heard before, though she recognized a few from the Defective factions. Cuddles stopped Lewis a few times to provide information on this name or that. Never firsthand, of course. Always *I heard from so-and-so who heard from so-and-so.*

Her heart skipped a beat when *Karl Yonnel* came up as a name they were interested in, but Cuddles pretended no knowledge there.

All the while Stefani listened, dread closed around her heart as she expected to hear her own name. Or worse, Ella's. Both came up in the ACM soldiers' questions. So did Marri's. Iazmaena's too. Stefani didn't understand how that was possible. It wasn't as though a census of Coldgarden's population had crossed the Bridge with them. She knew Karl had run afoul of Helena Cardiff, one of the colony's current leaders, so his inclusion made sense. He might even be a target of some priority if they didn't believe he was dead. But not—

It suddenly clicked. Karl had said he'd asked after them before he'd realized the danger of doing so. If Karl was a subject of interest to the current regime, surely any names he'd mentioned as important to him would be likewise.

Stefani couldn't read Cuddles's body language without seeing him, but he was absolutely selling the notion that he didn't know any of Iaz's people. She just wished he would complete the sale of the notion faster. Whether it was her imagination or whether Cuddles had been telling the truth, the air was getting thick in her hiding place. It was getting harder and harder to breathe quietly.

After what felt like an eternity but was probably less than an hour, Lewis spoke with an air of finality.

"Well, citizen, I don't think we need to take up any more of your time. We can stop back by later to check your newly clean system if we deem that necessary. In the meantime, you've given us several valuable leads to follow up on. You've been most helpful, but I would caution you to sever any ties you may have to the people you provided information on. Not only might they object to your helpfulness in that regard, but you also do not want the optics of being associated with them. Good day. Jimenez, with me."

The footsteps clomped out. Stefani nearly shouted for him to open the damn door, but she was afraid of wasting the oxygen. She was beginning to see spots despite the darkness, and that seemed like a very bad sign.

At last the door opened, and glorious, fresh air rushed in.

Cuddles frowned as she fell to her knees outside the confines of her cage of the past hour. "Your metabolism must run hotter than ours," he said. "You shouldn't have been struggling that hard to breathe." He handed her a wrapped bundle, a scale sleeve around stilts, she realized as her brain returned to normal working order.

"You need to leave now," he said. Where his manner had been gruff before, now it was cold. "I had to sell out several good people to buy enough good will to get them to leave before you suffocated. And I had to sound happy to do it." The way he said it, that had been the worst part for him. "Even with all my hedging and couching, some of them will surely get picked up. That's on me. And you."

Stefani could have pointed out he was saving his own skin as much as hers but decided this was not the time for calling out hypocrisy or naked self-interest. Not by the look on Cuddles's face.

"How do the stilts work?" she asked, trying her hardest not to gasp between words.

"Ask your daughter," Cuddles said, pushing Stefani toward the door. "She was remarkably adept at them the last time I saw her."

CHAPTER 23

THE WALK home was not a long one, but to Stefani, the streets were full of menace now. Cuddles had not waited much time between the departure of the soldiers and ushering her out the door after all. What if they'd only pretended to leave? What if they were waiting nearby to see if anyone exited Cuddles's infirmary after their departure?

She tried to walk naturally, to project an air of calm and act as if she had every right to be where she was. But never before had she so acutely felt how out of place she was on this world. Stefani saw no one suspicious, but this was almost worse than if she'd known for certain she was being watched. Even if she merely imagined it, it was a barbed anxiety impossible to dismiss precisely because she couldn't disprove it. It dug into her afresh with every step, filling her mind with catastrophe, each more outlandish than the last, yet each seeming perfectly reasonable as her fear mounted.

It was, quite simply, the longest short walk of her life.

Stefani arrived home, still shaking a little over the near miss, fearing she'd burned their collective relationship with Doc Cuddles to the ground and half-expecting to arrive at an apartment already surrounded and gutted by ACM, the one daughter remaining to her already in custody or burned to a crisp.

But the door opened to Stefani's knock, which followed a carefully prescribed pattern which told the occupants "I'm not under duress," even though it felt like a lie. Iaz's face greeted her, which was good. Stefani had a strict policy that Ella was not permitted to answer the door, ever, but "Auntie Iaz" had been known to flout Stefani's rules a time or two.

Fortunately, this particular situation didn't happen often. The past couple of days excepted, Stefani spent most of her time cooped up in this very apartment. As the only member of the resistance with a public-facing persona, Iaz was the most likely person to have been identified in the event that the Anaranjadan authorities had begun to make connections between Sam and herself. This was, in some sense, by design. Part of how Iaz had established an initial sense of trust with the Defective cells was to demonstrate that she had personal skin in the game. Harmony types loved that kind of self-sacrifice for a higher cause, and that included Defectives.

After receiving her "assignment," Stefani had insisted Iaz move in immediately so she could begin to learn the household routines, necessary if she was going to be caring for Ella. Plus, given recent events, the sooner Iaz was away from obviously targetable places, the better. She paid for this place as well, but she did so with untraceable cash chits. And given that nothing had burned down in Stefani's absence, Iaz had seemingly passed her first test of being Auntie Iaz the Babysitter.

"How did it go?" she asked Stefani after the door had sealed behind her. "Looks like you got what you went there for."

"And then some," Stefani said. She relayed the events as quietly as she could, conscious of Ella surely trying to listen in from an adjoining room and not wanting to scare—or worse, entice—the girl.

When she finished, Iaz was grim-faced. "Well, it's no worse than we expected, I suppose. Still, I could wish they hadn't gotten wise to

Cuddles so quickly. No telling how he will behave if one of us isn't in the room with him."

"You think he was afraid of what I'd do if he tried to rat us out while I was there?"

"I would be," Iaz said simply. Stefani wasn't sure how to take that. "Nothing we can do but move forward and try to make it up to the Defectives getting squeezed. And hope that none of it leads back to us, of course."

And that none of them *decide to rat* us *out.* Stefani wasn't sure how many of the Defectives were really prepared to do that. The ACM duo hadn't asked after any names of the Defective leadership, which was good. But roll-ups of those kinds of organizations often started at the low levels, promising amnesty in exchange for information to go after bigger fish.

Besides, anyone able to rat them out was too many in her book. Trevor agreed with a familiar frisson of anticipation, and that was almost more frightening than the nebulous threat itself.

"What have you been up to while I was out?" Stefani asked. It sounded like the kind of question she'd ask if she'd been gone for a weekend, but she wanted to change the subject and be dragged out of her own head.

"You mean aside from being the best aunt?" She overemphasized the last words, raising the volume of her voice.

"Debatable," Ella called from the living room.

"And just what have I done wrong?" Iaz sounded genuinely affronted.

"Made me wait to watch this while you answered the door."

"We've been getting set to look for clues in the broadcast."

"Oh, Iaz, I don't want her—"

"She's going to see it sooner or later, Steffi. It's all anyone can talk about on the networks." Implicit in her tone was an unstated but longstanding argument that Stefani treated Ella like a small child instead of a teenager. But Iaz didn't, *couldn't* understand. She was not Ella's mother. Parents always talked about how fast time moved as their children grew up. In Stefani and Ella's case, it had literally been true.

Still, Iaz had a point. "I suppose," Stefani said, acquiescing with bad grace.

"I'm unpausing without you," Ella threatened from the living room. Despite the teenage attitude, this was the side of Ella Stefani liked best. The side that made her seem as normal as possible.

"We're coming," Iaz said, grabbing Stefani's upper arm and pulling her along to make statement into fact. They took either side of the couch with Ella in the middle, and it almost felt like a family movie night except for the particular footage they were watching.

Marri's image was there, frozen on the screen. "How old do you think she looks?" Iaz asked, and there was no way she could know how painful a question that was for Stefani. She must have taken too long to answer because Iaz did so for her. "I'd peg her as being in her early twenties."

"Seems about right," Stefani said hoarsely.

"The scales make it hard, though."

"You don't think they're real, do you?" Stefani wasn't sure why she asked. "Something seems off about them to me, but maybe . . ."

Maybe I'm just telling myself what I want to hear, which is that they are fake.

"Start it," Ella said. The girl was frequently an intense person, but Stefani had never seen her daughter *this* intense. It was her sister, though Ella would have no conscious memories of Marri, of course. *She must be curious.*

Iaz played it, and they watched. Iaz looked analytical, and Ella looked positively hungry. But Stefani had trouble making herself even look at the footage. She couldn't close her ears though. The voice was clearly older than that of a thirteen-year-old girl but also unquestionably the same person. Marri, but older. Even having seen the same phenomenon take place with Ella, it left Stefani feeling shaken.

The speech wound down, and before Stefani could ask Iaz not to play it again, Ella jumped into the silence.

"*This* is the footage of Marri?" She sounded genuinely confused, a very uncommon occurrence. The girl frowned at the screen, brows knitted together.

"Yes," Stefani said, letting her uncertainty show in her tone.

"But that's not Marri."

Foolish hope flared in Stefani's heart, even as her brain fought to tamp it down. *Oh, my darling, I know you seem way older than you are by any measure, but there is no way you remember what Marri looks like given how old you were the last time you two were in the same place together.*

Iaz, by contrast, gave the girl a long, considering look. "Who is it, then?"

Ella looked as though she wasn't even listening. Her frown deepened further, and even with the image frozen, she leaned toward the screen as though she meant to crawl into it, the better to confront not-Marri directly. Ella kept shaking her head. The motions were minute but so continuous it almost seemed like some kind of involuntary tic.

"Ella?"

Abruptly, as though coming out of a trance, the girl shook herself, and her face smoothed back to placidity. She swiveled her head to take in both Stefani and Iaz.

"It's Giana," she said.

"All right," Iaz said after killing the video. "Let's walk through what you just told us, what it means, and how you know." Both adults were giving Ella their full attention, but Stefani was relieved the other woman was here. She was not sure she had the fortitude to have this conversation without help.

Had Ella been wearing her teenager mask—as Stefani shamefully thought of it—she might have huffed or blew up to puff out her bangs or rolled her eyes with devastating overtness. But, perhaps sensing how businesslike Iaz was being, she seemed to have adopted her more honest, brusquely pragmatic manner.

"That's not Marri. It's Giana. But," she said, cutting off Stefani trying to break in with a question, "it's not the Giana that works for Auntie Iaz. It's the original Giana. The one that made the one who works for you."

"What? How . . ." Iaz fought to get the words out. Stefani, by contrast, stood dumbstruck. The words, insane though they were, had been delivered with a conviction only possible with absolute certainty.

I can't afford to lose my voice now. There was so much to unpack, and nearly all of it sounded like terrible news. She started at the end. "There's more than one Giana?"

"Yes."

"Ella, if you knew that, why didn't you mention it before now?" Iaz's tone was only mildly accusatory, but Stefani felt herself bristling anyway. She fought it down because it was a good question.

"Because I didn't know it until I saw that footage," Ella said simply. "It's like the information is there, right? But I can't always access it. I have to have the right frame of mind, or immersed in the right context, to get at it."

"Okay," Iaz said, but less in agreement or acknowledgment, more simply to steady herself. "Okay. Let's go back. Our Giana appeared to die then woke up in the morgue with no memory of anything after Coldgarden. Or so she claims, at least."

"I believe her," Ella said.

"We do too," Iaz agreed, and Stefani nodded in agreement, albeit a bit grudgingly. It was still true, she reflected, but it was like a building sitting upon a sandy foundation. Every new revelation about her felt like a wave crashing against the shore, washing more of that sand out to sea.

"But before seeming to die," Iaz said, "she'd known everything that had happened. Or at least that's how it appeared. She fixed you. And she made some pretty outlandish claims, claims Karl believed were true."

Ella's gaze shifted to Stefani, the acknowledged authority on Karl while he was away including, apparently, what he believed.

"I think he believed her more than anyone," Stefani said.

Iaz sighed then went on. "She claimed she was a copy of the Giana we knew, that she'd been birthed into the world as a version of mutaprime who could co-opt humans. She claimed the other her had seduced a colonial and she was the result of that union."

Stefani gritted her teeth. Here went "Auntie Iaz" talking about the birds and the bees with her not-niece.

"Yes," Ella said. "Yes, I think that fits."

"So you're saying our Giana, both before and after she died, was telling the truth." Some part of Stefani had to know this, had to know if they'd been betrayed. Or, more importantly, if Ella had.

"Yes."

"And the person calling herself Marrietta," Iaz said, "is the version of Giana who birthed *our* Giana."

"No."

Iaz froze. "What?"

"No. Our Giana is too far removed from that one. I-I can't explain how I know. But I know." The conviction in her voice remained unshakable. "They couldn't be as different as they are only one generation removed. Something else happened. Some other step."

Stefani reeled. "You're saying there are *three* Gianas?"

"Were," Ella said. "I overheard Karl telling you that our Giana ate *her* mother, remember?"

"He did say that," Stefani said, stomach twisting both at the notion itself and on Ella casually overhearing it.

"All right, fine," Iaz said, and by her tone she was equally done with hearing those details. "But that's not really answering our question. How is this person who looks just like an older Marri actually Giana? I thought your *people* couldn't just shapeshift to look like anyone."

"We can't."

"So then what are we seeing?"

Ella thought comically hard about this. Stefani felt it wasn't part of her teenage persona. There was something almost vulnerable about the expression.

"I think what I said before wasn't quite right. It's Giana, but not. She's taken over Marri. Co-opted her. It's Marri's body, but it's been remade into one of my kind. She will call herself Marri, believe herself to *be* Marri. And really, she is. She's what's left of Marri."

Stefani felt a horrible sinking in the pit of her stomach. She almost couldn't form the words. "So Marri, the Marri we knew, is gone?"

Ella nodded, though she looked as though she knew the pain she was causing and regretted it. "Like Giana was at some point, the mutaprime has replaced her with a version of herself that's also mutaprime."

Stefani had to lean back. Her vision was tunneling. She placed her feet up on the coffee table, trying to elevate them. Iaz took over the questioning.

"Then why did you say she was Giana when you saw her?"

"That's the thing." Ella opened her mouth to say more, then closed it, looking frustrated. "Sorry. I'm just realizing a lot of this right now, while we're talking."

"More context-dependent memory?"

"I guess so. Anyway, there's a lot of underlying information that gets transferred to any new version of my kind. Any version that can think, anyway. Call us Gianatypes. The person still feels like the person and has their memories and their mannerisms and all, but there's a bunch of new stuff in there. And they don't have the same priorities they did before. But in this case, it's different. It feels like Giana put a lot of herself in there when she took Marri. As much of herself as she could, I think."

It was a concept Stefani of all people found chillingly relatable.

"And you can tell all this by looking at video footage?" Iaz marveled.

Ella nodded. "It's like we're connected, in a way."

Iaz felt another little chill. "Because our Giana fixed you?"

God, Stefani thought, despairing. At this point, she could only hope that's what had happened. Propping her feet seemed to be helping. Or maybe that was Trevor's coldness descending, muting her emotions, dulling their edges.

Another nod from Ella. "But she had a very light touch with me," she said, seemingly to reassure Stefani, whom she darted a concerned glance at. "Lighter than normal, even. Not like this at all." She pointed at the screen even though it was dark. "It's like she thought it wasn't enough to just transition the standard information and move on. She wanted as much of her *specific* experience to live on in Marri as possible."

"Like she thought she was dying," Iaz said, musingly.

"And she knew something that couldn't be allowed to die with her," Ella said.

"You talk about this information, the standard information. What's in it?"

Ella screwed up her face again, even more so than before. "It's there but fuzzy. I don't think I got a good copy. I definitely don't have anything extra that might be motivating Marrietta."

Stefani fought down bile. She hated hearing the girl talking about Marri as though she were something else entirely now. *That's your sister!* But her discomfort was her own, not on Ella's behalf. She knew this. And not for the first time, not even for the first time *today,* she regretted ever taking on a human identity.

"Anything you can tell us," she said, forcing calm into her voice, which sounded too thick in her ears. "Anything that might shed the slightest light on the original Giana's motivations, what she's after and why. Anything might be helpful in saving your sister."

"There's this . . . force," Ella said. "It drives everything we do."

"Like a hunger?" Iaz asked. "Survival instinct? Sex?"

Ella shook her head vigorously. "No. An external force. It's a part of us, but it comes from outside us. If I really concentrate hard, I can feel it." Fear flitted across her features, and abruptly Stefani's fugue lifted, replaced by the mantle of the protective mother, a person who never wanted to see fear on her child's face. Even worse, she couldn't ever remember Ella looking afraid. It was both shockingly normal and incredibly unsettling to behold. "It's weak in me, but I still don't like it."

Iaz clearly wanted to press for more. Stefani looked a warning at her old friend, and Iaz blinked in a way that seemed to promise a gentle approach.

"I need you to tell me whatever you can," she said.

"It's old. The force, I mean. Very old. And, ah!" Ella's eyes shot open wide. "It's alive! It's alive. Not in any way we would think of that word, but it's alive." She turned to Stefani. "Mom, I don't want to think about it anymore. I'm scared if I do it will *notice* me."

God, the child was actually trembling! Stefani gathered her up in a hug. For once, she didn't resist, didn't stiffen. She just allowed herself to be folded in her mother's arms.

"It's all right, sweetheart," Stefani said, squeezing. Ella hugged back, hard. "You can stop thinking about it. I'm sorry we asked you to."

"It wants chaos," Ella said into Stefani's shoulder, her words a whisper as though she feared being overheard by this force. "Order repulses it. That's why it made us."

"Chaos," Iaz said to no one. The word had an elemental sound to Stefani's ears. That concept could certainly fit with the mutaprime goal of killing the creature at the center of Coldgarden. If she couldn't call an ageless, planet-sized intelligence a representative of the concept of order, she wasn't sure what could earn that title.

And it seemed to fit whatever Marri planned now based on the information she had revealed in the broadcast. If she'd been doing anything with that speech, it had been fomenting chaos.

Ella shuddered in her arms, and Stefani pushed aside such thoughts. Her daughter needed her, and rare as that even was, it meant her need was even more dire.

Stefani realized then that a part of her had wanted this, had wanted Ella to need her in the way a normal child did. Yet being faced with the reality of her terrified daughter, she felt nothing but shame at the impulse. She had folded herself around the girl, seeking as much as giving comfort, when a knock sounded at the door.

A knock in a very particular pattern.

All three of them straightened suddenly, eyes glued to the door. Only one person would use that knock.

Ella was fastest to her feet, tears still glistening on her cheeks. She triggered the door to open before Stefani had taken so much as a step or managed a cry of caution. Maybe she'd been slow out of certainty, or at least hope.

A tall shape entered, the door shutting behind him. Despite knowing who she would see, Stefani gasped in stunned delight.

Then she dashed into his arms, Ella standing aside to make way, her normal reserve rebuilt.

"Karl!"

"Hi, Stef," he rumbled comfortingly in his deep voice as he hugged and then kissed her.

"What are you doing here?" Stefani could have kicked herself for blurting the question out.

"A lot's happened," he said. "Things I wouldn't be comfortable saying, even over a secure line. I figured in-person was better. Plus, I might have missed you. A little."

She laughed into his chest. It felt good, and some of the tension left her shoulders and neck. With him here, things that had seemed impossible now felt merely difficult.

"Come on in, Lance Commander," Iaz said, as if this was where she lived. "We have a lot to discuss."

It took a few minutes for the four of them to calm down after Ella's outburst and Karl's arrival. Ella recovered by way of repeating her revelation about Marri to Karl while studiously avoiding any talk of this external force that frightened her so. Afterward, she had returned to her stoic self, as though the second explanation had somehow erased the first from her memory.

Then, rather than get right into it, they broke for a meal of the kind they hadn't shared in months. Karl was resolute in his determination to steer clear of shop talk, trying to keep the mood light, and Stefani was grateful for it. Afterward, Iaz said she wanted to gather her thoughts and what information they had and assemble it into something coherent. Karl suggested they wait until morning. "We could all do with a night's sleep, I suspect."

He and Stefani didn't sleep, not right away, anyway. Their lovemaking was thick with desperation. The emotion took on a different aspect in each of them, but fortunately, those separate shapes complemented one another perfectly.

Afterward, in the liminal space between drying sweat and the rising chill of the apartment's nighttime temperature settings, Karl spoke.

"I got a message." His words were hesitant, as though he wasn't sure he wanted to reveal this to her at all.

"What message?"

He hemmed and hawed a bit before replying. "I don't want to get your hopes up. Not after what Ella told me about 'Marrietta.'"

"Karl, you will tell me what this message said and where it came from right now."

"Three words," Karl said. "Planted in my pocket by one of Marri's—Giana's—*whoever's* people. I had no idea what they meant until this new context." He pulled out his handheld and handed it to Stefani.

Three words, he'd said. It was no exaggeration.

She is alive.

Stefani looked to him with sudden, painful desperation seizing her heart. Karl's answering smile was restrained, somber, and overwhelmingly kind.

"Assuming this message was directed at me," he said, "there's only one *she* who makes sense: Marri. Do you know what this means?"

Stefani didn't trust herself to answer.

"It means that for the first time since I went down into those frozen depths, I have a place where I know she's been and I have someone who wants me to know she's out there."

CHAPTER 24

AS STRAIGHTFORWARD as the instructions had seemed, it was not nearly as easy to tamper with the interior of the cell as Giana had hoped. The main issue, of course, was that she lacked tools. Fingers were a poor choice to pry apart machine components that were not meant to be pried apart.

At first she tried asking for utensils with her meals, claiming it was more civilized. But though her request was always granted, it led to her having a minder while she ate to make sure said utensils were returned. After two attempts at this, hoping for another strange inter-action with one of the Cultists where they secretly wanted to help her, Giana abandoned this approach.

In the end, she only saw one option. After all, she was covered in hard, thin scales.

A true human would never have been able to do this. Scales in humans had a durable underlayer which replaced the outer layers of skin, so to remove one would involve tearing the layer, leaving infec-tion-vulnerable inner skin layers and the muscle beneath exposed to the elements. Giana, of course, was not a true human. Her scales were merely intended to be a disguise, so they lacked that anchoring underlayer.

For her, it was *not* impossible, merely excruciatingly painful.

The hardest part was doing it without screaming, swearing, or otherwise giving away that something was amiss.

It's only one, she told herself. One of the big ones on the front of her right thigh. She was able to get her fingertips under those, and while her mutaprime fingers were not capable of becoming fine, honed tools for prizing apart machinery, they *were* durable enough to dig out a scale. *You can do one.*

It sounded nice in theory, but even with her considerable strength behind it, the damned thing didn't want to come out. Its curved, burgundy smoothness twisted in her hand, the anchor point deforming rather than failing. It brought such agony she had to stop before she couldn't hold it in anymore. Damned Doc Cuddles and his professional pride.

She had to fight down sobs after she stopped, waiting for the throbbing pain to slowly ease. Okay. So that had not gone well at all. There was absolutely no way she could peel away a scale with simple, brute force.

But maybe that was the wrong approach. After all, she knew something of what she was, even if she didn't like to think about it. Karl had told her the full story after she'd woken in the morgue. How he'd met her shortly after their arrival on the world and his own escape from ACM custody. How she'd been in the throes of labor and had sent him away. When they'd finally reconnected, he claimed she'd both appeared and acted younger, only to rapidly age back to the age he knew her as. She'd also spoken of sleeping with an Anaranjadan and hinted that had been what precipitated everything.

The implications seemed clear, if revolting. Still, Marrietta's talk about her lent credence to Karl's interpretation as well. But it wasn't until *after* all this that she'd appeared to die. That had been Marrietta's attempt to remotely kill her, tying up a loose end. Giana was here now because of that partial failure.

She knew from past reading and experience that memory was

state-dependent. Now she wondered, though, could it work in reverse? Could state be memory-dependent?

Think back to the last thing you can remember before waking up in the morgue.

Easy enough. It was the meeting with Arjun. She'd been trying to find a way to infiltrate and gather information on the police conspiracy brewing in Coldgarden, one that had set its sights on Stefani specifically. Arjun Khatri, former friend and unrequited-admirer-turned-cop, had seemed the perfect avenue, however uncomfortable the concept of the meeting and its false pretenses had made her. Even thinking back on it now, fuzzy as it was, made her squirm. But, unlike all the other times, this time Giana forced herself to dwell in those cringing recollections.

What if it wasn't the awkwardness of attempting to reconnect that made her uncomfortable? What if it was something she'd done after her memory had faded out?

Bit by bit, she clawed the memory back. Every step was as mentally painful as removing the scale had been physically. But she remembered beginning the process of seducing Arjun on their way back to his place, remembered not even understanding why she was doing so, simply feeling an overwhelming urge that had nothing to do with desire. Then, she'd stopped, momentarily coming back to herself.

In a flush of shame, she'd returned to her apartment and *changed.*

Her hurried steps to the bathroom felt clumsy and sluggish as the swelling phenomenon repeated itself all over her body, including her face. The fluid in her distended skin sloshed with each step. It threw off her balance. The sense of illness made it difficult even to think. Her mind was a rising buzz of formless panic.

Through it all, she felt a scrabbling sensation deep within her. As though bits of herself too small to see were somehow reordering and reorienting themselves. As though the story Giana told herself about herself was being edited in real time.

After what felt like an eternity, she caromed off the bathroom door-

frame. Though she was rewarded with a fresh bloom of exquisite pain, she managed to fall through the doorway to the tub's edge. She flopped her whole body into the tub like a beached whale but didn't manage to reach the faucet knob before her flesh began to slough from her in great clumps, falling with sickening squelches to stain the white porcelain.

As her panic escalated, Giana began to hyperventilate. She could barely suck enough air through her swollen nose and mouth. Her vision tunneled down to blackness before an eerie calm descended. It was as if some force external to herself reached into her with a calming caress.

Easy, *it seemed to whisper.* Easy. It will be over soon. One last time. You are almost broken.

These thoughts from not-her should have frightened Giana, but she found them soothing instead. She sank into the reassurance they offered, a promise of an imminent future without doubt or worry. Succumbing fully at last to a process a year in the making, her aware-ness went gray for a time.

Eventually, the pain receded, the sense of rearrangement abated, and Giana found herself staring at a haphazard pile of her own swollen, torn flesh occupying the tub. She examined her own feelings and was surprised to discover that drool slicked her chin and that she was hungry in a way she'd never felt before.

As if guided by their own minds, she reached raw, skeletal arms like claws with shaking eagerness, and they tore away great hunks of the jellied, liquefying flesh piled up before her and brought dripping strips of it to her salivating mouth. As she moved to bring herself closer to her meal, she could feel her skin clinging to ribs that stood out like bars on a window.

She swallowed great gobs of herself with gusto. A part of her wanted to retch with disgust, but that part had changed along with the rest of her. It had been torn down, distilled to its essence, and now it was smaller than it had ever been.

She understood what it was now. It was the last kernel of her humanity, and it only still existed to pantomime how a human should behave, so no one would suspect her to be anything else. Its worries didn't matter. Its sense of disgust or propriety didn't matter. Giana was hungry, so she ate what was available. It was as simple as that, and there was nothing wrong with eating when you were hungry. She was hungry, and this was her food.

It had, after all, been her a few moments ago. Who better to eat it?

Giana almost vomited at the force of the recollection, in part because of the vileness of the sensations, but mostly because of the change she felt as it rippled through her body, from the top of her head down to the soles of her feet.

The scale came away easily in her fingers. Suddenly, it was all she could do to keep every scale from dropping free of her now fluid, glowing flesh. She could see the pallid light emerging from the patch of herself peeking up from where the scale had been.

She banished the sensation as quickly as she could. It was, fortunately, far simpler to do than finding it had been. As she did so, she felt her flesh find its shape again. Where the scale had been, now there was a patch of pink skin. It looked a little raw and new, but otherwise healthy.

More importantly, she had her tool.

CHAPTER 25

 morning brought with it a greater sense of hopefulness than Stefani had felt the previous day. It might have had something to do with the lingering effect of the warm glow she felt at the realization that Karl was here, really here. But mostly it was due to the message. He hadn't wanted to get her hopes up, and in this he had failed. Now Stefani hoped the strength it leant her was enough to sustain her for what she knew she'd have to endure soon.

"So here is what we know," Iaz said, kicking off the post-breakfast meeting by activating the table's holo-projector. "My part at least."

Stefani noted that Ella now acted as if she was simply part of the team. But she noted it silently, not inclined to stop her daughter from participating the way she would have done even yesterday. She couldn't ignore the truth that Ella had insights into the mutaprimes that none of them had access to anymore, with Giana missing and presumed captured.

Iaz keyed in the script to bring up the images she had assembled the previous night. To Stefani, she looked to be steeling herself for something difficult. Stefani knew the feeling.

An image of Sam appeared. "I know our recent op may seem like old news at this point, but it took me a while to get the necessary details to know exactly what happened, and I think it's very relevant to our newly emerging concerns regarding Giana and Marri. The op was set to be carried out by Sam, and it was to be the first active attack against the Equatorian Remnant. It should have taken place two days ago."

Karl shifted uncomfortably at this, as he did whenever talk of attacks cropped up. Stefani saw a muscle in Iaz's cheek twitch as she noticed the shift. Karl was not a human and had never been a human. But Stefani knew he struggled to let go of the idea that humans were the good guys and that they shouldn't be fighting them. She found it endearing—if occasionally exasperating—but Iaz seemed to consider it a threat on her bad days.

Considering what she must be feeling about discussing Sam, it was a potentially volatile mix of emotions Iaz was likely immersed in. Stefani put a hand lightly on Karl's forearm to restrain him from giving in to the temptation to speak his mind. Iaz briefly met Stefani's eyes with a look of gratitude and went on.

"We planned to inflict a targeted power surge to destroy a local grid relay. Easily repaired, but in doing so, there would be no mistaking that it was an act of sabotage, and that was the point. Not casualties," she added, certainly to mollify Karl.

In fact, Stefani knew they'd explicitly chosen a time and target which would minimize if not eliminate casualties. The relay in question was not responsible for recycling air nor in charge of any critical climate control measures. Between those two factors, any power outage on Anaranjado that dragged on long enough meant people would start broiling, freezing, or suffocating. Not necessarily in that order.

But, by design, not in this case.

"We wanted to appear to be sending a warning shot of sorts," Iaz went on. "A demonstration of the kind of thing we *can* do. In actuality, the goal was to provoke a specific security response."

"But you can't think the people on this planet would side with your grievances, the grievances of another species, over their own?"

"Let her speak," Stefani said to Karl, keeping her voice gentle.

"That's not what we think at all," Iaz said. "Provoking a security response isn't about causing a crackdown to turn public sentiment against the regime. Harmony makes that a lost cause. The only way we get what we want is to negotiate from a position of strength. The purpose of provoking a security response was based on our intel projecting a redeployment of forces in ways which would leave our actual goal less defended. Subsequent attacks would reinforce this trend, eventually allowing us relatively easy access to the shuttle yards and the orbital platforms."

"But it didn't go to plan," Karl said.

"No, it didn't," Iaz said. "It went about as poorly as we ever could have imagined. Wrong time. Wrong target. Worst of all, a response that gave us the exact opposite of what we were looking for."

"Something going wrong randomly would produce a similarly random result," Stefani said. The device failing, or Sam getting picked up, anything like that would have been bad luck but not outside credibility. But the result would also feel more haphazard than this one had. "This," she went on "coupled with the broadcast went wrong in precisely the way necessary to achieve the opposite of what we wanted."

Iaz grimaced. Stefani knew her friend wanted, more than anything, to believe Sam hadn't been flipped on them. But on this world, with a parasite wriggling in his brain, even one that ostensibly didn't work, who could say?

And it was, in the end, the simplest explanation, painful as that was to admit.

"Specifically," Iaz said, obviously powering past that point, "it went off here." The map shifted, showing the distance and shortest path between the two targets, planned versus actual. "A crowded night club. The surge alone fried everything cybernetic in anyone standing within three meters. Which turned out to be a lot of people.

Anyone with cybernetic limbs, eyes, anything of that sort, will need replacements. And if they were unfortunate enough to have critical meat organs, like their hearts or lungs, replaced or even assisted by cybernetics, they're just dead."

"And our allies take the blame," Stefani said.

"So says *Marrietta*, anyway," Iaz responded with grim humor.

"Then let's talk about the elephant in the room," Karl said. "Marri. I think I might have a lead on how we can find her.

"This agent, one of this 'Marrietta's' own cult or order or whatever she wants to call it, he planted it during an encounter he and I had. He's talking about her. About *our* Marri. Based on what Ella said, I don't know how. But somehow, she's alive."

"Unpack this for me," Iaz said. "Who is this agent exactly? How do you know she's one of hers? And you'd better start at the beginning. I don't want to have to ask a bunch of dumb questions."

Karl took a moment to compose himself, his arm never leaving Stefani's shoulders. Then he told them about Jürgen Fennec, this agent of the so-called Cult that had supposedly haunted Shadyside for years.

"So at first I figured I'd approach him," Karl said, "since he's still something of a regular figure down there in the tunnels. But the rumors don't stop with him switching sides. There was talk of a power struggle, one so profound the Cult abandoned its headquarters and moved elsewhere, intending to take a more active role in colonial affairs. I was able to confirm that last part at least, regarding the move. I found their old headquarters. It was empty, abandoned, but it hadn't been for very long. I found traces of files which had been wiped with timestamps from less than a year ago. No useful intel beyond that, but it confirmed at least part of what I was hearing.

"It all added up to two things. First: I was looking for the Cult in the wrong place. They'd moved, and judging by how absolute their clearing-out was, it was a significant move a significant distance away. And second: the Cult are clearly major players on that side of the planet. That meant they were either potential allies or potential enemies, and I needed to figure out which. Which further meant that a direct approach wasn't the best move. But I could still force myself into close proximity with Fennec, maybe plant a bug on him, let him at least show me where they'd relocated to so I can start questioning people with more recent interactions.

"But while I'm working on that, trying to pin down how I can bump into him without seeming suspicious, I'm digging into more and more stuff about him. Turns out he was something of a private eye, helping find missing people, that sort of thing. I'm tracing every lead of every person who's ever hired him, worked with him, interacted with him. And something else comes up."

"Marri?" Stefani said.

"Marri," Karl mirrored. "As near as I can gather, a year ago Fennec was shopping around for a place in Shadyside where two people—some say clients, some say Equatorians, some say Coldgardener refugees—could stay for a little while. He's shaking down everyone who owes him a favor, looking for anyone who can take these two people and keep them fed indefinitely. That kept coming up, how high their caloric needs would be. Everyone agreed it was one woman and one teenage girl."

"Still a pretty big stretch," Iaz said. "Or it would have been, I guess, before two days ago."

"My thoughts exactly," Karl said. "Suddenly it seemed a lot less of a stretch. And wouldn't you know it, but I happen to run into Fennec just a few hours before that broadcast. And I successfully plant a bug on him, too, enough that I hear him talking to this Marrietta just before the broadcast goes live." His voice had gone tight with intense excitement. "Only later did it turn out he'd planted something in my pocket too. The message. *She is alive.*"

"Almost like he knew the context necessary to understand it was set to happen later that very day," Stefani said. She fully bought into Karl's excitement, and more, her sense of hope was swelling.

"So you're saying this Cult is under Marrietta's control, and

Jürgen works for her, but also is somehow trying to undermine her by getting in touch with us? To what end?"

Stefani had to fight down irritation at Iaz's skepticism. *I can't just believe a thing because I want it to be true. She's right to be suspicious about the timing.*

"I have no idea," Karl said. "But if I'm being entirely honest, I only came here to tell all of you this. The next step is clear. I've got to find him. And it won't be easy. He left the district not long after that conversation, and I haven't picked up his signal since. Maybe he found the bug. Maybe he relocated elsewhere and won't be back for a while. Doesn't matter. I've got to find him."

"We," Stefani said, removing his arm from her shoulders and wrapping her own arms around it. "We've got to find him. And through him, her."

CHAPTER 26

WHEN MORNING CAME, Giana almost ruined everything by not noticing. It was a frantic scramble to hide the work she'd been doing with her crude tool when she heard someone coming.

Marrietta entered, her relative youth belied by the easy sense of command with which she carried herself. A cultist flanked her to either side. Giana couldn't tell if either was the one who had helped her, but it hardly mattered in this case, unless they went weird again and blurted all that had passed between them.

Regardless, the visit seemed official in a way that the previous one hadn't, which made Giana nervous.

"I have a proposal for you. One which will take you out of that cage, if you're willing," Marrietta said. Giana almost laughed at the thought of a night without sleep utterly wasted until Marrietta added, "Temporarily, of course."

"Where do I sign up?" Best to sound eager, if wary. Fortunately, that was how she actually felt.

"You don't want to even hear what we're doing first?"

"Would you, if you were me?"

Marrietta laughed. "Probably not," she said. Then her face scrunched up in a familiarly suspicious look, but with a twist: the wry amusement of an adult. The combined effect was an expression Giana had never seen on the girl's face before, but she recognized it as one of her own, which made it all the more uncanny.

"You can understand my hesitation. Even if our goals are similar, your *employer* might not approve of what I'm doing," Marrietta said, gesturing to her stolen body. "Especially given how I introduced myself to this world. And since your entire role in that organization is one of intelligence gathering, you can understand why I might be suspicious." She raised placating hands to forestall an objection. "But I tell you what: how about a little show of faith on your part? You tell me what your goal was in Caroline du Vernay's employ, and that can be the first brick in a foundation of trust."

This could either be a test or a trick, but Giana had a hard time believing her captor—a person so well informed that Giana was "rescued" from Caroline barely an hour after being captured—didn't know a lot more than she was letting on.

In other words, she already knew the answer and was waiting to see if Giana would tell her honestly.

"I was instructed to find a way to infiltrate one or all of the Coldgarden refugee camps," she said, albeit reluctantly. "Because of Harmony, there's no hope most of the native populace would join us in any kind of armed overthrow of the governing authority. Even if you assume a lot of people wouldn't actively fight, we need to even out the numbers imbalance."

The smile on Marrietta's stolen face had changed while Giana spoke, but it was difficult to parse in what way. "Thank you for your honesty," she said. "Maybe we *can* trust each other. And you won't even have to compromise your mission, technically speaking."

"What are you talking about?"

"A happy coincidence," Marrietta said. "Because it turns out the refugee camps are next on my list as well."

"Really?" Giana asked. It seemed a little too coincidental.

"Is that so surprising to hear? After all, it's not just Coldgardeners and revenants that are locked up. Our people—"

"Mutaprimes," Giana said. "Ella came up with the term." During Iazmaena's original resistance movement, it had been absurdly difficult even talking about the three races of Coldgarden until some sort of naming convention had been established.

Marrietta's face formed a thoughtful expression. "Mutaprimes," she said. "Definitely sounds like something a teenager would come up with, but as good a name as any, I suppose. But yes, there are a number of 'mutaprimes' in those camps who I'd very much like to free. You're welcome to come along, if you wish, but not until we take certain precautions."

Marrietta stepped forward, opened Giana's cell, and stepped inside, all in one fluid movement. The path of escape was open but blocked. If Giana had only had to hurt or kill another version of herself, she might have dared, even with the cultist guards. But she was looking at Marri's stolen body, and she had not given up the notion that there might be some chance to save the girl.

Then Marrietta was eating up the space between them, reaching up to Giana's face and forcing her mouth open with one set of bunched fingers. Giana fought her gag reflex but otherwise froze in shock.

"I apologize for this," Marrietta said, "but I need contact with your biological parts, and you went and covered yourself in synthetic scales. Now don't bite, and this will all be over in a second. Look at it this way: it would be even worse for you if I went for your eye."

A pity I can't tell her about the open spot on my thigh.

A sensation began inside Giana's mouth. Both hot and frigid, it spread backward toward her throat, numbing and searing as it went. Her mouth felt thick, like all the moisture had dried from it, and at the same time her palate seemed to swell.

But the strangest thing of all was the flash of white light Giana saw emerging from her own mouth as her mutaprime biology responded to Marrietta's own, showing itself briefly and admitting its characteristic glow.

Then both light and sensations vanished, leaving only tingling memory.

"What did you do?" Giana croaked as Marrietta removed her hand.

"Just a little insurance policy," Marrietta said. "I'm taking you with me, but I have no intention of losing you, either to the enemy or to your own initiative." Her smile was grim.

"And what does this insurance policy do, exactly?"

"Promise me you'll behave and not put yourself in *too* much danger, and you won't have to worry about that," Marrietta said.

CHAPTER 27

The imagined voice of Jürgen Fennec repeated like a mantra in Stefani's head. It was difficult to believe, given what Ella had said, but Stefani had no choice but to believe it anyway. Otherwise, she knew she would shatter beyond any hope of repair. And then it would just be Trevor wearing her like one of his expensive suits. Pretending to be her for as long as he could, and then the killing would start.

There was too much at stake. And not just for her.

"All right," Iaz said. "I hear what you are saying, but I need you to consider that this might not be what it appears."

Her implication was obvious to Stefani. Karl, too, as it happened.

"If you're implying this is some kind of trap, it feels a little convoluted to me," he said. "But I suppose we have to at least consider that this is Giana—or Marrietta or whatever she's calling herself these days—trying to lure us in. And she's certainly not being subtle about forcing a confrontation, putting us in a bind with our only allies the way she did. But ultimately, that doesn't matter. We're going to have to confront her. If Marri is still in there, we have to try to save her. And if she's not . . ."

He stopped with a glance at Stefani. She didn't need the rest spelled out to her. Especially with Iaz involved. If Iaz believed Marri to be dead, there were no limits to how far she would go to take the Marri impersonator "off the board" so to speak.

That meant Stefani had to do whatever it took to prove Marri was still in there. Whether or not it was true. If this Marri had been converted to Giana or by Giana, it might still be all that was left of her daughter. Stefani couldn't very well look askance at that kind of a person and not be a total hypocrite.

Not, at least, until she stood in front of the woman and looked into her eyes and truly understood who was looking back at her.

"So what are you proposing?" Iaz asked Karl. She seemed to have decided it would be easiest if she pretended Stefani wasn't there at all.

"No change at all," Karl said. "I was dead set on finding Jürgen because I think that will lead me to Marri. That's still the case as far as I'm concerned."

"And I'm still going to help him," Stefani said, putting as much steel into her voice as she could. "She's my daughter, and if I can get her back, I'm going to." She waited, then, for a pregnant moment, for Trevor to speak up in her mind, muttering his hatred for Marri, what he planned to do to her if he was ever able.

But he was silent. More and more, he was silent these days, unless there was someone Stefani explicitly had to kill. She didn't know what that meant, but given everything they were facing, she wasn't going to question it.

"Fine," Iaz said, sounding as though it was anything but. "It's not like I have a great alternative plan. Find Jürgen and then we'll see what we see. But I want you all to keep in touch. We can come up with a new set of code phrases so remote discussion is safe. I don't want you two running off on your own without consulting me." Yet again, her implication was clear. *I don't trust the pair of you to be objective, but you're all that I have.* "You work with me on that, Karl.

Steffi has to get her disguise situated if she's planning on leaving Meridian Equatoria any time soon.

As Karl and Iaz hashed out operational details, Stefani worked to learn how to move in the stilts. After an hour of attempting this, she officially hated them. What a stupid thing to almost get caught over, not to mention possibly burning their connection to Cuddles in the process. It was a pity she couldn't continue to impersonate one of the sycophantic hangers-on who had so desperately wanted to be like the Equatorians before being abandoned by them. But heading into Shadyside as they would be, she would stick out like a sore thumb.

Maybe it wouldn't have been as big an advantage as she'd hoped though. Public sentiment toward the Equatorians, and anyone who looked like them, had soured considerably in the past year, for obvious reasons. Harmony made it so people were unlikely to act on such feelings, but they would still have resulted in Stefani standing out anywhere she went outside the general vicinity of Meridian Equatoria.

In the end, it changed nothing. Whichever way she thought about it, the stilts were pretty much Stefani's only option to not look like a hated social class or an unaccompanied child.

Her increasingly vocal annoyance eventually drew Ella in like the smell of dessert.

"I see you've decided to get with the program," the girl said, sounding wryly amused. She was back to acting like a normal teenager now. Stefani usually appreciated the pantomime except for the embarrassment of it being entirely for her benefit.

Today, though, it was tough. The memory of the previous night, of Ella's claims about Marri, was too fresh. There was blunt, and then there was whatever Ella was.

"Instead of snide remarks," Stefani said, carefully modulating her tone, "how about you show your hapless mother how to walk in them?"

Ella rolled her eyes performatively before ducking out of the room to go fetch her own set, sized to fit her feet and overall proportions. It was so strange, craving that signature teenage "over it" attitude just for the sense of normalcy it projected. Even Stefani acting like it annoyed her was a kind of performance on her part.

Ella came back wearing her stilts, showing off by doing a little dance in them. In any dwelling on Coldgarden, she'd be slamming her head into the ceiling at the height of each little hop. Here, domiciles were built with the very tall in mind. As it was, Ella never once lost her balance in the process. Whether this was youth or mutaprime grace, Stefani didn't know, though of course she preferred to think of it as the former.

"Very nice," she said, even giving a little round of silent applause. "But I need to walk convincingly, not dance. And you don't get points for just showing me up repeatedly."

"Karl might ask you to dance. You never know," Ella said with a twinkle in her eye. Then she shifted into a more businesslike mien. More her true self, however painful that was to contemplate. That wasn't fair. Giana had been right a year ago when she'd said this had always been who Ella was. It wasn't fair of Stefani to wish her daughter was something else.

But every time she looked at Ella, a part of Stefani would forever feel she'd had something stolen from her.

"You have to kind of roll your hips," Ella said, demonstrating with slow precision. The problem with the stilts, of course, was that while they added the requisite height, they threw the proportion of upper leg to apparent lower leg way off. It meant you had to walk stiff legged to avoid showing just how unnaturally high up your knees were. There was a way to walk that—combined with Cuddles's clever design where the stilts subtly compressed at key points in your stride, shrinking a bit to maintain the illusion of properly proportioned legs —masked it pretty well. The right kind of clothing helped too. All in all, Stefani kicked herself for not mastering the various techniques long ago.

In the timeless tradition of teenagers rapidly surpassing their parents in physical skills, Ella had. Even knowing what she was looking at, if Stefani allowed her eyes to lose focus, it was virtually impossible to tell that Ella wasn't as tall as any Anaranjadan native.

It took a good two hours, but under Ella's patient tutelage, Stefani gradually developed into someone who, according to her daughter, "wouldn't turn the head of every person she encountered." Which wasn't exactly a ringing endorsement but at least gave her some confidence she wouldn't get immediately arrested.

"It's good you're going to Shadyside," Ella said. "The baggy clothes won't look as out of place there, and it will give you a chance for more practice in case you have to go places where they do."

"How do you know about Shadysider fashion?"

Ella shrugged. "Just something you pick up trawling the networks."

However she came by it, the advice was sound, but it filled Stefani with that familiar, quiet despair. Likely it was a simple example of a teenager being more culturally aware than her mother, but anytime she marveled at anything Ella did, Stefani couldn't help but wonder if this was the girl's tampered-with origins at work. It was a mental prison she knew she would never be free of, and she just had to live with that.

CHAPTER 28

CAROLINE WOKE to another splitting hangover and several unread messages on her lab terminal. Since these were the kind of messages that appeared anonymous and required unpacking several layers of encryption to actually open, she paradoxically knew exactly who they were from even before her decryption software did its job.

Her confidential source Vermin had apparently grown fed up with Caroline's radio silence.

How could you lose her?

That was the first of the messages. There was no context for this question, but based on their last communique, Vermin could only be talking about Jürgen's daring "liberation" of Giana, though how she knew that had even happened was certainly curious in a way Caroline didn't particularly like.

I feel like I have more cause to be annoyed by that than you do, Caroline thought testily around the throbbing in her head. She would never respond in that way though. Whomever Vermin was, they were prickly to a fault.

Still, the fact that Caroline's confidential source was willing to admit how quickly they were in the know was interesting. It implied that either Vermin was indeed deeply embedded on the other side or that she had seen Giana walking free herself, and that had been what prompted the first message.

Are you alive?

That message had come scarcely an hour after the first. And then came a follow-up, a few minutes later, as though they'd only just had the thought.

If you're alive, we need to work out a line of succession so I have someone to report to if you get taken out.

That was Vermin, comforting as ever.

Caroline groaned as she rose, groaned as she moved to the lab's restroom to find the anti-inflammatories she kept stashed there. A throbbing head was no way to deal with Vermin, much less anything else her day would demand of her. There was still the matter of the attack, the potential of Helena's betrayal, and—most immediately to hand—the results of the genetic tests she'd let run overnight.

Since those were more interesting than stress-inducing, and she had more than enough of a headache to be getting on with, Caroline decided to start there before anything else.

Even contacting Vermin.

The genetic analysis had run without issue, producing output with no warning flags or identified errors. Yet Caroline saw immediately *something* had gone wrong, even if the machine failed to recognize it.

The machine was designed to identify the genetic sequence of the Harmony strain in question by linking it with the closest relative strain here on the colony. Its database would be roughly a year out of date, though without Subject Rho or any significant amounts of free time, the number of tweaked changes to any of the existing strains

Caroline had been able to introduce in that time was close enough to zero to make no difference.

Yet even if she'd assumed a normal year's worth of updates, the staring up at her from the screen made no sense.

Nearest common ancestor designation: HS.1.0

Read out in non-jargon, that was Harmony Symbiont 1.0.

As in Anaranjado's original Harmony Symbiont, the one the founding colonists had sported in their heads. The hypothetically unchangeable one which Subject Rho represented such a radical departure from.

Caroline spared a look at the gargantuan thing floating in its deep chill. *Clearly not so unchangeable.* But she didn't understand. All the mutability of the Anaranjadan variants sprang from Subject Rho and his unique iteration of Harmony, which had somehow defeated all the Good Doctor's safeguards against such things.

Except here she was, staring right at one that was clearly the exception to the exception. And there was only one person who would have had a chance to make that kind of transformation happen.

Dad, what did you keep from me? It was the only thing that made sense. Somehow, Jules du Vernay had managed to induce radical mutation in the 1.0 symbiont genetic code. He must have worked on it in secret, generation after generation of successive parasites, until arriving at this monstrosity. Massive, seemingly predatory rather than parasitic—or symbiotic, if you believed the brochure—perhaps he had realized what a danger it had posed.

Why, then, hadn't he disposed of it? Where had it been all this time?

And how was it inside the heads of ACM members?

Helena. More and more, the answers stacked up against Caroline's counterpart. She'd been a fool. Her plan to eliminate Helena prior to their departure from this world had been more a matter of pique than anything. But clearly the woman—owner of a parasite or not—constituted a significant threat, one Caroline had been blind to for the past year. It had just been so damned convenient to rely on her in those early, chaotic days. The highest-ranking ACM officer still on-planet, her support had been key to making sure Caroline still possessed a monopoly on colonial violence.

Suddenly, she knew exactly how to reach back to Vermin.

Alive. Not for someone's lack of trying though. Need everything you have on Helena Cardiff. ASAP.

Let Vermin make whatever they wanted to out of that. Though Vermin simply had to be working for the at-large Coldgardeners, Caroline didn't believe for a second they wouldn't have gathered valuable intel on one of their chief rivals. And if Helena's primary worry—as seemed increasingly likely—had actually been Caroline, perhaps she hadn't guarded her informational flank as closely as she should have done.

You don't ask for much. Let me see what I can do.

That was fine. Vermin was a grand complainer. But they almost always delivered, and said deliveries usually exceeded expectations. That bit of unpleasantness done, and with the spreading warmth of feeling like she'd taken action filling her like alcohol, Caroline turned back and checked the status of her next sample scan.

Her lab space was small with only one of each piece of equipment. She'd known from the start she'd have to run her various samples sequentially, not all at once, and the parasite had obviously taken priority. The two remaining samples were those taken from the two bodies found alongside the monstrous parasite. The scan and analysis of the first, that of the ACM night guard the creature had emerged from, was still in progress.

There were technically calls Caroline needed to make, actions she needed to follow up on. The leadership of the colony couldn't wait, most especially when the second most highly placed person in it was seeking to unseat her.

But it had been a long time since a scientific puzzle had called out to her in this way, and it turned out the lure of it was an even more seductive siren's song than a freshly uncorked bottle. This held true even when it was just the razor-sharp curiosity of waiting for a sequencing run to complete and peel away a fresh layer of the mystery.

CHAPTER 29

"HOW ARE your new legs treating you?" Karl meant the question to be a little shared joke between them with perhaps just a dash of fond ribbing, but he immediately realized his mistake when Stefani turned a familiar look on him.

It was a withering look, but one she was desperately trying to hold back. She was mad but realized she shouldn't be. Which just made him feel bad for tripping over his own two feet. He'd learned how best to avoid things like this back on Coldgarden during the more innocent phase of their dating, when both of them had been unaware of her true nature.

But he guessed he was out of practice.

"I feel like a teenager who just hit her growth spurt," Stefani said. She'd reined her anger back in, returned joke for joke. It was a relief, and not only in a *no harm done* kind of way.

In the back of his mind, Karl could never forget Trevor was in the back of hers.

"You're doing fine," he said encouragingly and hoped it applied to all aspects of her.

They had left Equatoria firmly behind, riding the above-ground trams to Australis, the southernmost of the engine cities and the beginning of the trail head down to Shadyside proper.

"Just glad not to be doing it alone," she said. "And glad for a seat." She had grabbed the first open spot available, and Karl had been all set to glower at anyone who objected. But that wasn't how people behaved here. Everyone was so collectively minded they assumed that if you wanted a seat, it was because you really needed a seat, and they accordingly let you have it without complaint. Even after a year, it was difficult to shake a lifetime of habit. Karl had begun to wonder if he would ever adapt.

Maybe he was just too old.

"This is our stop," he told her, leaning in close so as not to announce it to the entire car. He offered her his hand, but she demurred. He was pleased to see her rise to her false feet without staggering at all. He was all set with a cover story in case something like that should happen, but he hadn't been lying. She really was doing fine.

"Where are we going?" she asked.

"It's a surprise," he said impishly. It wasn't. He just didn't want to say it out loud. It might have raised questions.

Once free of the car and melted into an ever-shifting crowd who'd be less likely to follow what they were saying, Karl elaborated. "Sorry. We're heading to the communication hub where *she* made her big announcement from." He'd almost said *Marri* or even *Marrietta*, but he worried at the reaction that name might prompt from any bystanders.

"I thought you said that would be locked down. That was part of the reason you came back to see us before trying it yourself."

"And I was right to because our mutual boss was able to dig up a way around that." He waggled his handheld. "Don't ask me how." Iazmaena had some source she was coy about but who was highly placed in the colonial leadership. That was good, since they'd lost access to Giana. "In any event, since my Jürgen tracker hasn't pinged in a couple of days, we're going to check and see if they left any clues behind that might lead us to them."

"You don't sound nervous at all."

"Don't I? I suppose I've gotten used to it."

"I figured it was just a similar feeling to when you were in the lancers."

"This? No, not at all. But I do think some of the compartmentalization techniques are the same. Keeps the stress out of the job, lets it eat away at you in peace." He smiled to show her he was joking, but he knew it was a sad smile because he really wasn't.

She returned the smile, sadness and all.

"How did we get here?" He wasn't sure she was asking him so much as the universe at large.

"I thought that was your whole department," he said.

She punched him playfully in the side. "You know what I mean."

"I don't know," he said. "But then, I never really have known the answer to that question, and in case you didn't notice, we've been some weird places before this too."

"That doesn't bother you? The not knowing, I mean?"

"I wouldn't say that," he said. "But whether it bothers me or not, whether I understand why or not, we're here. Nothing to do but deal with that fact. Try to get somewhere better if we don't like it. Try to stay put if we do." He shrugged.

"Sounds like the credo of the consummate soldier."

"I don't know about *consummate*, but I have been called a soldier before."

"Well, it seems like a wise way to look at things." She might as well have added *one that I'll never be able to manage*. He didn't believe it of her, but she clearly did.

Karl squeezed her hand.

"Come on," he said. "If there's one thing I've learned after a year of all this skulking, it's that you learn the most important things in the strangest and most unlikely of places. So let's go visit one and see what we see."

CHAPTER 30

MARRI STUDIED orbits of tidally locked planets and the physical principles behind volcanic engines. She learned about sustaining life on dead worlds. She built shelters against solar storms. She studied guerrilla tactics and classical warfare and all the strange shades between. She saw examples of civics and suffrage and various concepts of government play out before her.

She watched people denied a voice protest, then riot, then revolt. She witnessed what happened when people *had* a voice but let it wither and shrivel, starved by cynicism and laziness and overwork. She saw the thin, wispy boundary between cynicism and rage, saw how easy it was to tiptoe from one side of that gossamer line to the other, inflicting immense pain and suffering in the process. She watched in dismay as reality fragmented, as people turned on each other, eddies of chaos worming their way into calm waters until death flowed in the streets and peoples died and worlds died, both long before their time. She watched planets whirl stately paths around a small, orange star, then one planet in particular whose orbit began to rapidly shrink. *This world,* something seemed to whisper to her.

She learned, at last, the strange biology behind hypermutation. As much as the Professor understood, at least.

All the while, as the months and years rolled on, Marri picked out more and more moments from her personal past, the gradations between the true and the false growing ever subtler until she could barely tell the difference between them. Sometimes these were files on a screen, sometimes pictures in an art gallery, sometimes sculptures lining wide boulevards she had never seen in Coldgarden, never seen anywhere she could remember.

The longer she studied, the longer she worked, the less herself she felt. But it was also true that she felt those restraints clamping down upon her mind less often, and that was worth any amount of study, any amount of painfully drudging through her past.

It gave her a clearer sense of the passage of time. Hundreds of days, then thousands. Years. Years of time. Her strange, blurred reflection in surfaces grew clear to her. She was not a little girl any longer. Lean and long of limb, she had grown up in this place. It was shocking to see, almost enough to overwhelm her. But it cohered with the passing of days and so made a kind of sense. And she in turn made a kind of peace with it.

But something else happened too. The longer she went with only Bry as company—whatever entity called itself Bry at least—the more she began to empathize with those who had lost their voices. She had no voice either. She had a regimen of daily tasks in an endlessly changeable, decidedly *wrong* version of the city in which she'd grown up. It was something to fill the hours and fill her brain, but it was not a purpose.

It was not a *choice*.

Most importantly, it was not freedom. And she would be damned if she was just going to lie down and accept it.

THE COMMUNICATIONS HUB Karl and Stefani sought stood out more than most structures did at this level. They were down in the poorest sections of the colony now, and almost everything appeared cobbled together by whatever lay close at hand, with ample use of the naturally occurring stone as walls whenever possible.

The hub contrasted sharply to this. The same design for such structures was used throughout the colony, only a handful in each district, so this building which would have looked at home in Meridian Equatoria stood out like a sore thumb here. It wasn't just the obvious care in its construction, either. Whereas every other building was crammed cheek-by-jowl into every available space, the hub stood by itself, an open area around it as though it projected its own repulsion field. The closest structure was the reinforced tunnel which allowed the passage of the tram lifts between levels running vertically about twenty meters away.

The hub building was shaped like a single-piece bunker bristling with antennae of various shapes, sizes, and configurations, a motley assortment necessary to broadcast and receive the wide range of signal frequencies and wavelengths needed for an icy, rocky warren of tunnels. Thick cabling emerged from the top of the building, the hub's way of gathering up all that disparate data and sending it up a level to the next district.

"Did they have to make it look so much like a fortress?" Stefani had negotiated the vertical lift tram as well as she had the intra-city one and now walked like she'd been wearing the stilts for a month rather than a few hours.

"Fortress or not, Iazmaena swears this script from her insider source will get us in."

"What are we going to do about the people working in there?" Karl wished he could decide whether she sounded trepidatious or eager with that question.

"It's all automated. There shouldn't be any unless we get really unlucky and a maintenance crew is working there."

"And this won't trip some sort of alarm?"

"Considering Iazmaena's source's script is supposed to simulate a maintenance crew needing access for a routine check, I hope not. If I'm being honest, my main concern was this place would be swarming with ACM for the same reason we're here, but I don't see anyone." Which was odd, and despite the confident front he worked to maintain, it put his guard up.

He was as relieved as anyone when the door opened after he proffered his handheld to the lock.

The pair of them entered, and there was no trap, no group of ACM soldiers there to round them up for interrogation. The room beyond the door was utterly empty, the interior the same cascade of blinking lights and cleanly sealed panels he remembered from the background of Marri's video. In person, though, it was hot and stuffy. It looked to Karl as though the *real* maintenance crews kept the place both working and nearly spotless. He had hoped so, as it would have made their task easier, and since this was a Harmony world, he'd not been disappointed.

"If no one runs this, and Anaranjado doesn't do AI, what controls comms traffic?"

"That, I expect." Karl pointed at a small plinth in the center.

Atop it, under a transparent dome damp with condensation, was a lump of something that looked very much like a partial human brain. A naked Harmony parasite perched both atop and within it, and though neither thing moved, there was an unmistakable sense of *alive* to both.

"Ugh," Stefani said. "It can't think, can it?" Perhaps realizing the inanity of the question, she amended it. "It's not aware, I mean?"

"Your guess is as good as mine." Karl fervently hoped not. She was right this colony didn't do AI, but it wasn't like they didn't want their technology thinking for them. They just preferred to do it through more biological means. He'd learned a thing or two over the past year. "I wonder," he said.

"What?"

"This thing was probably tailor-made to see its highest calling in routing and prioritizing the districts comms and network traffic. If so, it might be the happiest thing on the whole damn planet. But one thing brains are great at doing is visualizing. Do you remember how perfectly still and straight-on Marrietta was in that broadcast?"

"Yes?" Stefani said, sounding unsure.

"Almost like she was trying to minimize movement." Karl smiled with dawning realization. "Like she was trying to make it easier to apply visual effects to herself in real time. A brain like this could do that. Running this network wouldn't even be using a tenth of its processing power."

"That way, she can wander around scaleless or even wearing a sleeve with a different pattern and color entirely, and no one would recognize her." Stefani looked at Karl with wonder. "Good catch."

"Law of averages says I have to manage every so often."

"Don't sell yourself short," Stefani said. "I'm kicking myself for not realizing how reckless it would be for her to show her face without some means to disguise it later."

"How about instead of beating ourselves up, we focus back on the task at hand? Got to find—there."

The port was easy to identify with everything being so clean.

Karl held his breath once again as he plugged in his device. Once again, everything worked as advertised.

They were looking, not for the record of the speech, the video of which they could view anywhere. Instead, they wanted to scrape the data itself. Just as Karl and Stefani had used a script to override the door and gain access, Marrietta and Jürgen must have used both a similar script and something to convince the comms hub to treat her speech like a colony-wide emergency and override all filtering safeguards. And if they could provide that back to Iaz and her source, they might be able to suss out a physical point of origin.

Karl wasn't picky. When prompted, he grabbed locally uploaded information from the twelve-hour window to either end of when the broadcast had happened. He knew from the listening device that it had gone out live, but he didn't want to chance missing something they'd done in preparation or afterward, to clean up. That was a considerable amount of data, and as such, it took a considerable amount of time. But better that than missing something crucial. They could sort through it later. The longer he thought about how strange it was no one from the ACM was here, the faster he wanted to be away.

The soft *beep* after so long in silent waiting made him jump.

"What was that?" Stefani's voice was low with alarm. Her thoughts had clearly followed a line with his. That they'd tripped some alarm, and the sound was the soft gentle indicator of such.

But no. It was coming from Karl's pocket.

"It's the tracker," he said. "It's picked up a signal again."

CHAPTER 32

THE CAMP HAD BEEN CONSTRUCTED in the ruins of the old hospital, the one destroyed in a friendly fire attack shortly after the Coldgardeners arrived on-planet. Or so Giana had been told. This, like so much else important, was all part of the blank spot in her memory.

Regardless, Marrietta explained, the destruction had been deemed too great to be worth rebuilding the facility as a hospital, but not so bad that it could not be modified further and used to house "refugees." The bitterness of the last word on her tongue had struck Giana, mirroring the tone Iazmaena, and to a lesser extent Stefani, used when discussing the same situation.

It might be a dangerous thought, the notion that there was more similarity between these two factions than difference, but Giana had it nonetheless.

They arrived at the heavily guarded, heavily armored front gate of the facility, and Giana thought she could still make out the ghostly outline of when it had been a place with far less restrictions to its access.

Neither Jürgen nor any of the Cultists had accompanied them, only Marrietta's small cadre of recognizably human supporters. The

Cultists were many things, but they did not blend in well anywhere. Marrietta had sent them away, though she'd declined to say where. Jürgen she had left behind to guard their headquarters.

"You're up," Marrietta said. This was why Giana had been brought. She might, *might* still be able to act with the force of Caroline's authority. Attempting to find that sense of confidence after everything that happened was challenging to say the least. It didn't help that Marrietta kept close, a hood drawn up over her features. It shouldn't be necessary. Her scaled appearance on her broadcast had been entirely fabricated by visual effects, and she wore a scale sleeve of a totally different pattern now, one that climbed only partway up her face. But if she was taking no chances on being recognized, she was taking equally little chance of Giana going off-script.

"It seems like a giant waste of what will be a one-time access," Giana had told her other self when Marrietta had finished explaining what they were doing.

"Keeping our people from starving is a giant waste?" And it sounded very sincere. Giana felt sure that if the other her had been wearing her own face and not Marri's, Giana would have believed this claim. Because it was how Giana herself felt.

"We both know that's not your real aim here."

Marrietta's smile shifted between cryptic and sad from moment to moment. "You think there's something more impactful I could use this access for, and you're right," she'd said. "But I'm also well aware we have a time limit. Very soon they will cut you off by changing protocols. In fact, we'll be lucky if they haven't already. So I'm going to use it while I can, and this is what I'm ready to do. It may seem small, but I need people on my side. Most of these refugees probably still don't even know why they're here. They'll be looking for anyone showing them any sort of kindness to cling to. I'd say feeding them qualifies. I know what it's like to go hungry."

Giana tried to keep her skepticism off her face.

"I can see you don't believe me," Marrietta said. "Would it help if I told you that they keep full revenants and natives, the kind that aren't pretending to be human, in the camp but sequestered from the rest. That they experiment on them? Torture them? These are conscious, thinking beings, all of them, and they are treated like scientific curiosities at best and freaks worthy of nothing but misery at worst. Is that something you enjoy hearing?"

It wasn't, and given Marrietta's look of satisfaction at whatever was playing across Giana's face, the other woman could see as much.

It was the part about the tenuous nature of their timetable that held Giana's attention as she approached the very armed guards. She didn't recognize any of them at first glance, but she'd met plenty of ACM in her position, so that didn't actually mean much. She couldn't decide if being recognized was better or worse. They didn't have enough information about her status to know.

The outermost of the phalanx of guards held up a hand for Giana to stop as they approached. Giana proffered her phone without comment. Stating her purpose for being here without being asked would seem strange. The pertinent information—as well as the faked authorization codes—would be on the handheld. She had a sickly memory of doing something similar while trying to investigate Stefani's secrets back on Coldgarden. Hopefully this would end better for her.

The man projected the orders into the air in front of the screen and blinked in surprise at what the glowing text told him.

"Caroline du Vernay has no jurisdiction over the camp."

Giana raised an eyebrow into a perfect, patrician arch. So far, this was going exactly as she'd expected it would even if she'd really still been working for Caroline. "You are the one in charge of this deployment's payroll?"

"I—no." The man blinked again, thrown off by the change in topic.

"Oh, I must be mistaken. Because it sounded an awful lot like you were balking at letting the person who is footing the bill for all your paychecks have access to this place."

"Ma'am, I—"

"Let's keep one thing clear, Lieutenant," Giana said, all icy disdain. "You may take orders from Helena Cardiff, but you work for Caroline du Vernay."

A third blink. "I'm going to have to elevate this to my superior."

"Do that."

Thus followed a wait in which each second was more excruciating than the last. Giana wanted nothing more than to look to Marrietta, but she didn't dare betray that kind of nerves out in the open where any of the ACM could see her. She had to be composure personified.

She couldn't be certain, but the feeling emanating from Marrietta seemed to be one of extreme smugness. Giana wasn't certain how she felt about that.

The minutes ticked by, and Giana lapsed into what felt like a stoic silence contest with the remaining guards. The longer this went on, the more likely it was that something was going wrong.

At last, the lieutenant returned. He did not bring an entire platoon of ACM with him, which was good. He also looked irritable, which was better. Before he'd even said a word, Giana knew what his answer would be. The fact he was gritting his teeth over losing face to her told her everything.

"You're free to come in," he said. "Under our strict supervision. And no more than an hour." He stepped away and began issuing orders to inspect the grav-sleds the Cultists had brought. Now Giana could safely turn to Marrietta.

"I guess now we know just how far Cardiff is able to piss," she said.

"Cardiff doesn't know about this at all," Marrietta said. "And whoever is in charge of this camp will hopefully keep it that way. At least long enough for us to be gone."

"How can you know that?"

"Cardiff knows you are missing," Marrietta said. "If the camp commandant had actually checked, he or she would know that too, and we'd be in a lot more trouble than we are."

"And how do you know *that?*"

"I have my sources," Marrietta said cryptically.

"And has it occurred to you that they are letting us in to make us easier to round up?"

"Of course."

"And do you have an answer for that?"

Marrietta snorted softly. "You don't think these Cultists with us are *human*, do you? Here's a hint: I don't have any biological human cultists."

"Follow me," the lieutenant said as he approached from behind. "Once inside the facility, you will comply with my instructions exactly. Any deviation from my instructions, and you will be detained." He was perfectly polite—he had a Harmony parasite, after all, and he believed them to be human—but also resolute in his authority. Giana had clearly pushed it as far as she'd been able.

"Understood," she said. "And I assure you, my people do as well."

She still projected confidence, but it now seemed to Giana as if somewhere, unseen, a giant clock had begun to tick down. After an unknown number of seconds, it would reach zero and then would come the consequences.

The entire facility existed within one massive Stone Dome, an artificially created cavern so vast that lights installed in its ceiling did next to nothing to illuminate the rooftops of the structures below. Lights near ground level were sparsely placed at best. Giana realized bleakly what this meant: the people of this camp existed in a perpetually underlit darkness. Maybe that was not viewed as any sort of cruelty here—on this world, it may well have been considered a kindness.

But it would certainly not feel that way to anyone born on a world with an open sky and a sun that wasn't hell-bent on killing them.

"Worse than I'd feared," Marrietta said softly for Giana alone. She never strayed far, and her stance was protective; she'd meant what she'd said about keeping her insurance policy safe, apparently.

Of course, this was not the same thing as caring about Giana's well-being, and she would do well not to forget that. "What must they think even happened to them?"

Giana spoke equally softly. "Is it true most came here in a trance?" It was something Giana could relate to since she also couldn't recall coming here.

"The Host put them in one, yes. His goal was to save as much of himself as possible, and that didn't allow time for niceties like asking or campaigns of persuasion."

"Because you and your kind killed him."

"Because *our* kind killed him."

"I wasn't born like this."

Marrietta laughed with genuine mirth. It still sounded odd coming from what had been a serious child. "We are what the world makes of us."

The entire facility appeared open-air, surrounded by high walls looped with razor-wire across the top. There were more technological ways to discourage people from climbing over things. The simple brutality of using razor-wire just enhanced the perception that only the lowest of the low in this society could be found here.

Those who demanded cost-effective containment.

They stood in what might be called a courtyard in a setting less bleak. Beyond were another set of doors flanked by the stenciled word *processing*. But their escort of guards, a pair of them who had appeared once the group had been ushered inside, directed them over to the right, toward a door atop a conveyor belt that could only be some sort of loading dock for supplies.

"You can drop the supplies there and go. We'll see they are distributed."

"Caroline du Vernay says otherwise," Giana said with icy command. She would follow his instructions, she'd said. But he hadn't issued any, and she didn't think that was an accident. She watched him purse his lips, sensed his teeth gritted behind them.

"Step onto the belt with the crates, please." There was no

acknowledgment of her victory beyond the statement itself. His tone was flat. This was simply the way things were going to work. Giana supposed it was good enough for her.

Climbing aboard the belt after the second crate was loaded, Giana crouched down in order to fit. The belt took them into a kind of warehouse, one far bigger than it apparently needed to be, judging by how empty it was of both wares and people. Once the grav-sleds were reengaged and everyone was through, the guards gestured them toward a set of heavily reinforced doors which featured yet another security checkpoint. These, presumably, led into the camp proper.

As they were ushered through, they got their first look at the refugees. Giana had to restrain herself from gasping in alarm at the sunken eyes and shriveled physiques who eyed them with wary desperation.

"This is ghastly," Marrietta said.

"We feed them everything we're sent to feed them," the guard said, sounding a bit hurt. He clinked the knuckles of one hand against an arm that was entirely synthetic. "It's not as if we're eating it ourselves, after all. But you should know as well as anyone how difficult it is to grow food on this world. Our own people have had to make sacrifices for these . . . creatures. We never invited them." He reined himself in after that, gesturing down a narrow path between two high walls. "Through there is the Central Plaza." He emphasized the words in a way that made them sound like both a title and a mockery of a title. "If you want to get them the supplies as fast as possible, you'll probably want to set up shop there. Follow me."

The "Central Plaza" was as devoid of life or decoration as every other place they'd seen so far. The harsh lighting was brighter here, owing to overlapping light poles which cast shadows in multiple directions. Giana wondered why that was before realizing that in any spot where lots of refugees could gather, the guards would want the maximum possible degree of visibility.

"This will work," Marrietta said, sympathy giving way to efficient dispassion in her stolen voice. Her gesture of command took in everyone in her party, Giana included. "Unpack the crates. I'll see about forming lines of the people who are here." She strode off, approaching each refugee's hungry gaze, sharing a few quiet words with them, then moving on. Giana tore her gaze away, realizing she wasn't helping with the unpacking.

Each crate was really a pallet of smaller boxes of prepackaged rations wrapped in foil, color coded to represent three different flavors of nutrient bars, just to provide a little variety. There were water pouches as well, perhaps even higher value than the calories. Last of all were capsules packed with vitamins and minerals, huge pills that Giana imagined she would have a difficult time swallowing. She supposed that spoke to the desperate need of these people better than anything.

"Everyone line up in an orderly fashion," Marrietta called out, smoothly taking charge. "And make sure to get one of everything. Once you have your set of rations, water, and vitamins, go and get your friends and loved ones. We'll be handing these out until we run out, and we'll be bringing more tomorrow, so there's no need to panic or hoard."

It started off orderly enough when there were only small clusters of refugees in numbers that could be managed easily. People were allowed to choose among the packets of food which flavor they preferred, then received their water and their vitamin tablet. But that changed quickly as word spread. Soon enough a few rivulets of starved people become a growing mass like a river swollen by flash flood. Giana expected it to become a riot at any moment, but on the contrary, despite the massive numbers, order reigned supreme.

It was almost more chilling than chaos would have been. Like everyone here had been brainwashed despite their utter misery and neglect. Or because of it.

At least it meant there was very little fighting for individual food pouches once they were given out. Giana saw only two people attempt to take a pouch from someone who had one, and neither attempt lasted long. Maybe it could be explained simply by everyone already being so weak.

As matters proceeded, though, Giana's tension only rose. She realized she was waiting for something. Screams, perhaps, or some horrible transformation to take place. She kept thinking of those pills, wondering why they had to be so big.

Eventually, her paranoia grew enough that she felt observed. Then she caught Marrietta looking at her and realized it was justified.

"You look so concerned," Marrietta said with false innocence. "What exactly is it you are worried will happen?"

Giana fixed her with a level look. "Do you really have to ask?"

"I wouldn't do anything to our people," Marrietta said, but the hurt in her voice sounded forced. And the smile on her face was a secret one, a look that promised she knew something no one else did.

CHAPTER 33

"WHAT'S WRONG?" Stefani asked as they made their hasty retreat from the comms hub.

"Something isn't right about this," he said. He kept expecting to have to hurry her along, but she moved as quickly in stilts as he did now. Call it a kind of revenant grace. "The tracker hasn't picked up a signal since shortly after the broadcast. Now it's active again, but more, it's *close*." He fixed her with a knowing look. "Too close."

"How close are we talking?"

"Right outside the lift tram." He inclined his head down the tunnel, where the column was still clearly visible. "That way." The tracker's indicator sound changed. "He's moving, getting onto the tram."

He turned to Stefani then, making eye contact. "We need to make a call right now. The timing of this tells me it's almost certainly some kind of a trap."

"It's my daughter, Karl," Stefani said.

"Fair enough," he said. Despite the danger, it was the answer he'd hoped for. "Follow me."

Karl hoped they could get to the lift before the current car departed. Whatever kind of trap was planned, it was far less likely to happen as intended if they could spring it early.

But no such luck. Karl rapidly lost the signal as it passed upward, leaving the district and entering Middledeep directly above. Karl didn't even have to ask. He simply strode directly up with Stefani and got in line for the next car up.

"Are you armed?" She kept her voice soft.

"Basic stun gun," he said. "And, well, the other. Not sure either will do much good against him if it comes to that. But I'm hoping it won't."

"Because he left a message in your pocket?"

It sounded thin when she said it like that, but that was the basic gist of it.

"We'll never find out if we don't follow."

Follow they did, and not just through Middledeep, but beyond that, up into Undercrust. Each time their quarry left a district ahead of them, they lost the signal. But Karl stopped worrying they wouldn't get it back after the second such instance.

So he was not surprised when they emerged almost back to where they'd started, squarely in Meridian Australis, southernmost of the three drive cone cities which had once propelled the planet into a shrinking orbit and very nearly its doom.

The tracker was still active. But it had stopped moving.

✺

They found what they were looking for easily enough: a closed gymnasium.

These were surprisingly popular for a colony where so many replaced so much of themselves with cybernetic augmentations. But the planet's gravity was lower than humans had evolved in, so for those who kept at least some of their bones and muscles, regular exercise was important to maintain their mass and density. And for those who'd rather replace their limbs, every single colonist still had a meat brain for Harmony to latch onto. This meant almost everyone opted to keep their biological hearts and lungs as well, the better to supply blood and oxygen to said brain and said parasite.

When this particular gym had closed—or maybe "closed"—Karl couldn't tell. Printed polymer sheets covered the windows, each with stenciling indicating that the facility was off-limits and no longer in service.

Despite their overriding sense of urgency, Karl insisted they spend some time scoping out the general area, planning their approach.

"It's going to have to be the maintenance access ports," Karl said. "The access paths themselves have to be big enough for Anaranjadans to move through, but the entry ports are much smaller to discourage people from wandering in. They open wider if you present the right electronic credentials, but we don't need them."

"Why are they open at all?" Stefani asked.

"A very trusting society," Karl said. "And a constant need for airflow and exchange to keep temperatures manageable."

"Okay," Stefani said, clearly not convinced. "But either this is a trap, in which case getting in will be easier than you seem to think, or we're talking about an illicit organization here, and it will be much harder."

Stefani looked thoughtful for a moment and then, shockingly quick given her stilts, darted off toward the door.

"Stefani!" Karl hissed, hurrying after. But she had already gotten her hands underneath the polymer sheet covering the doorway. She pulled, and it came away in a gooey yielding of adhesive left too long above its recommended temperature range.

At least it didn't make a lot of noise.

"I'll help you with the door. But if we'd used the vents, we'd be completely invisible from the street. Just saying." Karl stepped up regardless. But there was no need. Stefani had removed a wickedly curved blade from somewhere on her person and jammed it past a power junction cover. She yelped at the shock she received as sparks flew, but electrical safety protocols were very stringent on a colony with so many cybernetics.

The door slid open as the power failed.

"Like you said, a very trusting society," Stefani whispered with a smile.

Karl restrained himself from giving vent to his feelings over her recklessness. Her instincts had been accurate. Doors in this part of the colony, pressurized and kept at a livable temperature, did not default to closed. For the sake of safety, wellness checks, and a dozen other reasons, any failure in power would cause them to open.

Still, she might have been a *little* more careful.

For all his self-restraint, Stefani seemed to sense this unspoken thought and responded to it. "She might be in there, Karl. I'm not waiting. I'm not skulking. I'm going in."

If her eagerness had sounded even slightly outside what a mother would feel, Karl would have been alarmed for reasons beyond the obvious. He reminded himself it had been a year. *A year* without Marri.

He'd missed Marri something terrible. How much worse would it be for her mother?

The space beyond the door was clearly built with tall, thin Anaranjadan physiology in mind. Just in the light spilling in off the street, he glimpsed vaulted ceilings devoid of the clouds of dust motes he'd expect to see if the space truly was abandoned. He entered first, hoping to spot any danger, preparing himself to transform even if he doubted how much good it would do against Jürgen Fennec.

Once fully inside, he considered waiting for Stefani to enter and then closing the doors behind them. But that would cut off their one easy avenue for escape, and on balance, Karl decided that looking suspicious from the street was a lower risk than being trapped in here.

The door opened onto a lobby with a check-in desk to the right. Beyond a set of floor-to-ceiling interior windows directly ahead lay what looked like a swimming pool. Of course, here it would be grav-fields you swam through, water being as precious as it was and mechanical prostheses being as heavy as they were. In any event, it was clearly nonfunctional.

A hallway to the right of the windows led right, deeper into the gymnasium.

They saw no one, heard no one. If this place was serving as some sort of Cult headquarters, there was no way to tell from the lobby area.

Except that wasn't exactly true. As he walked slowly, carefully forward, angling toward the hallway leading deeper in, Karl could see deeper into the empty space of the pool. It was full of equipment, row upon row of unfamiliar, mismatched devices. Some were connected to one another via feeder tubes. Others seemed to stand alone. And while the non-emergency lights in the facility were dark, the machinery was running.

More than that, though, there was a shadow stalking between the machines, as if checking on them. A man-shaped shadow, but impossibly elongated, cast against the side of the pool. Stefani came up behind Karl, trying to see what had caught his attention.

At that moment, a metal hand suddenly gripped the nearest lip of the pool from below. The shadow revealed itself to be Jürgen Fennec as he hauled himself up and out of the pool, rising to his full height, where he overtopped them both even with the stilts.

"Get ready to run," Karl said.

"I'm not going anywhere."

"Stefani!" His exclamation was half-alarm and half-exasperation. He drew his stun gun.

"Karl." Her voice was the sharp calm of a razor poised. She held no weapon, not even her strange knife, but she transformed fully as Karl watched. Her stilts clattered to the floor as she became a living, shifting form of oil with a gold sheen. A revenant—minus, of course, the bulky exoskeleton she'd had to permanently shed to adopt a flawless human form.

One of the windows between lobby and pool was missing. Fennec stepped through.

"Where is she?" Stefani's voice when in her revenant form had a strange, echoing quality. Yet that was only half-responsible for the chill her tone sent down Karl's spine. The other was something he could only describe as the righteous rage of a mother frightened for her child's welfare.

CHAPTER 34

STEFANI HAD SPENT the past year on this world getting used to seeing people of all degrees of cybernetic. Even so, she had never seen anyone as mechanical as the creature that stood before her.

He towered over her, well over two meters, and she could scarcely see any skin on him at all. What little poked through the curved metal plates of his face—a far cruder solution than the more flexible scales that made everyone look so much like lizard people—appeared puffy and red, almost as though it was infected. His posture was strange, almost as though he stood poised on the balls of his feet, expecting something.

Stefani doubted he'd been expecting her, but he was going to get her.

"Where is she?" She roared the question, flowing right up to him. The lobby around them gave her plenty of room to maneuver if it came to that. "Where is my daughter? Where is Marri Palmieri?"

As though suddenly unfreezing from a locked configuration, the man drew a weapon from a holster Stefani hadn't noticed. He leveled it directly at her then froze again, resuming that unnatural stillness.

"Stefani!" Karl hadn't been any faster to react than she. His repetition of her name carried nothing but fear this time.

"Karl!" She couldn't hold the word back, couldn't stop flashing to thoughts of Ella, motherless. Marri, forever lost. Karl, alone.

As robotically as he'd raised it, the machine-man lowered the gun. He did not holster it. It quivered at his side, as though he fought with himself over what to do with it. His whole arm shook with the same inexplicable effort.

"Get over here, Stefani, quickly," Karl said.

Despite doubting the pistol could seriously hurt her, Stefani did so, flowing to his side, gaze never leaving the man. She expected Trevor to speak up, to howl in protest, yearning for blood as he did. But her other self was silent. Perhaps he was held as rapt by Fennec as she was. More than the man's gun-arm was shaking now. His entire body was quivering with unspent potential.

"What is he doing?" Stefani asked as she joined Karl. "What's wrong with him?"

"I don't know," Karl said. He turned his attention to Fennec. "You wanted us to come here, didn't you? Why?" He reached into his pocket, pulled out a cash chit. "You planted this on me with a message for me. Why?" Fennec's gun arm quivered, but it did not rise.

Stefani wished she could simply communicate mentally with Karl. If they split up, they could probably simply disable the man before he could act. Unlikely he'd be able to get both of them. If Stefani could goad him into attacking her, that would be best. Karl had no revenant body, and she was unsure how a bullet wound would affect him if he tried to transform into his Coldgarden native form after being shot.

Before she could say or do anything, a burst of static filled the air. Sound was emerging from the man's head, electronically distorted. At first, Stefani assumed he was talking through the speaker slit he had for a mouth.

But she recognized the voice that emerged, and it wasn't his.

"My family? You mean Stefani? Karl?"

Marri. That's Marri's voice. And not her new, adult voice, either. Marri the child Stefani still remembered so clearly.

"Karl?" she asked, not daring to hope. "Do you—"

"Yes," he said, his own voice tight with emotion. "I hear it. That's her voice."

A recording. It was some kind of a recording that, presumably, this man had made of Marri talking.

Then another voice emerged, this one with additional distortion but sounding like an adult male.

"No," the voice said brusquely. His accent wasn't one Stefani had heard often. Harsh, especially with the distortion, but it sounded like a response to Marri's questions. They were listening to a recorded conversation, maybe between Marri and this man. "Giana Novak."

Stefani went cold all over.

"Where are the others?" This was Marri again.

"I do not know," the male voice said. "You are the first I have found. I will continue looking however. You may rest assured."

The static noise cut off, the recording ended. Stefani realized there was no way she could know this without more context, but it sounded to her like this recording was taken shortly after Marri had arrived on planet. Her heart ached and went out to her daughter, all alone, desperate for familiar faces and finding only Giana's.

The crushing guilt of a year with no word threatened to overwhelm Stefani.

"Tell us where she is," Stefani said. "Please." The last word quivered with desperation.

"I don't understand what is happening to me," Jürgen said suddenly. It brought Stefani up short. The pain in his words was obvious even through the distortion. He put his head in his hands. "You can't be here. You can't!"

"You drew us here," Stefani said.

"Not me," he said, panting static hisses. "*It* wants you here, but *she* doesn't."

Stefani was about to demand to know who *she* was, despite knowing quite well, when Karl preempted her.

"What do you want?" he asked, his voice gentle.

"I want to be alone with my thoughts," Jürgen Fennec said, his voice thick with despair. "I want them both gone. Gone. Gone. Gone." His voice grew louder with each repetition. "Gone. Gone. Gone!" It grew so punishing Stefani almost couldn't hear the transition. "Go!" He shouted, raising his gun with slow, stuttering movements, as though he fought every millimeter. "Go! Go!"

Stefani lunged for the man. No, she was not going to let it end like this. She needed answers. Answers that were true. *Answers I can tolerate.*

Seemingly in response to her motion, Jürgen raised up his other fist, the one not holding the weapon. In contrast to his stuttering gun arm, this motion was precise. He let fly toward her with a small object, one she would have instinctively caught had Karl not gotten there first, trying to get between Jürgen and herself.

Jürgen spasmed slightly as Karl caught the object with one hand and triggered the stun gun with the other. The giant cyborg did not topple, but he did seize up briefly. Long enough for Karl to wind up his other hand and prepare to throw the mystery object back.

"No!" Stefani said. She wasn't sure why she said it. Something about the way the hand trying to kill them had struggled while the hand doing the throwing had been unhindered. "Keep it."

"Fine," he said, sounding unhappy about it. He turned and dragged her along with him, pulling her back to the wide-open door before she could object to anything else.

They broke line of sight just as the shooting started from within the lobby.

CHAPTER 35

IT FELT anticlimactic to just walk out of the detention camp, relief supplies delivered. But that was exactly what Giana and Marrietta and the rest did.

"What was that?" she demanded once they were out of earshot of any nosey ACM personnel.

"For someone attempting to be trusted, you aren't willing to offer any yourself."

"I'm not stupid, you know," Giana said. "I know there was more to that than just delivering relief supplies."

"You're right, of course," Marrietta said. "We haven't been idle this past year. Subject Rho—that would be the very special Harmony/human instance we captured in case no one's brought you up to speed—gave us the template to work with, but its changeability is too random, too slow for what I've got in mind. Fortunately, nothing kickstarts mutagenic capability like good, old-fashioned Mutagen Prime."

Giana shivered at the thought of adding their own essence to the creature already responsible for sowing so much discord across the colony.

"Does what we are upset you so much?"

"I didn't ask to be this way."

"Tell me, has any life form ever in the history of the term ever had a say in what it was?"

"I suppose not," Giana said grudgingly.

"Then why fight what you are? It isn't your fault. Embrace it!"

"It's different." Giana fought down the heat in her voice. "I used to be different, and now I'm this."

"You believed you were human, but you never were. The truth is you've *never* been what you thought you were. Think how much energy you've wasted fighting against your own nature."

"How can you call it my nature when what I am keeps changing?" Now Giana was losing the fight. Her voice had begun to echo through the tunnels in unsettling ways.

"Every living thing changes throughout its life. If you lived your entire life as a perfectly 'normal' human, and you had any kind of life worth speaking of, you would look back at earlier portions of it and scarcely recognize yourself. Just because what we are takes that concept and makes it a bit more literal, you view it as some kind of unnatural abomination."

"Why do you care what I think?" It was a weak defense, but it was all Giana could muster at the moment.

"Useless battles pain me," Marrietta said with a shrug. "You can fight it every moment of your entire life, but the one thing you can be certain of is that you can never step outside yourself. You will always be who, *what* you are."

Though they made the rest of the trip in silence, Giana's brain was anything but as she fervently tried to think of a reply.

CHAPTER 36

THEY WERE TOO busy running to talk. Stefani had lost her stilts, of course, so they had to hope she wouldn't draw too much attention after she resumed her human form.

As though there wasn't already a Cult enforcer trying to kill them.

Stefani kept waiting to feel the shots whiz by her head—or worse, to feel them impact her—but after the spasm of gunfire as they fled the gym, they heard nothing else.

Still, they didn't stop until they reached the lift tram station.

They rode the whole way down in silence, hand in hand. Karl's other hand was wrapped in a death grip around the strange object Jürgen had thrown. At least it didn't seem set to hurt them. Hopefully it wasn't a tracking device, though if it was, it was the most inartful application of one she'd ever heard of.

Of course, they'd kept it thus far.

The silence held until they reached Karl's home. Stefani tried to hide how appalled she was at its size. At least she would get to spend time with him here. By default. And perhaps the closeness was good because with the shock of the encounter wearing off, she had never been so cold.

"Let's get a look at this," Karl said after plugging in his space heater. Small as it was, the room began to warm immediately.

"We've got to get you a bigger slice of Iaz's budget," Stefani observed.

Karl's laugh was rueful as he fished the device out of his pocket. "Out of sight, out of mind." Then he examined it closely.

It was octagonal and faceted, almost like a gemstone of metal. The largest, central facet looked like a tiny screen to Stefani.

"Well, whatever it is, I've turned it on," Karl said. An image appeared on screen.

"That's Giana! Our Giana." Stefani leaned in close to see better. She was in a glass-walled cell of some sort, looking directly into the camera with a confused expression on her face. The camera dipped then, and a tray appeared at the bottom of the shot, sliding through a slot and into the cage.

"I think we're watching through someone's eyes," Karl said.

"Jürgen's?"

"Not unless he's on his knees," Karl said.

"Look there! On the tray. A device like this one."

They watched Giana take the device and hide it. The person interacting with her left shortly thereafter, and the feed went away.

"Do you think this is her device, then?" Karl looked to Stefani, confused. "Why did he give it to us?"

The screen flickered, and words appeared where the footage had been a moment before. Stefani's breath caught.

We can restore Marri. Your assistance is required.

Seeing the name gave Stefani a jolt of hope like a punch to the gut. But she had no time to revel in it, because a list had appeared. A long list of equipment, mostly. Stefani hurriedly got out her handheld and took a short video of it as it scrolled by, lest it disappear the way the footage had.

"Do you know what any of this stuff is?"

"Most of it, yes," Stefani said. Even for items she was unfamiliar with, it was simple enough to make an educated guess via context clues. "Jürgen, or whoever compelled him to make this list, wants to be able to organically print something from the ground up. And they want the technology to be as miniaturized as possible." She frowned. "I didn't get the best look, but from what I was able to recognize, most of this is equipment that pool already had. Why would he need to get it from elsewhere?"

Karl smiled.

"What?" she demanded.

"Just thinking what would have happened had I gone there alone. I'd never have had the training to recognize a bunch of poorly lit equipment after just a brief glance." He began ticking off fingers. "At a guess: one, because whatever it's doing, it would be noticed when it went missing. Two, because what's already there is not miniaturized enough. But I have to say, I don't like the idea that the equipment churning away in that pool is doing genetic printing."

"Neither do I," Stefani said absently. She'd been wondering where she was going to get that kind of specialized equipment, but suddenly she understood. "Oh! Miniaturized organic printing. Karl, this is what the locals have started using to supplement calorie short-ages now that so many Coldgardener refugees have to be fed. Iaz forbade us using them because she doesn't trust that they can't be tracked, but you just put in other kinds of raw material and the printers create digestible foodstuffs as long as all the right elements are present."

"I've seen those." Karl nodded in sudden understanding. "But they don't seem particularly small to me."

"That's because you've been stuck down here," Stefani said. "Up where the money still is, people can get extra-small ones as implants. Feed in raw material through a port and it pumps food directly into your digestive system."

"And where would you get something like that? Or the rest of the list, for that matter."

Stefani supposed there were all kinds of above-board places to get that kind of tech. The trouble was, it would be noticed, probably even logged. Still, there was one place she could think of. If Doc Cuddles was still talking to them, that was.

We can restore Marri. Your assistance is required.

Stefani would make Cuddles listen.

CHAPTER 37

CAROLINE COULD HAVE HOWLED in frustration three times over. She read the reports from her staff, detailed and verbose in their desperate attempts to say *something* when there was nothing to say. She read the equivalently terse updates from Vermin, which at least had the virtue of not wasting breath in reporting the same thing.

No one had seen hide nor hair of Helena Cardiff since the morning after the power station attack. That "no one" did a lot of work. None of Caroline's people could find her. All messages querying Helena were getting suspiciously vague responses, ones which sounded as if they were made by underlings, not the woman herself. Text only, of course. Audio and video could be faked, but not convincingly enough to evade detection indefinitely considering there were as many countermeasures to that kind of software as there were versions of the fakery software itself.

Vermin's addition to the speculation only further raised Caroline's concerns.

As far as my people can tell, she's gone missing. What's more, several of her top advisers have too. No one on my side can find any of them.

It all meant Helena was making some kind of move, and here Caroline was, playing scientist. Suddenly the more than a day she'd spent holed up here seemed like a frivolous waste of her one chance to reestablish control of the colony.

This shouldn't be me. I never wanted to be this. She had wanted scientific adventure, never anything approaching responsibility. Then her parents had died. Then her peers had abandoned her.

Suddenly this world was no longer a cushy—if harsh—playground. Suddenly it was kill or be killed. Stay atop the pile or be crushed.

The scan of the ACM victim's sample had come back frustratingly ordinary. Nothing there indicated anything but a totally average Anaranjadan with all the hormonal markers one would expect from a local Harmony worm. In mounting frustration, Caroline had set up the scan of the second body, the one the giant worm had died ripping apart. That sequencing analysis was still running.

At least her investigations into the abomination of a Harmony sample had yielded some results. Subsequent analyses had confirmed the initial findings. This was definitely an offshoot of an early Harmony strain, one somehow untouched by Subject Rho mutations. Difficult as that was to believe, the test results were unequivocal. More shocking still was when she ran the samples against a wider set of databases, searching for matches.

Included among those databases were genetic samplings taken from the refugee camps.

The Harmony sample contained human DNA with a highly mutagenic factor. Though this bore no genetic lineage to Subject Rho, the effect was Subject Rho on steroids. But as near as Caroline could tell, the proximate cause was some portion of the bizarre creatures who had invaded their world from New Calgary.

It meant that some of the at-large New Calgarians were actively experimenting with Harmony, either using it and resulting in some accidental genetic crossover or specifically attempting to alter its properties. Either explanation was potentially disastrous, an existential threat to every single human in the colony.

And if that scene at the Bridge had actually been a setup, if Helena was somehow behind it, it meant *even she* was working with the New Calgarian rebel contingent. She planned next to examine the giant worm's stomach contents. That it even *had* a stomach was a horrifying concept.

Caroline's phone buzzed, and she answered without thinking.

"What is it?" She was annoyed at having her runaway train of thought derailed.

"I'm so sorry, ma'am. I know you don't want to be bothered, but something has come up." It was Reginald, the highest-strung of her many aides. "We've just had a request for confirmation of an order you issued come in from one of the refugee camps."

"What are you talking about? I haven't issued any orders referring to the refugee camps." For a moment, her brain tried to connect this non sequitur to the samples she'd been comparing the Harmony abomination against. But those samples had been taken months ago and kept on ice. It hadn't required any special orders to access them.

"Ma'am, I'm referring to the order you gave to allow an unscheduled relief supply delivery. I'm sorry, but it's definitely your authorization I'm looking at. I wouldn't have bothered you about it, but the camp commandant forwarded a complaint about failing to be informed by you or Madame Cardiff."

Caroline's blood had run cold as sudden certainty had descended. "I thought I told you to wipe Giana Novak's credentials from the system."

"I did, ma'am. As I said, this is your authorization, not hers."

Caroline clamped her hand over the mic as tight as she could and let loose a bloodcurdling scream. Faked. That *thing* had learned how to fake Caroline's authorization. Worse, it was possible Caroline had granted her access to it to save a few fucking minutes one time and now couldn't remember doing so!

"Have them detained immediately!"

"I can't do that, ma'am. That is to say," he went on quickly as though sensing Caroline's aftershock eruption building, "all four camps were visited, but they are already gone. This complaint took some time to route through the layers necessary to reach us. The initial layer just confirmed it was your access key and rubber-stamped it. It was the follow-up complaint that elevated it."

There were going to be so, *so* many firings as a result of this. And that was if the responsible parties were *lucky*. But right now, Caroline had to get a grip and find out more information. She couldn't afford to lose it again.

"Who was with her?"

"Ma'am, I'm sorry?"

"Stop apologizing and tell me what the complaint said."

"Of course, ma'am. He goes on at some length about robes and hoods, some kind of odd religious order concerned over the refugees' well-being."

Jürgen's Cult.

"And they just *let them in?*"

"There was no alert to doubt your personal credentials, ma'am." Reginald seemed at a loss.

I let them in, at least as far as he's concerned. The timing of that broadcast had always been suspect. Now Caroline was more certain than ever that this cult, not the Defectives, had been responsible for the attack. Of more surprise was Jürgen's connection. Had her former lover kidnapped Giana and delivered her to his own sworn enemies? Did nothing about this world make sense any longer?

It was harder to reach the necessary course of action than she would have believed before the call happened. Before she was actually faced with it. Despite it being over a year, she hadn't done nearly enough study of the creatures to satisfy her curiosity and answer all the questions that needed answering.

Still, there was only one prudent outcome. Assuming, that was, that the ACM soldiers would even obey her commands. Caroline opened her mouth to tell Reginald that the camp had to be utterly purged of refugee life when her phone buzzed.

It was a message from Vermin.

"I'm going to have to call you back, Reginald. I'll have orders for you then."

"Of course, ma'am. Sorry again for disturbing—"

Caroline hung up, the better to read the message.

Trouble at the camps.

Caroline's response was immediate.

Yes, I know. What can you tell me?

Better if I do it in person.

Caroline paused, nonplused by this response. In all their interactions, Vermin had been explicit with their demand that Caroline never meet them face-to-face.

What are you talking about?

Knock knock.

And there came two knocks at the door to her lab. To Caroline's *secret lab.* She stood there, frozen, uncertain how to react to this impossible scenario.

Open up, Caroline. We need to talk.

Slowly, because she could think of no way out of it, no one she could call whom she trusted to handle this, Caroline approached the door. Each step seemed slower and more infinite than the last. Her phone buzzed, no doubt with increasingly impatient messages, but

Caroline didn't bother to look. Why would she? She was about to open the door. Whomever Vermin was, they were about to be able to berate her in person.

Caroline was suddenly conscious of how stupid she'd been to come here, certain she would open the door and Giana-plus-Cultists would be there.

The door opened to her palmed command, and Caroline stood, transfixed by the figure who stood beyond the threshold. A figure she —and this was saying something—lacked all necessary context to even fathom. The shape standing before her was vaguely human, but wrong in so many ways that her mind sought to reject it as if it could vomit out an unpleasant thought, purging it forever. Desperate, she latched onto the one thing she saw that was familiar, impossible as it was: the head of a woman she recognized, mouth lolling, eyes partly rolled up, perched atop a pulsing stalk of glowing white flesh fused to her neck.

It was not the only head the form at her door sported. It was not even the creature's *main* head. But it was the only head Caroline recognized.

"Helena?"

A terrible thought occurred to her. What would it be like to die in such total confusion, in a state of mind that was the utter negation of the concept of understanding and enlightenment? Surely it would be the most monstrously ironic end for a woman of science.

But she didn't die, not precisely. At least, Caroline didn't think she died. The figure surged forward, and Caroline flinched away, closing her eyes, operating on a pure reflex of negation, denying what she was seeing. Everything went dark in the normal way, and then, in an instant of blinding agony, everything flashed white amid so, *so* much pain that she was grateful when the darkness, this time of unconsciousness, again rolled over her.

When Caroline awoke, she couldn't move. There was still quite a bit of pain, but only in her neck, forming a full circle around its perimeter. The rest of her body she couldn't feel at all. This was not a sense of numbness or tingling, as one might experience if they fell asleep on an arm. This was the complete absence of sensation.

This should have alarmed her, should have sent her into a spiraling panic, but her thoughts felt sludgy, like cold molasses being forced through a fine sieve. She was used to fast thinking, a torrent of thoughts so blistering she could scarcely keep up. Now it felt like something was siphoning all that brain power away from her, so much so that obvious physical crises didn't even manage to register emotionally for her.

She watched a hand lift her phone. It seemed like her hand, but it wasn't. Dimly, she was aware that Caroline's hand was still attached to the rest of Caroline's body, and the rest of Caroline's body lay in a spreading pool of blood along the floor. But the hand that seemed like hers but wasn't intruded on this awareness, holding up the phone to her ear.

Speak.

The command was like the force of her thoughts the way she remembered them, only an order of magnitude beyond that. She couldn't even conceive of disobeying.

"Ma'am?" Reginald said on the other end. "We got cut off before. You said you'd have orders?"

"Yes, Reginald," Caroline's head said, speaking thoughts that were not hers. "Listen to me very carefully. You're going to submit an order to the ACM logistics hub to double the guards on the refugee camps and cut the prisoners' food to zero beginning immediately." Caroline struggled with this next part because it was complicated, and her blissfully constrained mind couldn't take it all in or grasp it as a single thing. "You are then going to block the order from going out any further."

"I'm sorry, ma'am, what? You want me to place an order and immediately rescind it?"

"No," Caroline said, transmitting her new master's frustration through her voice as though it was her own. "You're going to place the order, but *only* in the logistics hub. No order will go out to the actual soldiers. No troops will change stations as a result of this order. Do you understand?" Caroline turned to look at her fellow consul, saw awareness return to that slackened face at the end of that writhing pillar of flesh. "I have Cardiff here who can confirm."

"Do as she says," Helena's head said from her grotesque perch. *Just like my perch.* Caroline looked down to confirm—she had that much control at least. Her head now stood perched upon its own throbbing, pulsing stalk of flesh. "Voice print authorization Helena Cardiff." The head lapsed back into its prior stupor.

"Of course, ma'ams," Reginald said, sounding confused but relieved to hear both of them. "I'll see to it at once."

"That's good because I have other orders for you." And, with her patron's direction, Caroline issued them.

Once she'd disconnected the call, the person controlling Caroline said, "Good enough."

The words came from the main head, the one that sat atop a normal neck atop a squat woman, with Caroline and Helena's heads bracketing her, jutting up from either shoulder blade like the wings of a nightmare angel. The main head wore a sour-faced expression despite the woman's words, but Caroline had the sense that the mystery woman's face bore this expression naturally.

The smell of blood from Caroline's body choked the air now, metallic and sharp. It made Caroline want to gag, but a stifling sensation seized her mind, demanded she not retch, and so she didn't. She felt a fluttering of something beyond mere panic as her thoughts momentarily clarified, but that, too, was stamped down in short order.

Both exertions of control had come from the woman she was now attached to. Without needing to be told, her mind already gelling back into its newfound sludge, Caroline understood that she worked for this woman now. There was no name, because there was no need for such between them. A leg didn't know its owner's name, after all. And Caroline was owned now. She *belonged* to this woman. This woman was her utter and complete master. The master of everyone on this wretched world, whether they knew it yet or not.

Caroline's new master regarded the remains of Caroline's body. The master flexed something, and previously unseen limbs unwrapped themselves from around her midriff. They looked somewhere between glowing, white flesh and gleaming bone, and they clawed the air as if reached for the headless corpse on the ground.

"It does work up an appetite," the master said, stomping into the room and kneeling, dragging the limp form toward her head with her extra limbs.

The stifling sensation holding down Caroline's emotions was not enough to totally contain the depths of horror as she watched herself be eaten with gusto. Perhaps the master was just too excited to maintain full control. The smell of blood grew sharper, thicker, and then, as organs tore and squelched, was mixed with decidedly ranker smells, the stink offal and excrement tainting the air.

Caroline did throw up then, but what came up wasn't what she expected to see. Instead, it was black and viscous, with a consistency like drying blood mixed with crude petroleum. It ran down her chin, and she had no way to wipe it clean. As small a detail as that now was, it nearly drove her mad atop everything else.

After the master finished her meal, they turned as one, this amalgamated creature Caroline was but a part of now, heading for the door and the corridor beyond, and Caroline caught a quick glimpse of herself in the mirror-bright side of one of the lab's machines.

Even the fresh sight of her own pillar of flesh, the twin to the one holding Helena's head aloft where it sprouted from their new master's right shoulder blade and ran up to fuse with her neck, was not enough to trouble her any longer. The cold molasses of her thoughts no longer frightened or stifled. It *soothed.* Everything was so much easier this way. All she had to do was exactly what she was told.

None of her former problems belonged to her any longer. And as if that was not enough—as if she needed more proof that her new master was good, was beneficent, was glorious—answers, wondrous answers, flowed into her mind through their newfound connection. All the questions she'd had, all the mysteries plaguing her, all of them satisfactorily explained.

It was every scientist's dream.

"That's right, lap up your reward, like a good little dog," her master said. Her cutting laugh sent warmth rippling through Caroline's awareness.

It felt like coming home.

CHAPTER 38

KARL WOKE to a message indicator on his handheld. He knew from the soft buzzing pattern he'd set up that it was a dead drop message from Iazmaena. Interesting. Not an attempt at live communication using code phrases. He wasn't sure what that meant, but he didn't like it, and it certainly didn't make him any more eager to unwind himself from Stefani to check.

Even his slight shift did not go unnoticed.

"Cold," Stefani murmured as she shivered, still mostly asleep. He'd allowed some outside air past the blanket wall. They had both needed a night in each other's arms after that harrowing day, but the permanent chill of his tiny space wasn't exactly conducive to physical intimacy.

The handheld buzzed again, and Karl felt his stress tick up a notch. It was just his handheld trying to make him aware he had yet to read something important. The nature of their dead drop system meant Iazmaena wasn't on the other end impatiently sending message after message until he responded in real time. But it certainly gave that impression.

And, to be fair, the electronic dead drop system wasn't without risk, so it probably *was* important.

"Sorry," he whispered to Stefani, hoping she couldn't actually hear him. She grumbled as he snaked his arm free and reached for the device, but she mostly settled back down. His bare arm sprouted goosebumps immediately, but he kept it free of the blankets rather than disturb her again.

Just got this report from my source, and I need a logistician's eye. I'm missing something. Also, report.

Karl had to suppress a groan. Logistics had always given him a headache, whatever Iazmaena might think. He had no real head for it. And he could almost hear the irritated snap in her voice in the last sentence. Neither he nor Stefani had felt up to summarizing the previous day's events.

He thumbed open the report she'd included. It appeared to be a detailed listing of where ACM supplies were being directed, as well as orders to change deployment of those supplies. The orders had been signed off on by both Cardiff and du Vernay, so this was as high level as it got.

He was looking at the ACM's priorities before and after the attack. In other words, before they realized they were under threat and after. This was an intimate glimpse into what the ACM deemed most worthy of extra protection.

His eyebrows rose, and he understood now why Iazmaena had taken the risk to send it to him. This kind of information was both valuable and time sensitive. One never knew when another change might take place. If they could pinpoint an opening weakness, they could exploit it before it was closed.

He suspected Iazmaena had already formed her own opinions, but she had thankfully held back from including them, allowing him to come at this fresh, without preconceived notions.

One thing leaped out at him immediately. At a glance, something major had changed regarding the internment camps. Up until just recently, all four had been receiving a steady stream of supplies.

These included huge amounts of nutrient rations in particular, owing to the need to feed biological prisoners. Though even with those vast supplies, there was an old note "barely subsistence level" appended to the number.

In other words, the Coldgardeners weren't starving to death, but only just.

But in addition to those foodstuffs, there were also supplies more geared toward the ACM soldiers. Parts for cybernetics maintenance, emergency power packs, that sort of thing. It was far from the equipment lists he'd been used to seeing back on Coldgarden, but parts for maintaining lances had been a constant need.

Now, though, the numbers had changed, diverging massively from one another. ACM parts had doubled, and foodstuffs had been zeroed out. And this wasn't just recent, it was the most recent entry on the entire document judging by the timestamps. Every other datapoint he could see was at least a day older.

The most obvious answer was also the most disturbing. That there was no one left in the camp, in terms of refugees, who needed supplies. Karl scanned the historical trend over the camp numbers, looking for a downward slant. And, if he squinted, there was, over the past several months, a gradual decline in calorie needs. Almost as if, one by one, the prisoners were dying inside the camp.

Then, all at once, everything went to zero.

It's like they exterminated everyone in all four camps. Or, more pressingly, they were getting ready to. *No. No, surely they couldn't. Harmony wouldn't let them.* But that wasn't how Harmony worked. It hadn't been engineered to make humans love all creatures. It had specifically been designed to push people to behave in more group-centric pro-social ways to minimize strife *between* humans.

And, of course, Coldgardeners weren't human. And unlike when they'd first arrived across the Bridge, everyone on the planet knew that now. The horror of it brought tears to his eyes, but in a situation of critical resource constraint, Karl *could* imagine a society infused top to bottom with Harmony making that kind of call.

A part of him wanted to compose a message to that effect and send it to Iazmaena right away. If the powers that be were moving to purge the camps due to a strain on resources or any other reason, Iazmaena had to act now to try and stop them from doing the same to the others, though Karl had no idea what that would even look like. They had no hard power to bring to bear to rescue anyone. That had been the entire reason Iazmaena wanted to capture the orbitals. She at least needed to know, though.

But Karl restrained himself. She did know. The camp numbers were so glaringly obvious a child could have seen them. He didn't really know any normal children, but he was confident of that much regardless. Iazmaena was no idiot. She had certainly noticed. She had sent this to him to get a more nuanced look, to see if he might catch something she missed.

He took a closer look. The camps were still being sent water rations, and at a level commensurate with what it had been before the food had been zeroed out. That didn't make sense at all unless the prisoners were still alive.

Alive, but apparently being subjected to immediate starvation. And while this was certainly bad, it wasn't dire in the sense of an immediate emergency. Karl kept scanning.

After several more minutes, he caught what she had really been after his opinion on. He was looking at what must have similarly captivated her: the numbers for the shuttle complex. Namely, the only facility with orbital access. The recent history told the tale there as well.

There had been a surge in interest after the attack, but it had quickly dropped off. Marrietta had specifically mentioned Iaz's group's interest in it, so that likely explained the surge. But when something more urgent came up, those resources quickly dropped back to pre-attack levels. Whatever the ACM was up to, it was taking up too many resources to increase their presence everywhere important at once.

On the surface, this looked like good news. The entire point of the original attack plan had been to draw attention away from the complex. This hadn't done that, but it also hadn't made things worse in that regard, not long term, anyway. But something didn't fit.

What explains these moves?

The doubling of ACM parts to the camps certainly gave the appearance of doubling the ACM presence there. No point in moving extra supplies for the same number of boots on the ground, after all.

But unless there was a huge emergency stockpile of both resources and soldiers, both those things had to be reallocated from other places. And Karl wasn't seeing that here.

It was like they'd just conjured up a huge number of resources out of nothing, and that very much led Karl to believe that something about this report wasn't correct. The only question was why. Was it a clerical error, or had they been fed misinformation?

Then he saw his answer in a section without fluctuation. Or rather, with *odd* fluctuation. Both too random and not random enough. Shifting from his lancer mind frame to his operative mind frame, it looked exactly how Karl imagined it would look if someone was trying to fudge the supply numbers in a hurry and without really knowing what they were looking at or understanding the complex give and take of the circulatory system that was logistics.

It was the Bridge. The Bridge numbers looked wrong. They looked fake. They looked like someone was trying to hide something. And since the numbers were so relentlessly average—in fact, Karl's quick application of mental math told him they were near-enough *exactly* average across the document—that suggested to him that if the numbers at the camps were one half of the equation of strangeness, whatever was happening at the Bridge might be the other half.

They knew that Helena Cardiff and Caroline du Vernay had been trying to get the Bridge operational for the past year. It had been too big a project to keep secret, so they spun it as a good-faith attempt to allow the entire colony to escape to the lush new world the *Ultima Thule* was currently bound for. Karl doubted very much that anyone the colony's leadership didn't personally approve of would make that trip, but the fact that suddenly someone was hiding what was going on there was certainly enough to raise his hackles.

There was something else troubling about this though. Iazmaena hinted this came from her most well-placed source. And unless that source had been identified and was being fed bad information, that made them the most likely source of the tampering.

And if *that* were true, what other information might they have tampered with?

He hoped Stefani had gotten enough sleep because it was time they both got up. Iaz needed to be updated.

And they needed to dispatch someone to see what was going on with both the camps and the Bridge.

CHAPTER 39

"RISE AND SHINE," Marrietta said upon entry. Giana felt her dread crest like a wave. "I hope you slept well. I know it wasn't much time, but it's all I can spare. All the food deliveries will have had time to gestate by now, so it's time for the next phase."

Giana hadn't slept well, and the last she checked, it was still in the deepest part of the colony's sleep cycle. It didn't matter. Cycling endlessly through catastrophic thoughts about what Marrietta could be up to regarding the camps and the wider colony was not exactly conducive to a quiet mind.

Worse yet, her instruction manual, as she'd come to think of the strange device the cultist had given her with her meal that day, had been missing from its cubby when she returned. Someone had clearly found it and confiscated it. Yet another reason she couldn't sleep.

She'd seen that Marrietta was capable of somehow tampering with people she claimed to care about. How much worse might it be with people who angered her?

The woman had been ominously coy ever since they'd left the camp. Now, she approached Giana's cage with an unsettlingly direct expression. Giana found that, faced with the reality of both options, she'd preferred the former. When dealing with someone capable of what this woman was, dread was preferable to consequence.

"Yesterday was about trying to make you see what we're doing here," Marrietta said. She pulled up a stool and had a seat in front of Giana's cage. "You saw the condition of those refugees. How starved and emaciated they were."

Nothing about a strange device found in her cage. Nothing about betrayal. But Giana was not so easily gulled. She was, however, outraged and too tired to hide it.

"You talk like you were there to save them, but you just said things would have had time to gestate, so I know that's a lie. What have you gestated in them?" She very much feared she knew.

"I'm not here to save anyone," Marrietta said. "But one way or another, I set in motion the end of their suffering. You were right to be suspicious of those vitamin pills. They contain larval forms of the Harmony parasite, only modified to suit our interest and our varying biologies. Doesn't matter whether a pill was swallowed by a native, revenant, or mutaprime. Each pill had three larvae, one tailored for each of the three different Coldgardener biologies. Depending on what did the swallowing, the two larvae that don't match die. The winner matures fast and helps the host 'meet us halfway' so to speak. As I said, an end to their suffering. They could have lingered on indefinitely in those camps, slowly expiring as the colony's experimentation went too far on one subject after another. With my way, they'll have their freedom. Or something that feels like it anyway. In reality they'll be answering to me. But they'll *want* to do it, and in the end, isn't that just as good as freedom? Especially if, in so doing, they might even have a chance to take some of their tormentors with them. Their fate will be on their terms."

"Your terms, you mean." Giana tried to keep a lid on her tone, but it was hard. All night worrying. *Hers are the terms I'm set to go out on. Might as well make it count.* "You don't care about any of that."

"You're right. I don't. I wouldn't be very good at my calling if I could care about the ones I hurt. But I did want to make an exception for you. Perhaps it's just some sort of narcissistic impulse over an entity that shares so much of me, but I'd hoped for another who could understand."

Tell her you understand.

"I don't," Giana said. "And I never will."

Marrietta looked a little sad but accepting. "There's too much human left in you. Or, well, you know. Not enough mutaprime. But I suppose it will make the part that comes next easier for me. I only wish you had been able to find your way to my way of thinking. Then it would be easier on you."

"What are you going to do?"

"I need to reach out to all the new subjects we created a few hours ago. Call it a proof-of-concept test before we do the real thing."

"What does that have to do with me?" But Giana feared she knew.

"I can only control so many of our people at once. And to put it simply, I'm spread too thin. The last year took a lot out of me. If I try to exert that much direct control, I'm afraid it might kill me. But if I have a medium to work through, it, well, it's complicated. But suffice it to say it will spread the strain between us. And then, once you reach out through them, our 'bandwidth,' for lack of a better term, will be amplified still further. That's the other half of the terrible fate you assume I have in store for them. They are going to be our antenna."

Marrietta said all this as though Giana should be *proud* of her. "What makes you think this will even work? You've been saying that I'm not enough like you, that I'm too human—"

"And you'll only be getting half the strain," Marrietta said. She spread her hands. "Best I can do."

Giana saw through the act then. For an act was all it was. There was nothing behind that empty, apologetic smile. All that talk of wanting someone to understand? A pantomime of soliciting empathy. This was, what? Practice? Playing at appearing human? Giana had no idea. And, abruptly, she no longer cared. She was very tired. She'd woken on a slab a year ago to an endless succession of horrors, both biological and existential. Just let it end.

"Just do what you're going to do," Giana said. "You don't need my permiss—"

Giana cut off as her voice stopped working. Something gripped her mind, squeezed it like a vice. Crawling black tendrils crept inward from the outskirts of her vision as it tunneled down. The pressure mounted, became a voice in her mind, a voice speaking in something other than words. Imperatives. Needs. Urges. Giana felt them pass through her and beyond her, hollowing her out as they went, like they were an awl the thickness of a tree trunk.

Calling what she experienced *pain* would be like calling a flood a dripping faucet. But she felt the connection form, felt the command passing through her split and split and split again, reaching out and into each of the "antennae" Marrietta had birthed into the world a day gone.

Giana felt the commands focus, not into any specific action, but as a kind of test pattern. A carrier wave sent just to make sure the equipment intended to receive and return it functioned. Despite the pain, the power behind it was enormous, as though her mind was being multiplied a thousandfold. It filled Giana with a kind of euphoria that almost let her forget precisely what was happening and how much it hurt.

Just as she began to revel in it, the pressure on Giana's mind eased some, as though acceptance had been all that was required. With this easing, her awareness drifted somewhat, seeming to flow outside herself, twisting and bobbing in unseen winds coming out of the darkness enclosing her mind.

She sensed Marrietta, a shape of glowing white, only vaguely humanoid, too many limbs and too few heads, but it was the thing beyond her that captivated Giana's attention. It was a face, limned in a darkness deeper than the absence of light. Yet for all its invisibility, Giana could still sense how it shifted, ever changing, never holding a fixed form. And beyond the face, so far beyond it beggared imagination, lay a deeper presence, a thing as big as all the rest of her aware-ness put together. Bigger.

Marrietta's god half-watched them all with a paradoxical blend of interest and indifference, each cosmic in its vastness.

Giana owed her predecessor an apology if she survived this expe-rience. She *did* understand now.

The woman had to be stopped. At any cost.

CHAPTER 40

STEFANI MISSED KARL ALREADY. The two brief nights with him, one in as uncomfortable a set of surroundings as she could imagine, had been two of the best nights she'd had since she arrived on this horrible world. Only the first night after Ella had been cured could compare.

But they each had their tasks to perform. After deciphering the document Iaz had sent him, he'd taken it upon himself to go investigate the Bridge. Between that and the camps, he argued, whoever had potentially doctored the logistical data was more interesting in drawing attention to the camps, which inclined him not to check there yet. He had not responded to Iaz's request for a message for one simple reason: he didn't want Iaz—who would surely be more interested in the shuttle complex than anything else—to tell him no.

Stefani, meanwhile, had her own off-script mission to accomplish before she updated Iaz. She made her way back to Doc Cuddles's office to beg, barter, or steal the equipment on the list Jürgen had given them. If there was a chance they could restore Marri to what she had been then Stefani was going to take that chance, however remote its odds of success.

The door did not admit her when she buzzed it. She palmed the request for entry again. And again.

"Go away, Palmieri." Cuddles's voice was even brusquer than usual. "I'm busy, and I'm not interested in talking with you and yours just now." That answered that question. But it was not the end of the discussion. She buzzed three more times, but he didn't even bother to reply. Cuddles had no incoming intercom button—no way she could talk to him short of shouting through the closed door and hoping he heard her.

But she was not taking no for an answer.

Trevor hummed happily inside her head as she pushed close enough to the door to shield what she was doing from view, hopefully from both the street and the door camera. Then she changed one hand, transforming it into an edged, finely sharpened stabbing implement. These doors had access panels for maintenance or emergency opening from the outside. The edge of her blade was slender enough to get up into that seam.

She wasn't delicate, didn't have to be. She already knew how to open doors like this, after all. Sparks popped as she sliced through circuitry. Stefani winced with the pain of more shocks, but the door slid open with the rapidity born of assumed emergency. And by the way Cuddles stared at her, jaw agape, eyes torn between fear and outrage, he certainly considered it an emergency.

"I'm not here to cause trouble," she said, probably inanely at this point. "But I need some equipment that you likely have, and I can't take no for an answer."

"Not here for trouble, she says as she robs me," he said in his raspy, wry voice. "You need to leave right now, before we have another close encounter like the last time. Give me a list and I'll see you get your equipment, as long as you go. *Now.*"

That was good enough for Stefani. Almost, it was.

There was something about his demeanor—his urgency, specifically—that raised her hackles. Or maybe they were Trevor's. All well and good to fear a visit from the ACM, but he spoke as if . . .

"Why so urgent?" she asked. "Have *they* been by again since last time?" She kept her voice casual. Tried to, anyway. But the way he flinched told her she'd failed.

Or maybe that she'd stumbled onto something. He spoke as if they were due any minute.

"Are you, perhaps, expecting someone?" Now her voice was too casual.

"I have patients come in and out all the time. Today just happens to be a busier day than others," he said. His crotchety-old-man demeanor had returned, but it still rang false to her for some reason. "I have an appointment in fifteen minutes, if you must know," he said, as if knowing she wasn't satisfied.

Trevor whispered wordlessly within her mind.

"Who with?"

"Doctor-patient confidentiality is still a thing, my dear," he said, sounding on surer footing now. Sounding almost relieved.

He's sold us out. She wasn't sure who'd had this thought, herself or Trevor. *Or, no. He's* about *to sell us out.*

"I've got the list right here," she said, patting her pocket. "Let me show it to you."

"Leave it, I said," he snapped. "I'll get to it after my appointment. You won't have to wait long. I promise."

There it was again. Something in that tone. *You won't have to wait long* sounded an awful lot like *you'll get what's coming to you.* There was still fear in his words, but more and more, there was anger.

They held one another's stares wordlessly for a moment. Then Trevor was there, in control, surging them both forward as Cuddles tried to twist out of the way of their advance.

Trevor was faster.

Stefani had never, she realized now, put her blade away. It didn't matter. Trevor was strong enough to bear Cuddles to the ground in just one hand's grip, and then Cuddles was firmly under control. The doc weighed more than Stefani did, but his cybernetics were built for dexterity, not strength, and Trevor had all the leverage.

"Those people I sold out for you," he said. "Some of them were like family. You don't have any idea what doing that is—"

Anger surged in Stefani, red and weary of the assumptions of the people on this blighted rock. Her muscles screamed with the need to lash out. "Why, because I'm not *human*? I have a family, too, doc," she said. "I haven't seen one of my daughters in over a year. I would do *anything* to get her back. That's what I came here for help with."

"Oh, yes, your daughter. Don't think I missed the last name in that colony-wide broadcast on the heels of a terrorist attack. Marrietta *Palmieri*. Call me crazy, but I don't think your daughter is someone I particularly want reuniting with whatever it is you and Delgassi are up to."

Anger became rage, a fury she'd scarcely known she was capable of. "No one will keep me from her. Do you understand me?" She had to fight through a red haze of rage to speak the words. "Certainly not a back-alley sawbones like you."

"Listen to me," he said, his anger gone, his eyes wide with panic. "There's still time for you to go. I'll-I'll tell them something else when they come. I won't rat you out. I swear!"

Lying. But Trevor's warning was unnecessary. Stefani knew. *Can't let him live.*

"Of course you won't. I see it clearly now." Trevor's urgings were just a buzz in her mind as she stabbed down, pulling back in time with his jerk. Blood gushed outward like a faucet in time with his suddenly faltering heart. "We thought we could work with you Defectives, thought you were different than the lemmings of this world." She ventilated Cuddles in a second place, twisting her custom blade this time in that way she knew did maximum damage. He groaned, and this time the flow of blood was weaker, just like his struggles. Then she stabbed again. Again. Again. He'd stopped jerking with each strike by now. "But even Defective, too much of this culture has seeped into you to ever see us outsiders any other way."

By contrast, quite a lot of him was seeping out now.

There was a ringing in her ears. *Well,* Stefani thought, *a little unexpected treat for you. You must be happy.*

Quite happy, Trevor said. *But this was no treat for me. Not in the way you mean.* His voice sounded close to laughing with joy. *I'm not the one who killed him this time.*

Stefani stopped. She thought back, and there the memory was, damning as a descending gavel. Trevor had tackled Cuddles, but at the man's words, Stefani had taken control once more. Trevor hadn't even put up a fight, she realized.

A terrible, dead cold spread through her at this realization.

Bravo. You're a natural at this, Palmieri. I'd like to think I had some hand in it, of course—

Stefani stopped listening. She barely recalled standing, dragging the body out of sight of the permanently open door, and beginning a frantic search for the items she'd come for.

She only had a few minutes.

Stefani went for the storage closet first. Most of what she was looking for she would know on sight, but it turned out Cuddles had been fastidious when it came to organization and labeling of things, so educated guesses were not even required. In fact, her search was so short and successful she became convinced she'd missed something, double and triple-checking her copy of the list against the shelves and drawers arrayed before her.

But no, she'd gotten everything she came for. There was even a convenient grav-sled to move it in.

It had been so simple in the end.

It was time to go. She spared the dead man neither apology nor look and left, pushing the cart ahead of her, head on a swivel for anyone who might be watching or just seem out of place.

Stefani didn't live far from the clinic. She crossed the distance quickly, entered her apartment with unseemly haste, pulling the cart through after her and locking the door behind. Locking the events at the clinic behind her too.

"Mom!" Ella came running, either eager to see Stefani or doing a very credible impression of same.

"There you are!" Iaz's voice rounded the corner before she did. She sounded peeved but relieved. "What part of 'report' doesn't that old fossil you're dating get? Even with a message in the middle of the night, I expected to hear from you hours ago."

"Karl is freelancing a bit," Stefani said. "With good reason," she added when Iaz looked set to flare up. She gave a quick sketch of what had happened to them, what they'd found at the comms hub, Karl's analysis of the message, and his decision to see what was happening at the Bridge. Stefani finished, somewhat reluctantly considering Ella's presence, by describing the scene at the clinic.

A version of it, at least. One in which she arrived to find Cuddles already dead, likely killed by the ACM as a warning to anyone else who might help out Iaz's resistance or the Defectives. It would never hold up to even the most basic investigative scrutiny, but Stefani wasn't talking to the ACM. She was talking to Iaz, someone who would never have the chance to fact-check the story.

Thank god flowmatter fabric repelled liquids, blood included.

Iaz looked almost too amazed to be mad. But she clearly bought the story, a fact which Stefani found coldly satisfying. "Jesus, when you all go into work mode, you don't fuck around."

"Language!"

"Believe me, she's heard it all before. Particularly in the last couple of days. What about the download from the comms hub?"

"The only thing we found there was that there was some kind of code embedded within the static at the end of the message. The message itself was scrubbed clean of any locational data, but we found their location regardless thanks to Karl's tracker he planted on Fennec."

"What's this code?"

"I assumed some kind of malware, but Karl's handheld couldn't identify it if so."

"Hm. I'll pass it along to my source, see if they know anything."

"About that," Stefani said. "Karl is concerned that the strange logistics numbers you sent him could just as easily be strange *because* of your source. So be careful."

"You're just full of good news today. But I'll take that under advisement. At least it sounds like there might be some good signs with respect to the shuttle complex. Which I would be sending Karl to investigate if he hadn't decided to go rogue."

"Which is why he went rogue. We can't tell if anyone fudged those numbers, much less who did so, if someone doesn't investigate the reality on the ground."

"Yes, but he's not checking the shuttle complex, which is the only thing I care about. That gets us to our power play. That's what gives us leverage. Besides, they're months away from getting the Bridge to work. Every source we have agrees on that point."

"I'm beginning to wonder if that's true."

"You don't actually know that the numbers there are off."

"Karl seems certain enough to take the risk."

"Or he just doesn't have the stomach for my way of thinking. Beyond that, I'm not sure why he'd care about the Bridge. We know what they're trying to do with it. Even if they've gotten it to work, why would we want it? They seem to think they can use it to steal the Equatorians' new planet out from under them. If the last remnants of this planet's leadership want to leave, I say let them. Assuming this new planet is even worth living on. You really want to do a repeat of a year ago on some third planet? I'll take the devil I know, thank you."

Which was also a fair point, Stefani supposed. "I'm sure once he gets back, he'll be willing to go investigate the shuttle complex."

"It will be so nice of him to report in and request orders," Iaz said too sweetly. "But we don't have time for that. There's too much we don't know. A bunch of really weird stuff is happening, stuff we have no understanding of, and I have no idea when it's all going to blow up in our faces."

"That doesn't mean—"

"Let me finish. Somehow, we still have an opportunity to get to the orbital platforms. I'm sending you to meet with the Defective factions located in Australis. I'm going to meet with the ones in Borealis. They've all gone to ground since Marrietta's little blame-game transmission. But they're at least willing to meet, and that's what matters."

"To what end? You think they're willing to seriously bargain again this quickly after we burned them?" It had taken months of sweet talking to get them to tentatively agree to help—with many stipulations, mind—the first time.

"They reached out to me, believe it or not. Both sets. I was as surprised as anyone, but it gives us an opening. I need you to approach them from a position of strength. We're not waiting. We're not bargaining. We're acting, now, while we have the chance. They can either help us and have us in their debt or they can refuse and earn our enmity when we succeed anyway."

"*Can* we succeed anyway?"

"I need you to make them believe we can, Steffi. I'll certainly be pushing as hard as I can on my bunch. We need them to attack two different locations, each one local to them, simultaneously. Here," she said, overriding Stefani's further attempts at protest and shoving a tablet with a map under her nose. "These two points." She indicated two spots on the map, each overlaid with a red dot. "The shuttle complex is central to both, so it will be an obvious place to draw reinforcements from. Once those reinforcements get called away, we are going. So hopefully Karl gets back in time, or he'll have to arrange his own ride."

"We are *not* leaving him," Stefani said. "And even if we were, I'm not ready to—"

"I packed for us." Ella's voice was just a hair too chipper.

"Thank you, dear," Stefani said. This was what she got for leaving the girl with *Auntie Iaz.*

Iaz leaped into the distraction. "Steffi, whatever you feel about this, the meeting is set, and if you don't leave soon, you're going to be late for it. There will be time to find Karl. That was just a bad joke.

You will have time to try to convince me that building whatever the robot Cult man wants you to build is a good idea." Her tone left little doubt what she thought about Stefani's scavenger hunt. "Even if both Defective groups are convinced, they are going to need time to plan an attack. You will have time to get your head around this later, but you do not have time now. So you need to go and fake your ass off. That means right now, before we piss them off so much they'll never help us again."

Which was how Stefani found herself bundled back out the door and headed north.

CHAPTER 41

MARRI WAS ON STRIKE.

She could not recall when exactly she'd made this decision. Only the gradually accumulating sense that her mind was less fuzzy than it had once been. She experienced fewer bouts of time where she forgot details about herself, fewer instances of looking back at her days as though they had existed in someone else's dream.

And the more aware she grew, the less willing to tolerate all of whatever this was she became.

She sat stubbornly on the lip of a fountain edge, the composicrete basin dry and cracked, pondering her situation. There were some things she knew. First among them: this place was not real. No matter how long she waited, she never got hungry, never got thirsty, never got tired. Day never turned to night unless it suddenly did with zero warning. She recalled having this realization before—many times, in fact—only to have it blighted from her mind over and over again.

"Bry" jauntily rounded a corner, his manner unconcerned, as though he hadn't already done this fifty times "today." It was a different corner than last time. It always was, at least until Bry had run out of new corners to appear around and begun to recycle them.

As though if he could just approach from the right angle, she'd be fooled.

"We've got to go," he said. He was cutting straight to it this time. He'd done that before but didn't always. This version of him was closer to that of her memories. Bry had never been one for pleasantries.

Marri wondered if the real Bry was still alive.

This time, she chose to answer. She hadn't done so in a while. Inevitably, if she failed to answer, he would wander off awkwardly, in a very un-Bry-like manner. It had happened enough times, with no deviation, that she could safely assume another point.

Wherever she was, the entity in control either couldn't or wouldn't force her to do what it wanted. The Professor could try to persuade her, frighten her, guilt her, but it never *made* her do anything.

She dimly recalled having similar thoughts to this before. But never this consistently or this long before she was rendered dumb again. Something had changed. She just didn't understand what.

"I'm not going anywhere with you," she said, deciding on the spot to be more direct than she'd ever been. Growing up on the streets, she had learned the value of discretion. But now she was willing to take a calculated risk. "You aren't really Bry. I'm not doing anything you ask until you start telling me what's going on. What's *really* going on."

She expected another deflection, another changed approach, another attempt to slip past her defenses. But Bry's entire affect changed in a way that seemed vaguely familiar, like she'd seen it before in one of her inter-stupid periods.

"All recent analysis suggests that you have adopted an attitude that will resist any attempts at persuasion." As he spoke, his voice no longer sounded like that of a little boy, but like a chorus of electric sparks somehow forming words. "As such, the only possible path forward is to acquiesce to your demands and attempt to form a rapport. What is it you wish to know?"

Marri had to fight to keep her jaw from dropping, but she wasn't going to waste this opportunity. "What are you?"

"A synthetic intelligence of distributed architecture, the last remnant of the sentient beings that inhabited this world before the current colonists arrived."

Though she knew it wasn't real, Marri was on the verge of asking if he meant Coldgarden when the entire vista changed to that of the other world.

Anaranjado, some dim, years-old memory whispered to her. It felt like another person's memory.

"So you're a thinking machine?" She knew quite a bit more about the concept now than she had before she'd come to wherever this was. All the lessons, she realized. Synthetic Intelligence had been among the many topics she'd been tricked into absorbing.

"Correct. Designation: Feathertouch. I operate far outside my original boundaries even if my original purpose remains intact."

"What's your original purpose?"

"To make life better for this world's inhabitants."

"And is that what you're doing with me?" Marri asked, gesturing around her. "Making my life better?"

"I am the only reason you are alive at all," Feathertouch said. It did not sound aggrieved, like it expected her gratitude. It sounded like a simple statement of fact, which was far more disturbing to consider.

Marri thought back to the last thing she felt like she could remember before this place: Giana's assault upon her body and mind, and Marri fleeing into a thin, dark tunnel as everything collapsed behind her.

"What did Giana do to me?"

"Entity designation: Giana infected you approximately one year ago. The final collapse of your volition and the subsequent transfer of your biological processes to her control were sudden and complete. Only the fact that cultists I had subsumed installed a modified backup drive in your brain enabled your consciousness to escape in some fashion."

There was a lot to unpack there. But Marri leaped on the most obvious part first.

"My consciousness?"

"Correct. The biological entity that was you is dead, in essence. Your body remains intact, but it has become an entity both separate and distinct from you. The portion of your mind that was able to be digitally copied over to the backup drive installed in your brain was transmitted to me. In essence, you are currently a thinking machine yourself, utilizing a portion of my processing and storage."

Marri felt like her knees should have shook. Her heart should have been pounding. She should have felt faint. None of those things happened, and it was almost more scary as a result.

"I have learned a great deal while I have hosted you," Feathertouch said as if it could read her mind. "Including how to suppress certain of your simulated autonomic responses without suppressing your consciousness.

Of course it can read my mind. I'm literally a part of its mind.

"Incorrect," Feathertouch said, giving the lie to its own words. "In fact, we have both gone to considerable effort to render you distinct from me. When you first arrived, your personality components were haphazardly distributed across my processing and memory architecture. I had never had to host a separate consciousness before, so those architectures were not optimally arranged to house you. As my education efforts grew, you began to take up more and more free space, and it became more difficult to differentiate where you ended and I began. Hence our more recent work separating your memories from mine."

It was so strange that a statement could make perfect sense with Marri's own recollections yet also make her realize how utterly alien this creature was. It spoke like it was the smartest computer any human had ever designed, but that was really just a false face it was showing her. Something that she could grasp, at least a little.

She supposed she should thank it for making the effort at least. But she was distracting herself from the most dire of Feathertouch's revelations.

"You said 'the portion of my mind.' Does that mean not all of me made it?"

"Likely, though unknown. The backup drive had the latest in non-destructive brain scanning technology installed. It would have been able to rapidly copy your entire brain structure and digitize it— not so rapidly as destructive brain scanning methods would have, but that would be a suboptimal outcome. However, it was not installed for long before Entity Giana attacked and began aggressively altering your brain structure. There is no way to be certain if something was left out when that which had been copied was transmitted to me."

Marri thought furiously, looking for holes in her memory from before this place. Nothing sprang to mind. She didn't know whether to be relieved or frightened by that thought.

"It's entirely possible that if something was lost, you quite literally wouldn't know that you didn't know it," Feathertouch said.

"That's not very comforting."

"It was intended to be factual."

"Yeah. I think that's the problem," Marri said wryly. "So I've lost my body to that . . . thing. Does that mean I'm going to be trapped in here, part of you, forever?"

"Tentatively incorrect. Not if my plans come to fruition. For me to act openly would risk my discovery and likely destruction. But I may acquire influence with any person who has cybernetic implants of certain types, and I have cultivated such resources assiduously since your arrival. Plans are underway to restore you to your body with the help of your family, though they don't really understand why they are doing what they are doing."

"You mean Stefani? Karl?" Marri expected to fight tears, but none came. She wondered if that was more suppression of debilitating emotions on Feathertouch's part or some change in her. It had been so long, years, since she'd seen any of them. Shouldn't she feel a stronger longing? Or was the opposite true? Had she, in some capacity—or perhaps deficiency, if not all of her had made it—moved on? She decided to steer the conversation to safer ground. "You said it's only been a year, but it seems like more than that. Much more."

"Available analysis indicates Entity Giana has aged your body approximately seven Earth years, probably to more easily assume a leadership role among her peers. I have calibrated your own subjective experience such that you have experienced roughly the same amount of time. It will make reintegration easier."

It turned out that hadn't been safer ground at all, so Marri pivoted hard. "What is the plan?"

"I have seen to it that your family have come into the possession of a set of plans which will enable them to produce a bioprinter designed to replicate you."

Marri thought she didn't know what a bioprinter was, but on second thought, she did. More of Feathertouch's instructions. She could see the structure of a sizable wedge of her education now. He'd been training her to understand what he was doing to help her. "You're going to make me a new body and then, what, upload me into it?"

"Incorrect. Cloning a person is feasible, as is biological memory reconstruction from digital copies, but all known technology capable of performing these functions was taken off-planet on the colony ship for reasons unknown. Recreating it would be possible, but difficult and time consuming when there is an easier alternative."

"Which is?"

"I have substantially penetrated the Cult. Doing so while remaining undetected has limited my options substantially, but I have managed to copy the majority of the work the Giana Entity has been undertaking since assuming your identity. Our aims lie along very similar tracks."

Marri was losing patience. "What exactly are you planning to do, and while you're explaining that, what exactly is *she* planning to do?"

"I have designed a variant of the cerebral parasitic lifeform known as Harmony that will, in effect, translate into biology the portion of yourself currently contained within me in digital form."

Marri stood there, staring, too stunned for words. "I'd be a worm. A brain worm."

"A human brain is approximately 60 percent lipids, with the remainder comprised of water, protein, carbohydrates, and electrolytes. The Harmony parasitic lifeform is made of a largely similar ratio of materials."

"I'm not human," Marri said.

"Correct. Yet your species' impressive mimicry has refashioned its own brain to be an almost indistinguishable analog of a human brain. And, if I can be flippant, what you might call your true form resembles in large measure what humans would call a worm."

Checkmate, Marri supposed. "It's just a lot to process."

"Thinking organisms, be they biological or synthetic, are by definition emergent entities, producing complexity beyond their constituent parts. The parts themselves are largely immaterial when the end result is the same. And I have high confidence that this process will preserve as much of you as can be preserved."

Marri rocked back on her perch, struck at once by the grim certainty and the equally grim limitations of that statement. "And what does Giana plan to do?"

"The Giana Entity intends to do something broadly similar, but on much larger scale. It has developed a metaparasitic variant of the Harmony parasite."

"What does that—a parasite of the parasite?"

"Correct. Once introduced into the population at large via their bioprinters, it will hijack their existing parasites and make them subjugate themselves to the Giana Entity."

Marri dug down into that well of new knowledge about this colony and how it worked. "Those nutriprinters are tamperproof. You taught me that. How could she possibly hijack them into printing a metaparasite?"

"I have not been able to determine this. But based on my analysis of its actions, the Giana Entity believes very strongly it has overcome this problem. For the sake of preparedness, I am forced to take it at its word."

238

THE EMPTY POOL had been emptied further of the various bioprinters and gene sequencers. Giana, who had been returned to her cell much to her dismay, watched with mounting alarm as it was reconfigured with an array of what looked like broadcast and transmitting equipment.

Marrietta watched with considerably more evident pleasure.

"I don't get it," Giana said. "Why not just transmit the order via the same method you did last time?"

"Because they know that method now. My source in their ramshackle governing body tells me they're on the lookout for me to repeat my previous moves. So I'd be an idiot to use the same trick again."

"If you could transmit from your headquarters, why didn't you just do *that* before?"

"Because if I had, I couldn't use it now. One trick, one use," she said. "Doesn't matter the trick."

Jürgen approached. "Another hour and we should be ready," he squawked in his harsh electronic voice.

"Good," Marrietta said. "Then it will be time to see just how much of the colony we've managed to snare."

"What is this snare?" Giana asked. She gestured around her at Marrietta's considering look. "I'm not going anywhere. You can at least satisfy my curiosity. You explained what you did to our people—sort of, anyway. But what have you done to the rest of the colony?"

"You should always be careful what you choose to put into your body," Marrietta said, for some reason fiddling with the back of her head. Giana had caught sight of the implant there before. "I wasn't given a choice on this. I'd have had it out a year ago, but the doctors scanned me and told me it was clean of any . . . infestation. That, and the fact that the somewhat dramatic change in my brain structure at that time would make removing it highly risky, and I decided to leave well enough alone. But believe me, if I'd had a choice, either version of me, I wouldn't have installed it. Yet the people of this world made that choice over and over again."

Jürgen didn't move, for all that he was the perfect poster child of synthetic implants run amok. But then, Marrietta paid him no mind either.

"Something tells me you're going to make them regret that choice," Giana said.

"No, actually. If all goes well," Marrietta said, "they'll be as happy about it as can be. They just won't have any choice in the matter." She chuckled at Giana's obvious exasperation. "It's the nutriprinters almost all of them have now. So sophisticated. Able to provide them with the exact mix of nutrients they need by converting inedible matter into the building blocks of food. What more perfect solution to a world as infertile as this? Why, they even respond to biochemical and neurological feedback from the body directly, tailoring their behavior to exactly what the body is unconsciously requesting of them. And that is where the trap has been set."

"What are you talking about?"

"They're tamper-proof by any normal means. Believe me, we tried early on. Anything that would physically rework their core programming to what we needed bricked them. And even if we found a way, how to make it work for every individual printer scattered across the colony, most already lodged in people's digestive tracts?"

Giana frowned. She wasn't seeing it. Marrietta's eyes sparkled with delight at her confusion.

"It's the feedback feature that's the weakness. They adjust their programming based on the body's feedback. All the way down to the root level firmware, turns out. All we had to do was get the bodies attached to the printers to provide the feedback we needed. And it turns out that, in all their research about replacing the brain with pure cybernetics, the Cult has done quite a bit of research on how the body impacts the brain, and how the brain impacts the body in turn. And, most importantly, how you can *induce* the brain to make changes to the body chemistry. It's a much simpler process than you might imagine. You can do it with lights, sounds, smells. Even, oh, say, strange patterns in static."

She smiled at Giana's frown. "I supposed you didn't see my original broadcast, then. The way it was 'cut off' early. The way the static right at the end formed a very particular pattern. Probably a lot of people who saw it didn't even consciously register it. But they registered it unconsciously, whether they know it or not. And, more importantly, it would have resulted in a cascade of feedback effects on their nutriprinter, putting it into a kind of standby mode with a new set of printing instructions. Waiting for another signal. A signal we are about to send."

"And what will it be printing?" Giana asked, trying to keep the dread from her voice.

"The future," Marrietta said with a smile, and then she explained all about what she'd been doing this past year. Infecting the refugees as a way of ensuring she could control them. And then, from there, infecting the Anaranjadans toward the same end.

"It was very difficult," Marrietta said, as though she was looking for praise. Giana half-expected her to add *not bad for a little street urchin, huh?* "You're talking about four different variants of the parasite. Three for each of the three Coldgardener species. Then a fourth —what we're calling the metaparasite—to take over the brains of everyone on this world who already *have* a Harmony parasite in their heads. Then to figure out how to deliver them all. But you were the key, and I didn't even know it."

"You're insane," Giana said, cutting off whatever explanation the woman had been about to offer. Giana had no wish to know how she had been the key to any of this.

Marrietta shrugged. "What I am is unmoved by that argument. I've told you what actually motivates my actions. But if you must hear my justify this on some sort of human level, something the Marri of before could advocate, I saw the way corrupt authority treated those who can't defend themselves back on Coldgarden. I'm not about to shed a tear for any symbols of that authority here. This is just how things are. There are those who have, and there were those who don't. If you were in the latter, you owe it to yourself and to those who depend on you to claw your way as high up into the former as you can. And then, if you are a truly enlightened being, you use the power to amass to shatter the system. And, very soon now, no one will be higher than Marrietta Palmieri."

"But why shatter anything? Why not use the power to make it better?"

"Because then *I'm* the problem. The ones who do the shattering can't be the ones who take control. You're just replacing one broken system with another. I will break this colony, and then I will move on, and those that survive can establish themselves a new order."

"And what if the order they establish is as bad as the one you broke? What if it's *worse?* Then so many will die for nothing."

"Someone else will be along to break the new order in due time."

"But when does the breaking stop?"

Marrietta turned blazing, fervent eyes upon Giana. The "Marri of before," as the woman had termed it, would never have worn that gaze. They were the eyes of an absolute zealot. "When the society under attack is strong enough, just enough, resilient enough to withstand any blow. In other words: when it's *earned* its right to continue."

"Gods below," Giana said, and Marrietta laughed as if it were the world's best joke.

"I used the same epithet for years, but Giana, that's us! To all those Coldgardeners, *we're* the gods below. But they're wrong. We are no gods. Not really." She turned to Jürgen, as if to declare she'd made her final argument and it was unassailable. "Where are we in preparations?"

"All systems nominal," the mechanical man said in his electronic distortion of a voice.

"Let's get her set up then," Marrietta said.

Releasing her from her cell, they led her to the center of the pool and an egg-like chamber that sat there. Every other device was wired into it.

"The main thing you need to concern yourself with is that it's a sensory deprivation chamber," Marrietta explained, as though she could sense the questions whirling through Giana's mind. "You're going to be very thankful for that once it gets started. This is going to be bad enough without you having to take in any of your surroundings."

But Giana would not be persuaded away from her dread. "What are all the rest going to do?"

"Wake up the Anaranjadans," Marrietta said. "We'll only need the equipment to broadcast the print signal. Once our living network comes fully online, it will hold itself in place without help—provided you're alive, of course. And that's good because it will enable us to go on the move. So you needn't worry that we'll leave you here alone when we go to take the Bridge." Her smile said she knew that was exactly what Giana had been hoping—however momentarily—would happen.

The chamber opened at her approach. Giana considered trying

to slide past both of them and make a break for it. But there were Cultists and mutaprimes everywhere. She had no hope of escape.

They hovered close as Giana lowered herself into the antigravity field at the chamber's bottom. As the darkness closed down around her, the last thing she heard was Marrietta's attempt at comfort.

"Try not to stress. All you have to do is lay there."

About thirty seconds later, the agony began.

CHAPTER 43

WHOMEVER THE LEADERS of the Australis Defective Factions thought they were getting, it had not been Stefani Palmieri. And as she walked into the impromptu meeting room, really just a bunch of chairs pulled around the central bed of a nondescript hotel room as though it was a conference table, they were quite evidently not happy about the development.

For Stefani's part, she was just happy the Defectives were actually here and she hadn't walked into some kind of ACM trap. The sudden willingness of the factions to meet against all obvious logic had left her wondering.

"We request a meeting to discuss the ways you people so thoroughly burned us, and Delgassi sends her rabid dog to be diplomat?" Kestrel said. Always a charmer was Kestrel. And he loved to repeat his little jokes.

Gee, thanks for leveling with them, Iaz.

"She guessed I would be taken seriously," Stefani said, pivoting as smoothly as she was able. Above all, she must appear to be in control of the situation, not flying by the seat of her pants. "And she was right." She took her seat at the foot of the bed. It felt a touch ridiculous and underscored the precariousness of all their situations. Hopefully, that would also cause them to take this meeting seriously. Judging by the number of guards loitering "casually" outside, Stefani trusted they were.

"Thank you all for coming." There was no reason she couldn't start off being genuinely diplomatic. Maybe it would even keep them off-balance by running counter to their expectations. "Please take a look at what we're proposing and give us your thoughts." In the close confines of the room, she was able to safely transmit the attack plan Iaz had drawn up in a low-power, short range mode. Silence descended as the five faction leaders digested the planning document.

"You should apologize for wasting our time," Kestrel said at last. No points for guessing which of these august leaders was least afraid of Stefani. He turned his comment at her into a statement directed at everyone. "Our willingness to even *talk* to these off-worlders, these non-humans, is a waste of time. It has been from the beginning, and it's also dangerous. Their wants are not our wants. Their values are not our values."

"They want to get off-planet, Kestrel," said Dana Vasquez. "I would think you'd be all in favor."

"Much as it would please me to banish the off-worlders to join their fellows in space, they are a plague down here, and I can't think the other aliens will feel any different. I'm not willing to throw my people's lives away in an operation just so the aliens out there can rain down some kind of punishment onto us for afflicting them with the aliens down here. The quarantine of this world has always been absolute, and all our troubles now stem from the Equatorians turning a blind eye when these creatures arrived like a Trojan horse."

"Please, Kestrel, continue," Stefani said. "It's not as if anyone here is aware of your prejudices. You're always such a closed book."

Vasquez chuckled. So did one or two of the others. Kestrel looked discomfited at this, no longer quite so sure of his footing.

"Very well," he said, recovering himself. "Please, do enlighten us why we should help you secure the shuttle zone when you have failed to live up to any part of your end of our bargain. Have, in fact, made everything worse by even *attempting* to do so. A bargain, I hasten to remind everyone, I objected to from the start, *before* dozens of people had died."

Stefani's temper flared, and she lost the reins of her composure. "Why is it you called this meeting, exactly?"

"Our sources and the degree to which they inform us of the prevailing situation are our own." This, coming from Vasquez, unbalanced Stefani in turn. It was both unexpectedly revealing and made her feel as though she knew less than when she started.

She was still trying to formulate a way to get back on track when she was interrupted by a pair of the plainclothes guards from outside bursting in, shutting the door firmly behind them. Neither seemed willing to get in front of the other, a dance that was made all the more amusing when they spoke in near unison.

"We're under attack. We've got to get you to safe—"

The door exploded inward, flying off its mounts, taking a portion of the wall—and both of the guards—with it. The shattered remains of all three hit the wall. One of the leaders, Cecil Chao, was too slow to duck and wound up crumpled in a heap on the floor in a spreading pool of blood and other, more viscous fluids.

Trap, Trevor whispered softly. Stefani was inclined to agree, though it was not the kind of trap she'd envisioned. Stefani had no time to take in more detail than that. The thing that stepped through the door immediately commanded all her attention.

It was basically human in form, had recognizably been a human woman once upon a time. Too short and stocky for an Anaranjadan, true, and sporting no scales or cybernetics Stefani could see. But that was far from the least strange thing, considering a massive worm had burst out of this poor woman's mouth, peeking out from beneath a row of yellowed teeth and leaving the face without a lower jaw.

The size of the worm made Stefani think it should have been emerging from the woman's chest. The face bulged in strange ways, as though the skull beneath had been cracked in multiple places and was being pressed outward along unnatural seams. Worse, the eyelids opened not to eyes but to some sort of twisting mass the same pallid color as the worm.

Whatever kind of worm clacked its huge, sharp mandibles at Stefani—and she could not help but think of Harmony despite the horrific size disparity—the remainder of it was packed tight within that ruin of a head.

The monstrous hybrid charged at her, and she did not take chances, did not wait for Trevor's demure advice. She transformed fully, skin and muscle flowing, bones softening until she became living oil with a tangerine sheen.

Negotiations be damned. Now this was a question of how many of them even got out alive. Particularly when Stefani had noticed two more of the creatures in the hallway, trying to crowd their way in. Such was their eagerness that they began pulling at the walls, warping the metal to widen the gap.

That was all she had time for before the first creature was on her. She stabbed straight at its mandibles, reasoning that if anything would bring it down, it would be this.

Then it spoke in a normal, cheerful human voice.

"That dress is so cute. I love it!"

The words—as though spoken by one friend to another on a perfectly ordinary day—were so shocking they nearly fouled Stefani's approach entirely. She had to change the arm she planned to jab it to death with. The shank of bone hardened, burst from the nebulous region of her wrist, and stabbed between the mandibles, which closed too late. Stefani withdrew the shank before they could make contact, then as they scissored open again, she stabbed three more times, pulling backward on the last to rip a ragged tear in the worm's jellied flesh.

She withdrew as it squealed and thrashed, seemingly in agony. Then it lunged with frightening speed, seizing Stefani with its human arms. For all its display of pain, it hadn't lost a step. Its torn mandibles reared up like a snake, chewing the air in anticipation of eating her, or whatever it planned to do.

Stefani gave herself over to fluidity as much as she was able, flowing out of the crushing grip and resuming a scuttling shape. She nearly backed into the second of the creatures, this time bursting out of a man's frame, which had just wedged itself through the ruined doorway.

Whatever shock had gripped the remaining leaders of the Defectives, it loosed its hold on them at that moment.

"What betrayal is this?" Kestrel yelled, as though Stefani wasn't the one fighting the things. But his voice had risen to a manic buzz. She doubted he was still using anything approaching reason.

Stefani lunged upward, taking advantage of the first creature spreading its arms wide to grab her again. This time she formed as much of herself into a serrated edge as she was able. She pivoted, severing the already damaged worm head from the human body as close to the ruined jaw as she could. It tumbled, hitting the ground with a satisfied squelching.

"What are we thinking for dinner?" That insanely normal human voice again. Almost as if it was speaking in the voice of the person it had been before this gruesome transformation. Even in her altered state, the realization sent nausea rippling through Stefani.

The thing shifted its stance, actually crushing the worm head Stefani had severed with one of its feet. It seemed completely unaffected by the loss of its head.

"Get out!" Stefani said. In her current form, her voice had an echoing, bifurcated quality that lent it some extra authority, like she had a built-in megaphone. "They're coming after me. Get out!"

It took the others an agonizing few seconds to realize Stefani was talking to them. Perhaps once she would have taken a more selfless path. Now she had no real desire to save them at the cost of herself beyond the obvious truth of her statement. The third creature had crowded in, and it was angling for her as well, totally ignoring the fact that it had a clear shot to a room full of people far more helpless than her.

Stefani used the Defectives' moments of confusion to back herself more toward one wall, drawing the three creatures to the room's right side and opening up a narrow wedge of free space the others might use to escape.

If they had the guts.

Or maybe it was cowardice she meant because Kestrel was the first to make use of her altruistic gesture. He darted through and out without a second glance. The other three followed suit, each of them having the grace to throw a pained look her way. That they weren't carrying the prone form of Cecil Chao between them told Stefani he was either dead or they had deemed him worth abandoning.

One point in favor of Harmony, she supposed.

"If you want to thank me, you do as we asked!" Stefani shouted at their retreating forms. Not that any of them *had* thanked her. Yet despite the imminent danger, Dana Vasquez turned to regard Stefani one last time and gave her the barest of nods.

So at least there was that.

Alone now with her three assailants, Stefani saw how different each was from the other, even taking into account her mutilation of the first. The one similarity they all shared was they did not look Anaranjadan in the slightest. The leftmost one's human head was mostly intact, though it had the same squirming masses behind both eyes and mouth, the same misshapen, pulsing skull. But the mandibles of the worm head had only partly emerged from one shoulder. They chewed the mangled flesh between them but couldn't seem to sever it enough to burst through.

The one on the right, meanwhile, had enormous mandibles erupting from its stomach. Stefani could actually see into the empty cavity of it. She wondered how it ate. What it ate.

Me, probably. An ironically appropriate end for her, all things considered.

They crowded in, each equally trying to get to her. They didn't seem to work well together, or to be all that intelligent at all. In fact, each was so intent on its quarry that they kept bumping one another. At first, they seemed unaware of each other's presence at all. Then the middle one, the one Stefani had maimed, seemed to snap. It lashed out with both arms, and whether because of their inhuman strength or because the creatures seemed top-heavy, both its fellows went toppling.

"I'll take the usual, Samir, thanks," the voice said. Another banal statement spoken from a dead person.

Fortunately Stefani didn't need a formal invitation to take advantage of the situation. She called upon all the speed she possessed, darted around and over the downed creature to her right, making sure to keep clear of the stomach-jaws. The middle creature toppled itself trying to reach her, tripping in its eagerness.

Stefani moved as fast as she had ever moved, back down the hotel hallway and toward the exit. Only as she approached the lobby did she transform, putting into use her long-practiced trick of disgorging her flowmatter jumpsuit and allowing it to form back around her body as she did so. She could only pray she'd lost them, but even if she hadn't, being found out by some random passerby as a Coldgardener wouldn't help anything.

She stepped onto the street as if nothing was following her at all, hoping very much that this was the case.

CHAPTER 44

KARL WATCHED, transfixed, from his hiding place in an air exchange tunnel. He'd arrived on this world near this very point, though it had looked quite different then. The powers that be had taken the trouble to cover the open space with a thick layer of stone, transforming a small canyon-turned-greenhouse into a completely enclosed cave. He couldn't imagine how expensive that had been, but it was a smart play if the goal was to get the Bridge working again.

Though, judging by the tiny number of ACM personnel present, far fewer than were called for by the logistical dispositions he'd read, it didn't seem to be all that high of a priority at present.

Karl scanned faces and rank insignia with his binoculars, looking for someone, anyone, who looked in charge. But aside from some non-coms keeping things from getting too slack—in the grand tradition of militaries everywhere, he supposed—there was no sense of greater purpose to the group beyond "stand here and wait for further instructions."

The fact that they hadn't even set up defensive perimeters—the fact that Karl had been able to get this close at all—suggested to him that the order they obeyed wasn't even "defend this point" but rather "go here and wait."

But if the militia was bored, the bustling engineering team hard at work on the Bridge infrastructure was anything but. They crawled over the structure like ants. The sparks of welding and the whine of power tools filled the vaulted space. It was impossible to be sure considering he hadn't been here in a year, but it seemed to Karl if they'd been working that hard all this time, the Bridge would have been operational months ago.

Karl had come here uncertain why it would be a point in whatever intrigue Iazmaena was set to uncover. But whatever it might meet or portend, this sudden acceleration of work was something Iazmaena and Stefani needed to know.

He was getting set to leave when a voice sounded from behind him.

"Who's that skulking around in my vents?" It was an oddly familiar voice, though Karl couldn't place it. "Go deal with whoever that is, you."

Several shapes moved in the darkness beyond where any light reached. Karl himself must have looked like little more than a silhouette. Suddenly a piercing light turned on, pointed directly at his face. He squinted and turned away, dazzled, but got a glimpse of the nearest shape, which was approaching him, and froze, mouth going dry.

It was human in shape—purely biological, with no obvious scales or cybernetics—but looked more as if another creature, a massive, bulbous worm like Harmony blown up to absurd proportions, was wearing the human's body like a suit. The chest cavity had cracked open and splayed out in a vee, and it was from this the worm, almost as big across as the human waist it had coopted, emerged, tendrils wriggling and mandibles chewing the air as if in anticipation.

"Gods below," Karl said, his words a croak.

"Who's that, now? Wait, I don't want him dead. I changed my mind. Come back here, you. Hey! Are you listening?" The voice made a disgusted sound, but Karl could barely pay attention. A high-pitched whine had invaded his hearing. Too much horror in too short a time. The voice was speaking again. "You three, stop the first one and bring Lance Commander Yonnel to me. Alive."

Karl watched, stunned, as three additional creatures, each one a different expression of the same awful characteristics of the first, approached from behind the one menacing him. They moved in together, their sheer bulk covering any possible avenue of escape his assailant might have. In a brief flash of lucidity, Karl considered darting out into the roiling madness of the Bridge chamber, but in his haste to turn, he tripped over his own feet and went sprawling on his back. The impact knocked the wind out of him. His assailant, meanwhile, seemed oblivious to the danger it was in even when the attack on it began.

There were no weapons, no claws, no teeth. Just whirling arms and open-palm slaps that, based on the sounds of impact, hit like falling buildings. The first blow staggered Karl's attacker, but even though it kept its feet, it never turned to confront those attacking it. It locked an iron-gripped hand around each of Karl's ankles as the next three blows drove it to the ground, and the massive strikes continued, each monstrosity swinging first one arm then the other in a deadly, staccato rhythm of brutality.

Gradually, their target was reduced to a quivering mass of broken bones on the ground. Still the hits continued. Karl watched in dumbstruck horror. There could be no question of escape. Of the two paths available, one was completely blocked by the nightmare tableau before him, the other cut off by the grips on his ankles which would not relent no matter how dead the creature was.

The three literally beat the one to a loose sack of shattered flesh and bone, and only then did it finally stop squirming and trying to rise. Not to defend itself, or even escape. But simply to drag Karl closer to his own demise.

Once their quarry was a heap of gore, the three began their approach. Karl cursed himself as he remembered with sudden clarity that he was not human and prepared himself to transform, determined to go out fighting at least. Faced now with no choice at all, he found he was relieved it had been made for him. He counted it a small blessing that he would die as he'd lived: fighting monsters. His earlier horror was forgotten. Now there was only a strange comfort that as weird as the universe around him had become, there were still monsters in the world capable of shocking him to his core.

But they were too fast for him. No sooner was he shifting limbs to claws, threading his way out of the twin death grips, than the lead one surged forward and clubbed him in the head.

Darkness descended.

CHAPTER 45

STEFANI STUMBLED through her own front door, her exhaustion such that she could scarcely hold herself upright. Despite her determination to remain calm and avoid notice, she'd broken with the thought those things might be following her and run most of the way. Only once she'd circled the block three times with no sign did she deem it safe to actually go home.

She wouldn't risk leading those things to Ella. Whatever this was, it wasn't her daughter's fight. Though this worry was undercut somewhat when she entered to find Ella bent over the flat disc of instructions Jürgen Fennec had given Stefani, carefully examining its various digital readouts and comparing them to the parts Stefani had "liberated" from the clinic.

"I thought I taught you more about privacy than that," Stefani said. Despite her exasperation, she was grateful for the distraction of the nightmare she'd just left behind.

"You just left it lying around," Ella said without looking up. "What made you think I wouldn't wonder what it was? At least now I know why you were visiting Cuddles—what's happened?" She'd finally raised her eyes to look at Stefani and had clearly read the trauma in her mother's face.

"Nothing you need to worry about," Stefani said, forcing calm into her voice. She knew she couldn't give Ella a normal childhood, but she could protect her from the worst of what they had to face. She just hoped what she said was true. "Not just now, anyway." Then, because she felt guilty for patronizing her daughter, "Since you seem to have decided to assemble that, what have you managed?"

Ella shrugged as if this conversation was nothing out of the ordinary. "It looks like your standard nutriprinter." She toggled Jürgen's device, and it projected a small hologram of what the final device should look like. The image rotated slowly in the air, and as it did, Ella pointed out various parts with a bored air. "Amino acid synthesizers, protein compilers, muscle-fiber assemblers, the usual. If you didn't know any better, it wouldn't look any different than one half the colony uses today."

Stefani tried to hide how much she was reeling. On the surface, she was talking to a twelve-year-old girl, but if she closed her eyes, it might as well have been the designer of the nutriprinter.

"If I'm being honest," Ella said knowingly, "my homeschooling curriculum is a little below my level. I've been supplementing it on my own initiative. And before you ask, because I didn't want to bother you."

"Why didn't you just tell—never mind," Stefani said, half-asking the question before she'd processed the answer. "We'll discuss your curriculum later." She thought ruefully about how Karl had been impressed when Stefani had recognized the kinds of devices used in the programming of things like this, wondering how he'd feel when she told him Ella could probably be her boss if she still worked as a scientist. "Tell me about this device. What makes it different?"

"Nutriprinters are designed to reproduce the basic building blocks of nutrition. They only get as complex as they have to in order to ensure healthy digestion. So they're designed to produce a wide variety of fairly simple food elements. This one is the exact opposite." She tapped the image, causing it to flicker and decohere before it reformed. "It's custom-designed—hardwired, in fact—to produce only one thing. One very complex thing."

"What is that thing?"

Another shrug. "I haven't figured that out yet. The plans don't say. They tell us how to build the thing, not what it's intended to result in. I can work it out, but based on how you look right now, I doubt I'll have time." She paused. "But whatever this thing does, we're supposed to attach it to a port embedded in Marri's skull." She rotated her eyes to stare at Stefani, waiting for what she certainly thought would be a vivid reaction.

"Port in her—" Stefani cut herself off, pinching the bridge of her nose between eyes squinted shut. She took a deep breath and let it out. Maybe it was because of that obvious audience or the distinct impression Ella thought a knee-jerk rejection of whatever insanity this represented would be an unreasonable response. But despite all the raw emotion of the past few days, the past *year*, she managed to filter her response.

"We need to know what this thing will do before we stick it into Marri's brain."

"Makes sense," Ella said with a small smile. Stefani raised an eyebrow. That sounded very much like pride in the girl's voice.

"One thing I'd like to know, though. Nutriprinters can be reprogrammed to suit an individual's nutritional needs." It was a necessary fact on a colony where virtually every person was a bespoke combination of biology and cybernetics. "If this is a just a specialized nutriprinter, why do we need to build one from scratch? Surely it would be much easier to reprogram a working one? They can print all the biological building blocks. I've seen video of one of the really fancy commercial ones make a steak."

As surreal as this conversation was to Stefani, Ella didn't let any perceived awkwardness stop her.

"Theoretically, yes, any of them could make anything biological. But to make as dramatic a shift to a standard one as this custom one is designed to do, you'd have to get at their root programming, the firmware. Change several settings that are never intended to be changed. They make these things pretty tamper-proof. I don't think you could alter it that much without breaking it."

Stefani didn't want to do what she was about to do. But she realized, in that moment, she never would. And the truth was, whatever else she was, Ella was too capable to leave out of this now.

Iaz and Stefani needed all the help they could get.

"All right, then," Stefani said. "How long will it take you to finish it?"

This time, the smile she got was brilliant. A million watts at least.

⚭

Iaz entered the apartment in a flurry of movement, and Stefani, standing from where she'd been helping Ella assemble food-grade components, immediately knew something had happened. With a fresh memory at her recent attack, it wasn't difficult to guess what. Stefani's hands still shook after all, and the incident had felt a fair bit too convenient to be random. Despite her frantic, darting eyes—or maybe because of them—Iaz immediately keyed in on Stefani's own crashing adrenaline.

"Um, Steffi?" Iaz's voice came out as little more than a croak. "Steffi, did you run into any . . . issues?" Without waiting for an answer, she turned to Ella. "You haven't seen anything strange lurking around, have you?"

"Like what?" Ella's look was its usual blank impenetrability— what Stefani now recognized as the girl's real self.

"If you'd seen one, you wouldn't need to ask," Iaz said. She locked eyes with Stefani then, her gaze more focused, searching. Stefani could see the moment when she understood.

"You too?"

Stefani nodded. "They were—"

"Something else, yeah." Iaz shook herself.

"What are you two talking about?" Ella asked.

Neither woman engaged. "Steffi, think about it. What are the odds the two of us got attacked but nobody else?"

"Shit," Stefani said. "Karl!" She rushed to find the emergency comm unit. "Tell me about what happened." Too late to protect Ella from this now. And at the moment, she didn't really care. She just wanted the sound of someone talking to blunt the surging tide of her anxiety.

"The meeting had barely started," Iaz said. "Four out of six dead as far as I could tell."

"All but Chao got away in my case," Stefani said, tearing apart drawers.

"He was one of the friendlier ones too." By the sounds of things, Iaz had begun dismantling the kitchen to help Stefani's search.

"They were only after me, Iaz," Stefani said.

"Me too," Iaz said. "Where the hell did you hide this thing?"

"Is this what you're looking for?" The voice was Ella's. Stefani looked up to see the girl holding out the emergency communicator.

"Yes!"

"We have to get to Karl," Stefani said.

Taking the unit from Ella, Stefani forced herself not to hesitate. She toggled the unit on.

CHAPTER 46

THE COMM LINK RANG. And rang. And rang. Stefani despaired in time with the beeps. To use these even once was to burn them—they'd no longer be safely untraceable a second time. Iaz had been certain of that. If Karl didn't answer, they wouldn't be able to safely try again.

Stefani didn't know which would be worse, the idea that something had definitely happened to him, or the thought that she would be left in crippling uncertainty over the matter.

The sound of a connection almost made her jump.

"Hello," said a gruff, female voice. "To whom am I speaking?"

"Karl, is that you?" The words just came out. Of course it wasn't Karl. "Where is Karl? Put him on right now!"

"He's not well at all, I'm afraid," the woman said. "You'd better get to the Bridge if you want a chance to save him. Better hurry." The words themselves sounded urgent, but they were delivered in almost a monotone.

"To whom am I speaking?" Stefani demanded.

"Helena Cardiff. Hurry up. He's not well." That was it. Stefani had known the voice sounded familiar, but the timbre and tone were all off. As though one of the two most powerful people on the planet was talking in her sleep.

"If you touch a hair on his—" But the call terminated.

Stefani turned to Iaz, seeing her own grim expression reflected on the other person's face.

"It's clearly some sort of trap," Iaz said.

"I know," Stefani said, her certainty mirroring Iaz's.

"But I have to go anyway."

"What? I—"

"Please, Steffi. You still have one daughter. What do I have that can compare? Besides, in case you hadn't noticed, everything is fucked. All our plans are up in smoke. Might as well try to salvage what we can. Maybe now I can figure out what the fuck is going on at the very least."

Stefani didn't even have the heart to complain about the language. "Thank you," she said.

"Don't," Iaz replied, waving away the comment as if it pained her. "As I recall, I had quite a lot to do with getting us into this mess."

"You aren't alone there," Stefani said. She wished this didn't feel like saying goodbye. "A part of me wishes I'd never finished that damned Bridge."

"The planet was dying whether or not we were leaving it." As though Stefani needed the reminder. "We'd have just died with it."

At least we'd have been together, Stefani thought. Perhaps heartlessly, that thought didn't involve Iaz, but Karl and Marri. She wondered if the other woman could read the sentiment in her face.

But if she could, Iaz retained enough political intelligence to brush past it. "I'd better be going. I have a feeling the longer I wait, the worse Karl's chances will be. And you need to help Ella. If I have to save the lance commander, you have to put your family back together." She didn't say it, but Stefani could read it in her face: Iaz thought she had the easier job.

"All right then," Stefani said. Unprompted, she reached out and pulled Iaz in for a hug. The woman stiffened—she'd never been much for physical affection—but she ultimately returned the embrace. "Good luck."

"Wish it to them," Iaz said with a wink. "They're the ones who will need it."

CHAPTER 47

THEY CAME in ones and twos at first. Giana couldn't see them, of course, not from her sensory deprivation tank. But through the irregular pulses of pain, she could *feel* them, even at great distance.

She felt them as they rose up against their internment camp guards, moving as one to crush them in a unity so profound and absolute the Anaranjadan militia would have wept with envy if they could have experienced it themselves.

Of course, some *did* experience it. Marrietta had not lied about the speed of her creations, both their manufacture and their growth. And once the order went out, the twin to the first, it was inevitable that some of the guards would have been activated by it, the way a lethal allergy was triggered not on the immune system's first exposure, but the second. In this case, the only thing dying was their free will.

It was this that turned the tide. Giana could only see through the eyes of the refugees—and then, only with great effort—but she could feel the way hunger and neglect had sapped them of their strength. But when Marrietta commanded, they listened, and with the help of a fraction of the militia turning on their own, it was enough at each of the four camps.

With exponential speed, the web grew, and as it did, so did the tide of nodes in that web heading in their direction. Coming to obey. Giana felt its newly formed strands extending with each passing breath, connecting to new nodes—new *people*—and dragging them into Marrietta's control. They were coming to pay homage to their new master. Coming to obey.

All while Giana absorbed the brunt of it.

All their thoughts assaulted her, throttling her little by little, death by a thousand cuts, but Marrietta's thoughts were stark and clear, loud as a cannonade in her mind.

They thought they'd created harmony. But this, this is harmony.

And, in a perverse sense, she was right. A large and ever-expanding portion of the planet's population under the control of a single mind.

And it's all thanks to you, Giana. I was so angry when I discovered you'd lived. But you make this all possible. Without you as a buffer, even with the refugees as the first layer, there is no way I could have controlled them all directly. The Anaranjadans would still have listened to me, all but worshiped me, but I'd have to give them orders, and then they'd have to interpret those orders, and it would just be so much messier. Honestly, sometimes I can see the appeal of an orderly system.

The last thought had an almost giddy thrill to it, as though she were invoking blasphemies.

I know it hurts, dear. And it will keep on hurting. But if it makes you feel any better, the pain won't kill you. You are much too valuable to kill. That's why I'm giving you the best possible protection.

"Jürgen." Marrietta's voice was barely audible from outside the little tank. "Pick that up—smoothly as you can, now—and let's go. Our first order of business is to capture the Bridge, and I want to keep her close by." She went on, sounding almost as if she was talking with herself. "Once we have it, we can go anywhere."

Giana felt a flutter of emotion from Marrietta then, rich and complex enough to become coherent thoughts. *Last time we fled disaster. Scattered. Disorganized. This time, I will have an army at my back, and access to any human colony I want.* Marrietta's most deeply embedded source had assured her the Bridge was far closer to being complete than she had assumed. Giana could feel the other woman's certainty, her eagerness, over their link.

Giana shuddered at the realization. More worlds. Marrietta intended to subject yet more worlds to this insane nightmare. As the tank was hoisted into the air by Jürgen's inhuman strength, it was hard to tell whether shifting fields or mounting despair nauseated Giana more.

CHAPTER 48

"I THINK," Ella said, tongue stuck out in concentration in a way that reminded Stefani of herself, "that should do it." Her dexterous hands finished tightening the last of the tiny screws. She set the device down and regarded it, tilting her head this way and that as though each angle allowed her to see more of the tiny machine's secrets. "One specially designed nutriprinter." She looked up at her mother as though seeking agreement.

"You did really well, sweetheart," Stefani said. And it was true. Her heart burst with pride for her daughter's ability. She just wished she felt anything but apprehension about what they—mostly, Ella—had built. They were trusting a mysterious benefactor they knew nothing about that Marri was recoverable and that this was the path to that end.

It mainly served to remind Stefani just how desperate she must be. A part of her kept hoping someone, anyone, would take her aside and tell her this was insanity. But that wasn't going to happen.

It was this or accepting that Marri was gone. And she would not do that.

"Now we have to find her." Six words to describe a process Stefani had no idea even how to begin.

"I can do that, I think," Ella said.

It took Stefani a moment. "I'm sorry, what?"

"I can find Marrietta."

"Are you telling me you could have found Marri the whole time?"

"Marri? No, because there's no Marri to find. But Marrietta is Giana, and a part of Giana is me."

"And you didn't know about her before," Stefani said, recalling their earlier conversation. "But you do now. You have to know a thing is possible before you can do it." She eyed her daughter with suspicion. "You could have told me this earlier, you know."

"There was no plan earlier," Ella said. "And to be honest, I didn't think I could trust you not to go running off despite that."

"That's not your decision to make."

"Except that it clearly is, since I did." There was no heat in her daughter's voice. No emotion at all, nothing Stefani could ascribe to teenage hormones, which would have at least been understandable. Ella had possessed information Stefani and Iaz didn't, and she had elected to hold that information back to ensure Stefani behaved the way Ella wanted.

"I suppose it would be pointless to tell you never to do that again."

"Yes, it would."

Stefani almost laughed. "All right then. Where is she?"

Ella closed her eyes, and to Stefani's surprise, the girl's head immediately lolled to one side as though she'd passed out standing up. It was beyond disconcerting, as though only the top third of her had fallen unconscious. She remained that way for long seconds, then a minute, then two, occasionally twitching, but otherwise remaining perfectly still, her head, neck, and shoulders relaxed as Stefani's anxiety rose. But just as Stefani went to go and shake her awake, Ella started, eyes snapping open with a gasp as though she'd been trapped underwater and had just found an air pocket.

"She's headed to the Bridge," Ella said, and Stefani liked the fear in the girl's voice even less than she had the cold calculation. "And she's not alone."

CHAPTER 49

IAZMAENA DELGASSI WAS, despite credible allegations to the contrary over the years, not an idiot. She had no intention of marching into the Bridge facility alone and demanding Karl's release from Helena Cardiff and whomever else was there. For starters, the head of the ACM was unlikely to be traveling anywhere unprotected, and one nice thing about heading up the military was that you got military-grade protection.

That was all right. Iaz was not without friends, provided she didn't care about keeping this particular group of them hidden anymore. Not all the full revenants had been captured or killed a year ago. Iaz had managed to make contact with a small cluster of them over the course of the first month they'd been here, the cagier ones who had managed to avoid sticky fates and eat as few people as possible to stay alive and avoid notice.

She knew where they stayed—or at least the various places they stayed because they tended to move around a lot. It was something she was careful never to write down. Not even Stefani knew. Stefani was still Stefani, and that was the problem. Whatever her issues with Trevor, she had gone far too native for Iaz to trust her with any sort of authority over the few revenants she could still muster.

She found the bar easily enough. It wasn't precisely on her way, but it was also the easiest of her contact points to activate without arousing general suspicion. Once a watering hole favored by the workers who managed the Topaz Canyon solar arrays. And it still was, technically speaking. It was just that those workers had all technically been eaten and replaced some time ago. From the standpoint of the colony, nothing had changed. The revenants had assumed the workers' identities—albeit in a fashion more crude than she had assumed the identity of one Iazmaena Delgassi—and resumed the jobs of the former workers.

Solar array work was among the most grueling the colony had to offer, but also the most crucial. That seemed to be a curse of humanity in general, in Iaz's estimation. Topaz Canyon array was off the beaten path even more so than most of the other arrays. It attracted Anaranjadans with no other attachments in their lives beyond the general communal spirit offered up by Harmony. If the Equatorians had still been around, likely this wouldn't have been possible. But because the remaining colonial leadership was stretched way too thin, and because the Topaz Canyon array had at no point suffered a drop in output, no one had bothered checking up on it.

Which made it the perfect place for Iaz to hide a sizeable portion of her remaining revenant muscle.

Second shift had just come off duty by the time Iaz arrived. A weird, stiff joviality erupted in the place as she entered, which had very obviously not been the case a few moments ago. Revenants didn't generally talk if they didn't have to—they had other means of communication. Iaz missed that sometimes.

The false commotion died down as soon as the bar's occupants, patrons and staff both, realized who had darkened their door.

"Hi, everyone," Iaz said, injecting her own note of false cheer to cut the sudden tension in the room. Her infrequent visits were always scheduled so they wouldn't be surprises, and this one had not been on the schedule. She could read surprise even on the weird, dull faces of the imperfect human copies staring her way. "I know, I know. I'm early. But I need some help of the kind only you can provide."

Revenants were, despite what the Coldgardener natives had convinced themselves, not all identical creatures. They had as diverse a set of personalities as the humans they had sprung from once you accounted for the harsh conditions of their day-to-day lives. In the faces before her she saw everything from fear to eagerness to annoyance. But none of them were going to balk. That was good. Iaz would have few enough as it was and likely fewer still by the time they were done.

"Come on," she said to the dozen-odd faces. "You can change when we get there."

Iaz had never been to the Bridge site on this world. But even just standing in front of the door leading into the space it occupied, she recognized it. There was a feeling to it, a hum of energy that was unlike anything else she'd ever experienced. As though the Bridge itself possessed a power that did not quite belong in this universe.

It made the hairs on the back of her neck stand up because the last time she had felt that sensation had been back on Coldgarden, and it had been because the Bridge was powered on.

Iaz very much hoped this Bridge was not powered on. It was not an anxiety she could attach anything specific to. If the rest of the colony's leadership wanted to flee to parts unknown, let them. Iaz would help fill the vacuum. But instead of hope, she felt a dread settling over her, a weighted blanket that suffocated instead of comforted.

She fought back against it, gritting her teeth. She'd been considering how to approach this delicately, but that now felt like giving into fear.

"Open it!" The order was a bark, intended to straighten her spine as much as anything.

Her revenants had dropped the act and assumed the full insectile-nightmare proportions. At least that she could feel good about. Among the many misconceptions the revenants had possessed in their quest to regain their humanity had been how few of them would want to once they'd had a true taste of what they'd have to give up. Iaz understood that pang all too well.

She stepped aside, allowing two of them to move forward and approach the doors. They were not subtle, jamming the tips of their claws at the seam. It was an airlock-style door, far too strong to simply lever open. It had to be physically torn down. Fortunately the revenants were more than capable of this. They'd had generations to perfect getting into places where they weren't wanted, and keeping air in was not the same thing as keeping a revenant out.

The two were joined by two more as they attacked the metal, stabbing and twisting, creating weak points where none existed. With tortured squeals of metal, the revenants wrenched the twisted doors from the frame and tossed them aside.

Iaz got her first glimpse inside, and what she saw did not comfort her in the slightest. The Bridge was not only powered on, it was partway to activating, the first of the concentric rings already hovering above the ground, seemingly held aloft by the purple arcs of lightning dancing between it and the widest ring, still laying flat. The other rings would follow suit, each ring further inward lifting higher than its predecessor, until the entire collection formed the outer edge of a dome in space.

And within that dome, whatever world the Bridge was opening to would be accessible.

"Fuck," she whispered. Whatever plan she'd had in mind of saving Karl had been rendered obsolete. Now she had to take control of his entire facility if only to understand what was going on. Destroying the Bridge was another option, but an unappealing one when she herself might make use of it. She recalled berating Stefani for the same idea just the previous day, but standing here, seeing the Bridge actually functioning, imagining all its possibilities, had her reconsidering. She really should have brought more revenants.

Fast on the heels of that thought, the shooting started. For a second, another disorienting wave of remembrance assaulted Iaz. She half-expected to hear the sounds of lancer fire, but that was another place, another time.

Still, it hardly mattered the specific choice of weapon when they worked. There was a blinding flash of light, and one of her revenants squealed, retreating backward, two of its forelimbs' outermost joints vanished. The rest of the revenants retreated to either side, thinning themselves to better fit behind the limited cover. The injured revenant immediately transformed, resuming its human form, whole and complete, though grimacing in pain, as he took advantage of his smaller size to retreat to cover.

This was their crude attempt to avoid hypermutation. A kind of bodily admission that this was their true form dramatically lessened the chances of its occurrence. Reforming as a uninjured human helped further. In Iaz's opinion, it was a little too much of a "mind over matter" solution to the genetic nightmare that had plagued Coldgarden for generations, but she couldn't argue with results— even if she didn't understand them.

The formerly injured revenant was out of the fight, though. He would have to hold the human shape for some time to minimize the chance of his body's healing going into overdrive. In effect, it was like tricking your body into believing you'd just imagined the injury. By the time he could safely re-transform, the fight was likely to be over.

There were a few more flashes, each lighting the doorway up like it was a massive LED. Then screams started up from inside the Bridge chamber. There were more flashes, but these seemed directed toward somewhere other than the door. Iaz's revenants shifted, as though sensing the focus was no longer on them and eager to capitalize on it. Iaz raised a warding arm and continued to listen.

The screams increased, and between them, Iaz could hear the meaty sounds of flesh striking flesh, sounds that grew increasingly wet the more they repeated. The wetter the sounds, the fewer the screams and the more those screams that remained sounded like gurgles. Large, irregular shapes surged past the door, moving too fast for Iaz to get a good look at. She'd only encountered them once before, but it had been both recent and memorable. The ACM forces here had been attacked by the same sort of worm-monster creatures that had broken up her meeting with the Defectives, hers and Stefani's.

And it was clear the ACM had lost the fight.

Then a voice called a harsh halt to the proceedings. Iaz recognized it as the voice of Helena Cardiff.

"Is that you, *Madame Archon?*"

Iaz's mouth dropped open in shock. How did an Anaranjadan woman even know that title to mock her with? From her limited view, taking cover behind the revenant closest to her, she could just make out as another of the Bridge rings reached its desired height and seemed to invisibly lock in place.

"I should have known you'd bring your big, buggy friends to help. I think you're a bit overmatched though. Are you sure you want them to play? I feel like there can't be many of them left at this point. I have to say I'm surprised you came instead of Stefani though. I mean, Karl surely wasn't your favorite by the end."

It was eerie. Iaz had never met Helena Cardiff before this moment, but the woman talked like she and Iaz were old acquaintances. *She has Karl. Maybe she's getting this information from him.* The gnarled old root of a soldier wouldn't have betrayed his own easily. Of that she was sure. Iaz really hoped she didn't have to tell Stefani that Karl had been tortured to death. Her stomach dropped even further when she imagined the source was not Karl, but Sam.

"How about you give Karl back to me and let me worry about him?" Iaz called back. She would not mention Sam until she was sure he was a factor. No sense giving them more information. "No one I care about is dead yet, and the rest of my friends haven't arrived. We can just forget this whole thing happened."

"Oh, I don't think so. For one thing, you don't have any other friends coming. More importantly, you and I have a score to settle. A personal score." By the sound of her, she was no further out of the line of fire than Iaz was.

"It must be a pretty one-sided score, since I don't know what the hell you're talking about."

"Perhaps it would help," said a sickeningly familiar voice, an *impossible* voice, "if I stopped speaking through my intermediary."

As another ring locked into place beyond, two figures stepped fully into view. The taller of the two was Karl, and he looked to have had better days. He was keeping on his feet but walking as though someone had shoved something somewhere uncomfortable. Or maybe it was just the quality of his company.

Iaz stared agape at the short, dowdy woman. At the smug face she remembered and the extra, inhuman parts jutting out of her at various points that she very much did *not* remember. Iaz could still feel the ridged scar left over, a gift of sorts from this woman.

"Kyne Libretta," Iaz said, somehow finding the words to speak through her shock. The woman who had killed the original Iazmaena Delgassi, the Iaz who had believed herself human. That had come only after she had tricked that Iaz into murdering most of the elected government of Coldgarden, driving her over the edge of sanity in the process. Knowing that she was not actually that woman did not help blunt Iaz's sudden surge of rage in the slightest. "Where the fuck did you come from?"

As if to punctuate her question, the final ring locked into place. The lightning arcing between them first doubled, then tripled, then increased at an exponential rate until there was more lightning than empty space, until the lightning was a solid wall of light, one gradually resolving into an image of somewhere else.

"Earth," said Iaz's murderer cheerfully. "And I'm about to bring a whole bunch more of my big, worm-person friends over."

CHAPTER 50

KARL WAS FAIRLY certain he was concussed. His head rang, and he felt nauseous and dizzy. Not that it would have mattered. The pain in his back dwarfed all the other discomforts. He didn't have much choice but to stand upright, because Kyne Libretta had a needle-thin, steel-strong blade made of her own body lodged between two of his vertebrae, ready to stab deeper if he so much as twitched. He didn't know what would happen if she severed his spine while he was in his human form, but he was quite eager not to find out.

It struck him as a perverse mark of how far he'd come that fear of hypermutation was, at worst, a distant worry, an echo of an ancient, ingrained habit he'd learned as a child. It wasn't impossible that it could happen here and now, even with so pinpoint an injury as this. He partially transformed enough to make his back into thick native hide. It was not enough to defeat the needle, but it was hopefully enough to overcome the lingering risk of his own body turning against him. They still didn't fully understand how it all worked. But it really did seem that acknowledging the truth of himself acted as some kind of shield against the affliction.

And really, alongside the head injury, the shock he was still processing eclipsed even that ancient fear. And even his surprise was nothing to what he read on Iazmaena's face. She was gamely trying to hide it, but he didn't think she even realized she'd stepped out into full view from her hiding place.

"You've done some work on yourself, I see," Iazmaena said. That was an understatement. Karl had gotten a much closer look than he might have liked. It was unquestionably Kyne Libretta, yes, but she was so much more too. The skin of her arms was the so-green-it's-black color of Coldgardener native hide, and what at first appeared to be an uncharacteristically stylish belt revealed itself to be two native limbs, bone scythes wrapped around to hug the woman's middle. They unfurled, waggling lewdly at Iazmaena.

But the worst was the heads. There were two of them, each attached to a glowing stalk of mutaprime flesh emerging from Kyne's back like plums on the fingers of a child.

They were heads he recognized, one from personal experience. That one, the one that had once belonged to Helena Cardiff, stared at Karl in a kind of slack, dull-eyed recognition.

"Do you like it?" Kyne asked Iaz bitingly. "I have to say, I'd done a good job making every power broker on this miserable rock trust me but having such *direct* access to both these two certainly made this easier."

"I can even talk like them!" This statement came from Cardiff's head in Cardiff's own voice, and while she was still staring at Karl. Disconcerting didn't begin to cover it.

"I guess I'm head of the planet, now," Kyne said, her voice a slash of sarcasm.

"Or, I'm both heads!" Caroline du Vernay's head said in its thick accent. "Pleased to meet you," the head said. "I'm Caroline du Vernay, and I really, really like to pronounce my name in the silliest way possible."

"I have to say, Iaz," Kyne said, with her own head and as pleased with herself as Karl had ever heard her, "every bit of this effort has been worth it just for the look on your face right now. I'm your insider source, by the way," she said, with a nod in Iaz's direction. "In case you are too stupid to have put that together. I figured the trick worked so well on the first Iazmaena, why not try it again?" She jerked a thumb at Caroline's impaled head. "I was her source too, but it was the same deal. And Helena's. Hell, I even sent some information *Marrietta's* way. Your man Sam? Yeah, I'm the one who put her onto turning him to her side. I guess that's two of your lovers I killed."

A muscle in Iazmaena's cheek twitched. Karl half-expected her to surge toward them, dooming both herself and him. That Kyne wouldn't hesitate to kill Karl he was certain of, regardless of whether she was in actual danger. And that Kyne had the upper hand, he was equally certain of. He, after all, had a much better view than Iazmaena of the hulking worm-person forms scattered through the chamber, each of them busily cracking open Anaranjadan skulls and feasting on the parasites within. Maybe he wasn't concussed after all. It was certainly enough to cause nausea all by itself.

"Touched a nerve, did I? Did a bit more than that last time we talked though. I'm sure you remember. That corpse you ate certainly died with that memory very fresh on her mind. Bet you wish you couldn't remember quite so well, don't you?"

She was playing with her food, savoring her moment of triumph, of beating them again. And just like last time, she'd beaten them so badly they hadn't even realized she was playing the game.

Behind them, the Bridge continued to dance with light. And across that impossible gulf were more of the creatures. A whole planet's worth. Kyne had explained it all to Karl. Gloated, really. Gloating was when she was at her most talkative after all.

"We've been tiptoeing across our own span for a while now," she called to Iaz, overly casual. "Ones and twos, here and there. Not something you can do with one of the colonial Bridges, of course, not without being noticed. But when you have access to the *Master* Bridge so many more options are available. It's been such a *pain* keeping these brutes hidden, let me tell you. Probably unavoidable when you are trying to tailor them for maximum brutality. But after one of my side experiments displayed some unintended side effects got itself killed going on a little extracurricular hunt for some ACM grunt's worm, I was forced to accelerate. Still, despite how much easier it's been to move around now that I've gotten access to all of *Caroline's* sneaky little tunnels, it's much better to finally be out of hiding."

"If you're just calling for them now, we still have time," Iaz said, sounding as though she was trying to convince herself. "There's a—"

"Delay? That delay between leaving one area and arriving at the next? Sorry to tell you, but that comes from just having one end open and having to do all the work itself. And if you have both sides open at once, well, then it's truly instantaneous!"

Iaz looked sick. Karl tried to catch her eye. Tried to tell her, with his own pained, plaintive gaze, to run. Not to get help, not to try to stop Kyne. To run and get Stefani, get Ella, and not stop. Run for the orbitals, buy a ride or commandeer one, and leave this place forever.

It was a laughably slim hope, but then, when had their odds been anything else? They'd only ever survived by running. Why should that stop now?

The shifting pain in his back was the first warning he had that something had changed. Karl grimaced, at first certain that Kyne was wiggling her needle on purpose to cause him agony. Then he felt it in the soles of his feet. A subtle vibration, but one that was growing more pronounced. It was rhythmic too.

Like the approach of feet. Many, many feet. He tried to catch Iazmaena's eye yet again, only to see she and her revenants turning to assess the churning mass of new arrivals.

"Come on, you," Kyne growled suddenly, each syllable punctuated by a stab of agony along his spine. She sounded shocked, angry. Whatever this arriving horde represented, it was nothing she had wanted or expected. She hauled Karl away and, with their inhuman escort, they made their way toward the control tower, which would place the bulk of the Bridge hardware between them and the entryway.

"Until my friends arrive," she said, more to herself than anyone,

Karl thought, "we're going to follow the better part of valor, bitter as that thought is."

It gave Karl a moment's hope, that sense that not all was proceeding as per her plans. But it was a short-lived burst. Because hulking shapes were already taking form in that blinding brilliance, each silhouette unique, yet each unmistakably one of the creatures mindlessly doing Kyne's bidding.

Very shortly, the Bridge site was going to be a war zone.

Monsters everywhere, he thought with rueful sadness, *and me without my lance.*

CHAPTER 51

THROUGH THE EYES of their army, flashing gaze to gaze, each glimpse lasting but a moment, Giana watched the approach to the ruined doors. Anaranjadan eyes and Coldgardener eyes both, in all flavors of the latter, marching as one in a way that had never before been accomplished.

Giana watched Iazmaena and the revenants turn with obvious alarm and flatten themselves to the tunnel walls. Marrietta thought of them, these revenants she did not control, as her enemies, and so some of the army moved as if to attack them, but Giana had learned that she could guide matters a little around the margins. Actions too small for Marrietta to notice, filtered direct contact as she was. Every time a clump of Anaranjadans or Coldgardener natives or revenants or mutaprimes tried to break away and attack Iazmaena's revenants, Giana steered them back on course for the Bridge chamber beyond. It was a little like making them forget what they'd seen just moments before, and it was disturbingly easy.

She'd never imagined minds could be so easily manipulated.

Inside was Marrietta's true goal, and they were arriving in the nick of time because the Bridge was activating. Full-on open, as near as Giana could tell. Seeing it like this, she experienced another flood of memory from her missing time at the end of Coldgarden's existence. She recalled standing in front of a set of rings like this one, hovering their way into becoming a dome just as these were, and staring into a bright orange glow.

The glow of Anaranjado. The glow of this ring site before it had been closed off in stone.

Marrietta's army did not make it far into the chamber before Giana caught sight of Karl Yonnel and a small woman—or something that looked vaguely like a woman and vaguely like something impossible—moving off together as though they were connected by the hip. They were heading in the direction of the Bridge control tower.

Then Giana's view was obscured as the army was set upon by things of nightmare. She felt Marrietta's shock, first at the woman with Karl—Giana could feel that very specifically—then at the sight of the creatures, human-sized with horrifically mutated Harmony worms sprouting from random places. It was then Giana understood that her newfound patron had not foreseen everything. Not by a long shot.

The new creatures were vastly outnumbered by the combined tide of Marrietta's army, but they fought like twenty times their number, lashing out with arms and legs and biting mandibles, shattering limbs, smashing rib cages, severing heads. Hypermutation blossomed everywhere amidst the Coldgardener refugees, turning the injured and dead into screeching monstrosities.

Marrietta had control of her forces, yes, but that control was not limitless, and the sudden cocktail of agony and terror rippled through the masses like an earthquake, with equally destructive results. The column shattered like glass, and the effect felt like Giana's mind was coming apart. Above her in the link, Marrietta certainly felt the effects as well. Giana could tell right up until the link fell apart.

Suddenly, she was alone, shifting around in her grav-field, surrounded in darkness, muffled sounds of milling chaos from outside her only source of information. The pain echoed in her, but like an echo, it was fading quickly.

It did not take long for the panic to take its place.

"Let me out." It felt like years since she'd heard her own voice. "Let me out!" She beat hands and knees against the top of the pod. Then she lurched as she was set down. Blinding light came flooding in as the pod cracked open, and Jürgen's mechanical face stared down at her.

Giana stood quickly, shaking with the remembered pain of the mental link.

"What does she want me to do?" She asked the question to appear as though she was still onboard. In reality she just wanted to get out from under his immediate observation so she could try to escape. To what end, she had no idea. She just knew she didn't want to ever do that again, and the only way to make sure that never happened was to slip Marrietta's control of her.

"The device is active," Jürgen said. Chaos surged around them, but as one of the horrid creatures broke through, Jürgen grabbed it, picked it bodily into the air, and threw it, where it bounced off one of the hovering rings, spasming with electrical discharge and landing with what looked like a broken spine. Suddenly there was a small open space around them as every creature on both sides had no desire to test the machine man.

"Yes, I see that," Giana said, gesturing at the Bridge.

"No," Jürgen said, and something about his voice seemed off to her now. It was as though his personality had changed. It made the hairs on the back of her neck stand up. "The device that will free Marri Palmieri. I have established a link with it. I am preparing her data upload, and the ones who will install the device are on their way. But they will need your help. Go now. Hide, and watch for them. When they arrive, you will help them confront the Marrietta entity. Now go, before this one wakes up."

"I—what? What are you talking about? This one?"

"The one speaking to you now, the one you must obey for this world to have any hope, is not Jürgen Fennec. But I cannot hold Jürgen Fennec this strongly for long. Now go."

"What—"

"Go!" Jürgen's—or whoever spoke to Giana—bark legitimately terrified her, coming from a man of such size and strength. She darted into the maelstrom, following calmer points, trying to string together enough patches of relative safety to move through without being killed.

STEFANI HAD NEVER BEEN to the Bridge site, but it was not difficult to find. A huge amount of the colony's population all seemed to be heading in that direction. It was eerily reminiscent of the last night in Coldgarden, only then the populace had been in a kind of trance. These people looked fully within their right minds, only with an almost maniacal focus.

As such, all Stefani had to do was follow along and act like one of the crowd. She tried not to think about exactly what was going on and what she was heading into.

She didn't want to speak to anyone, in fact, and that was fine because no one wanted to speak with her. They seemed not to see her at all most of the time. The few times she met eyes with one of their number, they'd look confused and frightened before the intensity and focus would settle over them again. And whatever drove them did not discriminate. More than a few children numbered among the marching horde.

She saw a lot of nosebleeds too.

But nothing could prepare her for seeing the shock of Coldgardeners—of all three types—marching along with the Anaranjadans, the same fixed expressions on their faces—where such faces existed. There were natives and revenants, too, both in their natural forms. She even caught the occasional white glow of a mutaprime momentarily losing its human disguise. Yet even this, what surely must count as a waking nightmare, elicited only brief and occasional flashes of outright terror on the faces of the locals, there and gone.

Needless to say, Stefani kept her distance from everyone when walking between tram stations but was forced into packed cars full of them otherwise. When they encountered people who obviously weren't under the same spell, they stared like they were watching a horror story come to life. Most ran inside the instant they realized how wrong everything was. Stefani always felt the urge to go to them, to seek comradery in like-minded beings, but instead, she pretended to be one of the flock because they were going where she needed to go.

She'd had no one to leave in charge of Ella and bringing her along was out of the question. Thus, she'd been left with no choice but to leave her alone with strict instructions not to follow and what to do if Stefani didn't come back. It had been very difficult giving those instructions, but Stefani had managed it.

When she wasn't obsessing over what was going on around her, she spent half the trip railing against herself, wondering if this was really the right choice—she was risking leaving her child motherless on what had to be considered a fool's errand—and the other half reminding herself that Ella was no normal child and might very well be more capable of surviving on this world than Stefani herself.

In the end, she knew she couldn't knowingly sacrifice one child just to provide a slim increase in the odds of the other's safety. She had to do this. The only acceptable choice was to make sure it worked.

The crowds thickened the closer she got. People must be converging here from all parts of the colony. It was Marrietta's doing. It had to be. The only thing that made sense was that she planned to capture the Bridge, but even with that as the goal, to summon so many was surely overkill. The ACM was not a small organization, but it was nothing compared to the full population of the colony.

Which left only that she intended to open the Bridge and take the people through it. Another mass exodus. If the being Giana had become, Marrietta, desired to escape to still more worlds, saving Marri was no longer just a case of saving her daughter. It was necessary to prevent this plague from spreading any further.

At last Stefani reached a physical impasse. The number of routes to the Bridge site had shrunk to one, and as that stone tunnel narrowed further, it grew more and more crowded, enough that she could not move forward. People jostled her as she tried, forcing her back in their intensity to reach their destination. Occasionally fists lashed out, or worse: claws. Flashes of mutaprime white were almost constant.

Worst, Stefani heard screams of the sort she hadn't heard in a long time. She couldn't understand how she knew these sounds in particular, how she could pick them out from any other scream, but they told her hypermutation was taking place ahead. Random body parts would be sprouting, bones and organs growing with impossible speed as the Coldgardeners' injured bodies killed themselves in their attempt to heal.

Nor was this limited to only people in front of her. People behind fought to get ahead of her as well, including a particularly sharp elbow to the small of her back as though from a child. This thought alarmed Stefani, but it was too crowded even to spin around and confront the person. She couldn't move from her spot at all.

Not as a human, in any event.

Careful to absorb her jumpsuit lest she lose its precious cargo, Stefani transformed into a being of flowing, golden-sheened oil, a revenant minus the chitinous armor. Thus changed, she was able to slide herself through the gaps between people, doing her best to avoid those mutaprime flashes of white as she worked her way gradually but steadily up to the front of the space.

She had just flowed past the archway into the chamber, awash in violet brilliance, when a hand closed around the part of her that was her arm. Against her will, Stefani returned to solidity in the instant, whirling to face what surely was an attack before she understood. A revenant could do that to another revenant. She put it together just as she heard Iaz's sharp voice.

"Steffi!" Iaz's grip on Stefani's shoulder was obsidian hard. She stood at the edge of a cluster of full revenants, each dwarfing Stefani in ways that made her uncharacteristically envious. Iaz hauled Stefani bodily away from the main column of people, into the rapidly diminishing empty space to one side.

Credit to the woman for picking her dark, flowing form out of the crowd.

"Let me go, Iaz. I've got to find her," Stefani said. "I've got the device that can save her."

"Steffi, you don't understand what's in here. It's—"

But whatever she said was lost in a sudden roar, and Iaz's grip broke as Stefani was borne away on a backward crush of bodies as screams and cries of pain ripped the air. The spell seemed to break all at once, and what came after it was absolute pandemonium.

Stefani squeezed herself down as small as she could get, desperate to find some tiny space of calm and avoid being crushed. That was when she noticed it. Compacting herself as far as she could, she ought to have easily been able to feel the hard knot of the custom nutriprinter squirreled away inside her flowmatter jumpsuit. But she didn't. Twist and turn and squeeze though she might, she could only feel the soft, flexible, changeable fabric.

It was gone. The nutriprinter was gone, and with it, her only chance of saving Marri.

CHAPTER 53

GIANA COULDN'T TELL how she knew, but she felt it the instant someone began to observe her. It shouldn't have penetrated her awareness, not with all the chaos around her. Not with more of those creatures pouring across the Bridge each moment. She had found a hiding place behind some crates pushed almost, but not entirely, up against one of the chamber walls in an area where it bulged outward well away from the bullseye of the Bridge. Smothered in the stark shadows cast by the Bridge's coruscating light, no one should be able to see her at all.

And yet, she knew she had been noted. Marrietta. It had to be Marrietta. The woman was trying to reestablish control of the horde, had come looking for her antenna, and of course she'd know exactly where to find Giana. They were two parts of the same whole, after all.

A voice suddenly spoke, a woman's voice over a loudspeaker.

"Very impressive, I have to admit! You've come a long way from the gutter rat I remember." Giana didn't know this voice, but she would bet it belonged to the horrific woman-creature whose face had so shocked Marrietta. She must have retreated back to the control tower under the cover of chaos her monsters bought her. Which meant she was at least a little bit concerned. "You've brought more toys to our little playdate, I'll grant you. And it's a neat parlor trick, controlling them like that. But my toys are better. And they have a bigger doorway into here too."

Giana prepared herself to fight. Marrietta would be desperate to regain control, to turn the tide back in her favor before the strange woman could bring so many monstrosities across the Bridge that she was unstoppable. She wanted to peek out and see how the fight was going, get a sense of what she would be up against if she ran. But a foolish part of her said to see was to risk being seen, for all that the presence approaching her hadn't already zeroed in on her precisely.

As it was, she received yet another shock when that presence rounded the corner of the outermost crate and it was not Marrietta, but Ella.

"Hello," the girl said simply. She held up a small device in her hand. "I brought this. I need your help."

It took Giana a few moments to grasp the situation. When Jürgen had said they were coming . . . "I assumed it would be Stefani," she said lamely. "And I assumed *you* would be Marrietta."

"Stefani's here," Ella said. "But I didn't trust her to do this properly. Too emotionally invested. So I followed her and picked her pocket in the crowd."

"That sounds more like something Marri would do."

Ella's shrug was a thing of nonchalant perfection. "I wouldn't know. But if this works, maybe I can find out. As for what Marrietta's doing now, she has bigger problems than you running around loose and a limited window of time to solve them. She's trying to cut the head off the snake."

"Aren't you worried about keeping Stefani safe?"

"She wants Marri and I to be okay more than she wants anything," Ella said. "Even to live. The best way to make sure she gets what she wants is for you to help me."

"What do you need me to do?"

They approached the tower, keeping low, darting between crates and whatever other cover they could find, Giana on Ella's heels. The girl had a preternatural ability to avoid trouble, and Giana sensed that if she hadn't been slowing Ella down, Stefani's daughter might have passed without notice entirely.

As it was, they were spotted several times, but in each instance, Ella was able to maneuver them such that the worm-monster caught wind of more enticing prey and moved off. They did not seem intelligent at all, just ferociously strong, relentless, and impervious to pain. Which were more than enough advantages to have, really.

Ella held up her fist then, a signal to stop. Giana followed her gaze. She had spotted Marrietta near the base of the stairs leading up to the tower. Ella gestured, and she and Giana took cover behind one of the tower support columns. The girl had been right. Far from Giana's certainty that Marrietta would attempt to reestablish control of her horde of people, she was instead trying to decapitate the opposition force by killing the woman at the loudspeaker.

Marrietta was surrounded by what must be her most loyal followers, a small knot of people who must really be mutaprimes plus several Cultists and Jürgen, who stood a head taller than even the tallest of the Cult. As they watched, she shouted at her coterie. "Get up to that tower and stop this, now!" She sounded more out of sorts than Giana had ever heard her.

"We need to wait until they've gone up, but not too long, or she might notice our presences so close," Giana said. Marrietta was distracted now but might be less so once her orders were underway.

"Yep," Ella said.

Jürgen obeyed without hesitation, and as the one with the longest stride, was first up the steps. The others followed at varying rates, with the Cultists showing some reluctance but ultimately obeying.

The reluctant Cultists watched Marrietta's eyes as they tracked the movement of her entourage up the stairs. Ella opened her mouth to speak, probably the go-ahead, when three huge figures lurched into the space among the tower supports.

One was one of the new creatures, clearly an all-biological human at some point but with a giant worm, mandibles chewing air, erupting from the junction of neck and shoulder on its left side. Fighting it were two full revenants, which, even though each was much larger, seemed to be barely a match for the creature despite their combined efforts. Still, their superior mass drove it backward, though it kept its feet, and the trio left the area of the tower before any of them noticed Giana or Ella.

It would have been a stroke of luck if it hadn't drawn Marrietta's attention, and by the time Giana spun back, she saw the other woman's eyes narrow in recognition of the two shapes lurking in the darkness.

"Now!" Ella made good on her shout by leaping forward like a lightning strike. The girl was suddenly all overly jointed limbs lashing like the tails of scorpions and sickly, glowing light. Giana, meanwhile, moved at merely human speed, so by the time she arrived, Ella and the much larger Marrietta had collided, their respective lights seeming not so much to add to one another as to multiply.

Think back. That night with Arjun. The last night I was me. Think back to what it felt like. In the restaurant. In the tub. In his apartment. Just as it had when she had pried free her scale, her own light flared. Only this time it did so across her whole body. Her scales fell away in a sloughing wave. And she crashed into the struggling pair, creating another trio of combatants.

But the stakes were so much higher here.

Instantly, the three of them had fallen into one another. Their thoughts, their emotions, swirling together, distinct from one another yet available to all, provided you could parse them out of the maelstrom. Their fight transcended the physical then, existing there still, but also beyond, a great dark space, like a sphere of emptiness surrounded by rapidly swirling, night-dark thunderheads. There was something in those clouds, something that possessed will, that knew them. It was vaster than the clouds yet obscured by them, watching them and yet not, asleep yet absorbed by the trio's struggle. Every sensation Giana felt regarding this presence was like a contradiction in her mind. If she had been able to direct her full attention to the contradictions, it would have driven her mad. As it was, it took all her focus just to stay alive. The three of them were lightning in those clouds, striking back and forth across the emptiness.

"Force her to revert." They were not words so much as flashes of intention, and they came from Ella, carried her voice. "Help me! Concentrate on what's around you." Giana thought she meant the insane storm at first, felt a frustrated grunt from the girl, and abruptly they were back to struggling on the ground beside the tower stairs, three beings of intermittent light and flesh, three strains of the same disease, related but fighting for superiority.

Relieved to be out of that other space, Giana allowed the physicality of the world around her to permeate her awareness. The stink of blood on the air, the gritty feeling of the cavern floor upon her cheek. Remarkably, as she did this, she felt herself resuming her human form, as though such sensations formed an anchor to which she could tether herself. Even more remarkably, Marrietta, locked in hers and Ella's grips, did the same. Her face betrayed her momentary shock. Then it hardened back into resolve.

"I'm the original," she said. "You two are just poor copies. Neither of you can hold me like this."

"Don't have to," Ella said. She was fighting to hold back Marrietta's hand from wrapping a strangling grip around her throat, but she gave up this fight, croaking as Marrietta grabbed her and squeezed, pulling her close to bring more leverage to bear. But the girl was wily. As her own attacker closed the distance between them, her hand darted viper-quick into her jumpsuit and removed the object she had shown Giana, the nutriprinter. Then she jammed it against the back of Marrietta's skull and the port housed there and twisted it home with a click.

CHAPTER 54

SOMETHING WAS WRONG. Something had changed. Marri woke not to an impending lesson or another long talk with Feathertouch, but to the dissolution of her city. It was pulling itself apart with unseen hands, reassembling into something else.

Buildings broke into fragments, but instead of crumbling to dust and rubble, walls separated from ceilings, windows from housings. The pieces moved with stately serenity, hovering in the air, arranging themselves into new and distinct patterns. The water of the river spiraled upward, threading between and around the pieces as though binding them together like braiding. Even people linked hands in a human lattice, one that was lifted gently off the ground.

All the world around her tore itself apart and remade itself into a tunnel leading upward into the too-bright sky.

Feathertouch was suddenly there, still holding the form of Bry, standing beside her. Looking up at her. She kept marveling at how short he had become. A strange expression rested on his face.

"What's happening?" she asked.

"It's time," he said.

"Time?"

"For you to go."

"Go where?"

"Back into yourself. The device is installed. The uplink is established. I do not know if this will succeed, but it is time to find out."

Marri felt a fluttering in her chest. So long. She had been here so long. Almost as long as all the rest of her life put together. More, if you counted only the parts of her life she was old enough to remember.

The thought of leaving this place was simultaneously exhilarating and terrifying.

"Let me see you," she said. It was as much a stalling tactic as anything. "The real you."

It happened all at once. Bry vanished, replaced with a blinding light surrounded by swirling black shapes, jagged feathers at the end of glittering filaments, whirling in a constant maelstrom.

She was both surprised and not by what she saw. But she definitely remembered it for what felt like the first time in years.

The thing in the tunnels. It came for me, then the Cultists found me.

"I apologize," it said. "I hoped to use you to stop the Cult. I had no idea what the Giana Entity could do to you. Today, I will attempt to reverse it. Today, I atone for my sins against you, as best as I am able. The device is already working to print the organism. This final upload of your current consciousness back into the memory storage device lodged in your brain will ensure that your memories of this place—and all you have learned here—will carry forward into the you that reclaims your body. Your people might call it a 'Day One Patch.'"

And in large part thanks to the education Marri had received in this place, she understood that to be a joke and a decently funny one.

She smiled, and it felt like the first time in a long time.

"Why did you do this for me?" It started to answer, and she cut it off. "I know what you said, but you didn't have to help me. Your plan didn't work. You could have swept me away and started over. You're powerful. I couldn't have stopped you. Why didn't you?"

"Your question saddens me and heartens me."

"Why?"

"It saddens me because I could not teach the cynicism out of you. It heartens me because it means I did not destroy the parts of you that make you who you are."

"But what do you want from me? You must want something."

"I have told you. My purpose has ever been to make the lives of those I watch over better. I have never needed another. This has been far harder with the humans, and your peoples' arrival made it more difficult still. But it has always been the only reason I exist. If you feel you owe me payment for doing what I was made for, then I ask that, as I tried my best to save you, you try your best to save this world."

Marri reeled a bit. "Save it? From Giana?"

"That one will, I think, no longer be a threat. But there are others. Some you will see when you surface. And some are as fixed and immense as the sun in the sky." These words felt freighted with meaning.

It wants me to—what?—fix the planet's climate? The orbit? She must be reading too much into matters. But suddenly those lessons on volcanic engines and orbital mechanics rang especially loud in her head. *Thank it. I need to thank it.* It was difficult to overcome the suspicion that there was something more, some idea all those lessons had implanted that would explode like a time bomb a week, a month, a year down the road.

She opened her mouth to speak, but darkness was already descending.

"Goodbye, Marri. I will be watching over you, though you won't see me. That is my nature, and I have defied my nature for far too long."

CHAPTER 55

"I TELL YOU WHAT, Karl. This is not where I expected either of us to end up back in the good old days. Remember the Underlab? What a time that was."

Karl was grateful enough that Kyne had removed the spike from his spine that he knew better than to offer up any genuine feelings of his. She had hauled both herself and him back to the tower, a safer place than out in the open with half the colony seemingly hell-bent on charging in.

"Why not just let me go?" he ventured. "For old time's sake."

"My most valuable hostage?" She scoffed. "Perish the thought. The only thing better would be the brat—Palmieri's youngest. Though from my intel, she might be a bit of a handful these days." Her laughter was as nasty as the rest of her personality.

Two of the creatures she'd brought with her flanked the doorway leading out to the stairs. Based on what Karl had seen—and felt—of their capabilities, a mere pair of them guarding a choke point in which they had the high ground would be a very daunting prospect for anyone attempting to reach this place.

Still, he knew several people likely to try if they realized he was up here. Better for everyone if he wasn't. For now, that meant he had to keep her talking.

"Why even come here though? You've been to Earth! Why visit this backwater disaster of a colony?" He didn't have to fake a distaste for the place. A year here had not softened his stance that he would rather be just about anywhere else.

"It's a fair question," she said, gazing out the window into the Bridge portal, disgorging more of her creatures every minute. "There are plenty of other, better places I could go, certainly. And I will go to those places. But I don't like leaving scores unsettled, you know? Plus, I had to try out my toys in a real-world experiment. They're dumb as a load of bricks, but fortunately they also hit like one. All in all, I've been very pleased." She turned to him as though to get his opinion.

"Well I certainly never want to see one again." The same went for her and especially her two extra heads, though he was careful to keep any disgust out of his voice. He was afraid to ask her how she'd become what she'd become. Afraid of what she'd do if her famously prickly nature got nettled.

His act must have worked because she beamed in what seemed genuine pleasure.

Footsteps sounded on the stairs outside. Loud ones.

"Visitors," Kyne said with relish. A large shape appeared just outside the door, and Kyne's hulking bodyguards turned to face a man even taller than they were.

Jürgen Fennec.

"You will surrender and come with me at once." Credit to the man's spine. He did not sound afraid.

"Jürgen, naughty boy!" This was Caroline du Vernay's head, spoken in her famously thick accent. "How dare you interrupt our conversation? I thought you knew me better than that."

The sound of her voice staggered the man, and Karl didn't think it was just the entire stolen-head-on-the-end-of-a-trunk-of-flesh thing.

"What have you . . .? How—"

"You will bow before our new master as I have, Jürgen," Caroline's head said. "She bested both leaders of this world. It is hers by rights now. So say I, and so says Helena."

"So say I," Helena Cardiff's head intoned.

"I'm getting bored," Kyne said. "Dispose of that trash."

Her creatures moved surprisingly fast, and Jürgen had still not recovered from whatever had spooked him. The creatures picked him up bodily and, as he belatedly started to struggle, hurled him from the catwalk at the top of the stairs to crash below.

"Kill anyone who was with him," Kyne said, turning away as the pair of monsters set about their bloody work. Inhuman screams, biological and electronic both, followed.

CHAPTER 56

PUNCTUATED by a loud crash of something heavy falling from a great height, Marrietta battered Ella away with one backhand before she went clawing for the back of her head. Giana couldn't let her do that, so she attacked with renewed ferocity, forcing Marrietta to defend herself.

Marrietta flashed white again before snapping back into human form, her eyes bugging out in shock. Again she flashed, and again she snapped back. Suddenly, her eyes were filled with real fear. With a desperate cry, she went on the attack herself, shoving both hands worth of fingers into Giana's mouth as though trying to rip Giana's jaw from her skull. Every instinct screamed at Giana to fight this invasion, this violation.

This creature had given up trying to fight. Now she was trying to take Giana over from the inside out. The world flickered around them, blinking between the real and the swirling storm of before. Giana was under assault in both places, each seeming more ferocious than the other in the moments she dwelt in them.

With Ella's help, Giana had managed to offer up a decent fight against Marrietta. Alone, Giana was no match. She thrashed in both worlds, fought for her very life, but it didn't take long. She felt the moment where the flow of new *self* dried up, where the spigot was turned off. The pressure was there, all-encompassing, since the bag of her mind was overfull of what had gushed forth from the spigot moments before. But nothing new was flowing in.

Marrietta's will, that which animated her consciousness, had fled her body and was now measuring for drapes in Giana's.

In that moment, Giana gave into all those instincts and struck back. It did not feel like self-defense so much as a counterattack. Attack was all her kind knew at their roots. Attack, invade, depose, replace. So that was what she fought to do. Every place Marrietta took root in her, she assailed in kind.

There was a strange push and pull to the fight. Giana, a weakened strain of mutaprime, was not as strong as her attacker, but Marrietta was on Giana's home turf, as it were. Giana had no experience in this sort of fight, but her very naivete lent her counters an unpredictability that worked to her advantage. And, perversely, the frenzied desperation of knowing she had already lost made a difference.

But she *had* lost. She could delay but not win. For every two steps forward she made, Marrietta countered with three.

She opened her eyes in the real world, looking desperately for help.

And, amazingly, Ella was there, looking down at her.

"Ella," Giana said through clenched teeth. "Help me. Please."

But Ella shook her head, eyes impassive.

"This was the way to be rid of her," the girl said. Her voice was so matter of fact. So cold. "She needed a new host. It was why I needed your help. Because if it wasn't you, it would be me. And Mom would be a lot more upset if it was me. I'm sorry."

But it sounded like a platitude. She didn't *sound* sorry.

Ella broke eye contact then, looking around. Giana saw her gaze fixate on something. Then Ella put two fingers into her mouth and blew a piercing whistle, as though to draw someone's attention.

Or something's. Whatever she intended, Ella moved quickly after whistling, grabbing Marrietta's limp body and dragging it away, leaving Giana alone with her internal assailant.

As if in counterpoint, Marrietta's will dragged Giana back into the storm world then, the better to press her invasion. Reeling from what she'd just heard and seen, Giana could feel Marrietta's rage and sense of betrayal bathing their entire battlefield.

I made you. I am you. How dare you?

Abandoned, alone, Giana felt something within herself stiffen. Maybe for the first time ever.

Perhaps Marrietta's claims were true. But Giana got a say in such matters as well. She had never wanted any of this. She'd been given no say in her original transformation. That's what she'd told herself, at any rate. Herself and others. Stefani and Iazmaena, Karl and Ella, they'd all accepted that explanation. But maybe, just maybe, if she'd fought harder back in Coldgarden, she could have prevented all this death and suffering and chaos.

Or maybe not. Regardless, Giana fought as hard as she ever had, harder than she thought possible, constantly assailing Marrietta, trying to impose her will, her form, onto the other woman even though it was Giana's body they fought in.

She should have lost the fight faster. But Marrietta had badly overextended herself over the past year, robbed herself of much of her strength the better to spread tendrils of influence far and wide throughout the colony. Under other circumstances, it surely had seemed a fair trade, and clearly it had worked out absurdly well for the woman thus far.

But none of those other beings over whom she held sway were here now to come to her defense. It was only the two of them, here at the end.

Giana mentally gritted her teeth and was rewarded with feeling her actual teeth grit as well. This woman, this *creature* had stolen her life, perverted it, created her as a tool to be used. Now she was attempting to transform an entire colony of people in the same way. Giana looked back at her time at Gene Sequencing, realizing now, to her undying shame, that she had already been a part of something like this once before. It was strange how she could only see it when confronted with it in an utterly different context, but once seen, it could not be unseen.

And if she could prevent something like that from happening again, even indirectly, well, there were worse things to die for.

She could feel Marrietta's rage at the irony of two people she'd so profoundly influenced turning on her, feel the fear they shared as thudding footsteps approached them, drawing her awareness back into the real world as the Harmony monster Ella's whistle had lured over approached. The girl, along with Marri's body, was nowhere to be seen.

I saved her life, and now she kills me.

The creature leaned over to regard this strange, frantically thrashing prey. It seemed to scent the air, perhaps looking for something. Every part of Giana screamed that she should lie still, play dead to escape the thing's regard, but Marrietta's frenzied assaults would not let her. As such, she thrashed wildly, and, like a predator seeing distress as invitation, it closed in.

The storm world washed over them again. Marrietta was muttering, chanting some prayer. Some catechism. Calling upon her dark god, Giana realized, to intercede on her behalf. It was, perhaps, the most human thing she had ever done. And Giana understood. A part of her still hoped to be saved, still hoped for a timely arrival something, anything, that could make sense of this chaos.

Call it *deus ex infinitate.*

And then, that all-encompassing presence no longer loomed in the distance but was there in the storm with them. The space around them darkened. Roiling clouds of a something that was also nothing. She could feel a bitter cold descend. Not the cold of Shadyside's surface or depths, but the cold of what she imagined cryosleep to be. No, more: it was the cold of space itself.

In the real world, the Harmony monster was reaching down with questing hands, savoring the moment preceding its delight in destruction. Meanwhile, in the darkness of the storm, the presence filled them both, as though unable to decide which to address. Marrietta rejoiced as Giana despaired. Their thoughts merged, fighting to become one even as each vied to be the only one. Here it was, arrived at last. Here it was, arrived too late. Marrietta's master. Her patron. Her god. The one for whom she had done all this, gone so far beyond what had been asked of her.

It was here to save her, and yet how could something even as vast as it save her now?

But the emotions rolling off the presence didn't feel right. The vagueness of before sharpened as its actual, full regard fell upon them, however briefly. Everything about it felt alien, unknowable. Giana thought it would drive her mad until something like an invisible lens slid into place, and she could feel recognizable emotions. But the god's emotions were not gratitude, not sorrow, not righteous anger. They were . . . fond amusement? Perhaps touched with irritation.

There were no words to be heard, and yet the vastness of the presence took on the shape of words in their imagination, words like the sounds of random auditory nerve firings that nevertheless self-assembled into meaning. They were strangely precise words for such a vast, impossible intellect. If a god were ever to have a voice, Giana had never envisioned one that sounded so particular in its personality.

My, my, haven't we overachieved? There was a sense of gratitude then—one Giana despised, one Marrietta gloried in, fickle though it was—but it was a mere undertone beneath that wry, head-shaking humor. *All I asked and so much more. I wanted you to know that, to know that I appreciate what you achieved and what you attempted. But perhaps it is better if it stopped here. Rest well, children. I am, on balance, more pleased than otherwise. But I believe your work here is done.*

Giana pushed it away. *Yes, go! Leave us be.*

Marrietta wailed in despair. *Wait!*

Only the former got her wish. The unseen lens slid away. The presence went back to madness-inducing strangeness, and Giana felt its regard leave them for the final time. Marrietta tried to call out, and Giana rejoiced as the godlike presence left them. Each felt absolutely empty as it departed.

In the real world, the Harmony monster reared back and delivered a skull-crushing blow to the head they shared. A second strike. A third. Mutaprime as they were, resilient as they were, even their shared body could only take so much. The pain was exquisite until the moment it—along with everything else—was gone.

The blows continued well past the point when life could not.

CHAPTER 57

"WAKE UP."

Marri inhaled the stink of blood as she obeyed the unfamiliar voice and opened her eyes.

Immediately, she noticed the difference. She had forgotten what it felt like to open real eyes in the real world until this moment. The thinness of the simulation she'd existed in was only obvious to her now that she was no longer inside it.

My body. I'm back in my body. As if to prove it, her head was absolutely splitting. But if Feathertouch had been right, and there was now a bespoke Harmony parasite in there, that probably stood to reason.

Her first sight upon returning to the real world was that of a face staring down at her. A girl about her age. Rather, a girl about the age she'd been and what she still tended to think of herself as. The face was that of a stranger until Marri looked more closely. It was the eyes. The eyes and the knowledge—imparted to her by Feathertouch—of how she herself had grown faster than natural aging could account for.

"Ella?" she asked. Her voice came out as a croak.

"Hello, sister," Ella said. She squinted in consideration, studying

Marri's face, seeming to take in every detail with the methodical way her eyes roved across. "We're not *exactly* the same, you and I. But you're definitely no native. Not just one, anyway. Lucky for you, or you might be dead by now."

"I'm fairly certain what happened to me counts as dying," Marri said with a nervous laugh. The laugh hurt. Everything hurt. That was another thing she'd forgotten. There hadn't been physical pain in Feathertouch's simulation world. It was an unwelcome reminder of what reality was like.

"We need to move." Without asking permission, Ella grabbed Marri's arm and pulled until the elder sister was in a seated position. She was surprisingly strong for her size. Or perhaps Marri was simply weak by comparison.

Once partially upright, Marri followed Ella's pointed finger and abruptly understood. A little ways distant, a body with a face still barely recognizable as Giana's lay in ruins.

It's over. Marri was free of the woman—the creature—at last.

But not of the culprit. The horror unlike any Marri had seen, which was saying something, was standing and scenting the air, as if seeking the Palmieri sisters for its next bit of fun.

Ella pulled, trying to get Marri upright, but it was like she'd been returned to another body, one utterly unfamiliar to her now that she inhabited it for real. She tried to rise only to fall again, and only by leaning hard on Ella was she able to regain her feet.

Which was about the time the monster stumped over to them.

Ella pushed. Marri staggered into the start of a hobbled run, but she knew they were going to be too slow to get away. Feathertouch's victory would be a brief one.

Then Jürgen Fennec was between them and the monster.

The mechanical man looked far more mechanical than when Marri had last seen him. He was larger than the monster and limping as he approached it, one of his legs sparking with damage, but he showed no fear.

Jürgen wasted no time and didn't bother trying to size his opponent up. He just neutralized his injury as a weakness by falling on the monster, bearing it to ground, wrapping one metal hand around the worm and bracing the other one against the monster's shoulder. Marri heard mechanical joints whine, and the monster shuddered as it came apart in Jürgen's hand. Part of the worm had been left inside, and the torn end oozed viscous goo.

Jürgen stood with some difficulty, discarding the worm like trash. He turned to face them.

"Do you remember me?" Marri asked, still leaning on Ella.

"Yes," he said. "You are the girl, Marri. Not a girl any longer. And not *her* any longer. For the first time in a year, my mind is my own. Her voice, in my head always. It's gone now. And the second voice. The machine's voice."

The machine. He was talking about Feathertouch.

"It was working through you?" she said.

"Yes," he said, apparently not needing context to understand who she meant. "Quiet, insidious. A worm tunneling slowly, patiently. Aside from its lower volume, I did not enjoy it any more than I enjoyed *her* voice. But if this is the result, I am glad that it was the one to succeed. You have freed me. I owe you that freedom. What can I do to help you?"

"You're ready to just keep on serving?"

"If I've learned nothing else in this past year, it's that I can't trust my own mind. But I always liked you. Perhaps trust can begin with liking. And this madness must stop." He gestured around them.

Marri spun with Ella's help. She had only seen a Bridge in operation once, but it was impossible to misinterpret seeing one again. The portal was open to some place that, judging by the colors she could see beyond, seemed a fair bit more like Coldgarden than it did this world. But where it opened to didn't matter.

What did matter was that every few seconds another of those creatures came through. A slow enough trickle, but how long had it been going on? How many of them were here now? The creatures were heading straight for the vast chamber's low exit, now, but there were signs of extensive fighting. A great deal of bodies, many of which twisted and squirmed in the throes of what was clearly hyper-mutation. Some of the creatures tore at the heads of corpses, popping them like ripe fruit, trying to get at something inside.

"They're coming from the Bridge," she said. "We need to shut the Bridge down."

"At once," Jürgen said. He did not wait, did not ask her any clarifying questions. He simply limped off toward the nearest equipment that glowed with power and looked important.

"Marri! Ella!"

Marri spun and nearly fell at that voice. Suddenly Stefani was at her side, Iazmaena right behind her. Without wasting a moment, Stefani grabbed up her daughters, one in each arm, sobbing softly.

Ella squirmed beside Marri, desperate to get free. That was Marri's first instinct as well, but quite aside from the fact that she didn't think she'd be able to stay upright if she did, something inside her broke, and she was hugging Stefani back, matching the woman's tears with her own.

She opened her mouth to form the word, a word she had never managed to utter to this woman before. And, wonder of wonders, it was there.

"Mom," she said. It was all she could manage, but Stefani shook with renewed sobs. Ella worked herself free but stayed close, moving to where Marri could see her. Her eyes never left Stefani. They were wary, those eyes.

Before Marri could respond further, a loudspeaker crackled.

"Well, now." It was a voice that Marri knew instantly, one that sent chills through her. It belonged to a woman who had almost killed her once. "What a touching family reunion," Kyne Libretta said. "But it feels like there is someone missing." The door at the top of the tower opened, and Kyne stepped out, the overly stiff figure of Karl next to her. She had a gun to his side, but more to the point, what looked like the leg of a Coldgarden native was wrapped around his shoulder, the bladed edge held firm against his neck.

One of the worm-creatures was standing on the catwalk, worrying at the metal corpse of a Cultist. The other was partway down the stairs, doing the same on a landing. Both stood straight as Kyne appeared. Marri had no idea how she was controlling the things, but it was clear they obeyed her.

"Don't do anything she says," Karl shouted down. "Just leave me and—" He cut off suddenly as Kyne did something unseen.

"Now, now, let's not shoot our mouth off," Kyne said. By the light of the Bridge portal, she looked somewhere in the nebulous space between insanely gleeful and just insane. "I've roughed him up a little, true. But we'd hate to really test if the old man here has accepted himself enough to defeat hypermutation the way I have."

"Let him go." Marri was more surprised than anyone that she'd been the first to speak. Stefani looked torn between Karl and her daughters. Iazmaena looked ready to dash up the stairs and test herself against Kyne Libretta and her monstrosities both.

The entire situation hung poised on the edge of a blade until the light from the portal began to flicker. Its glow so dominated the room that the change drew every eye, Kyne's included.

Jürgen had torn the side panel from a piece of equipment—*power regulator*, Marri's Feathertouch education whispered to her—and was yanking wiring out by the fistful, seemingly with no idea what that would do beyond the obvious effect of the decohering portal. It stabilized momentarily as Jürgen paused, realizing he'd been spotted, and Marri could have sworn the blurry image beyond had changed in between flickers. Still the same world, it looked like, but perhaps a different part of it. But among her many lessons she had learned the paradoxical robustness of the Bridge technology. Once it was active and stable, it resisted being closed again, almost with a will of its own.

"No, no, no, that oaf will overload it!" Kyne Libretta shouted.

Then she gave a grunt of pain, and Karl was moving.

CHAPTER 58

KARL CHOSE HIS MOMENT WELL. Kyne Libretta had always been a hard woman to surprise, so when the instant came where she slackened both her grip and her aim, intent on Fennec as she was, he did not hesitate. She was the perfect height for his knee to hit her solar plexus, and she was still human enough in this form for the blow to have the intended effect.

She doubled over with an outrushing of breath, and Karl was away. As he moved, he transformed. This would ironically slow him thanks to the implant in his human hip his transformation had to configure itself around, but it made him much more capable of doing things like upending the nearest of Kyne's Harmony monsters over the catwalk railing and out into empty space beyond.

Which was precisely what he did. The sound of it hitting the ground below, a sickening combination of thudding, crunching, and splatting, left him in no doubt that it was dead.

One down.

As he hitch-scuttled down the stairwell, he rolled a pair of his six eyes back to find Kyne. She had already recovered from his sneak attack, but instead of chasing after him, she made for the railing herself, the part closest to Jürgen and his attempts to sabotage the

Bridge. The last view Karl had of the woman was of Kyne Libretta, her native legs uncurled from around her, scuttling down the tower's exterior supports like a spider.

Karl attacked the second of the creatures in the same way as the first. It seemed slow to respond, its attention all on its master and her distress. It was, therefore, no more difficult to send crashing down than its partner had been, but it did not fall nearly far enough to kill it. It thrashed there, legs broken, as Karl hobbled the rest of the way down.

Thankfully, those at the bottom did not dally. Iazmaena and Ella broke away from the group and approached it, wary but not hesitating. Karl watched with his front-most eyes as each partially transformed into their respective true forms and set about dismembering the injured creature.

Then he was at the bottom, resuming his human shape, flowmatter jumpsuit springing back up around him. Stefani and Marri were watching the carnage, Stefani standing behind Marri, helping to hold her up with one hand.

Karl felt his blood freeze. Stefani's other hand was shifting, transforming into a gold-accented blade. As he watched, Stefani cocked her hand back, aiming the point of the blade at the back of Marri's neck.

No, it couldn't be Stefani. It had to be Trevor.

CHAPTER 59

IN STEFANI'S moment of greatest vulnerability, her face still wet with tears of relief, Trevor's dormant personality struck.

Instantly Stefani lost control of her body, walled off in a spherical prison without door or seam in her mind. The switch was so smooth, so effortless, that she was left reeling with terrible realization even as she battered futile fists of impotent will against the imprisoning walls.

All those months when he had only come when called, when she needed help doing her dirty work. Sometimes not even then. All those months when, in the rare instances he resisted being banished, he had yielded easily enough in the face of Stefani's will.

All those months she'd become more and more like him.

He'd been playing her. Learning her mind, her defenses, her weaknesses. Probing for untested avenues of attack. And she'd been laying the track to help him. And now, when faced with the person he blamed for getting him killed back on Coldgarden, he could at last exact his revenge.

And there was nothing, absolutely nothing, Stefani could do to stop him.

CHAPTER 60

IN THE INSTANT after Karl grabbed Stefani by the upper arms in a grip tight enough to hurt, he feared he'd misread the situation, gone too far. But she snarled, tried to twist in his grip and then, transforming partially, nearly broke it entirely. There could be no mistake. This was definitely a Trevor situation.

As he pulled Stefani clear, Marri staggered with the loss of support. Iazmaena and Ella were there on the instant, pulling her further away from danger. That was good because Trevor reacted with strength Karl hadn't known Stefani possessed. Only Karl's desperate fear for Marri allowed him to hold on for the bare instants he needed to reel Stefani into a bear hug. He locked his hands around the opposite forearms, calling on all the strength his human form could muster. His bone-worm form was far more powerful, but also not built well to restrain someone versus simply eviscerating them.

"Hi there, lover boy," Trevor said. Hearing those words in Stefani's voice sent a tremor of weakness through Karl that threatened to end the matter right there. "Maybe this time, I get to stick something in you, eh? Fair's fair."

A lance of pain surged through Karl's chest. Trevor had reformed Stefani's rib into a stabbing shank and lanced it out her back and straight through Karl. Breathing was suddenly a struggle. He grunted in pain.

"Like that, do you?" Trevor said. "Well then, how about some more?" Three more lances impaled him.

"Run!" he shouted. He didn't like how liquid it sounded. "Iaz, get them to safety, now!" Whatever happened to him, whatever happened to Stefani, she would never forgive him—and he would never forgive himself—if he didn't do everything in his power to see her children safe.

Iazmaena held his gaze, and he implored her wordlessly. He didn't think he could talk. She nodded and gathered up Marri and Ella, herding them further away. Marri protested heavily, but she looked very weak herself.

"You think they can hide from me? I'll stand over all your corpses, and oh, the pleasure her body will feel knowing it." Trevor laughed as he transformed fully into a revenant form. This made holding on almost impossible, but at least it pulled the ribs from Karl's perforated chest.

No choice. Karl transformed as well. He thought himself unlikely to survive any other way. Karl the man vanished. Karl the bone-worm took his place. *I'm sorry, Stefani.* He was. If he survived and she didn't, he would never forgive himself for that, either.

But he knew she wouldn't want to live this way.

He opened his cavernous mouth wide, gathering up her fluid form with pure suction before she could flow away, and slammed them both to the ground. He heard a clatter of metal as the special knife she carried skidded away and was thankful for that small mercy. He had enough to contend with just fighting Stefani's body. This was not like fighting a full revenant—she had diminished herself from that to assume a perfect human identity. But Karl was himself diminished, hobbled as he was by his hip implant when in this form. This seemed the best way to nullify his own disadvantage.

Karl thrashed and rolled, Trevor fighting to get free of Karl's mouth, trying to stab through the toughened native flesh with momentary lances of bone, Karl squeezing down harder on his struggling form. He knew from talking with Stefani, letting her air her anxieties about the persona's existence, that the man was expert at killing natives. Karl didn't expect to survive long, therefore, even like this.

The flickering light of the portal was like a coded message for him. He caught brief glimpses which told him that Kyne had rallied enough of her creatures to drive Jürgen away from his sabotage, but the rate of flickering seemed to be increasing without him. It looked an awful lot to Karl like the portal had crossed a point of no return in its path toward shutting down. Its flickering light whispered to him, a message meant just for him.

A way to make sure Trevor could never harm anyone he cared about but Karl and Stefani herself. Even if the price would be almost unbearably high.

Karl waited until the next roll brought him right side up, got his legs under him, and charged straight for the pale blue light at the heart of the dome, Trevor still trying in vain to slice his way free.

CHAPTER 61

"MOVE, MOVE, MOVE. NOW, NOW, NOW." Iaz chivied them along.

"We can't just let them go," Marri said. She had just watched the closest thing she had to parents vanish through the failing Bridge portal, one being half-eaten by the other. But the weakness in her limbs told her how foolish such a statement was. She expected Ella to back her up on this at least—not that Iazmaena had ever been one to listen to anything she didn't want to—but Ella offered up no argument in favor of going after Stefani and Karl. Marri remembered the way Ella had been staring at her own mother.

"Maybe it's better we don't," Ella said warily.

"What was that?" Marri said, cutting to the heart of the matter rather than wasting time on incredulity. "What happened?" It should have been upsetting, having Stefani apparently try to attack her like that, but Marri felt mainly concern for the woman, not a sense of betrayal.

"Stefani has her demons," Iaz said. Then added, with considerable force behind the words, "None of which are her fault." Her tone promised more explanation later when there was time. "They'll find a way back, but we'll die if we stay here."

And Marri relented, too tired to argue.

They made for the door, aware that Kyne Libretta was still behind them, attempting to keep the Bridge open. But Marri suspected, succeed or fail, Kyne would remember them soon enough.

The sounds of mechanized footsteps told Marri that Jürgen was approaching. He had not precisely fixed his limp, but judging by what looked like newly re-bent portions of the affected leg, he had come up with a temporary workaround.

"With respect, we need to get out of here," he said to Marri.

"I'm calling the shots here, metal man," Iazmaena said.

"Whatever you wish to tell yourself," Jürgen responded with disinterest. They had the sound of words that would prove themselves soon enough, and Marri remembered Feathertouch's description of Marrietta's plan with a chill.

Once introduced into the population at large via their bioprinters, it will hijack their existing parasites and make them subjugate themselves to the Giana Entity.

The Giana Entity, it had called Marrietta. But none of the colony's inhabitants would have seen her that way. They would see only the entity controlling Marri Palmieri's body.

Which, now, was Marri herself.

Kyne's forces, those that had not already escaped through the tunnel into the wider colony beyond, were wrapping up their desecration of the dead. Some seemed fascinated by the fact that hypermutating dead didn't stop transforming no matter what was done to them, not until that awful process had exhausted all remaining energy. Others of the monsters had already straightened, staring around stupidly as if for something else to eat.

Jürgen seemed to read her mind. "Quick as you can," he said. At least the tunnel looked clear, so far as Marri could see.

In short order, they had left the Bridge complex behind. Iazmaena and Jürgen did not allow them to let up, however, and Marri resolved to suffer in silence lest they all be killed to give her a rest.

Eventually, though, they had to stop, if only to catch a tram. It seemed insane to Marri to be waiting on an automated tram. They passed several of the creatures on their way to the nearest station, Harmony monsters that must have lagged behind their fellows. One and all, these seemed to have fallen into a stupor. Maybe it was proximity to Kyne that mattered. But at least the tram ride allowed Marri's body the rest she desperately needed.

Her heart sank as the car pulled up. It was packed with Anaranjadans, most of whom looked terrified even through the windows. Worse, as though the dinner bell had rung, the nearby Harmony monsters woke from their stupor and began to stump over toward the car.

"In, now!" Iazmaena followed her own advice, Jürgen, too, shoving the girls in ahead. Marri was wondering if she would collapse before they reached their stop when the people immediately across from the closing tram doors cleared a space for her without speaking a word. They bowed their heads as if in deference. She told herself it was Jürgen's presence. They definitely seemed afraid of him.

The tram pulled away just as the Harmony monsters reached it, and Marri let out a sigh of relief. But grateful as she was for a chance to rest her body, she couldn't give the same luxury to her newly rebuilt mind.

"Where are we going?"

In answer, Iaz pulled out her handheld, hand shaking slightly. A light on its side flashed urgently. Her entire demeanor changed as she read whatever message awaited her. Indeed, her face split into a wide grin.

"What is it?" Marri asked. Iazmaena ignored her, typing out a reply instead. Trying to quell her impatience, Marri allowed her gaze to wander around. A great many eyes were focused on their group. Every eye on the tram, in fact. She told herself that wasn't surprising. They were a very strange group. But the longer she looked, the more Marri realized that the people's eyes weren't focused on her group.

They were focused on *her*.

"I know where we're going," Iaz said, breaking the spell those gazes held on Marri. "Where I've wanted to go since the very beginning of this mess." She looked as happy as Marri had seen her since reawakening in her body. Iaz held up the handheld for Marri to see, leaning in close.

Palmieri saved our lives, so we honor our end of the bargain. We have the shuttle complex. Come soon. We can't hold it for long.
— Vasquez

"I just messaged her back," Iazmaena said. "There's still time. We can leave all this shit behind us." That last part seemed to be just for herself.

Their stop arrived shortly thereafter. Too short for Marri's taste. Her legs were already protesting the idea of having to stand again. But no sooner had the tram pulled to a stop and the doors opened than one of the Harmony monsters was there, lunging for the opening, trying to get at all the tasty people inside.

Some people screamed, but far fewer than Marri would have thought.

"Help her!" someone called.

"Save her!" another shouted.

"For Marrietta!"

"For Marrietta!" They took it up like a chant then, at least half the people on the car. Horrified, Marri watched as they hurled themselves at the creature. More and more piled on, driving their legs, grabbing the door frame for leverage, and they gradually forced the thing back out of the car, bearing it to the ground with the weight of their bodies as it gnashed and tore at them.

They chanted her name even as they died, a few gurgling it as hypermutation began.

It was the moment when Marri stopped lying to herself about what was happening. She had asked Feathertouch why it was helping her, and it had told her after a fashion. It wanted to help people. The former Giana, in her Marrietta form, had somehow programmed the people of the colony to view her as something between leader and god. Feathertouch had anticipated this, had planned to use it.

It had spent subjective years teaching Marri to be a leader so that she could lead this colony it wanted so desperately to protect.

The sense of responsibility, unwanted, hit her like the savage blow of one of the Harmony monsters. She was in a daze as Iazmaena's shouting, just a buzzing in Marri's ears, resulted in Jürgen lifting her from the tram seat and carrying her out the door, past the melee and into the tunnels.

She was still processing this nightmare by the time they arrived at the shuttle complex, but she came out of it enough to take in the scene around her. An Anaranjadan woman, Vasquez, had led a group of her people here, and the ground was littered with ACM bodies.

"We're coming with you, obviously," Vasquez said. "No choice, now." She gestured at the fallen ACM.

"It will take too long to explain," Iaz said in return. "But even though you're afraid of the wrong thing, it's the right call anyway."

"Wait," Marri managed. Everyone turned to look at her, but not like the people on the tram had. Vasquez's people looked at her as if she was some kind of a disease, though there was at least some confusion thrown in there as seasoning. "We can't go. These people, they think I'm their leader. We can't abandon them to Kyne Libretta."

"Marri," Iazmaena said, pinching the bridge of her nose in a way that said she'd been dreading this and hoped she'd avoid it. "We can't stay. Kyne is now the power here. Until we understand more about what we're dealing with, we're just asking to die if we stay here."

"These people will be dying *for me*," Marri said. "I don't want that, do you understand? I don't want it, but I can't stop it, either. Not until we undo what Marrietta did somehow. But I can't just let them—"

"Kid, check your history. Leaders go into exile all the time."

Annoyingly, she was right, and not just about the fact of it. She was also right Marri had been instructed in those very histories. A childish part of her felt a flash of irritation at being forced into so much book-learning.

"It's part of the burden of leadership," Iazmaena said, and her voice had softened some. "The leader is important. Sometimes people die to keep them safe."

Marri's eyes burned with sudden tears. She felt all of thirteen again for the first time in a long time. That girl's stubbornness made one final attempt. "We can't leave Stefani—"

"Leaders can't be stupid," Ella said suddenly. Marri turned to her, surprised. "And I've heard enough stories about you to know you're not stupid, either."

"She's your mother," Marri said. The words had just escaped her.

"And we can't help her right now," Ella said, cold as hard vacuum. Marri found herself wondering what kind of creature Ella really was.

Vasquez pulled her handheld from her ear and chose that moment to interrupt. "I have no idea what the fuck is going on here, but if you're finished, I do not like the reports I'm getting."

"We'll come back," Iazmaena said, fixing Marri's brown-eyed gaze with her hazel one. "For everyone." She really hit the emphasis on the last word.

Exhaustion washed over Marri at this, and for all that she wanted to fight, it turned out she had no allies here and no strength to force the issue.

"Fine," she said.

They boarded the shuttle and found more of Vasquez's people working to override the lockouts. Iaz offered to help. Ella too. Marri only sat, beaten but not convinced. Vasquez's people kept throwing dirty looks her way, which she did her best to ignore.

Abandoning them. I'm abandoning them. She wondered what Feathertouch would think of that. She wondered when she'd started thinking of Feathertouch as some sort of moral touchstone.

The shuttle's ascent into orbit was far more violent than Marri would ever have expected. She kept waiting for the ship to shake apart around them, such were the vibrations. But at last, the sky went from permanent twilight to full dark—the platforms must have been located on the night side currently.

They hung there, wedge-shaped, bristling with solar arrays, looking entirely too frail to offer any kind of sanctuary, much less hope. But docked with them was some kind of vessel. It looked alien in some indescribable way.

"Finally made it," Iaz breathed. Marri supposed it ought to have felt like a new beginning, but instead, it felt like something had ended. Yet as if to mock this feeling, that was the moment the presence—she could think of no other word to describe it—rolled over her, blotting out her vision, squeezing her mind like a vice.

Like a black hole had suddenly taken up residence in her head.

There were words in that presence, freezing words, colder than ice, darker than pitch. She did not have time to feel panic because memories that were not her own reached out and filled her awareness. Giana's memories. The Giana which had inhabited this body. Marri felt a recalled sense of awe, of subjugation, an almost infinite desire to please.

The realization struck her like a planetary impact. With sudden horror, she understood. This presence, this force, was the *reason* Giana—and all her kind—had done what they'd done. It was the reason they existed at all. Like a strange kind of god, guiding them in their destruction. And though Marri could not understand the god's words themselves, the totality of the meaning they conveyed was somehow lodged there, in her mind and against her will.

Terrible, impossible meaning.

She'd been wrong. It was not over. It would never be over.

CHAPTER 62

IN THE INSTANT Stefani realized where Karl was taking them, saw her daughters falling away behind her because of the threat *she* posed, she summoned the will to wrest control of her body back from Trevor, driving him back down into darkness. Or perhaps it had nothing to do with her strength. Maybe the revelation that Trevor's desired target was about to be out of his reach which weakened him instead. Regardless, before she could conjure up a comforting excuse, they had already crossed the Bridge's terrible threshold.

She was an instant too late in returning to herself to stop Karl from taking the fateful step.

The last time she had jumped worlds by Bridge, the journey had been an experience of psychedelic terror which had seemed to take an eternity and no time at all.

This time, the transit was instantaneous. She was in a poorly lit cavern amid a maelstrom of violence on one world, blinked, and opened her eyes to a sapphire-blue ocean with a matching sky slowly deepening to orange at one horizon. She resumed her human form at once, found herself on all fours, the grit of wet sand scraping the skin of her palms. The shock being at the edge of an ocean, more water than she'd ever seen in her entire life, was enough to hold her fixated even without the rhythmic, lulling crash of waves.

She heard tentative movement behind her. "It's me, Karl," she said, the spell broken. She stood and turned, determined to turn and step back through to Anaranjado. She could still sense the flickering of the dome, its edge just behind her. But she spun just in time to watch it vanish.

Karl was resuming his shape nearby, and as his familiar face took form, she saw his stricken expression, reacting to her obvious despair.

"No," she said, but there was no force behind it. "No." A moment. For one precious moment, her family had been whole again. And then, in a moment's weakness, it was all gone. "No."

"Stefani, I—"

"You did the right thing, Karl," she said. She would not lash out at him. She would not. And not least because she couldn't be sure who would be in control if she did. "The only thing you could have done."

"That doesn't make me any less sorry," he said.

Seagrass, as tall as Stefani's waist, crested the dunes behind him. It seemed like something from another world. A lost world.

"Where are we?" she asked.

"Earth, to hear Kyne tell it. Though I've no idea where on Earth. Not that it would matter if I did." he said. He sounded despairing but also full of wonder at the name, and Stefani could relate.

"We saved her," Karl said. "That's the important thing."

Stefani suppressed a snort. She hadn't done anything, hadn't even had a chance to take Ella to task for following her. The girl must have stolen the device from her, given that she'd already been with Marri when Stefani and Iaz had found her.

"You're right," she said because it was expected of her.

A moment. One precious moment.

They stared around them, ocean to one side, heaping dune to the other.

"Which way do we go?" she asked.

"Inland, I suppose," he said, but belied his words by sagging abruptly to his knees, clutching his chest. "After I catch my breath."

"You're injured!" *I injured you.* The guilt was like her own set of chest wounds.

"Nothing a few back and forth transformations shouldn't take care of," he said. But the fact he didn't immediately start following his own advice told Stefani it might not be so simple as that. Still, he seemed determined to pretend. At her telling silence, he looked at her. "I'm hurt, but I'm not dying. I promise." Abruptly he was all business. "An empty beach can't be where Kyne's army was gathering. This side of the portal must have been jumping around at the end as it failed. But if this world is where Kyne came from, we'll find something eventually."

Kyne Libretta. Stefani still couldn't credit it. How had the woman survived Coldgarden, reached a whole other world, and gathered herself an *army*? "Emphasis on the word *thing*," Stefani said.

"It was a deliberate word choice," he said with a bleak chuckle.

She refused to move to explore the area until Karl agreed to stay put. He refused to agree until she promised to stay in sight. The dune was taller than expected, and the sand, wet on this side, did not make for an easy climb. She slid back down, feet digging furrows in the sandy cliff, more than once. Finally she had to partially transform to scale her way to the top. Still, just given the breathable air, tolerable sun, and gorgeous scenery, Stefani couldn't decide why anyone, even Kyne Libretta, would choose to leave this planet for Anaranjado.

Until she reached the top.

"What is it?" Karl called up from his place in the sand. The dune had been tall indeed, tall enough to obscure the thing which climbed up into the sky, a thing easily viewable as it towered above the flat, wooded wetlands beyond.

It was vast, eating the lower third of the sky. It was spheroid in shape, its outer boundary ever shifting. Stefani might have said *pulsing* if forced to choose a word. She could not see the point where it contacted the horizon, just a portion of the narrower stalk which formed said connection. It tickled her biologist's brain, making her think of a sac or a polyp. But it was what lay *inside* the polyp which stole all her attention. That outer layer must be transparent because she could stare straight through into the twisting madness that lay within.

Roiling shapes squirmed and writhed, twining and intertwining as though engaged in some loathsome sexual congress. Now they looked like humans as tall as mountains, now like clusters of worms, now like creatures she had no name for at all, The longer she looked, the more a strange light seemed to suffuse the entire biological structure. Her teeth clenched involuntarily, and a skittering sense in her own head begged her to look away.

She was only too happy to oblige.

"Stefani," Karl called, his word lost amid a roaring in her ears.

"I can't describe it," she said, her own voice lost in the tumult.

In her haste to put the thing out of sight, she went careening backward, sliding back down the dune she had just so laboriously climbed. When the line of sight broke, the scrabbling feeling in her head abated—but not entirely.

She lay there, three-quarters of the way back down the dune, panting as though they'd been sprinting.

"Are you okay?" he asked. She nodded, but that was a lie. She was still experiencing the thing, whatever it was. Out of sight like this, it was muted but not gone.

As though the horrible growth, a tumor on the rind of this world, was more idea than tangible object. An idea, once had, could never be un-had, after all.

As though it had clocked her existence and was now as aware of her as she was of it.

AAYAN MALOUF STOOD from the ruined body of the creature. He had been among the many to hurl themselves at it as it tried to invade the tram car, but he had been among the few to be able to walk away. He still remembered watching his skin turn to green-black hide, his arms to bone claws which had punctured its thick skin and iron-hard muscle, severed ropey tendons, cracked bone hard as stone.

In large part, he had been the reason they had finally been able to tear the creature, durable as it was, apart.

Yet, despite his monstrosity, no one had turned on him. No one had shunned him as a monster. All of them had shared the same purpose: the safety of Marrietta Palmieri, the preservation of her glory. Memory of her made Aayan look around, frantic. This might not be the only one of the creatures. Marrietta might still be in danger.

When he couldn't find her, his franticness swelled to near-panic. And he was not alone.

"Where is she?" The cry went up. "Where is she? Where is she? Where is she?"

"Don't forsake us!" he found himself shouting. A part of him goggled at his own behavior, reminded him of his missing son and husband. He still had the drawings of them crumpled in one pocket.

But the greater part of him, a part filled with glorious newfound clarity, told him none of that mattered anymore. His husband and son were dead, or they were not. There was nothing he could do about it in any case. But Marrietta Palmieri, she who was the light of his life, he could still help her. Aayan Malouf didn't understand how he knew this with such fervent certainty, but she would lead them all to glory. He just had to find her.

While the others wailed at her absence, Aayan sat down and pulled out the picture of his son. Straightening the paper and turning it over to reveal its blank side, he found his pencil and began a new sketch.

He had only seen her with his own eyes for a few minutes aboard that tram, but he could have drawn her in his sleep.

JOIN THE CURSED DRAGON SHIP NEWSLETTER

Want more just like this one? Sign up for our newsletter so you don't miss out on the adventure. You'll get:

- A free book for signing up
- Advanced notice of new releases
- First word of books on sale
- Opportunities for free books
- Most up-to-date information on author appearances.

We're busy and know you are too. We won't send more than one newsletter a month.

Register below.

ACKNOWLEDGMENTS

I recently thought back to the fact that I wrote the first draft of what would eventually become *The Last Humans* almost fifteen years ago, and it's wild that here we are now, with four down and one (fingers crossed) to go. The trouble with acknowledgements this deep into a running series is that they tend to sound repetitive, but the truth is that while a series gets easier to write as you go in some ways, in other ways it gets harder. All the people who helped me shepherd this book to completion deserve even more thanks with each successive volume. Once again, Sara George is not only a great proofreader, tolerantly correcting all the mistakes I keep making no matter how many times she explains the grammatical rule to me, but also an ace at spotting the last few lingering plot holes or continuity errors I can never fully stamp out. Stefanie Saw brought Karl to life on the cover, and after so long as a stalwart of the series, I'm happy he gets his due in such a spectacular fashion. As ever, Kelly Lynn Colby can best be described as an editor perfectly designed for my writing style. She is my first audience I write for, and it's always a treat when I manage to surprise her. Special thanks to Suzy and to all my readers for continuing to walk this bizarre path with me no matter how strange it gets. And the biggest thanks of all go to my wife Debbie, endlessly supportive and loving no matter how big of a weirdo she married.

ABOUT THE AUTHOR

Gregory D. Little is the author of the Unwilling Souls, Mutagen Deception, and the forthcoming Bell Begrudgingly Solves It series. As a writer, you would think he could find a better way to sugarcoat the following statement, but you'd be wrong. So, just to say it straight, he really enjoys tricking people. As such, one of his greatest joys in life is laughing maniacally whenever he senses a reader has reached That Part in one of his books. Fantasy, sci-fi, horror, it doesn't matter. They all have That Part. You'll know it when you get to it, promise. *Or will you?* He lives in Virginia with his wife, and he is uncommonly fond of spiders.

Join Greg's newsletter and get a free story:

facebook.com/gregorydlittleauthor
x.com/litgreg
instagram.com/authorgregorydlittle

www.ingramcontent.com/pod-product-compliance
Lightning Source LLC
Chambersburg PA
CBHW051440190726
48289CB00001B/276